a Tenacity romance

A Lovely Condition

ANITA BLOUNT

Printed in the United States of America by
Kindle Direct Publishing, an Amazon company.

Book design by Tracey Hudson Countz of
Moon Diva Illustration and Design

Cover art by Artist,
Bobby Walters of Hattiesburg, MS

ISBN 978-1-63821-733-6

**FOR MY HUSBAND,
BUFF BLOUNT,**

who makes my life wonderful.
Without his help and support, this
book may never have been published.

CHAPTER ONE

Anna pushed her light brown hair over her shoulder, began refueling her shiny new BMW, and prayed that returning home from her self-imposed exile was the right thing to do. After four troublesome years away, she was driving headlong into a trove of memories, many of which shaped her life in valuable ways, others that altered it tragically. What she needed now was courage.

Looking around, she recalled the tranquil pasture that once occupied the spot where she stood. Anna was only eight or nine years old when bulldozers destroyed the field, but she still remembered the small herd of horses that grazed there, particularly a brown and white pinto she pretended was hers.

When the people of Tenacity, Mississippi discovered an Interstate would bypass their small town, it was all anyone could talk about. Some feared it would kill what little commerce they had. Others were grateful unfamiliar vehicles wouldn't overrun their town, filling it with exhaust fumes and disturbing their peace. Years later, no one could deny the town had suffered financially, but Anna thought they had dodged a bullet.

She'd driven on one interstate or another all day and couldn't say she was impressed by the commerce they attracted. In the past hour, she'd seen at least ten billboards, a secondhand auto parts store surrounded by defunct automobiles, a concrete factory, and a neon sign towering over a hot pink motel. The strip mall she'd just passed contained a liquor store, a vape shop selling something called ape vape, and a contemporary boutique, its signage boasting, "We have the fashion if you have the passion."

Anna slid into the driver's seat to begin the last stretch of her journey, barely avoiding getting drenched by a sudden rainstorm. Gripping the steering wheel, she leaned forward, peering into the downpour, listening to the rhythm of the windshield wipers. She was looking for the unmarked exit leading home, if she could still call it that, and to a lifetime of memories she wasn't sure she could face.

There. She almost missed it. Turning onto the gently curved timeworn road, Anna smiled despite her misgivings about her decision to return. For she knew that around the bend and over a rise in the terrain was the tunnel of foliage that had intrigued her since childhood.

The three-quarters-of-a-mile section of road, known to locals as the corridor, was bordered on both sides by giant oaks, their limbs reaching across the passage to congratulate one another on their longevity. No one knew who planted the trees or why, but Tenacity residents believed the corridor embodied a mystical quality, and the trees stood guard over their small, out-of-the-way town.

Anna paused at the rise in the road, drinking in the view, remembering how it felt to ride through that shelter of dense foliage—the dimmed light, the quieted sounds, and the odd feeling she was traveling from one world into another.

When Anna was a child, she and her mother called the passage 'the enchanted corridor' and imagined otherworldly creatures living among the branches. It was a game Margie enjoyed playing with her daughter, but young Anna was a believer.

Convinced fairies hid behind the foliage to peak at passersby, Anna waved vigorously at every rustling leaf. And no matter the weather, she insisted on lowering the car windows so a fairy could fly into the car and go home to live with them.

To young Anna's disappointment, a fairy never flew into their car. But adult Anna considered the imagined world of the corridor a monumental gift, as it was the inspiration for her epic first novel.

Ending her nostalgic musings, the young author drove into the corridor, the canopy of leaves immediately hushing the sound of the rain. She opened the car windows, absorbed the familiar surroundings, and allowed the earthy humid air to welcome her home.

Anna was grateful the years hadn't diminished her sense of wonder. The corridor was still glorious, still mysterious, and it stirred in her a feeling she couldn't quite describe—something almost spiritual.

"I'm here," she said aloud, addressing the unknown force that lured her back to this place. She'd tried to resist, tried to ignore the compulsion to return, but eventually, she obeyed the silent command. "You called," Anna said to the air, "and I came. Now what?"

The warm sunshine of a lovely spring afternoon greeted the young novelist as she exited the corridor. The weather change was so abrupt and so pronounced Anna imagined a perfect rainbow curving over the road and a chorus of celestial beings singing the "Hallelujah Chorus." Smiling at her flight of fancy, she welcomed the brief distraction from the conflicting feelings vying for her attention. Anticipation mingled with apprehension while delight dueled with melancholy.

She'd led a charmed childhood in Tenacity, with a loving mother, good friends, neighbors who felt like family, and Max, a boy she began loving when she was six years old. They were blessings, and Anna appreciated her blessings. It's just that thoughts of those happy times came with an acute awareness of what she'd lost.

Anna understood loss was an inevitable part of living. She knew she should deal with it and get on with her life. If only it wasn't so damned difficult.

Continuing her journey, she drove past a sagging metal gate, flooding her mind with thoughts of the carefree summer days of her youth. On warm Saturday mornings, her mom and Max's mom would pack a picnic lunch, buckle their swimsuit-clad children into the backseat of the Robinsons' car, and head to the creek.

Max's mom, Carol, always opened and closed Mr. Jordan's gate, while Anna's mom drove over the rusty cattle gap. For the kids, the journey through the pasture was part of the fun. Amid uproarious laughter and exaggerated bouncing, they rode across the uneven path through the pasture, shouting names they gave to Mr. Jordan's cows.

Anna's mom drove to the end of the path and parked beside cars and trucks belonging to friends and neighbors. Then Margie, Carol, and their excited children followed a narrow footpath through the woods to the creek, their arms burdened with gear, flip-flops throwing dirt and sand onto their bare legs.

On one of those visits, Anna's mom snapped the photograph she kept on her bedroom dresser when she was alive. Max and Anna wore wet swimsuits and big smiles, their skinny arms wrapped around one another. The photo was one of the few items Anna took with her when she left home.

Teen age visits to the creek took on a different tone. On warm summer nights, Tenacity youth gathered at the creek, leaving their vehicles in the pasture where Anna's mom used to park. The boys would cut a load of wood, haul it to the river in the back of a pick-up, and build a bonfire on the sandy shore.

Anna delighted in those nights; the beauty of the fire against a dark sky, cool night breezes, the comradery of friends, and the feeling of remoteness the darkness offered—until Max ruined it for her. She still remembered his long body stretched out on the sand, resting on one elbow, facing a giggling Susie Edwards.

He leaned close and whispered something in her ear, before giving her a long, slow kiss and easing one of his legs over hers.

The scene was both agonizing and seductive. Anna knew about her neighbor's many girlfriends, if you could even call them that, but watching him devour one of them hurt far too much.

5

Continuing to drive toward town, Anna shook her head, as if trying to dislodge that long-ago night. She slowed at the 'Welcome to Tenacity' sign, telling visitors they were entering the home of the Tenacity High School Wild Gators, winners of ten state football championships. She stared at the sign, weighing her options one last time. If she continued driving in the same direction, she'd hit Main Street just beyond the Methodist Church.

A right turn at Main Street would take her past the farms on the outskirts of Tenacity and right out of town. No one would ever know she'd been there. But that was the coward's way out. She'd made a decision, and she'd stick to it. It was time to face her demons. Anna turned left.

About a half mile down the road was the pristine white sign proclaiming Historic Mill Village as the oldest neighborhood in Tenacity. Anna looked around and smiled. Snowy white dogwood trees dotted the area as far as she could see, colorful azalea blossoms graced every yard, and yellow daffodils burst forth in unexpected places. Claude Monet couldn't have imagined a more charming scene.

It was a spring day such as this, when six-year-old Anna and her mother first laid eyes on Mill Village. She remembered sitting in the back seat of Katherine Bell Lee's big yellow Cadillac, listening to the real estate agent recite village history in her syrupy accent.

"There was nothing here when the mill was built but wilderness and the river. Times were tough, and jobs were hard to come by. Workers came from way off to put in long hours for pitiful pay. But the mill owners built a grocery store, a post office, a church, and, of course, those sweet cottages. The people worked hard, but they had it better than some folks back in those days. Then the mill burned down, and the owners packed up and left. All those workers had to find a way to survive."

"What did they do?" Anna's mom asked.

Katherine Bell continued driving slowly. "There's a sign in front of the courthouse that tells the story. Every Tenacity schoolchild learns to recite it. I still remember every word."

We're proud of our heritage and cling to the values of our ancestors. Life was hard for the mill workers who founded this town. They planted gardens, foraged for food, canned what they could, hunted, and made everything they owned. Everyone worked: men, women, and children. But they also found time to sing, make music, and tell stories. No matter what curve life threw them, the people shared what they had, supported one another, and every Sunday, walked to the little white church by the river to give thanks for all they had.

Although Margie found the story inspiring, she was ready for it to end, anxious to find a home for herself and little Anna.

But Katherine Bell hadn't finished. "Our ancestors were as resourceful as they were hardy. They took advantage of the area's two most important resources: the woods surrounding them and the deep Tanakbi River and started a logging business. That's how our town was born. Our founders called it Tenacity because that's what it took for them to survive.

"Here we are," Katherine Bell said, slowing the Cadillac and ending her story at exactly the right time. "This is where the cottages begin." The area was what people today would call a transitional neighborhood. Some houses had been restored, while others still needed a lot of work. But Anna's mother fell in love with Mill Village, just as she did with the sturdy white cottage that became their home.

Anna pulled her BMW into the driveway of that same house. Only this time, she was a grown woman, and she was completely alone. Feeling relieved the long drive was over, she stepped from the car and stretched, a little surprised the neighborhood and the house she grew up in still felt like home. The yard looked different without the pine trees that once grew there. She'd paid to have them removed after her mother's effort to clean pine straw from the roof resulted in her fatal fall. Anna pushed the thought away, determined to keep a positive attitude.

Because her interaction with her contractor had been limited to e-mails, telephone calls, and texts, she was anxious to see the changes Fred had made to the house. The new floor-to-ceiling windows were a great addition, she thought, moving to the street for a different view.

Standing at the edge of the road, she tried to picture the house in a different color palette. Maybe light gray with white trim and an apple-green door. Maybe yellow. She wasn't sure. She only knew the trim and the porch banister had to be white. Tomorrow, she'd walk over to Cole's Hardware and look at paint samples.

She was beginning to get excited about the renovation, still finding it hard to believe she had the money to make it happen. The decision to alter her childhood home hadn't been an easy one, but Anna was convinced it was the right thing to do. She was tired of feeling like a victim, and this project was a big step toward accepting the past and moving forward.

She noticed the porch swing hanging placidly behind the dilapidated, overburdened trellis, its heavy vines returning to life with the coming of spring. That old wooden swing was the scene of many significant events in Anna's life. She flashed back to a childhood memory of being simultaneously thrilled and terrified as she and Max pumped the swing so high it hitched, threatening to toss them over.

As teens, they spent mellow summer evenings on that swing, listening to crickets and talking quietly, Max's long legs never leaving the floor as he glided them back and forth. He'd held her hand and kissed her, while sitting on that swing. And it was on that swing, that Max uttered the words that shattered her heart and destroyed her dreams.

CHAPTER TWO

The last time Anna saw Max was at her mother's funeral, four years before, two years after he left town. She was sitting on the pew reserved for family members with the people she felt closest to: Max's parents; her best friend, Samantha Lindsey; and Cleo Shoemake, who worked in Anna's home for years.

The building was filled with church members, co-workers from the law office where Margie worked, and townspeople who wished to pay tribute to a respected member of their community and offer support to her daughter.

Maybe it was intuition or a sixth sense, but for some unexplained reason, Anna turned toward the back of the church at the exact moment Max pushed open the heavy sanctuary doors. Their eyes met and held, until the handsome man slid into the pew next to the grieving woman and wrapped his strong arms around her.

Overcome with emotion, Anna buried her face in the neck of the person she loved most in the world and silently sobbed. Max kept his arms around her, until she regained control, then took the tissue Samantha offered and blotted Anna's tears. Giving her a sympathetic smile, Max enclosed her slender hand in his and held it firmly throughout the service, hoping to transfer some of his strength to the young woman he'd known most of his life.

When the time came, Max and his dad escorted Anna from the church to the Andersons' sedan. Carol and Alex, Max's parents, sat in front, while Anna sat in the back, flanked by Max and Samantha. The day was unusually cold, the kind you want to spend in front of a crackling fire with someone you love. Instead, they were on their way to the cemetery to bury a good woman, who surely would have enjoyed many more years of life, if not for a senseless accident.

Anna looked past Max to stare out the window. It seemed to her on that cloud-darkened day that nature mourned with her. She felt a kinship with the passing deciduous trees, for just as they were forced to stand in place and endure the icy winds, eighteen-year-old Anna had no choice but to endure the losses in her life and accept her new circumstance.

Samantha watched from the corner of her eye, as Max removed his gloves and then one of Anna's. He clasped her hand in his, took it to his lips for a deliberate, wistful kiss, then held it close to his heart. In response, she rested her head on his broad shoulder. When Max leaned his head down to rest on Anna's, Samantha turned to look out her window, feeling like an intruder on the tender moment.

The five people sitting in the car, Samantha realized, were the only people who knew the romantic nature of Max and Anna's relationship. Samantha knew how devastated Anna was over the situation that tore the two

11

apart, but today was the first time she'd seen evidence of how Max felt. Judging from the adoring way he looked at her friend and the reverent way he touched her, Samantha suspected he was as deeply affected as Anna.

Everyone in town knew there was a bond between the two, that they were close family friends. But the look that passed between them when Max entered the church may have triggered speculation that there was more to the relationship than commonly assumed.

When the car stopped, Max replaced Anna's glove and then his own before helping her from the car. The grieving girl's companions waited patiently while she tucked a woolen scarf into the neck of her overcoat. Then Max and his dad escorted her to her mother's grave site. There were tears, of course, but for the most part, Anna maintained her composure throughout the service. No one spoke on the trip back to the church where Max's vehicle waited. When Alex stopped the car, Max affectionately grasped his parents' shoulders, and his mother patted her son's hand in a show of understanding and sympathy.

"Mom, Dad, I'll see you later. Give me a minute with Anna, will you?" Holding out his hand, he helped the sad young woman from the car and stood facing her. "This is as far as I go." She answered with a nod, looking down, too emotional to speak.

Max desperately wanted to make things better for her but had no idea how to go about it. "I want you to remember you're not alone. You know that, don't you?" Anna remained silent. "Let my parents help you. They want to. And keep in touch. Please. I can't lose you. If you need me, I'll find a way to help."

Max gently lifted Anna's chin and looked into her beautiful face, not ready for the jolt of emotion that pulsed through his body or the intensity of his need to kiss her. Resisting the urge, he held her face in his hands, wiped a tear away with his thumb, and said nothing, lest his voice betray the depth of his emotion.

Anna wanted to throw her arms around him, hold on tight, and beg him not to go. She wanted to tell him how devastated she felt and how much she needed him. Instead, she bravely lifted her chin and looked into Max's deep brown eyes, filled with sympathy and regret. "Thank you for coming," she said, grateful he'd managed to come alone. She appreciated it more than he would ever know.

Max pulled her into his arms like a condemned man allowed one last embrace. Then he firmly kissed the top of her head and reluctantly released her. Sending Anna one last regretful look, he turned and walked away, eyes cast downward, shoulders drooped, arms that held Anna moments before, feeling utterly and unnaturally empty.

Max's parents and Samantha tried to give the couple privacy by looking the other way, but Samantha couldn't help glancing their direction. That one quick glimpse dispelled any doubt she may have had concerning the depth of Max's feelings for her friend. The look on his face was tortured. The man was definitely in love, but it wasn't with his wife.

The drive from the church to the house Anna had shared with her mother was woefully silent. Seeing Max and Anna say good-bye had been heart-wrenching. Samantha would always remember the look of sad resignation on Max's face and the sheer devastation on

Anna's. Those two were like magnets, irresistibly drawn to one another, yet unnaturally kept apart.

On that ride, Anna experienced an epiphany. Max was wrong. She was alone. She'd buried her mother that day and with her went any chance of finding other relatives. Her mother never even revealed her father's name. To make matters worse, Anna watched the man she loved leave to be with someone else.

Samantha would offer support, but she wasn't much more than a kid herself. And no matter what Max said, there was no way she could stay in touch with his parents. If she did, she would never get over their son. And if she was to have any kind of life at all, she had to move past her obsession with Max.

Exiting the car with a dry face and a straight spine, Anna walked boldly into the house she'd always called home to face the mourners waiting to convey their sympathy. She grimly trudged through the rest of the day, finally thanking the women from the church who'd come to do whatever needed to be done. They were wonderful, even making sure the house was tidy before leaving and taking food dishes to return to their owners. Anna was grateful but relieved to be alone.

She wandered through the house, scanning its contents, overwhelmed by the thought of sorting through her mother's belongings. Her sentimental side immediately warred with her practical one. There were so many details to be addressed: social security, insurance, bank accounts, taxes, bills, credit cards, death certificates, a headstone. *One thing at a time*, she told herself. Then she walked out, locked the door behind her, and drove away in her mother's car.

Before Anna left town, she stopped to see Miss Katherine Bell, who still sold real estate when there was a need. Her large, old-fashioned kitchen was her office, her kitchen table doubled as a desk, and she still drove the big yellow Cadillac Anna and her mom rode in when they first saw Mill Village.

Still dressed in the clothes she'd worn to Margie's funeral, the real estate agent, who had become a friend, held the door open. "Come in. Come in, sweetie. You must be tuckered out. You ought to be resting after all you've been through today. Sit down. How about something warm to drink, some tea or hot chocolate?"

Sitting in one of Katherine Bell's big, upholstered chairs with a cup of hot chocolate sounded wonderful, but Anna was afraid if she did, she wouldn't get up for a very long time.

"No, ma'am. Thank you. I can't stay. I have to get back to school."

"Not today! Surely you can wait until tomorrow. It'll soon be dark."

"No, ma'am, it's a long drive to Tuscaloosa, and I need to get back to UA. Exams are coming up. I'm here because I need your help." Anna had several in-state scholarship offers when she graduated from Tenacity High, but she'd chosen to put distance between herself and Max.

"Well okay, honey," Katherine Bell said. "Sit down and tell me what I can do."

Anna chose a straight-backed chair, not wanting to get too comfortable.

"I want to put the house up for rent. Can you rent it without me being here?"

15

"Sure. We can use the internet for the paperwork. But things will have to be done to get the house ready. We'll need to cut the grass, give the inside a thorough cleaning, and store the items inside, probably including the furniture. People who rent houses often have their own."

Seeing the overwrought look on the girl's face, she asked, "Do you want me to take care of that for you? I'll be glad to. Give me your e-mail address and leave a key to the house. We'll talk when you're ready."

"You'd do that?"

"Sure. It won't be the first time. Is that what you want?"

Anna nodded. "Yes ma'am, thank you. You don't know what a relief that is. If you'll send me the bills, I'll find a way to pay for the work that has to be done." Anna started for the door.

Katherine Bell ached for the girl. "There's another option to consider. You could sell. I mean, if money is an issue. I wouldn't have any trouble selling the house. Your neighborhood is really popular these days."

Her neighborhood. That was the problem. It was her neighborhood, and she couldn't imagine permanently breaking that connection. "No ma'am. I'd rather rent it."

When the real estate agent held out her arms, Anna leaned down to hug the petite woman.

"I understand," Katherine Bell said. "Don't worry. You just concentrate on school, and I'll see that everything is taken care of here."

"Thank you so much. I'll send the address of a storage place near me so I can go through things when I have the time."

16

"That sounds like a fine idea, dear." Katherine Bell looked into the sad eyes of the young woman who had just buried her only relative. "Honey, are you going to be all right?"

Anna fought back tears. "I will. It'll take time, but I'll be okay."

She had no idea that four years later, she'd still be working on being okay. She handed a house key to the sympathetic realtor, hugged her once more, then drove away from Tenacity and everyone in it, determined to deal with her loss in her own way.

CHAPTER THREE

Now, Anna was back in Tenacity, standing in front of the house she hadn't seen since the day of her mother's funeral. She chastised herself for being morose. *No good can come from re-living the saddest day of my life,* she told herself. *I'm a successful woman and have no right to feel sorry for myself.* Then she repeated what was becoming her mantra. *Everyone experiences sorrow, and I'm grateful for my life.* Once again, Anna resolved to face the issues she'd pushed aside, deal with them, and move forward. *I will not wallow,* she promised herself.

Her eyes fell to the well-used footpath between the Robinson and Anderson homes. The years hadn't completely erased the evidence of hundreds of visits between the people Anna loved most in the world, and try as she might, she couldn't help feeling the heavy weight of loss that had kept her from returning until now.

Allowing her gaze to wander to the house next door, Anna wondered if the Andersons had sold it or if renters still lived there. When Max's parents moved to Clarkston, they told everyone they were moving to eliminate Alex's daily commute, which was probably true. But Anna knew they also wanted to prevent the awkwardness and hurt that visits from Max and his wife would cause.

Now that Anna was back, she would contact Carol and Alex. She was strong enough now. And she would ask them about Max. She knew he and Janine had a daughter. Were there other children? The thought hurt, but no matter what was happening in Max's life, she sincerely hoped he was happy.

When an SUV with darkened windows pulled into the driveway next door, Anna looked back at her house, not wanting to appear nosy. The driver of the SUV, however, had no qualms about eyeing the tall, stylish young woman standing in front of the house next door.

The man shifted into park, threw open the door, and sprang from his vehicle, leaving the engine running. "Anna, is that you?"

She knew that voice. She remembered when it rang with childhood laughter and when it began to change, dropping and cracking as he approached manhood. And she remembered how its mature, deep tones could turn her body into a pool of desire.

Instructing her racing heart to slow, Anna turned to see the beloved face of the man she couldn't forget. For years, she'd only seen this beautiful man in her dreams. And now, as if by magic, he was rushing toward her. The years fell away, and it seemed only yesterday he'd held her in his arms. Max broke into a huge grin. "Anna!"

He crossed the distance between them in a few long strides, wrapped his arms around her slender body, pulled her close, and swung her around. Setting her back on her feet, he held her at arm's length and looked again.

19

"You're here!" He shook his head in disbelief. "And you're so beautiful! How I've missed you! I've really missed you," he said with laughter in his voice. He hugged her again.

Stunned, Anna struggled for control of her emotions, finally managing to ask, "Max, what are you doing here?"

He flashed his devastatingly sexy smile. "That's what I was about to ask you."

Anna attempted an unruffled expression, hoping her voice didn't betray the impact his presence was having on her. "I'm moving back into the old house."

Max looked genuinely surprised. "Say that again." When Anna repeated her words, Max whooped.

Confused by his behavior, she said, "What?"

"Anna, do you know where I live?"

"The last I heard, you were living…"

Not letting her finish, he shook his head. With a satisfied smile, he nodded toward the house next door. "I live there, in our old house."

"You're kidding!" Anna said with obvious delight, before her brain kicked into gear and turned delight into dismay. She'd made progress in her attempt to accept the challenges life had thrust upon her, but living next door to Max and his family was too much to ask. She didn't think she could even live in the same town.

The injury his marriage inflicted on Anna's heart had diminished only marginally in the last six years, lessening at best from a sharp pain to a dull ache. She was still vulnerable, and inserting herself into a situation like this wasn't smart.

Seeming to read her mind, Max pleaded, "You're staying, aren't you? You're not leaving?" He didn't give

20

her time to answer. "Come for supper. I want to hear all about your life. And you can meet Gracie, my daughter. Janine's parents will bring her by in a few minutes. Gracie's a great kid. You'll like her."

Still a little stunned, Anna managed to form a cohesive sentence. "Well, Max," she said, shaking her head slowly, "I don't think that's a good idea. Janine and I have never gotten along very well. She wouldn't approve of you inviting me to supper."

She remembered watching Janine walk through the school halls, looking smug with Max's arm over her shoulders, seeming to guess how Anna felt about the boy at her side. Then there were the comments Anna was meant to overhear. "Her mom and Max's mom are best friends. He has to be nice to her."

Max shook his head, wondering about what she'd said. "Janine won't be there."

"Even worse. I don't think she'd be happy to find out I visited you and your daughter when she wasn't home." Max cocked his head, narrowing his eyes as if trying to solve a mystery.

"Anna, Janine no longer has anything to say about what I do. Hasn't in a long time."

It was Anna's turn to look puzzled.

"You do know we're divorced, don't you? We divorced shortly after your mother's funeral."

"No. I didn't. I haven't been in touch with anyone from Tenacity since Mom died, except Katherine Bell, who managed the house rental, and lately, Fred Carson."

Max didn't ask why. He simply put an arm around her shoulders for a side hug and resolved not to let her get away. "Now that you know I'm a free man, you have no more excuses. You're coming to supper."

"Give me a few minutes. I haven't been in the house yet, and I'm anxious to check out the new addition."

"I walked over and looked the other day," Max said. "Fred's doing a good job."

Anna did want to see the new construction, but she also needed time to digest what she'd just learned. She couldn't remember a time when she didn't love Max Anderson, but she'd spent years trying to resign herself to the fact that he was no longer part of her life. She didn't know what to do with this new information. A few minutes earlier, she was focused on putting Max out of her mind. To learn he was divorced and living next door was overwhelming.

I should have declined Max's invitation, Anna thought. She believed that, but she simply couldn't resist the chance to spend time with him. So now she had to regain control of her emotions and find the courage to take the familiar walk next door. She would meet Max's child, sit at his table, and pretend not to be dumbfounded by the turn of events.

CHAPTER FOUR

Max was in the kitchen buttering bread and telling Gracie a friend would be joining them, when he heard the doorbell ring. Wiping his hands on a dishtowel, he rushed to answer it. Five-year-old Gracie trailed closely behind.

When he opened the door with a big smile on his face, Anna was struck once again by how handsome he was—not the beautiful boy she used to know, but a magnificent, virile man. She had trouble believing he was real.

When Max placed a welcoming kiss on her cheek, Anna breathed in the scent of him, a blend of spicy cologne and his own unique bouquet. Resisting the urge to fall into his arms, Anna hoped he'd affect her less once the shock of seeing him subsided. But that didn't seem likely, when just breathing the air surrounding him threw her off balance. Unfortunately, she seemed as vulnerable to his charms as ever.

Pulling away from the assault on her senses, she looked down into the interested eyes of a beautiful little girl with olive skin and dark curly hair. She was a feminine version of young Max, with one obvious difference. She had Janine's bright blue eyes. As painful as that was for her to see, Anna had to admit that Max and Janine produced a stunningly beautiful child.

Anna extended her hand. "You must be Gracie."

The five-year-old put her hand in Anna's. "Yes, ma'am. You're pretty. I like your toenails. See, Daddy, she paints her toenails. Aren't they pretty?"

Max, whose eyes were on Anna's face, slowly let his gaze travel down her body to the tips of her feet and back up again. "Yeah," he said in a seductive voice. "Definitely beautiful." Anna raised her eyebrows. *Really? In front of your daughter?*

A mischievous grin adorned his face while Gracie continued her discourse. "Daddy says I'm not old enough for toenail polish, but I think I am. Don't you?"

"Oh, no, you don't, young lady. I'm not getting in the middle of that discussion. That's between you and your daddy." After a moment's hesitation, she added, "and your mom."

"Gracie, don't you think we should let Anna come inside before you start grilling her?"

"What's grilling?"

"It's asking too many questions." He ruffled her curls. "Come on in, Anna. It isn't the Taj Mahal, but it suits us. Doesn't it, Gracie?"

"Ah huh. I like it better here than at Grandmother and Granddaddy's house."

"Let that be our secret. It might hurt your grandparents' feelings if they heard you say that."

Gracie's curls bounced when she nodded. "Okay, Daddy."

"Gracie lives with Janine and her parents when she isn't here with me," Max explained.

Anna looked around the room, remembering how it looked when Max's parents lived there. It was simpler now, more masculine. There was a tan leather sofa, a matching recliner, an upholstered chair, and a sturdy coffee table on a multi-colored rug. Anna could picture Max relaxing on the sofa, watching the big-screened television that sat in a wall of shelves, his bare feet propped on the interesting-looking table.

"Nice coffee table," Anna observed. "Is there a story behind it?"

"Not really. It's just something I made from some barn wood I came across."

"So, you're still finding ways to use abandoned wood," Anna said, remembering the ladder he made as a child.

She wandered closer to the shelves for a better look at the photographs positioned at intervals between rows of books. There was Gracie as a toddler, a picture of her taken recently, some snapshots of Max and Gracie together, and one of her with his parents. Anna was secretly happy not to find one of Janine or her parents.

"Your work?" Anna asked, running her hand over the perfectly smooth shelf.

"It is."

"It's beautiful. You're a skilled craftsman."

"Carpentry is one of my talents." There was that grin again.

Gracie took Anna's hand. "You want to see my room?"

"Go ahead. Gracie can give you the tour while I finish in the kitchen. She'll tell you everything you want to know and more."

25

Anna laughed. "I'm beginning to get that."

"This is my princess room," Gracie announced with a Vanna White gesture.

"Wow!"

The child was delighted with her guest's reaction. "I know. Isn't it perfect?"

The room was a little girl's dream, pale pink walls, fluffy pink curtains, a Disney princess bed with a sheer canopy, and even a chandelier. Anna walked around the room noticing the details. "Who did this for you?"

"I picked out everything myself, but Mimi helped. She sewed the curtains and the ruffle around the bed. And Daddy painted the clouds on the ceiling and put up the stars. You don't see them too good now, but they glow when it gets dark."

Max appeared in the doorway, the feminine room emphasizing his masculinity. "I know it's a little over the top. I told Mom the sky was the limit, so she and Gracie took me at my word. They may have gotten a little carried away."

"No, it's wonderful! Really." She turned around for another look. "What little girl wouldn't love this?"

"You ready to eat?" Max asked. "I try to keep Miss Piglet here on some semblance of a schedule, but I can feed her now, and we can eat later if you're not hungry."

"No, now is good. I'm starving and something smells delicious."

"I am not Miss Piglet!" Gracie insisted, grinning and grabbing her father's arm. Max lifted his arm straight out from his body, lifting the child off the floor. "Daddy, Daddy, let me down," Gracie giggled.

"All right, little bit. Scoot to the bathroom and wash your hands." He gave her a playful swat on the behind, while she giggled and scampered away to do his bidding. "And use soap," he called after her.

The adults were laughing as well, until the intimacy of being alone in the hallway caused them to sober. Max couldn't believe how much he wanted to wrap his arms around Anna and kiss away the wall that time and circumstances had put between them.

But they'd only reconnected about an hour before, and Anna seemed almost wary of him—or nervous. He couldn't tell which. Their lives had changed drastically, and they needed to get reacquainted. Max knew he needed to be patient.

"Gracie is adorable," Anna said.

"I have to agree. She's pretty special."

Telling himself to be satisfied with a touch, Max placed his warm hand on that sensitive spot low on Anna's back, guiding her toward the kitchen. She knew it was an automatic gesture, that Max was only being polite. Nevertheless, his touch made her heart pound. *Calm down*, she told herself. *You're not a girl crushing on the popular boy in school. You're a grown woman, and he's a grown man with a child.*

No one spoke on the short walk to the kitchen. Gracie ran past them, sat at the table, and began singing a song about peanut butter and jelly. She whisper-shouted the word jelly, shaking her hands jazz style.

"No peanut butter and jelly tonight," Max said. "We're having spaghetti casserole."

"Yeah!" exclaimed the child, before bursting into a rendition of "On Top of Spaghetti," pretending to sneeze at the appropriate places. Anna finished the song with Gracie, who was all smiles.

"Enough singing and sneezing," said Max. "It's time to eat."

Anna made a face, as if they were both in trouble. "What can I do to help?"

"It's all done." Max held out a chair for Anna.

He knew his way around the kitchen, she noted. He had set the table before her arrival and placed a bowl of salad beside each plate. After taking the casserole dish from the oven, he positioned it on a trivet on the counter. "I'll serve the plates from here," Max explained. This is too hot to put on the table."

"You didn't make this yourself, did you?" Anna asked.

"No. It's something I had in the freezer." He intended to change the subject quickly, but Gracie was quicker.

"The ladies in town want to go on dates with Daddy, so they bring him food. He's not interested in dates, but the food is real good."

Anna chuckled. *Max was right; this child is delightful.* Beginning to feel comfortable, Anna cocked her head, looked at her host, and put him on the spot. "And who is responsible for tonight's main course?"

"That would be Mary Beth Miller," he admitted, looking a little sheepish. "I know that because her name and telephone number are printed on the aluminum foil with permanent marker."

"I see," Anna said with a knowing chuckle. "And, of course, the dish will need to be returned."

"Right," Max agreed, drawing out the word.

28

Gracie jumped back into the conversation with more interesting information. "Daddy doesn't have a girlfriend, but Mother has a boyfriend."

"Does she now?" asked Anna, amused at the turn of the conversation.

The child continued in her animated way. "Yes, his name is Doug McKinnon." Anna's eyebrows shot up, sending a questioning look at Max. His nod confirmed it was true.

Anna remembered Doug as a poor kid who sometimes came to school with a black eye or a split lip. He and his brother always blamed the damage on each other, but everyone suspected their alcoholic father was responsible. She was surprised Janine would be interested in someone with his background.

Max seemed to read her mind. "Doug has done well for himself. He started out fixing up old cars and selling them. I guess he learned by trying to keep his old man's rusty excuse-for-a-truck running. Somehow, he saved enough to buy into a convenience store, where he worked part time. Now he owns several. Calls them Wag-A-Bags. I have to hand it to him. He pulled himself up by his bootstraps. He has custody of twin boys from a marriage that didn't work out."

"And they're real mean," Gracie interjected. "Nobody likes them."

Max took bread from the oven, placed it in a napkin-lined basket, and opened a bottle of Chianti to pair with the spaghetti.

"Wine?" Max asked his guest.

"Thanks. This is your mother's table," Anna said, remembering the happy times their families spent there.

"Yeah. It's so heavy that my parents didn't want to move it, so they left it here for renters."

After Max poured wine, Gracie announced it was time to say the blessing. It was something Max's family had always done. Really, almost everyone in town did. Anna remembered asking her mother why they didn't. After that, the blessing became a regular occurrence at their table, but Anna realized it was something her mother hadn't grown up doing.

Gracie reached across the table, trustingly placing her small hand in Anna's, while Max's large callused one lay on the table in invitation. With her heart in her throat, Anna placed her slender hand into Max's warm welcoming one and was bombarded with feelings that threatened to overwhelm her.

For just a moment, Anna pretended to have what she wanted most in life. She imagined the three of them as a family, sitting at the supper table as they did every evening. And later, she and Max would read their child a story, tuck her into bed, then retreat to their bedroom to participate in their own nighttime ritual.

That's how it was supposed to be, and for a time she believed that's how it would be. But Anna experienced the devastation of having her heart's desire within her grasp and having it wrenched away. She could never let that happen again.

The sing-song cadence of Gracie's prayer brought Anna back to reality. "Amen," the child said emphatically. When the blessing was over, Max didn't immediately let go of Anna's hand. Instead, the man who refused to disappear from Anna's dreams, the man she thought she'd never see again, caressed her hand with his thumb and pressed his lips to her knuckles, like the hero of a historic romance novel.

"I'm glad you're here," Max said, looking directly into Anna's eyes. If there was ever any question whether the attraction between them still existed, the jolt of electricity passing between them at that moment provided the answer. The allure was as strong as ever, and the fact that they were now consenting adults elevated the thrill.

Anna looked down, hiding her blush by focusing her attention on the food. "Mmm," she purred, taking a bite of the casserole. Max's body stilled. He dreamed of hearing that sound tumble from Anna's lips. But in his dreams, she was in his bed, her body moving rhythmically under his. Anna felt his eyes on her before looking up to see how dark and intense they were. This time, she couldn't stop the blush from exposing the delicious attraction he stirred in her.

Anna felt slightly ambushed. The surprises were coming so hard and fast she couldn't adjust to one before being hit by another. She took a deep breath, hoping her discomfort was inconspicuous, and tried to appear in control of her emotions. It would help if Max would stop looking at her that way.

CHAPTER FIVE

Max and Anna pulled away from their intimate moment when Gracie decided to continue her interrogation. "Do you have a boyfriend?" Silently thanking his daughter for the question, Max lifted his eyebrows, waiting for the answer.

"Not really"

"You're so pretty; I thought you'd have a boyfriend," chirped Gracie.

Not understanding why, Anna felt the need to explain. "I've been very busy."

Rescuing their guest, Max told his daughter, "Anna wrote a book, and some people are going to make a movie about it."

"Maybe," Anna corrected. "They only bought the rights."

"They should. It would make a great movie." Turning to Gracie, he said, "After we've finished eating, I'll show it to you. There's a copy on the bookshelf."

Gracie squirmed off her chair, "I'm finished."

"Whoa," chided Max. "Didn't you forget something?"

Gracie slid halfway onto the chair and dutifully asked, "May I please be excused?" before Max finished saying, "Yes you may."

Gracie was off her chair, running to the living room. "Which one is it?"

Anna looked at Max, "You read it?"

"Just a minute," he said to Anna, holding up a finger. "Gracie, not that one. It's a big book to the left of the television." He motioned toward himself. "This side."

Max returned his attention to Anna. "Of course I read it. My girl wrote it. I knew you had an imagination, but wow." He ran his hand lightly down her arm. "You're talented. I'm very proud of you."

Lots of people had congratulated her on the success of her book, but there'd been no one to say, "I'm proud of you." And from Max, the words were precious.

She stood, blinking back tears. "Let me help you clean up."

"No. Spend the time with Gracie. I'm used to my kitchen. It'll go fast. Help her find your book."

Anna did as she was told and pulled the large volume from the shelf, placing it on the coffee table. Gracie's first comment was, "Wow, it's really big. Did you write all that?" Without waiting for an answer, she began leafing through the book.

Understanding what she was looking for, Anna apologized. "I'm afraid there aren't any pictures."

The child nodded. "I guess grown-up books are like that."

"Yeah," Anna commiserated, making a mental note to write something for Gracie with illustrations. Her artistic skills were pretty good.

Max called from the kitchen, "Anna, will you autograph your book for me?"

She considered the request before answering. "No. I don't think so."

Surprised, Max walked out of the kitchen, eyebrows furrowed. "Why?"

Anna shrugged. "I need to think about what to write."

Returning to the kitchen, he yelled over his shoulder. "Whatever you say, but I won't let you forget."

"Wanna see my books?" Gracie asked.

"Of course. I'm a librarian."

"You mean you work in a liberry and let people check out books and stuff?"

"That's right. Before I came here, I worked in a library in Tennessee."

"Are you going to work at our liberry?"

"No, I'm going to write another book."

Gracie hurried to an area of the living room Anna hadn't noticed, one that delighted her librarian's heart. In the corner was a small floor lamp next to a low bookcase. A child-size bean bag chair sat on a previously round rug, cut and bound to fit the corner.

Children's books, puzzles, and board games resided on the lower shelves, while framed snapshots of Gracie with pre-school friends and various family members sat on the higher ones. There was a photograph of Janine, but Anna was mollified to see it was relegated to the child's corner, as if meant only for Gracie.

"Max," she yelled toward the kitchen. "I love Gracie's book corner."

"I knew you would. I thought of you when the idea came to me."

Gracie chose a book from one of the shelves, asking the expected question. "Will you read this to me? It's really good. It's about a little house that lived in the country, but people built big, tall buildings around it and made the house sad. But don't worry. It gets happy again."

"*The Little House!*" Anna exclaimed. "That's one of my favorites. I used to read it at story time in the library where I worked."

Gracie wriggled onto the living room sofa and leaned her warm little body against Anna, her breath stirring the hairs on her new friend's arm. Enjoying the closeness, Anna put an arm around Gracie and pulled her close, surprised by her rapid attachment to the child. She began to read.

When Max walked out of the kitchen and saw the pair on the sofa, he was struck with yearning and regret. He could never wish anything that would prevent Gracie from being part of his life, but if wishes could alter reality, he'd wish the scene before him was what it appeared to be, a mother reading to her child.

"The end," Anna said, closing the book.

Gracie's blue eyes sparkled, and she spoke as if confiding a secret. "Wanna see Daddy's favorite book?"

"Sure. If it's all right with him."

"Daddy, can I... I mean may I show her your pirate book?"

"Of course. You know where it is." Gracie ran toward a room in the back of the house.

"You're still reading pirate books?" Anna teased. Saying nothing, Max leaned against the door frame, as if posing for a magazine shoot, and waited for Anna's

35

reaction. When Gracie returned, carrying a rusted metal box, Anna had to blink back tears.

Eight-year-old Anna had given a lot of thought to that purchase, spending an entire afternoon searching the bookshelves in the back of Mr. O'Neal's drug store. It cost her three weeks' allowance, but it was perfect. It even came in its own treasure chest.

After she presented it to Max, the book stayed in the tree house, protected from the elements by the metal box. But on the day Max married, when sixteen-year-old Anna climbed into the treehouse for comfort and a private place to mourn, the book was missing.

"You took it and kept it all these years," she almost whispered, touched that the book meant so much to him. "I wondered what happened to it."

Gracie suddenly became animated, "I know you! You're my daddy's friend who built the treehouse with him! There's a picture of you and Daddy at Mimi and Paw Paw's house. You were little kids, standing in front of a weird ladder."

"I'd love to have a copy of that," Anna said.

Max left his spot against the door frame to sit in an upholstered chair, facing Anna and his daughter. "I'll see that you get one."

Grateful for the lightness Gracie's excitement brought to the nostalgic moment, Anna finally began to relax in the strange, yet familiar setting.

"Your dad and I used to re-create stories from that book. And we made up a few of our own." She launched into a narrative of memories designed to delight the adorable child. "We pretended the treehouse was a ship on the high seas. And, of course, there were sharks in the water below."

Gracie giggled, casting her eyes toward her dad. "And what else?"

"Well, your daddy would pretend he was a bad pirate and would terrorize my teddy bear by tying his hands behind his back and making him walk the plank."

Gracie giggled again. "Did the sharks get the bear?"

"Oh my, no! Then your dad would play the part of the hero and jump into the raging sea to rescue Fluffy."

Max was all smiles, not sure what he appreciated most, the story, Gracie's reactions, or Anna's enjoyment in the telling.

"Fluffy?" he said with feigned annoyance. "I'm sure I never rescued anything named Fluffy!"

"I think you insisted on calling him Black Jack or something."

"Black Bart," Max corrected.

Anna leaned toward Gracie and confided in a loud whisper, "But his name was really Fluffy." Gracie snickered and nodded vigorously, her dark curls bouncing, enjoying their conspiratorial liaison.

"Then what happened?"

"Your dad would hold the bear in his teeth and climb a knotted rope all the way back up to our ship."

Gracie's giggles progressed to outright belly laughs. "Daddy did that?" she was finally able to ask.

Anna's expression was serious. "Cross my heart." And in a theatrical British accent said, "He was really quite splendid."

Anna looked at Max and batted her eyelashes coquettishly. Their eyes met, and once again, laughter abruptly morphed into heated attraction.

"I hate to bring this delightful evening to an end," Anna said, a little flustered, "but I need to get to my motel room."

"There's always a bed for you here," Max reminded her. He didn't qualify his statement.

"And tomorrow, the whole town would be talking."

"Don't go," Gracie begged. "Stay longer."

"It's your bedtime, young lady." Max picked her up and gave her a kiss.

"Now tell Anna goodnight." Gracie leaned away from Max, wrapped her arms around Anna's neck, and kissed her on her cheek. Swinging her to the floor, Max gave his daughter a playful swat and said, "Now go brush your teeth and choose a book for bedtime."

"Can I wait until Anna leaves? Please?" Gracie said dramatically, her hands in prayer position.

Max employed the backhanded grammar correction he learned from Anna's mom. "You can, but you may not. Here's the deal. You go brush your teeth and hop into bed, and I'll let you miss your bath tonight. In a few minutes, I'll come tuck you in."

"Yea! No bath! Bye, Anna." Gracie skipped from the room.

Anna smiled. "I take it she doesn't like baths."

"She hates having to stop what she's doing to get in the tub, but once she's in the water, she doesn't want to get out. Go figure. I probably started something by letting her ditch her bath, but I want you to myself for a minute."

"She's wonderful, Max—smart, happy, adorable. You did the right thing all those years ago."

"We did the right thing. We made that decision together, if you remember. But losing you was painful, and it never stopped hurting."

"I understand all too well, but I'm not ready to talk about that. I'm tired. I need to get to my room and get some sleep."

"Okay. But let me take you out to dinner tomorrow night. There's a catfish place on the other side of the river. Not easy to find, if you don't know where it is."

"You do know it's not your responsibility to feed me."

"I know, but there aren't many places to eat around here, and Lucky's is one of the few options. I'd like to show it to you. It's a come-as-you-are place, blue jeans or shorts. Of course, I vote for shorts," he said with a mischievous grin. "Give me your number, and we can decide on the details tomorrow." Anna punched her number into Max's phone and thanked him for a lovely evening.

Max followed his guest onto the front porch. When he slid his hand under her elbow, Anna turned to look up at him. Gently, he cradled her face in his large hands and kissed her. The kiss was tender and sweet, but the look in his eyes said it was only a preview. "Goodnight my sweet Anna," he crooned. "Thank you for coming home. Call me when you get to Clarkston."

"I'm not driving all the way to Clarkston. I'm at that little motel beside the gas station, right before the turn off to Tenacity."

"Okay. Just a minute." He walked to the door and yelled inside. "Change of plans, butterbean. We're taking a quick trip to make sure Anna gets to her room safely."

It didn't matter how often Anna said she'd be fine, Max insisted on following. "I'm not sure that's a safe place for you to stay. You should shove something against the door tonight. And keep your phone close by. Don't hesitate to call if something doesn't feel right."

"Since you've already told Gracie she's going for a drive, you may escort me. But you can't do this every night. I've been alone a long time now. I'm used to taking care of myself."

No matter what Anna intended, Max thought the words sounded accusing, and they wounded a vulnerable place in his heart, a place where guilt already resided. At least on this night, he could make sure she got safely to her room.

Anna sat on her bed, dazed, attempting to absorb the recent changes in her life. Max had called her his sweet Anna. But she wasn't his anymore—except as a friend. She could never stop being his friend.

Since making the decision to return to Tenacity and conduct a total-immersion-stop-loving-Max Anderson program, she'd resigned from her job, given up her apartment, driven back to her hometown, kissed Max, and met his precious child. It was too much to contemplate, at least for now.

Physically and emotionally spent, Anna took a quick shower and pulled on an oversized t-shirt. Grateful for clean sheets and a soft bed, she expected to fall asleep at once. But she couldn't persuade her mind to abandon the images swirling in her head. Her thoughts bounced from the events of the evening, including the tender kiss on Max's front porch, to a time when she and Max weren't much older than Gracie, free of responsibility and full of joy.

CHAPTER SIX

Experienced in exchanging one home for another, six-year-old Anna understood the loneliness of leaving friends and moving to a new town, but she was bored. Cleo, the middle-aged woman hired to watch Anna, was sympathetic.

"Honey, why don't you ask the boy next door to play? He's new here, too. All I've seen him do is ride his bike up and down the street. He probably wrapped up his school year early to move here and hasn't met anyone yet. I bet he's lonesome."

Anna had been watching the dark-haired boy and thought Cleo was right. Then one day, while sitting on her back porch, Anna saw him walk across her backyard toward the woods. "What are you doing?" she called.

"Just going in the woods."

"Why?" Anna yelled, jogging toward the boy.

"Might climb some trees."

"Can I come?"

"I guess so, but girls don't climb trees."

"Why?"

"Don't know." He shrugged. "They just don't."

Anna followed closely behind, as her neighbor expertly wound his way through the thick bushes. Noticing him scanning the area, she asked what he was looking for.

"A climbing tree. I need a tree with good climbing branches." Finding a satisfactory one in the center of a clearing, he competently grabbed the lowest branch with both hands, swung his legs upward between his arms, looped them over the limb, and pulled himself upright.

Anna jumped toward the limb several times, not quite tall enough to catch hold. The boy looked down and said bluntly, "See. Girls can't climb trees."

Anna walked away without a word, and then returned dragging a large limb. Standing on it, she imitated the boy's climbing method, made her way onto the tree's lowest limb, and sat beside him. Then she gave her neighbor a big smile. The boy, who introduced himself as Max, smiled back.

In the days following the tree climbing experience, Anna watched for her new friend.

"Why don't you go over and ask him to play?" Cleo asked. "Y'all had a good time the other day, didn't you?"

"Ah- huh."

"Yes, ma'am," Cleo corrected.

"Yes, ma'am. I haven't seen him outside."

Cleo looked up from loading the dishwasher. "We know somebody's at home, 'cause there's been a lot of racket coming from over there. Sounds like hammering."

Almost on cue, they heard a voice from the backyard. "Anna, are you there?"

"I'm here," she yelled, eyes sparkling.

43

"Come on." He gestured toward the woods and headed that direction.

Anna glanced at Cleo for permission.

"You go on, little missy, but stomp on the ground every now and then. Warn the snakes you're coming so they can get out of the way." Cleo watched the children from the back porch, grinning when she saw Anna stomp the ground before entering the thicket. *Who knows,* Cleo thought. *It might work. It's what I do.*

"I made something for you," Max told Anna, hurrying through the woods.

"Slow down. Give the snakes time to get out of the way."

Arriving at the clearing, Max gestured toward the tree. "That's for you, to help you climb up." Leaning against the tree was the unconventional ladder eight-year-old Max put together without the aid of a tape measure or saw. The vertical rails of the ladder were different lengths, as were the steps, which extended beyond the rails to varying degrees.

"Go ahead. Try it. Dad made sure it's safe."

Anna scampered up the ladder without hesitation. "Thanks, Max. It's great!" The six-year-old girl thought the ladder, as well as the boy who made it, were absolutely awesome.

"I'm home," Max's dad called after a long day of construction work.

"In the kitchen," Carol answered, from where she stood, stirring a pot of purple hull peas.

Standing behind his wife, Alex nuzzled her neck, kissing the sensitive spot below her ear. Carol turned and pulled him down to her level for a proper welcome home kiss, then playfully batted him away. "You go on now, before I burn supper."

"How much longer 'til it's ready?"

"I've started the vegetables, but I still have to fry the chicken and make the cornbread."

"Where's my boy?" he asked, looking around.

"Max said he wanted to show the neighbor girl what he made for her."

Alex smiled a big smile. "I think our boy's smitten. Said he made the ladder so his friend wouldn't hurt herself climbing the tree. Anna—I think he called her. He's being protective."

"But he's just a baby."

"Still." Alex kissed his wife on the cheek. "I'll go check on him. Meet the girl. See what they're up to." Before leaving the kitchen, he opened a drawer and took out his favorite camera. "We'll want to remember this." He found Max and Anna sitting on a low limb, swinging their legs, talking. "Hey, man," Alex said cheerily.

"Dad! See our climbing tree."

"I see. Looks like you found a good one. I presume this young lady is Anna."

"Yes, sir. She's a girl, but she likes to climb trees."

"It's nice to meet you, Anna. How did the ladder work out?"

"Good," they said together.

"I made it 'cause Anna needed help climbing up," Max explained, making it clear he needed no assistance.

"You used it, too," she reminded him.

"Yeah, but I didn't have to."

She didn't argue.

"You know," Alex said, looking at the old oak with an appraising eye, "this tree would make a good tree house."

Excitement filled Max's eyes. "Do you really think we could build a tree house?"

"I do."

Max looked earnestly at his dad and tried to sound confident. "You'll help, right? I'll probably need some help."

Alex played along. "Sure, I'd like to help." He looked at Anna, sitting quietly on the limb, anticipation in her eyes. "It's going to be a pretty big job. Do you think you could give us a hand, young lady?"

She flashed a huge smile. "I can! You and Max will need to tell me what to do, but I know I can help."

Alex smiled, noting Anna included Max in the expert category. *Well, he did build her a ladder,* Alex thought.

"Then it's settled. You think your parents will let you come over for supper tonight? After we eat, we can talk about what we want the treehouse to look like. Then we'll have to make a list of supplies we'll need." *Might as well make this a learning experience,* Alex thought.

"It's just my mom," Anna said. "I'll ask her when she gets off work.

"Where does she work?"

"She works with Mr. Parker. She's a legal 'sistant."

Anna's mom returned home that afternoon to an overly excited daughter, speaking rapidly about a tree house and something about Max's dad and supper and some sort of plan. Margie was trying to convince Anna to

46

slow down when Carol Anderson knocked on the front door and introduced herself.

"I live next door," she said, gesturing in the direction of her house. "Our children and my husband want to build a tree house, and I don't know who is more excited, the children or Alex. They think they have to start planning this very night. Will you come to supper and help me keep this project under control? That is, if you can eat vegetables and fried chicken."

That night was a turning point in all their lives. Margie and Carol became instant friends, and the Andersons became the extended family that was missing from Anna's life.

CHAPTER SEVEN

Anna awoke to a sliver of sunlight peeking through the opening of her motel room curtains. Once the fog of sleep dissipated, she recalled the events of the previous evening with Max and his daughter. Surprisingly, a good night's sleep had given her a more positive outlook on her future.

She reflected on her situation. She and Max were once in love, although they never said the words. They were young at the time, only sixteen and eighteen. But the loss of that love, as well as their friendship, had shredded Anna.

Max had flirted with her the night before. *Does he have residual romantic feelings for me*, she wondered, *or is it simply that I'm female?* Anna knew men found her attractive. She had a good face, her curves were in the right places, and Max liked women. Maybe that's all there was to it.

Not willing to dwell on questions for which she had no answers, Anna threw back the sheets, showered, dressed, and left the room with her ponytail swinging. A big guy staring at her from the truck stop made her feel uneasy, but the drive through the cool green corridor put her in the right frame of mind. She drove into Tenacity feeling almost confident about her decision to return.

As she approached Big Mama's Café on Main Street, Anna recalled cherished moments in the little diner. It was where she and her mother had lunch after Sunday church services and the place they celebrated good report cards and class performances.

She and Max used to go there for ice cream when they were kids, half running and half walking along the footpath leading from Mill Village to the cafe's back door. Anna conjured an image of them sitting on red vinyl and chrome counter stools, their bare legs dangling, licking melting ice cream cones—chocolate for Max, vanilla for her. Later, Big Mama's was where she joined friends after school to talk about boys and complain about teachers.

When the café opened in the Fifties, the décor was the latest style, and in thirty years the owners never deviated from the look. By the time the ownership changed, the style was considered retro, and the new owners had the good sense to replicate the original decor down to the last detail.

Anna parked in front of the café and looked down the street toward the town hall. Just as she hoped, pansies graced the window boxes. They were beautiful, but Mrs. Johnson, who'd worked at the courthouse for years, would soon need to replace them with something more heat tolerant.

The location of the simple brick building, which was Tenacity's first and only town hall, had mystified young Anna. The town square was its front yard, and Main Street ended where the square began. As a child, she worried that a big truck would speed down Main Street, drive between the two giant oaks in town square, and push Town Hall into the river. But the building still sat in its place, the seat of government for generations of Tenacity residents.

Hunger turned Anna's attention back to the café, where large cursive letters painted across the plate-glass window announced to passers-by that they'd arrived at Big Mama's. A quick look inside told Anna the town's favorite meeting place hadn't changed.

Pushing open the heavy glass door, Anna inhaled the combined aromas of coffee and bacon, embracing the warmth and acceptance she associated with the place. Looking the same as always in her white shirt and black pants, Miss Cora made her way across the black and white checkerboard tiles. The slender woman, with her gray ponytail, had worked at Big Mama's as long as Anna could remember. Cora greeted her with a hug.

"Anna girl, I heard you were back. We've missed you around here. And you went and got yourself famous," she said with pride.

"How did you know I was back? I only drove in yesterday afternoon."

"You know the gossip mill around here. I hear you didn't waste any time getting reacquainted with the town's most eligible bachelor."

"Now, Cora, you know Max and I are old friends."

"I know, but even a friend can't be blind to all that hunky maleness. Well, find a place to sit so I can get you some breakfast. I'm assuming that's what you're here for."

One of the three elderly men sitting at the laminate-topped table near the front window flashed Anna a smile. "Well, if it ain't our own Anna Robinson. We thought you'd done gone and left us for good. Got too big for your britches, being a big author and all."

Anna returned his smile. "No, Mr. McMillan. My britches, I like to think, are just about the right size, and this town will always be home."

"Well, it's good to have you back. You staying awhile?"

"Yes, sir, I plan to."

Lamar Bryant sat at the same table, drinking a cup of steaming coffee. "Welcome home, little lady. You sure did grow up pretty."

"And smart," added the third man.

"Thanks." Anna was genuinely happy to see old acquaintances.

Situating herself in one of the red and white vinyl booths, Anna took one of the laminated menus from the metal receptacle.

"Menu's the same as always," Cora told her. "Hasn't changed a bit since you left. What can I get you?"

Anna ordered breakfast number three and listened to the men's conversation while she waited. On this beautiful spring morning, they were already talking about next fall's high school football lineup.

"I tell you," Bryant said, "that Coleman boy's gonna be a good ball player."

"Which Coleman is that?" asked the man Anna finally remembered as John Collins.

"Ol' man Al Coleman is his granddaddy, and Ross is his daddy," Bryant explained. "Ross married one of those

McDaniel girls from over in Copiah County. Nice girl. Kinda pretty. Ross done all right marrying her."

Listening to the discussion of family lineages summoned a familiar knot to Anna's stomach. She tried to ignore such talk, but in a community where most people could recite their family tree, going back three or four generations, it was difficult.

The men continued their football talk. "Mark my words. That boy's gonna show us something next year. He was pretty good last season. Saw him the other day, and he's growing. I bet by next year he'll be a foot taller and at least a hundred and eighty pounds. I wouldn't be surprised if he set some records this year."

Bryant chimed in. "Bet he won't beat Jet's records. Nobody's as good as that boy was. He had that mean throwing arm, could outrun anybody on the field, and could spot a hole in the defense like nobody's business."

Joshua, the cook, was placing a breakfast plate on the counter. "You're right about Jet. It's a damned shame that Larson girl got her claws in him. He could've gone pro."

Anna looked at the pictures on the wall opposite her booth. There was a historic photo of muddy Main Street, from the days when overburdened animals and wooden-wheeled carts brought people to town, some collages of long-ago senior classes, and a framed newspaper article featuring the quaint, unchanging café.

Hanging next to a framed headshot of Elvis, Anna saw what she was looking for, a large action-photo of Max, or Jet as most of Tenacity called him, decked out in his Wild Gator football uniform. The photo was taken seconds before he threw one of his famous touchdown passes.

Max was a high school junior when the picture was taken. He was more than six feet tall, well-built, with his father's good looks, and was an intelligent, natural leader. More importantly, as far as the community was concerned, he was the best damned quarterback the Wild Gators ever had.

Like most small towns in the South, the Tenacity population turned out in force for Friday night high school football. Fans analyzed plays, made predictions, and held players accountable for their performances. But when they talked about Jet Anderson, their admiration bordered on hero worship.

It was at an exciting point in one of the home games when a commentator gave Max his nickname. Who knew if it was an impromptu comment or if the announcer had been waiting for the opportunity to unveil it? Anna guessed it was the latter. Whatever the case, the moniker stuck.

"Max Anderson is running the ball," the announcer yelled. "Look at him go! Like a jet, flying at maximum speed!"

In successive games, the announcer would bellow, "There goes the Jet, ladies and gentlemen, flying down the field for another breathtaking touchdown."

So, to most of the town, Anna's handsome neighbor became Jet, but as far as Anna was concerned, he would always be Max.

When Max and Anna were teens, every girl in school dreamed of dating Jet Anderson. He gave most of them the opportunity, at least the pretty ones. And schoolgirls weren't the only ones affected by his charms. The math department's student teacher fell completely under his spell, blushing profusely whenever the hunky quarterback walked into the classroom. She almost passed out the day Max cast a smile her direction and winked.

CHAPTER EIGHT

The day after Max's reunion with Anna, he sat in his office staring at a set of blueprints. He was supposed to be scrutinizing a house for his final stamp of approval before turning it over to the construction side of the business. But Max couldn't concentrate. He kept thinking of how amazing it was to see Anna again, to talk to her, to touch her. Then there was the kiss. It had been brief. Too soon for anything more. But he couldn't forget the sweetness of her mouth.

Passing the picture window separating his son's office from the spacious construction materials showroom, Alex noticed the bemused look on Max's face and wondered what put it there. Thinking maybe he could help, Alex turned around and entered his son's office.

During Max's fifth year of architectural school, his dad brought up the idea of the two of them going into business together. He'd share his recently acquired warehouse if Max would design a space suitable for them both.

So Max designed an efficient workplace with an upscale industrial look to impress clients. His dad implemented the plan, Max used the design as his final school project, and the space was ready for use when he graduated.

As new as Max was to the field, people immediately took notice of the talented young architect at Anderson Architecture and Construction. One of the local glossy magazines covered the office renovation, describing it as an innovative work environment that facilitated easy collaboration between client, architect, and contractor. Another article, which included a delicious headshot of Max, referred to him as Clarkston's hot new architect.

Alex walked through Max's open office door, a cup of hot coffee in his hand. "Morning, son. Busy already?"

Max looked up and spoke without preamble. "Anna's home. I told you she hired Fred Carson to renovate the house. I figured she was getting it ready to sell, but she's moving home. She left her library position and plans to write another book. She had dinner with us last night." He spoke as if he didn't quite believe it. "Gracie's already in love with her."

And so is Gracie's father, Alex thought. He settled into a comfortable blue leather chair. "How does she seem? Is she well?"

Max smiled. "She's beautiful. More polished, but still sweet. She's more... more mature." A worried look came over Max's face. "But she didn't seem at ease with me. She was pretty reserved."

"A lot of things have changed," Alex reminded him. "The two of you will have to get reacquainted."

"If she's so inclined."

"She give you any indication she's not?"

"Not really. But I couldn't read her. I've really missed her, Dad. I was ecstatic to see her, but I couldn't tell how she felt."

Alex decided to be blunt. "You hurt her, son." When Max flinched, he added, "I know that wasn't your intention, but it happened. She might not be ready to forgive you."

"That's what I'm afraid of, and I don't know what to do about it."

Alex hesitated before speaking, feeling the importance of the moment. "If you want her in your life…"

"I do," Max said quickly.

His father nodded. "I wish I could tell you what to do, but you're going to have to feel your way on this one. Do you want what little advice I can give?"

"Sure. Anything."

"You may have to be very patient."

Max nodded. "That's going to be hard. But I know you're right."

"I have faith in you, son. You can win her over, but I don't think charm will do the trick. You'll need to bring each other up to date on your lives. Buried feelings may get dredged up, and you may have to bare your soul. Then y'all can decide where to go from there. And don't discount groveling," Alex said with a grin. "Groveling is always good."

"Surely Mom never made you grovel."

"Oh, I did my share, until I identified my offenses and weeded them out of my behavior."

Max chuckled.

His father looked serious. "I don't mean to trivialize what you're facing. We both know you have a lot to make up for." Alex glanced at his watch. "I need to get busy. Give our love to Anna. Carol has worried herself half to death over that girl. Bring her by the house when the time is right. We'll look forward to seeing her."

Having taken advantage of a shower at the office, Max arrived at Anna's motel room in clean khakis and a golf shirt that showed off his toned abs and muscled arms. Anna opened the door and left Max standing there while she changed from slippers into a pair of flats. Then she plucked her phone from the charger and threw her purse over her shoulder. "Ready," she announced.

She looked amazing in a scooped neck t-shirt and skinny jeans. *Whoa boy*, Max told himself, curbing more impulses than he wanted to count. It took less than a minute for him to imagine holding her against him and pressing his lips to hers. The bed in the room did nothing to bridle his imagination.

Anna began talking the moment she opened her motel room door. "You wouldn't believe the day I've had. The moment I walked in the house this morning; Fred hit me with a list of renovation decisions to make. He flipped open his laptop, clicked on the favorites bar, and showed me option after option. I was able to make a few choices on the spot, but I need time to consider the others."

When Max opened the car door for Anna, she was still talking. "There are so many decisions to make." Then she realized what she was doing. "I'm sorry. I'm a motor mouth. I've been busy today and can't seem to calm down."

Max wondered if that was all there was to it. Was she nervous about being alone with him? He wanted to pull over and kiss away her uneasiness, but he wouldn't take a chance on making the situation worse.

After driving a couple of miles, Max turned off the interstate. He traveled another three miles before turning onto a gravel road barely wide enough for a car to pass. Nothing marked it but a homemade sign.

Anna looked around at the vast expanse of trees. "You weren't kidding about this place being in the boonies."

"It's not really that far from town. Just secluded. But it's unlikely anyone would happen upon it." About ten minutes later, he parked on a piece of bare ground with about twenty other vehicles. "This is it."

"Really?" Anna joked, looking up at a huge sign looming above the parking area. On it was a caricature of a large, open-mouthed catfish with bold letters printed above. "Lucky's" it said, "where everybody gets lucky but the catfish." It wasn't quite dark, but Anna could see the green florescent lights outlining the catfish.

Lucky's Catfish House was an unpainted building sitting between two bodies of water: a narrow, slow-moving creek on the left and a stagnant body of water on the right.

"You'll need to keep an eye out for mud puddles and more objectionable things," Max told Anna, holding out a hand to help her from the car.

"You didn't tell me it's a zoo."

"More like a farm. The Stewart family lives in the house at the other end of the parking lot. The animals belong to them. When the restaurant first opened, they had goats but couldn't keep them off the customers' cars. There are rabbits over there." Max pointed to a hutch.

"I bet Gracie loves it here."

"She does. There's a sow in a pen back behind the house. She had piglets recently, and Gracie got to hold one. I have some great pictures."

"I'd love to see them."

"And I'd love to show them to you."

Anna side-stepped a puddle. "Should have worn my shit kickers."

"You don't own any shit kickers."

Anna looked up and smiled. "You're right, I don't." She let out a surprised squeal when two large hands surrounded her waist, lifting her off her feet.

"Crap," he explained. "You were about to step in some."

"Thanks." Anna laughed, hoping Max couldn't tell how much she enjoyed having his hands on her.

The restaurant's dirt-and-gravel frontage was alive with activity. People chatted in a waiting line that extended into the parking lot. A mother took a photograph of her toddler sitting on an unpainted bench, petting a white cat. A boy, about ten years old, craned his neck to see what a man pointed to in the murky water. A little girl with a big blue bow in her hair held a carrot for a black and white rabbit to nibble. And a woman yelled at a couple of boys to stop chasing the hens.

Anna gasped in disbelief. "Those chickens are flying!"

"Anna Robinson, you mean you've lived here most of your life, and you didn't know chickens can fly?"

"No!"

"I'm not sure it's actually called flying," Max said. "They flap their wings and propel themselves upward. You see that they're roosting on the lower limbs of the tree, and getting that high seems to take a lot of effort."

Before Max and Anna got into line, a waitress motioned them forward. She'd waved at them minutes before as she ran past, most likely late for work. She was dressed like Anna, except her top was much tighter and lower cut.

"Hi, Max," she said loudly enough for those in line to hear. "Come on in. Claude is expecting you."

Smiling broadly at Max, she led them to a table and leaned forward farther than was necessary to give them their menus.

"Who is Claude?" Anna asked.

"He's the owner, and he's not really expecting us. You can't make reservations here. Jennifer was just helping us out. Being friendly."

Anna smiled. "Sure she was."

A few minutes later, a middle-aged man appeared with a bowl of turnip greens and a basket of hush puppies. "Redneck hors d'oeuvres," he explained, noticing Anna's confusion.

Max introduced Anna to Claude Davis. "Claude and his wife, Hildy, own this place."

"It's my first time here," Anna said politely. "It's a great place."

"Hildy and I started building this about four years ago. My wife's a good woman. Good with a hammer, good in the kitchen, and I'll get in trouble if I finish that sentence." He chuckled at his own joke.

"We opened with just this room, then added on with the help of some of our kin. We're open Thursday, Friday, and Saturday nights. When we're open, we're full. Like the sign out front says, we're lucky people. Good to see you, Max. Nice to meet you, Anna. If I don't get back to work, I'll be in trouble with that good woman in the kitchen. Thanks for visiting us. Someone will be here shortly to take your order."

Anna looked around at the strange collection of items hanging on the unpainted plank walls. On one wall, there were framed photographs of Willie Nelson, Johnny Cash, and a real bear sitting at a table with a family. On another were car tags, mounted animal heads, and several large-mouth bass frozen in the act of plucking bugs from the air. Through the window, Anna saw a resin alligator next to a sign that said, "Don't feed the gators." At least, she thought it was resin. It hadn't moved.

Before Anna could take in more of her surroundings, a young woman and a man with a guitar settled on the low stage.

"I'm Stephanie," the woman announced, "and that's Johnny over there with the guitar. I'm here to sing a few songs for y'all, and I'm happy to have my parents in the audience tonight. My dad was real sick recently, and we thought we were gonna lose him." She hesitated, regaining control of her emotions. "But he's here with us tonight, one hundred percent, praise the Lord."

People in the restaurant applauded.

"I hope y'all will indulge me for a couple of minutes while I sing him a little song." Stephanie launched into an emotional rendition of the country song "Dad, You're My Hero" and customers all over the restaurant wiped away tears. Anna was stoic.

Unlike most people in the room, she never knew her dad. Not even his name. How often, Max wondered, had she endured similar situations? He covered her hand with his to offer comfort and because he needed to touch her.

They ordered the catfish dinner, substituting a baked potato for the fries, just so everything on the plate wasn't deep-fried. While they waited, several old friends and fans of Anna's book came over to say hello.

"It's so good to see you, Anna," Gladys Waters said, trying to be heard over the music. "We're all so proud of you. Every time I see you on television, I call everyone I know to tell them to turn on the TV. What was Jimmy Fallon like?"

"He was nice, friendly. But I really didn't spend that much time with him. How've you been, Gladys? You look good."

"Well, thank you, but I know I've gotten fat. I have to cook for my family, and unfortunately, I like my own cooking."

Max had hoped he and Anna could have a conversation over dinner, start getting reacquainted. He wanted to know about her life after he left Tenacity. But mostly, he wanted to know if he had a chance with her. He wouldn't ask outright. Not yet. But he was hoping for a clue. He should have thought about the loud music.

Jennifer arrived with their meal, once again treating Max to a view of her ample cleavage. Since it was a crime in this part of the country to let fried catfish get cold, the other patrons left them to enjoy their meal. They listened

63

to the music, and Max resigned himself to a loud, superficial conversation. After paying the check, which included a big tip for Jennifer, he walked to the stage and spoke to Stephanie.

"We have a request for an old song," Stephanie announced, "a tune recorded back in the 1970s by Frankie Valli." The chords of "My Eyes Adored You" filled the room, and couples drifted to the dance floor. Max held out his hand, inviting Anna to join them. Holding her slender body close, he swayed to the music.

Anna relaxed against Max's warm strong body for the first time since she was sixteen. He seemed bigger now, more masculine. Being pressed against him and inhaling his spicy scent was the best feeling in the world. She could happily stay wrapped in his arms for the rest of her life. *What am I thinking? I'm not thinking. That's the problem. This man is my kryptonite. He gets close, and I go weak.*

Unaware of her thoughts, Max leaned down and whispered in her ear, his warm breath caressing her neck, "This song was written for us." The lyrics spoke of children walking home from school together, of unexpressed young love, and the sadness of drifting apart. It spoke of loss and regret.

Anna's feelings, already on a trampoline, bounced a little out of control. When Max felt her snuggle into him, he pulled her closer. Then he felt the tears. *Shit. The song was too much.* Saying nothing, he held her and swayed to the music.

Knowing he felt her tears, Anna looked up. "Do I look like I've been crying?"

"Nah. The light in here is dim. No one will notice. You're beautiful."

Max gave Stephanie a nod of thanks and dropped a bill in her tip bucket. With a hand on the small of Anna's back, he guided her out the front door.

In the SUV, Anna covered her face with her hands. "I don't know what's wrong with me."

"Nothing's wrong with you. You're perfect."

She rolled her eyes and threw her hands in the air. "I can't explain. I don't know why I was crying."

Max smoothed her hair. "I must be doing something wrong. I'll do better. I shouldn't have sprung that song on you. It's just that it says things that are hard for me to say, things I want you to know." Then his voice softened, and he looked even more serious. "I've missed you, blue eyes, for a very long time."

Uncomfortable with the intensity of his emotion, Max said nothing else. Instead, he wrapped his arms around Anna and kissed the side of her head. In turn, she buried her face in his neck.

Inhaling his manly scent, she was filled with desire and a myriad of other thoughts and emotions. She'd dreamed of just such a moment, but now that it was here, she didn't know how to react.

Max leaned in and kissed her. It was the kind of kiss women dream of; soft and sweet, as well as passionate. Then he buckled her in and began the drive home. Anna didn't think anyone had buckled her in since she was a child. It felt good to be cared for. When Max felt her eyes on him, he looked at her and winked. No one spoke, but Max took her hand, placed it on his leg, and covered it with his.

It took all his self-control, but Max gave Anna an almost chaste goodnight kiss and reminded her to lock the deadbolt when she got inside. As she walked into her room, Anna turned and said, "I've missed you, Max." It wasn't much, as declarations go, but he'd take whatever she had to give.

Lying in bed that night, Anna thought of nothing but Max. Dancing in his arms had been heavenly. His embrace felt warm, safe, and right, like she belonged there. But she knew feelings could contradict reality, and giving in to Max's charms could be dangerous.

Anna had lied to Max about her tears, but she couldn't let him know a six-year-old pain had reappeared and overwhelmed her. She was only sixteen when he left, but she'd loved him. She always would. And for that reason, he had the power to hurt her like no one else.

She'd spent the last six years trying to mend the heart he decimated. Would she ever learn? The first time Max broke her heart she was twelve years old, and it marked the end of a beautiful, carefree childhood.

CHAPTER NINE

Max and Anna began walking to and from school together when Anna entered first grade and Max was in the third. Margie intended to drop her daughter off at school each morning and have Cleo, the sitter, pick her up in the afternoon.

"Please, please, please, let me walk," Anna begged. "I'll stay on the sidewalk, and Max will walk with me. He said he would."

Since the school sat at the edge of Mill Village and they lived only a few short blocks away, Margie relented. "All right, if it's okay with Max and you promise not to go off on your own." The arrangement continued for years. Since they were the only kids on their street, it was the natural thing to do.

One momentous day when Anna was twelve and Max was fourteen, he told her not to wait for him after school. "I have something to do," was all he said.

"Okay. Hope today is a good one." It wasn't—at least not for Anna. When school was out, she breezed past noisy kids boarding school buses and began the short walk home. Suddenly, she knew what Max had to do after school.

Dismayed, she saw him on the opposite side of the street with Madison Marley, who looked up at him like he was some kind of superhero. At age fourteen, Madison was everything Anna wasn't—a petite, popular, ninth grade, junior varsity cheerleader. She even had the curves of a woman's body, while Anna was a tall, skinny twelve-year-old. Jealous and angry, she cast a reproachful look in Max's direction, but his attention was solely on Madison. The forlorn dejected girl kicked the ground, reluctantly continuing her walk.

Curt Gillis, a kid who never missed an opportunity to torture anyone smaller or weaker, saw Max with Madison and knew he had a target. "Come on," he said to his companions. "Let's have some fun." Stepping in front of Anna, walking backward to face her, Curt taunted, "Where's your boyfriend? Oh, yeah, that's right, he finally realized you're a brat."

A sixth sense told her to ignore him and keep walking, but instead, she talked back. "I'm not a brat, dummy. I'm probably taller than she is." It was a foolish thing to say, and she regretted it the moment it left her mouth.

An evil grin came across Curt's face as an avenue of torture manifested itself. "Yeah, but she has boobs," he taunted. Seeing his jab hit its target, the bully was emboldened. "You think she has any boobs under that shirt?" he asked one of his equally contemptible friends.

"Nah," answered the boy, enjoying Anna's discomfort.

"Maybe we should check," a third boy suggested, grinning as he and his friends began surrounding her.

Anna tried not to let them see how terrified she was. "Leave me alone, you bullies! Leave me alone!"

The boys were smirking, and Anna was on the verge of panic. She wanted to sink to the sidewalk and curl into a ball, but instinctively knew she should stay on her feet.

When she started yelling for help, the boys laughed. Max heard Anna, dropped his backpack, and jogged across the street. If he ended up in a fight, at least he wouldn't be hampered by a backpack. He tried to appear nonchalant. "What's going on here, guys?"

Curt looked up, surprised to see Max. "Nothing. We're just having a little fun."

Max assessed the situation. If things progressed to a fight, he'd be outnumbered, but if he yelled for Anna to run, maybe he could occupy them long enough for her to get away. He hid his anger, tried to sound casual, and hoped for the best. "Ah, leave her alone, Curt. She's just a kid, and you've scared her. Let her go."

Curt was intelligent enough to realize he wouldn't win the credibility battle if the incident came to the attention of school officials, so he backed off. "Come on, guys. Let's go. Leave the brat alone." Curt and his friends laughed as they walked away, and Max sighed with relief.

Completely humiliated, Anna managed to muster the courage to look Max in the eye. She expected him to put his arm around her and sooth her fears away. Instead, he gently said, "You're okay now, Anna. Go on home." Then he walked away.

She couldn't believe it. He walked away! For a moment, she just stood there, watching Max walk toward Madison. Anna ran home. Or maybe she walked. She wasn't sure. But she was sure her life had just changed.

Her absolute best friend in the world was no longer hers. And she felt a huge empty hole in her heart.

Max was reticent for the rest of his walk with Madison, thinking of how Anna looked at him when he told her to go home. He saw not only fear and embarrassment but also accusation in her big blue eyes, as if he'd betrayed her somehow. He hadn't. He'd helped. Saved her even. So why did he have a dark, sick feeling in the pit of his stomach?

After depositing Madison at her door, Max gave the situation serious thought. He wasn't a kid anymore, and he couldn't continue walking Anna home forever. He had a life of his own. The problem was, he decided, Anna was too dependent on him. Maybe if he kept his distance, she would venture out, spend more time with friends her own age, stop depending on him so much.

But Max couldn't help himself. He stopped by her house to check on her. It wouldn't hurt to check on her. He walked up the front steps and knocked. "Anna?" he called through the door. Her heart leapt when she heard his voice, but she said nothing. When there was no answer, Max tried again. "Anna, are you okay?" Nothing.

Inside, Anna sat hugging her knees, still bewildered by the events of the afternoon. She was too hurt and embarrassed to face her friend and glad no one was home to ask what happened. Before Max walked away, he did the only thing he could think of. Loudly enough for Anna to hear, trying to sound worldly, he yelled, "Curt and the rest of those guys are assholes. Don't listen to anything they say. And stay clear of them. They're mean sons of bitches."

She'd never heard Max curse before and would have teased him about it under other circumstances. But at the moment, she couldn't get past her own misery. Her pride was bruised, and she'd been so scared. She even felt a little sick to her stomach. *Why had those boys been so mean?*

It was Max's fault for walking home with that girl, Anna told herself, although deep down she knew it wasn't. He came to her rescue, and she should be grateful. But the boy who'd been her friend for as long as she could remember was leaving her, and she was devastated.

Anna resigned herself to walking home alone. When Curt and his friends tried to torment her again, she was prepared. "If you touch me, you'd better kill me," she shouted. "Because I'll call the sheriff, and he'll put you perverts behind bars. Maybe you'll like juvie," she mocked. The boys weren't sure they could be arrested for harassing a girl but decided they'd better not take the chance.

Carol and Margie were concerned about their children's aloofness toward one another, but neither Max nor Anna ever spoke of the incident. One spring morning the two friends walked to school together, and that afternoon they weren't speaking. Things were awkward between the friends for the rest of the school year and into the middle of the summer.

Just as the split happened, swiftly and absolutely, so did the reconciliation. It was a hot humid day. Dressed in shorts and a t-shirt, her hair in a ponytail, Anna mowed half the front lawn before shutting off the mower and going inside for a drink.

She sat at her mom's retro dinette set, her slender legs sticking to the plastic seat of the aluminum chair, and drank a glass of cold tea. Hearing the lawn mower start, she looked out the kitchen window to the front lawn. Max was behind the mower.

Anna watched until he finished, seeing the gesture for the peace offering it was. Pushing the screen door open with her shoulder, she shouted, "Max!" holding up a glass of sweet, iced tea. He smiled and wiped his face with the tail of his shirt, exposing a torso worthy of the attention she was giving it. They met at the steps, where he took the glass, nodded his appreciation, and mumbled his thanks.

"You're welcome," Anna said. "Thanks for finishing the lawn."

"Sure."

They sat on Anna's front steps and quenched their thirst in companionable silence, no longer children, not yet adults. Their relationship had changed, but they remained friends. Max wasn't sure how Anna was supposed to fit into his life, but he knew she belonged there.

CHAPTER TEN

The day after their meal at Lucky's, Max received a text from Anna. **Thanks for last night—the meal, the song, the dance, and the kiss. Sorry about the tears. Return to Tenacity arousing too many emotions. Need time to myself. Hope you understand.**

Max told himself it could have been worse. At least she thanked him for the kiss. He didn't know what she needed time for, but he knew she was telling him to back off. Okay. He didn't like it, but he could give her some space. He answered her text. **Enjoyed last night—especially the kiss. Don't worry about the tears. Here when you're ready.**

Every morning for the last week or so, Anna had driven to Mill Village for a run and a shower at her house before the crew arrived. Exactly five days after her text to Max, she sensed someone running up beside her as she began her second lap around the neighborhood.

"All right if I run with you?" Max asked.

73

"If you think you can keep up," she quipped, happy to see him.

"I'll do my best."

Anna hadn't seen Max since their dinner at Lucky's, although she received a brief text each night asking if she was safely locked in her room.

"Gracie's not with you today?"

"One of her mother's mornings. I'll pick her up after work."

"Is the shared custody arrangement working out all right?"

"Pretty much. Sometimes I need to call on Mom for help. But I never ask Janine to keep her on my time. I can't say the same for her."

"And that causes problems for you."

"Not problems. More like complications, but Gracie's worth it."

"The neighborhood's looking good," Anna commented, moving the conversation along. "Been any changes in ownership?"

"A couple. Miss Beula died."

"How old was she?"

"She died soon after her hundredth birthday. Her daughter moved in to help and stayed. She had some repairs done to the house and painted the exterior, but Chantilly is still pink and still has her gingerbread trim. You probably saw that Henry is for sale."

"I did. He's as dapper as ever, although the yard could use some work." Still running, she looked at Max. "I can't believe you remember the names I gave those houses. How old do you think I was?"

"Probably about ten. And I only remember a few. You were always naming things, like Mr. Jordan's cows and those horses on the other side of the Corridor."

"Sparkle. I loved Sparkle. I used to pretend he was mine."

"But you were most inventive with the houses. You saw personality in them, and the names seemed to fit. I should have known you'd end up doing something creative."

"You're the one designing houses."

"Maybe you influenced me."

They ran in silence until Max said, "Seeing you run makes me think of the day you made the track team."

"You remember that?"

"Yeah. I knew you were trying out, so I hung around to watch. Made me late for football practice, but it was worth it to see the look on Shoemake's face. You were faster than every girl on his team. Surprised the hell out of him. I didn't know the man was capable of a smile that big." Max knew his smile must have been as big as the coaches. Who knew sweet Anna could run like a gazelle?

Breathing a little harder, his words came a bit slower. "The next year, you took the team to state and won."

"I didn't do it alone."

"But it wouldn't have happened without you. Remember how excited everyone was?"

Anna remembered all right. She remembered hearing Max's voice as she approached the starting block. Looking up, she saw him on the sidelines, hands cupped around his mouth, yelling for all he was worth. "You can do it, Anna! Just run!" She flashed him a smile, shut out everything but the task at hand, and passed every competitor on the track.

For Anna, one celebratory moment stood out above all the others. In all the excitement, Max picked her up and swung her around. Then he did the most astonishing thing. He set her on the ground and planted a firm kiss squarely on her lips. Lying in the dark that night, teen-aged Anna replayed the moment, remembering how it felt to have his arms around her and his mouth on hers. She unabashedly basked in the thrill of it, for one night. Then the next day, she put it behind her and resumed the pretense of wanting nothing more than friendship from the boy next door.

Now, here I am years later, Anna realized, *jogging through the old neighborhood with the man next door, still pretending I want nothing more from him than friendship.*

Near the end of their run, Max said, "I left something for you on your porch. Please use it." A little winded, he veered off at his house and waved a hand behind him. "Work waits."

Then he turned. Walking backwards, he called to Anna, "Don't leave early tonight. I'm bringing take-out." He jogged inside without giving her time to respond. Max knew she wouldn't appreciate his approach, but he'd given her five whole days to herself. That should be enough. And he was afraid if he asked, she'd say no. If she wasn't there when he showed up, so be it.

Anna found a box on her front porch. The attached note said, "If I can't talk you into staying some place safe, please use these items." Untying the bow, Anna was touched by the unromantic but thoughtful items the box contained. There was a can of mace, a door wedge, and a heavy flashlight, with a note explaining the flashlight was useful as a weapon as well as a light. Even though she considered herself an independent woman, she appreciated Max's concern.

As she showered and dressed for the day, Anna thought about Max's announcement that he was bringing supper. It should bother her that he told her he was bringing take-out instead of asking, but it didn't. Since their dinner at Lucky's, Anna had been doing some soul-searching. She was ready to admit, at least to herself, that she wanted a romantic relationship with Max.

Could she trust him not to break her heart? If it happened again, she was afraid she'd never recover. That might sound overly dramatic, but it was a real concern. The man had the power to do that to her.

Max left work early to prepare for the evening. First, he stopped at a big box store to buy a thermal bag designed to keep food warm. Then he drove to the best Chinese restaurant in Clarkston and bought fifteen containers of take-out.

With the thermal bag in his arms, Max stood at Anna's screen door and watched the sexiest woman he'd ever seen. Tall and slender, wearing short shorts and a t-shirt, Anna stood barefoot, strands of hair falling from her casual updo. She was holding a paintbrush, studying paint swatches on the wall. Max was spellbound. Controlling his libido around her was a constant challenge. *The woman's going to kill me, and she isn't even trying.*

Max cleared his throat, hoping not to startle her. "It's me. I come bearing gifts." He held up the bag of food. "Hope you like Chinese."

"Who doesn't? I'm starving. Come on in." When she pushed the screen door open, Max sauntered in and gave her a quick kiss on the lips. He was gorgeous as always, wearing jeans and a navy golf shirt with a tasteful Anderson Architecture and Construction logo printed on the front.

The man was hard to resist. *If things are to progress beyond friendship*, Anna thought, *we need to move slowly, let things simmer. Our relationship should be a meandering stroll through a park—not a high-speed Olympic sprint. It would help if he could dial down all that masculine hotness.*

"Be right back," Max said, making a quick trip to the SUV parked in Anna's drive. He returned with a quilt, a bottle of wine, a corkscrew, two wine glasses, and a smile that rocked Anna's world.

"Looks like you've thought of everything."

"I aim to please."

Spreading the quilt on the living room floor, Max proceeded to take small containers from the bag. When Anna gracefully folded herself onto the quilt, Max noticed that the hot pink polish on her toenails was splattered with paint and wondered if it was weird to think a woman's toes were sexy.

"You think you brought enough?" Anna teased.

"I didn't know what you like, so I got an assortment."

Max held up a fork in one hand and chopsticks in the other. Anna reached for the fork. "I've never understood why people insist on learning to use chopsticks or twirl spaghetti. I'm an American. I use a fork."

About that time, the aroma from the cartons reached Anna's nostrils, and she made that sound of appreciation that sent Max's imagination straight to the bedroom.

He redirected his thoughts. "Tell me about your plans for the house."

"I will, but let's eat first. I'm starving." Sitting on the quilt, close to one another, they ate directly from the boxes, sharing as if it were the most natural thing in the world. Anna finally began to talk.

"I have lots of ideas for the house. But you're an architect. My plans may be all wrong."

Max shook his head. "You should do what you want. Fred will keep you straight on the structural requirements. The design should suit your needs, represent your taste. Go ahead. Talk to me. I'm interested."

"Okay." Anna was excited to tell him her plans. "This room, the kitchen, and the section of hallway separating them will become one large room, rising all the way to the rafters. It will be the only living space. No separate den or dining room. I'm going for the open casual look."

"It's what most people want these days. Keep going. I like what I'm hearing."

"The wall between this room and what Mom called the den will be pushed back to allow space for an open staircase leading to the attic." Anna was animated, her eyes shining. "It'll have a pretty white banister with clean lines."

Damn you're beautiful, Max thought. But he said, "This is fun for you, isn't it?"

"Definitely. I guess I'm an architect wannabe. It must be great to do that for a living."

"It is. Of course, it's different from designing your own place. But there's something to be said for creating something you don't have to pay for. What's going upstairs?"

"Since I'm repurposing so much of the downstairs, I'll put a guest bedroom and bath up there and maybe a sitting area. And if there's enough space, I'd like a storage room for Christmas decorations and things I should get rid of but can't seem to turn loose."

"My mom needs a room like that. By the way, Mom and Dad send their love and want to see you. I'd like to drive you over there when you're ready."

"That would be nice. I've missed them. But let me settle in first."

"Take your time. Just let me know when you're ready. Now tell me about the addition," Max said, reclining on his side, propping on an elbow. Anna was scraping the last bit of food from one of the boxes. Holding up a finger, she finished chewing the last bite of cashew chicken before continuing.

"Fred demolished the old back porch, which was in bad condition, and added twelve feet across the entire rear of the house. The hallway will continue down the middle of the addition, with a screened porch on the right side. My office, which is almost finished, is on the left. I had Fred install lots of windows, so I can look up from my work and see the woods beyond the yard."

"Sounds perfect. What else?"

"Good stuff." She proceeded to describe the placement of the office closet, a half bath, a laundry room, a coat closet, a pantry, and a master bedroom suite.

"I can picture it all. I'm impressed, Miss Architect Wannabe. You can work with me any time."

"For now, I'll stick with writing. I'm working on a second book, hoping *A World Apart* wasn't a fluke."

"Nah, you know you're talented."

Uncomfortable with the praise, Anna patted her flat stomach. "I don't have room for another bite. I can't believe I ate so much." Max began putting the empty cartons into the bag from the restaurant.

Anna started to stand. "You brought the food. I'll clean up."

"No need," Max said, tugging her arm, gently pulling her back to the quilt. "There's nothing to do. I'll take all this with me when I leave. How about more wine?"

"I'd better not. I have to drive to the motel."

"Yeah. How long are you going to keep doing that?"

"Not much longer, I hope," Anna said, sitting cross-legged on the quilt. "They're going to finish the master suite before they do anything else."

Max sat up and leaned on one knee, watching her. "Really? I'm surprised Fred agreed to that?"

"He tried to talk me out of it, explaining that having the subcontractors come twice will cost more and slow down the project. But I have to sleep somewhere, and I'm ready to get out of that motel."

"I wish you'd take my extra room." *Or share my bed.*

"We had that talk. You know I can't do that. But I'm using the travel lock you gave me, and I'll be settled in here soon. I need to get some writing done."

81

"That'll be hard in a construction zone," Max reminded her. You know how loud it gets."

"That's why we're soundproofing my bedroom. We can't get it completely soundproofed, since it has windows. but it'll be as insulated as we can get it."

"That's a creative solution, but if it doesn't work out as well as you hope, use my house. Cook, write, take a nap, whatever. It sits empty all day. I'll bring a key over tomorrow, so you can use it whenever you like."

Conversation between the two old friends flowed easily, until it turned to things that occurred when they were apart. Curiously, neither of them wanted to convey anything more than cursory information about those years.

Anna changed the subject. "Have you reconnected with any of your high school girlfriends since you returned?"

Max chuckled. "Quite a few of them are married with kids."

"How about the other one hundred and fifty?"

Max ran his hand through his hair, looking apologetic. "I guess there were quite a few."

"Yeah. You could claim to be the founder of speed dating."

He rubbed his hand across the back of his neck. "What can I say? I never understood why being a quarterback was such an aphrodisiac. But I was a horny teenager, and I wasn't complaining."

Anna shook her head. "I think you're being modest. You must know that being a quarterback wasn't the only reason girls threw themselves at you. You were pretty cute."

"You thought I was cute? I never knew." Then he flashed his irresistible smile and teased, "What about now?"

She looked at him appraisingly. "I don't think cute is the right word. Sexy is more appropriate." Anna was surprised that came out of her mouth, and so was Max, who went into full flirt mode.

"Well, Annaleah Robinson," he said, using her whole name. "That's interesting, because I think you're the sexiest, most beautiful woman I know. Do you think we have a chance in hell of resisting one another?"

"Of course. But we might have to work at it." Uh oh, she was flirting too. Not a good idea.

"Let's try something," Max challenged. "You kiss me, and I'll see if I can control myself."

Anna laughed. "Has anyone ever fallen for that?"

"No really, I dare you," he teased, ignoring her question. He lay on his back and put his hands behind his head. "Go ahead."

Having fun, Anna leaned over and kissed him on the cheek.

"I'm resisting. Keep going," urged Max.

Knowing she was flirting with danger, she kissed him on the other cheek. Max shook his head, looking stoic. "Still resisting. You can do better than that."

Anna kissed him on his forehead, his nose, near his eyes, his chin, and before she realized what she was doing, she was kissing the corners of his mouth. She'd taken the game too far. She was about to tell him he passed the test, when he cupped her head in his hand, wrapped an arm around her waist, and pulled her against his long hard body. Then he gifted her with a kiss that

83

could wake the dead. It was slow and easy, deep and sensual. Anna was floating on a cloud of pleasure when Max reluctantly pulled away, afraid he was moving too fast.

"Well, now we know," he quipped, breathing hard. "You're definitely irresistible. It's been substantiated by empirical data."

In her own attempt to lighten the mood, Anna fanned her face. "Whew. We proved something all right."

She stood and moved the bag of food containers off the quilt. Max wasn't ready for the evening to end, but he got the message and began gathering the remains of their picnic. Together, they folded the quilt, the last fold bringing them face to face. It was all Max could do to stop himself from kissing her again, but he was afraid he may have already taken things too far.

"I'll drop the bag in the motel dumpster when I follow you back."

"You don't need to do that. I can get to my room by myself."

"I know, but I'm following anyway. I won't walk you to the door if that's what you prefer."

He'd walked Anna to her door the night he took her to Lucky's, but after that, she decided a man at her motel room door might give the wrong impression.

Max kissed Anna, no hands style, his arms full of items to take to his car. *Leave them wanting more,* he told himself. *The problem is, I'm the one wanting more.*

CHAPTER ELEVEN

The next morning, when Anna was making coffee for the crew, she faintly heard someone call her name over the buzz of the electric saw. Looking in the direction of the open front door, she saw the adult version of a handsome, sandy-haired boy she went to school with. "Jeff," she yelled, walking over to hug him. "Jeff Windom. Come in. I'm so glad to see you."

She spoke close to his ear. "Coffee?"

"If it's already made," Jeff yelled.

"It is. How do you take it?"

"Black's fine."

Jeff happily watched his high school crush pour coffee into two mismatched cups she retrieved from an almost empty kitchen cabinet. He accepted the hot cup of coffee, followed his friend onto the front porch, and leaned against the banister.

Anna situated herself in a weather-worn rocking chair. "Now we can hear each other. What are you doing here so bright and early?"

"I heard one of my favorite people was back in town, and I wanted to see you." Jeff had always liked Anna, and if he was perfectly honest, he'd have to admit he enjoyed looking at her. That morning, she was wearing flip-flops that showed off her bright orange toenails, shorts showcasing long, toned legs, and a white v-necked t-shirt that couldn't hide her curves. With her hair pulled back in a ponytail, she was stunning.

Looking like the rancher he was, in cowboy boots and a western belt buckle, Jeff sent Anna a crooked smile. "I was driving by and saw an unfamiliar car in the driveway, so I stopped to see if you were here."

"I'm so glad you did. Tell me what you've been up to." *Besides filling out that tall skinny frame of yours and becoming quite the hottie.*

"The long version or the short one?"

"The long one."

"Okay. I graduated from Mississippi State with a degree in animal husbandry."

"Congratulations."

"Thanks. Unlike you, it took me all four years to graduate. I read in a magazine that you finished college in three years, like you did high school. Anyone ever tell you you're an overachiever?"

"It's been mentioned, but really, I had to. I couldn't afford a fourth year. So what's your plan now? Will you stay in Tenacity?"

"Oh yeah. I couldn't leave this place. I like to tell people I have a ranch, but that's a stretch. I have a few head of cattle. Started buying them back in high school."

"How did you manage that?"

"Dad began paying me as a cattle hand as early as middle school. In high school, I hired on with neighboring ranchers who needed help. Sometimes, I worked cattle auctions. Really, I did about anything that required some muscle and hard work."

Anna leaned back in the rocking chair, careful not to spill her coffee. "I'm impressed. So how big is this ranch of yours?"

"Thanks to Dad, I have more than a hundred acres between old man Sullivan's place and Samantha's. I have a prize Bull and a couple of dozen Brangus cows."

"Never heard of a Brangus."

"It's a cross between Angus and Brahman. They're beautiful animals, and half of mine are pregnant," he said proudly. "I've got a ton of plans I won't bore you with. That's pretty much my story." Jeff rested his cup on the banister. "The last time I saw you was at your mom's funeral. Then you disappeared. I wondered where you were and what you were doing. Then suddenly you were in the papers and on talk shows. You're famous."

Anna shrugged. "I guess you could say I got my fifteen minutes of fame. Some of it was fun. Some of it was a pain in the neck."

Max stepped onto his front porch with the intention of getting into his SUV for his daily commute to work. But he changed his plans abruptly when he noticed Jeff Windom's truck parked next door. *What the hell was Windom doing at Anna's?* Knowing it would make him late for work, Max sauntered next door, trying to look casual. He needed to let Windom know the field wasn't open where Anna was concerned.

He found the two of them on the front porch, laughing over a morning cup of coffee. After giving his neighbor a proprietary kiss on the cheek, Max shook Jeff's hand.

"Good to see you, big guy," Jeff said. "You're not going to try to deck me again, are you?"

"Humph. I guess that depends on your intentions?"

Jeff smiled and returned the volley. "Maybe I should ask you the same."

Anna looked puzzled. "Maybe y'all could let me in on the joke. But first, how about I get you a cup of coffee, Max?"

"That'd be nice. Thanks." She didn't have to know he left a full travel mug sitting on his porch.

Max had settled on the swing when she returned with his coffee. Anna sat in the rocker.

"Go ahead, Jeff. Let her in on the joke," Max said.

Anna eyed Jeff expectantly, and he saw she wasn't going to let it go.

Looking slightly chagrined, he risked an explanation. "It was a few years back. Remember how cool I was when I was sixteen?"

"I do," Anna joked.

"Good. Keep that in mind." Jeff began a whitewashed version of the encounter. "Well, I said something complimentary about you—in the locker room."

"Humph," grumbled Max.

Jeff defended his statement. "It was complimentary—in a macho locker room sort of way."

Anna crossed her arms. "Oh, I see. Locker room talk, was it?"

"Yeah," Jeff said, with a slight shrug.

Anna pretended annoyance. "And what exactly did you say, Mr. Windom?"

Stroking his chin, as if in deep thought, Jeff drawled, "As I recall, the last thing I said before landing on the locker room floor was, I'd like to tap that."

Anna pressed her lips together, trying not to laugh. "That was no reason for Max to hit you."

"That was nothing compared to Pops's lecture about respecting women and the long list of chores he gave me." Pleased Anna found his anecdote amusing, Jeff continued the story. "Kevin Bartell must have said something complimentary, too, because the next thing I knew, he was lying on the floor beside me."

Anna laughed out loud. "I remember Max getting into trouble for hitting you guys, as he should have, but I had no idea it involved me."

"Anna, half the guys in school had the hots for you. Didn't you ever wonder why you weren't asked out more often?"

Anna sat her empty coffee cup on the floor. "Are you insinuating Max thwarted my high school love life?"

"I'm not insinuating anything. I'm telling you he did."

Max looked at Anna, a serious expression on his face. "I was protecting you."

She was amused. In truth, she hadn't been that interested in dating. She wanted to be, but Max was the only boy on her radar.

Anna sent a mock look of defiance Max's direction. "Jeff took me to the prom."

Jeff stifled a grin. "Hey, you were gone, man. Married. She was up for grabs."

Anna was enjoying Max's discomfort. "Mom wasn't happy when I didn't come home that night."

Jeff caught on right away. "But what a night!"

"Yeah," Anna said dreamily. "It was my first time."

Jeff stood, ready to defend himself, if necessary. "That's taking the joke a little far. I was a gentleman. Tell him, Anna."

She grinned. "As I remember, you were so shy you had trouble working up the courage to kiss me good-night."

"Okay, I admit I might not have been quite as confident with the opposite sex as I pretended in the locker room."

Max frowned at Jeff, "You mean I decked you for no good reason?"

Jeff rocked back on his heels a couple of times. "You could say that."

After the three friends shared a laugh, Jeff put his cup on the floor beside Anna's. "Okay to leave this here?"

"Sure. I'll put it away later."

Jeff gave her one of his sexy smiles. "Don't forget I want to show you the ranch."

"I'm looking forward to it." Standing, she gave him a friendly hug. "Thanks so much for stopping by."

Max stood as well, and the men shook hands, exchanging niceties.

Jeff started walking away, then stopped and turned around. Totally ignoring Max, he fixed his gaze on Anna. "Just so you know, I'm not quite so shy these days."

Max knew that was an understatement. He'd seen Jeff in a few bars, always with a different girl. And if Max could help it, Anna wouldn't be his next conquest.

CHAPTER TWELVE

Minutes after the crew left for the evening, Anna heard a vehicle pull into the driveway. She walked onto the porch in time to see a pretty young woman with curly, strawberry-blonde hair emerge from a shiny, refurbished 1950s truck. With a huge smile on her face, Anna ran down the steps to greet her childhood friend. "Samantha! You came!" Samantha's big smile matched Anna's, as they hugged eagerly, tears in their eyes.

"Sam, I'm so glad to see you. I was afraid you'd be angry with me for leaving like I did."

"Oh, I am," Samantha said, still smiling. "We're going to talk about that and about how much I missed you senior year. I don't blame you for finishing early, but I really missed you."

They walked to the porch, their arms wrapped around one another's waists, then sat on the swing, excitedly talking over one another.

"I can't believe my best friend is a famous author. I'm sooo proud of you! Every time I saw you on television, I called to make sure my parents were watching."

"You're not living with your parents anymore? It's hard to picture you living anywhere but the farm."

"Oh, I'm still at the farm. Mom and Dad aren't.

"You're kidding! What happened?"

"You remember my mom's parents. They still live in Smokey Creek. They're getting older and beginning to need some help. So, when a house near them went on the market, Mom and Dad bought it. They declared themselves retired, gave me the deed to the farm, and moved."

"Wow, that's a big change for them. Are they happy there?"

"Yes. I think they are. That's where they're both from, and they have friends there."

"I can't believe you're in that big farmhouse all alone. Or maybe you're not alone. I don't see a ring on your finger. Is there a boyfriend? Someone special?"

Samantha stared at her hands. "I guess you don't know."

"I guess I don't. What?"

"I suppose you should hear the story from me." Sam took a deep breath. 'Okay. Here goes. I ran into Hal Jacobs one night at the Bar None."

"I remember him. A few years ahead of us. Serious type. Cute."

"That's him. We started dating my freshman year at community college, and that summer we got married." Samantha held up her hand before Anna could respond. "It didn't last."

"What happened?"

"I really hate to tell you."

"You know you can tell me anything."

Sam sighed. "Even though I tried to keep it quiet, I wouldn't be surprised if you're the only person in town who doesn't know. I'll give you the basics. But that's all. It's not my favorite subject." She took another deep breath and began.

"I told Hal I planned to finish college after we married, and he said that was fine with him. But after the wedding, I discovered he really didn't want me to. Because he didn't go, he couldn't understand why it was important to me. He resented the time I spent studying and complained about the cost, even though I only spent money my parents and I saved for my education.

"Hal works offshore on the oil rigs—fourteen days on, twenty-one days off. One night, he accused me of cheating on him while he was working. 'Carrying on with college boys' was the way he put it. He'd been drinking, we argued, and he hit me."

"No," Anna moaned. Sam only nodded.

"Oh, wait, it gets worse. I forgave him. And when he hit me the second time, I forgave him again. The third time, someone told him my truck was parked at the Bar None while he was out on the rig. Turned out, someone working there drove a similar truck. It wasn't even the same color."

Anna wore a pained expression as Samantha continued. "That time was really bad. I may be a slow learner, but I'm not stupid. That was the end. I wasn't going to be his punching bag for the rest of my life. The marriage lasted less than a year."

Anna hugged her friend, blinking back tears. "I'm so sorry."

Sitting up straight, Samantha symbolically dusted off her hands. "Well, it's over, and I'm smarter for it. Enough about that."

93

"That's all you're going to say on the subject?"

"For now. It wasn't the end of the world. I graduated from Southern Miss with a degree in elementary education and was hired to teach Mrs. Morgan's second-grade class. Can you believe she finally retired?"

Anna clasped Samantha's hands. "I'm so proud of you for getting out of that terrible situation and moving on. I'm sorry I wasn't around when you needed a friend."

"Don't think about that. You're here now, and I'm ridiculously glad you're back."

"I was wrong to leave the way I did," Anna admitted. "I know that now. In my defense, I was a mess."

"Of course. Your mom died."

"It was more than that. She was the only family I had. And after she was gone..."

Samantha finished the sentence for Anna. "You had no anchor—no safety net."

"I didn't. And knowing I had no financial back-up scared me. I was actually afraid of becoming homeless. Thank goodness, I had a partial scholarship, and my out-of-state tuition was waved. But I still had to pay for books, the rest of my tuition, food, rent on my studio apartment, and everything else. I was obsessed with supporting myself and getting a degree as quickly as possible. My concerns weren't unreasonable, but now I realize they were probably excessive."

"But you had this house."

"The problem was it wasn't paid for. That meant house payments, taxes, insurance. The logical thing would have been to sell, but I just couldn't lose Mom's house. It was all I had left."

"Thank heavens you managed to hold on to it. If you hadn't, you might not have come home."

"It feels good to be back. I didn't realize how much I missed Tenacity until I returned. I hope you understand why I left the way I did. Can you forgive me?"

"Of course, I forgive you, but I admit it's hard to understand why you left people who would have supported you. And you've always been so confident." Samantha grinned. "You worked in the school library, for heaven's sake, a cool girl sacrilege, right up there with riding the bus. But you didn't care what they thought. I've always admired you for that. I'm surprised my self-assured friend could…"

Anna offered some options. "Go nuts? Come unglued? Go off the deep end?"

"No. Well, maybe a little of that." Both girls smiled.

When someone in a passing car waved, Anna waved back, glad she'd had the old trellis removed. "I guess I thought Tenacity would remind me of Mom's death and what happened with Max. I needed to put all that behind me, so I stayed away."

"Did it help?"

"Who knows? Time passed and eventually the burdens became easier to bear. I didn't realize until today that pulling away like I did was selfish. I felt so sorry for myself, it never dawned on me someone might need my support. I'm truly sorry, Sam. Thank you for coming today. I'm so grateful to have your friendship."

"And I'm glad to have yours. Think we've had enough sad talk for one day?" Samantha wanted to know.

"Definitely."

"Got any coffee or tea? I want to talk about juicy stuff. Like have you seen Max and are the old feelings still there? That is, if it isn't too hard to talk about."

Samantha followed Anna into the house, laughing when her friend looked disgusted with herself.

"I've seen him all right. The feelings are definitely still there, but our relationship is complicated. The man flusters me. When he's around, I have trouble forming a cohesive thought. He makes my brain foggy."

Samantha's eyes widened. "You generated thousands of words for a novel and the only thing you can say about Max is 'he makes my brain foggy.'"

"That's about it."

"Are you going to pursue that relationship?"

"That's the big question, isn't it? Want to see what I'm doing with the house?"

"All right. I get that you don't want to talk about Max. Show me around after we finish drinking whatever you're about to pour?"

"I'd love to. And we're drinking tea. The crew and my morning guests drank all the coffee."

"Who visited this morning?"

"Jeff Windom. I was pleasantly surprised to see him."

"That doesn't surprise me," Samantha said. "He's always had a soft spot for you. What did the two of you talk about?"

"It was really the three of us. Jeff had only been here a few minutes when Max joined us."

Samantha laughed. "Now why doesn't that surprise me? Lord save me from territorial men! Did they lift their legs and pee on the porch?" Laughter drifted from Anna's house, and she couldn't believe how good it felt to be home.

✻

"Morning," Max said, running up beside Anna.

"Morning. Were you waiting for me?"

"Yup."

"What if I'd decided not to run today?" Anna asked.

"Eventually, I'd have given up. I've been running alone for years, but it's more fun with you. How's the bedroom suite coming? Tell me you're moving in soon."

"Well, the walls have been painted, and the floor is dry enough to walk on. I'm hoping the plumber will install the bathroom fixtures today. It shouldn't be much longer."

"It can't be soon enough, as far as I'm concerned. I hate you living in that motel."

"It's not bad. It's clean."

"Just not safe. Stay with me until your room is done. Or with Samantha."

"I'm fine, Max. It won't be much longer."

When they found themselves near the school, Max impulsively grabbed Anna's hand and pulled her toward the gym.

"What on earth are you doing?"

"Taking a walk down memory lane. Come on. No one is here this time of the year, at least not this early."

When they reached the back side of the gym, Max pressed Anna against the brick wall, his hands on either side of her head. Then he leaned so close their lips almost touched. "We had our first kiss here." His voice was soft and seductive. "You caught me by surprise that night. The dance. The kiss."

His toothpaste scented breath was warm on her face. "That kiss did it for me, Anna. I've been yours ever since. Or I should say, I've wanted to be. I've never cared for any other woman on so many levels. No one's even come close."

"Not even Janine?"

"Especially not Janine."

Anna was thrilled and a little shocked at his declaration. Until that moment, she thought Max's interest might be more about sexual attraction than anything else. Not sure how to respond, she said, "Just kiss me."

She didn't have to ask twice. The kiss was a little desperate, urgent. Memories, both treasured and sorrowful, mingled with their passion. When Anna wrapped her arms around Max's neck, his hands traveled down her body, grazing her breasts, cupping her perfect bottom, lifting, holding her tightly against him.

His need was intense, heightening even more when Anna wrapped her legs around him. The urge to take the euphoria to the next level was powerful. He was confident he could make it happen, but he wouldn't. Not behind the school gym, no matter how forcefully his body told him to.

Max and Anna leaned against one another, their foreheads touching, breathing hard. Together, they fought the desire to linger in that realm where nothing exists but passion.

Max broke the silence. "How about we walk home—slowly? I'm not exactly up to running right now."

Dazed by the jolt of emotion they'd just experienced, they clasped hands and silently drifted home.

Anna absently went through the motions of showering and dressing in the unrenovated bathroom of her house. Instead of greeting Fred and the crew, as usual, she slid behind the steering wheel of her car and left before they arrived. Driving with no destination in mind, she savored the lingering feelings of the morning's passionate kiss. Then her mind drifted to their first kiss, years before, one wondrous night behind the school gym.

CHAPTER THIRTEEN

At Janine's insistence, eighteen-year-old Max escorted her to the Tenacity High School Spring Dance. There were still a few more weeks of classes, but the dance was the last one of the school year and the last one ever for seniors like Max and Janine. Max wasn't particularly fond of gymnasium dances, but Janine wanted to go, so he took her. While she flitted around the room, he leaned against the concrete-block wall, disinterestedly watching the activities.

Max noticed Anna walking in with some guy, but since they were mingling and dancing with other people, he couldn't tell if they were on a date. At the end of a dance with one of her classmates, Anna found herself standing in front of Max. He nodded when they made eye contact, and she walked over to lean against the wall beside him.

"Having fun?"

"Sure," he said, a little sarcastically. When a fast song began to play, Max surprised them both by saying, "Want to dance?" He hadn't planned on asking. The words just popped out.

"Really?" Anna asked.

"Hell yeah." Smiling, he took her hand and led her away from Janine's group of friends. Because Max tried to keep his relationship with Anna casual, he'd never asked her to dance. But she looked so pretty, with her cheeks pink from exertion, he couldn't help himself. And asking her to dance wouldn't change anything.

They had fun, acting a little silly with the familiarity of the childhood friends they once were, but when a slow song started, Max began leading her off the dance floor. Anna stopped, still holding his hand. When he turned to see why, Anna looked directly into his dark eyes and said, "Dance with me." He couldn't say no.

The moment Max took Anna into his arms, he was lost. He'd dreamed of holding her, but the reality felt better than he'd imagined. Pulling her close, he leaned down, his face brushing hers, and breathed in the scent of vanilla and oranges. Her body was relaxed, soft and compliant against his, as they moved in unison.

Max forgot where he was—forgot about his plans to keep their relationship platonic. All he could focus on was the beautiful girl in his arms and his intense desire to kiss her. If he turned his head just a little, his lips could be on hers. Then, without his bidding, his leg eased into the space between hers, and his body began to stir.

He should never have agreed to that dance. Now that he knew how good it felt to hold her, he couldn't imagine never doing it again. But Anna didn't need someone like him—not for anything more than a friend. She was too sweet and innocent, and he cared for her, a lot. That's why he needed to keep their relationship platonic. It's also the reason it was so damned difficult.

When the music stopped, Max found the strength to back away. For once, he didn't know what to say. He wasn't thinking straight. He cast a glance in Anna's direction and mumbled, "Sorry. I have to go." Conflicted, he headed outside.

It didn't take long for a couple of girls to approach Janine, delighted to be the bearers of bad tidings. "Janine, did you see Jet dancing with Anna? He looked like he was going to take her right there on the gym floor." Janine pretended more confidence than she felt.

"Don't be silly. Jet doesn't think of her that way."

When she approached another group of friends and they all stopped talking, it wasn't difficult to guess the topic of their conversation.

"Are you all right?" one of the girls asked dramatically. "We heard Jet was dancing with Anna."

Putting her own spin on the story, she scoffed at the implication. "That doesn't mean anything. She's like a little sister to him."

With a smirk on his face, one of the boys scoffed, "If that's the case, somebody better call the cops. I hear incest is illegal."

"You don't know what you're talking about," Janine huffed. Then she walked away with laughter ringing in her ears. *Jet Anderson*, she thought, *you're not going to do this to me. You're not going to dump me for that… that library girl.*

Janine told herself to be smart about the situation. She wouldn't confront him right away. In fact, she decided she'd ignore the whole thing. *I can fix this*, she told herself. *When we're alone, I'll make him forget all*

102

about little Miss Perfect. No one's going to make a fool of me.

When Anna's dance with Max ended, she was stunned. Max dated a lot of girls, but he'd never asked her out. She didn't think he even thought of her in a sexual way. But that dance had been unbelievably hot! Max was as turned on as she was. She saw it in his eyes and felt it in his body.

After Max left the building, Anna found him leaning against the back wall of the gym, staring up at the sky. Out of the darkness, he heard her voice. "What's wrong, Max? Why did you leave like you did?"

He pushed away from the wall, and in a couple of long strides was looking into the innocent blue eyes of his longtime friend. "Why did I walk away? So I wouldn't do this."

He laced one hand through her hair, pulled her close with the other, and kissed her. At first, the kiss was hard and desperate. Then his lips softened, and it morphed into tender evidence of his affection. Max was surprised at Anna's easy, certain response. It felt like they'd been kissing forever. Well, there had been that one time.

"Mmm," Max hummed. "We're a lot better at that than when we were... How old do you think we were when we tried kissing?"

Anna laughed softly. "Probably around ten and twelve. Our experiment may have been a bit premature."

Wrapping his arms around her, Max rested his chin on her head. When Anna's arms went around his hard body, they both thought nothing had ever felt so right.

Max reluctantly broke the spell. "I'm afraid I didn't come to the dance alone."

Anna looked up at him, wishing she didn't have to let him go. "Neither did I. I guess we should find our dates."

"Before they find us," he quipped. But neither of them moved right away.

Forcing themselves apart, they reluctantly separated and found their dates. Max coaxed Janine away from her friends and told her he'd had all the partying he could take for one night. He was quiet as he drove her home, and she was smart enough not to mention Anna. When Janine saw where Max was taking her, she gently dragged a finger down the side of his face, leaned close, and murmured seductively, "We could park at the lake."

Max shook his head. "Not tonight." He took her straight to her house.

Once he was home, Max headed to the kitchen. His dad found him sitting at the table, smiling, a plate of leftovers in front of him. "What put that smile on your face? Or should I say who."

"Who," Max said, before taking a bite of a chicken leg.

"Okay then, who put that smile on your face?"

Max didn't normally discuss girls with his dad, but he felt like sharing this news. "Anna," he answered. "I like her."

Alex smiled. "You always have, son. You always have."

Max lay in bed a long time before falling asleep. He cared about Anna. She was intelligent and sweet, with perfect curves on her tall slender body. And her eyes... Those beautiful blue eyes seemed to look past the Jet persona into the deepest parts of him.

But she was only sixteen, young and innocent, and he'd passed innocent some time ago. With effort, Max had selflessly kept Anna in the 'friend' category. But their dance inadvertently put her in a division all her own.

One dance shouldn't have broken down the barrier he'd meticulously established between them. But that's what happened. That dance changed everything. When Max closed his eyes that night, he saw Anna's face and remembered how she felt pressed against him. And that kiss! She'd tasted sooo sweet. And she was into it. Yep. Anna was definitely out of the friend category. Now he had to decide what to do about it.

The next morning Max knew his moratorium on dating his long-time friend had come to an end. The first thing he had to do was break up with Janine. He couldn't keep dating her, feeling the way he did about Anna.

Max hated to admit it, but he didn't even like Janine that much. He sort of fell into the relationship. She'd pursued him aggressively. She was cute. And she was usually up for anything. So why not, he thought, and they became a couple.

Margie was finishing the supper clean-up when she heard the doorbell. Drying her hands on her apron, she left the kitchen and saw their young neighbor through the glass in the door. Max stood on the porch, as handsome as ever, appearing more intense than usual.

"Hi, Miss Margie. Is Anna here?"

"She is. Come on in. I'll get her." Max waited just inside, listening as Margie knocked on Anna's bedroom door. "Max is here, dear. He's asking to see you."

Anna appeared immediately, wearing slender jeans and a sweater. She was beautiful. No fuss. No make-up. Just naturally beautiful. Max's eyes danced and his crooked smile managed to look cocky, as well as a little shy.

"Hi," he said, with his hands in his pockets. "Go for a walk with me?"

"Mom, I'm going for a walk with Max."

"Fine. Don't be gone too long."

Once Margie heard the front door close, she looked out the window, only a little surprised to see Max take Anna's hand. Something had been weighing on Anna's mind all day, and there'd been something different about Max's demeanor when he came to the door.

The pleasure Margie felt at seeing them together was closely followed by concern. The kids were young, not yet ready for their forever love, and Margie knew her daughter's feelings for Max went deep.

When Max took Anna's hand into his much larger one, energy sparked between the friends, and there was no way they could deny what was happening. Grateful for the darkness that hid her blush, Anna hoped Max couldn't hear the pounding of her heart. They walked awhile before she asked in her easy direct manner, "What are we doing here, Max?"

"I'm going to break up with Janine," he told her.

Hope sprang into Anna's heart, but it was tempered with caution. "Really?"

"Really," he assured her.

"Why?"

Max squeezed her hand. "There's someone else."

106

"There always is," she joked, not daring to assume he was referring to her.

Max gently grasped her shoulders and looked into her eyes. "It's not like that."

He was in uncharted territory. He had a well-deserved reputation with girls, but his feelings for Anna were different, and he was having trouble expressing himself. He didn't know how to say what he felt, without making promises he might not be able to keep.

He'd never lied to Anna and wouldn't start now. "Anna, you may have noticed that I've kept you at a distance, at least until recently. You're not like other girls. At least, not to me."

Oh, *no. He's trying to tell me the dance and kiss meant nothing to him.*

Max felt her start to turn away but held her in place. "You're special. I've never wanted to hurt you."

Just let me go, Anna begged silently, afraid she'd burst into tears in front of him.

With frustration in his voice, Max shrugged. "But I can't stay away from you any longer. I think about you all the time."

Anna's heart sang. He wanted her. She and Max were finally going to be a couple!

She looked into his eyes and asked something of him, knowing she might be asking the impossible. "Don't hurt me, Max."

Pulling her close, he promised he wouldn't, hoping it was a promise he could keep. "Then you'll give me a chance?"

"I will," she told him, not sure exactly what that meant. Max gave her a sweet, tender kiss. And that night

Anna floated into slumber, happier than she ever remembered being.

CHAPTER FOURTEEN

For several days, Max sent disinterested signals to Janine, while she remained her usual perky self, refusing to admit anything had changed. The usual break-up strategies weren't working. He stopped calling, didn't walk her to class, and refused to attend a party she was excited about.

While the rumor mill already had them broken up, Janine pretended she was blissfully unaware of Max's transgressions. He finally realized there would have to be a break-up scene. Janine wasn't going to let him off the hook that easily. He decided to take her for a drive and tell her he didn't think they were right for each other. That didn't sound so bad. Then he could be with Anna.

When Max called Janine to tell her they needed to talk, there was excitement in her voice.

"You must have read my mind," she chirped. "I have something to tell you, and you're going to be so surprised."

Janine was always excited about something. He hoped that whatever was making her so happy would take the sting out of what he had to say.

Max was uneasy when he knocked on Janine's door that night. She had to be aware of the signals he'd been sending, but she wasn't responding normally. The girl was a little ditsy, but not stupid. She had something up her sleeve.

When Janine answered the door, she was more animated than usual. Grabbing his arm, she pulled him toward the car, not giving him a chance to talk.

"Drive to the lake," she directed. "I have something to tell you."

Max parked in a spot where they wouldn't be disturbed, and Janine began talking as soon as the engine stopped.

"You might be upset about what I have to tell you but try to keep an open mind. It could turn out to be the best thing for both of us."

Yes! Max thought, *she's breaking up with me.* He'd try not to show his relief.

"I know we're young," Janine continued, "but I think we're both mature enough to handle this. Try not to be upset."

"What are you trying to tell me, Janine? Just spit it out."

"I'm pregnant."

Max was so stunned he couldn't speak.

"Say something, Max."

He managed to get out the question foremost in his mind. "Are you sure?"

"Two different pregnancy tests were positive, and I went to the doctor."

A little frantic, Max managed to ask the next question that popped into his head. "How? We used condoms. You're on the pill. We were careful!"

Janine shrugged and said cheerily, "I guess it was just meant to be."

Max frowned at her nonchalance. "I can't talk about this now. I have to think."

As soon as he was able to function again, Max started the car and took Janine home. He was overwhelmed, unable to organize his thoughts. He had a football scholarship to State. He was going to be with Anna. How could this be happening?

Ironically, Max felt like a little boy as he knocked on his parents' bedroom door. When no one answered, he ventured in and woke his father. "Dad," he said, his voice quivering. "I need to talk to you."

Afraid something must be very wrong, Alex managed to wake up enough to say, "Sure, son."

He donned the jeans and t-shirt he was wearing earlier and walked to the living room with Max. When Alex turned on a lamp and saw his son's ashen face, he was instantly alarmed.

"What's wrong? What's happened?" Max said nothing. He just repeatedly shook his head and paced back and forth in the dimly lit room.

Alex tried to ascertain the immediacy of the problem. "Is anyone hurt?"

When Max continued to shake his head, unable to speak, his dad put his hands on his son's shoulders, led him to a chair, and told him to sit. Alex pulled up a chair to face him. "You're scaring me. You need to tell me what's wrong."

Max was about to speak when Carol walked into the room, tying her robe sash. Sleepily, she asked, "What's going on?" Max jumped up and headed out the front door.

Afraid he might get in the car and leave, Alex ran after his boy. "I'll deal with this, Carol." His voice begged for understanding. "Go back to bed."

Alex caught up with Max on the porch, put an arm around his son's shoulders, and led him to the steps. They sat side by side, staring into the darkness. It was a lovely spring evening, but neither of them noticed.

"Talk to me, son."

Max looked out into the dark yard and finally told his dad, "Janine's pregnant."

Alex dropped his head, feeling like he'd been gut-punched. He tried to hide his reaction. "And it's yours."

Max nodded, before burying his face in his hands. When he regained control of his emotions, he spoke with quiet anguish. "I'm sorry, Dad. I let you and Mom down."

Alex placed an arm around his son's broad shoulders, remembering what it felt like to be a teenage boy in a man's body, and they both quietly cried. Max's charmed life was taking an unexpected turn, a turn that would likely lead him away from the future the Anderson family had anticipated.

A part of Alex wanted to scream at his son, but he'd seen how girls shamelessly threw themselves at his boy. Hell, Tenacity High was a smorgasbord of teenage girls vying for his attention. He understood the temptation. *But I warned him,* Alex thought. *Dammit, I warned him!* It was too late for admonitions. Max would have to face the consequences of his actions.

After a few moments, Alex straightened. "We'll deal with this, son. It isn't the end of the world."

"Dad, I think she may have done it on purpose. She's so happy about it." A little embarrassed, he confided, "I mean, I used protection, and she told me she was on the pill. I don't see how this could have happened."

Max began spilling out his disjointed thoughts. "She says she's going to keep the baby. What about my football scholarship? And there's Anna. We were about to get together. I care about her."

Alex asked, "Do you care about Janine?"

Max looked at the step his foot rested on. "I know this sounds terrible, but not so much. I mean I don't want anything bad to happen to her or anything, but I don't love her. I don't think I even like her that much. Dad, what should I do? Should I marry her?"

He seemed to be begging Alex to find a way out of this for him. Alex shook his head, trying not to show how upset he was, and sighed. "This is one time I can't tell you what to do. What you and Janine have done will change both your lives. You're the ones who have to decide how to handle this. I will say it's difficult enough to make a marriage work when a couple is in love. And beginning a marriage this way, without love...well..."

He didn't finish the sentence. He didn't need to. "Just know that your mother and I love you and will support you in whatever decision you make."

When Max went quiet, Alex told him to try to get some sleep. "Your mind is reeling with this news. You'll have a better perspective in the morning." But sleep was a scarce commodity in the Anderson house that night.

Max was up early, his mind busily organizing the day. First, he would face his mother. Next, he would tell Anna. He couldn't let her go to school and be blindsided.

Max texted Janine, asking her to keep the news to herself until they made some decisions. She answered that she'd already told most of her friends, who were sooo excited.

Shit, Max thought. By the end of the day the entire school would know, and before dark the whole town would be privy to the information. It would have been nice to have a little time to absorb the news before it became Tenacity's hot new topic.

Max's phone rang. When he saw it was Janine, he didn't answer. Instead, he texted. **Not ready to talk. I won't be in school today. Need to think. Wish you had kept this to yourself.** As an afterthought he added, **Everything will be okay,** although he didn't believe it for a minute. He thought about telling her not to worry, but Janine didn't seem worried in the least. She was pregnant, keeping the baby, and happy about the situation. She was probably planning their wedding. Max wasn't happy about any of it. In fact, he was downright miserable. But life would go on, and today he had to decide what direction his would take.

Max smelled sausage and knew it was time to face his mother. When he walked into the kitchen and saw his mother's red, swollen eyes, he couldn't keep tears from forming in his own. Carol wanted to grab him and hug him, as she had when he was a child, but chose to help him keep his dignity. Ready or not, he was an adult now.

114

"Set the table, Max," Carol told him. "Breakfast will be ready in a minute."

Setting the table gave Max time to blink back his tears and collect himself. After Carol served their plates, she sat in the chair next to Max.

"Where's Dad?"

Carol covered her child's hand with hers, remembering when that hand, now much larger than her own, was small and delicate. "He'll be along in a minute."

Dad was giving him time alone with his mother. Max looked down at his plate, gathered his courage and said, "I'm sorry, Mom."

She patted his hand. "What's done is done. Now we look forward."

"I know. I'm not going to school today. I have decisions to make. I have to do what's best—not for me, but for the baby." He said the word softly, as if saying it aloud made it real.

Carol put her hand on his shoulder and kissed his cheek. "Don't completely dismiss doing what's right for you. You know your dad and I will always stand behind you, but what happens from here on out is up to you."

Max nodded, the weight of the impending decision heavy on his heart. He picked at his breakfast, not hungry, probably for the first time in years. When Alex appeared in the doorway, Max pushed his chair back from the table.

"Thanks for everything, Mom." He kissed her cheek and nodded to his dad. "And Dad."

Then the burdened young man sighed deeply. "Now I have to talk to Anna. I have to tell her before she hears it from someone else."

He saw pity in his parents' eyes. They knew he'd started to think of a future with Anna. They loved her and would have been thrilled to see the two of them make a life together. But he'd ruined that. Max stood, raised his chin, straightened his shoulders, and walked out the door to do the hardest thing he'd ever done.

When Margie Robinson opened the door, still dressed in her robe, she saw the intensity in Max's eyes and heard the urgency in his voice. "Miss Margie, I need to talk to Anna before she goes to school."

"Come on in, Max. I'll get her. It might be a few minutes."

He wouldn't meet Margie's eyes. "I'll wait on the porch."

Pacing back and forth, the troubled young man tried to think of the best way to break the news to the person he most wanted to protect, the sweet spirit he was about to injure in an appalling way. When Anna opened the door and stepped onto the porch, the look on Max's face told her something was very wrong. "What is it?"

"Sit down," he said, gesturing to the swing, "please."

They sat on the porch swing, and Max wasted no time. He took one of her hands in his, looked into her eyes, and began the telling.

"I've done something, and I'm sorrier than you'll ever know. I never meant to hurt you."

Anna saw the pain in his eyes, heard the regret in his voice. "Just tell me."

"There's no good way to say this, and I'm so sorry." He dropped his head, took a deep breath, and confessed, "Janine's pregnant."

Anna blanched. Her free hand flew to her mouth, and she felt like someone just punched her. Her hope of being with Max, the beautiful boy she'd always loved, was dashed with two words.

Stifling a sob and shaking her head, two staccato words came from her mouth. "No, no. Maybe it's a mistake."

Putting an arm around her shoulders, Max pulled her close and rested his chin on her head. "She's been to the doctor." Max held her close, giving her time to grieve the situation.

Anna pulled away, tears on her face. "I believed you wouldn't hurt me."

Nothing she could have said would have hit Max harder.

"I know. I'm sorry, Anna. You'll never know how sorry."

When she was able to focus on Max's face, Anna saw tears in his eyes and realized she wasn't the only one who was hurting. Forcing herself to be calm, she held Max's face in her hands and asked, "Are you all right?"

He looked into her eyes, acutely aware of what he was losing. Anna was incredible, and suddenly, without an ounce of doubt, Max knew he loved her. It wasn't infatuation. He really loved her.

"No. I'm not all right." Seeing the hurt and concern in her eyes, Max lost some of his control. Turning his head away, he wiped away tears he'd valiantly been holding back.

"I had to tell you this morning. Janine is already spreading the good news," he said sarcastically. "I couldn't let you hear about this at school."

Anna winced. "Thanks for the warning."

"I won't be at school today," Max told her, looking miserable and inconsolable. "I have things to figure out."

"Do you want company?" She didn't want him to be alone. Neither did she want to face the chaos this news would cause at school.

Damn, I love this girl, Max thought. But he said, "Are you seriously offering to skip school with me?"

"Yes, if you want me to."

"I do. I need you." Max's heart lightened a little for the first time since he'd heard Janine's life-changing news.

"Okay. Give me a minute to explain to mom."

Max gave her a small smile that didn't reach his eyes. "I'll tell my parents and come by in a few minutes. We'll take the bike and go somewhere we can talk."

CHAPTER FIFTEEN

Anna knew she was about to interject herself into a situation that was sure to cause more anguish. She didn't know how she could help Max when her own heart was so seriously wounded. But this might be their last chance to be together, and she wouldn't let the fear of pain steal their last moments.

She gave her mother a brief explanation before running out of the house. "It's very important. Carol can fill you in."

Max returned home, looking slightly more at ease than when he left. When he explained his plan to spend time alone with Anna, his parents looked grave.

His dad's lips formed a tight line. "Max, you know that girl cares about you, and she has a tender heart. Be careful you don't bruise it any more than you already have."

His mother touched his arm, and Max could see both sympathy and worry in her eyes.

"I understand," was all he said, before walking out and straddling the motorcycle. Anna was waiting in front of her house. Max handed her a helmet and helped her adjust it to fit. Her emotions were all over the place as she mounted the bike and wrapped her arms around his body. From a distance they must have looked like a carefree happy couple on a date. But they weren't on a date, and neither of them was the least bit happy.

They headed out of town, passing Samantha's place and the Windom farm, before crossing a bridge. When there was nothing but woods on both sides of the road, Max slowed a few times and then sped up again, until he found what he was looking for. He stopped and removed his helmet, signaling Anna to do the same.

"Are you up for a hike?"

"Sure. Where are we going?"

"You'll see."

He walked the bike into the stand of trees so it couldn't be seen from the road and parked it. Then he took Anna's hand and led her into the woods.

"Are you sure you know where you're going?"

"Of course. I've been exploring these woods since I was a kid. Used to ride out here on my bicycle and spend the day."

"Alone?"

"Yeah. I was oblivious to what could happen to a kid alone. I liked being out here by myself. It's peaceful. You can hear and see things you'd miss if someone was with you." As they walked, Max questioned his choice of a place to spend the day. He hadn't been this alone with Anna since they were kids, and the isolation of the forest was seductive. They walked hand in hand until the terrain changed to a steep slope.

"Can you climb to the top of that hill? I promise you'll be glad you did."

"Sure. What's at the top?"

"A   view   you   won't   forget."
Standing at the top of a bluff overlooking the river,
Anna looked around. "This is beautiful. I can't believe
I've never heard of this place."

"It's my favorite spot. I found it when I was about
fourteen. Haven't been up here in a while though."

"You don't bring dates up here?" Anna hoped she
didn't sound jealous, but she really wanted to know.

Max shook his head. "Never have. It's a private
spot."

They sat side by side on a large flat rock, silently
admiring the river below, until Anna asked, "What are
you thinking, Max? Tell me what we're doing."

He sighed, looking as if the weight of the world was
on his shoulders. "I have some big decisions to make. The
life-changing kind. And I need to make them today."

Anna moved close to Max and took his hand. "Okay
then, where do we start?"

Max shrugged. "I have no idea."

"You probably do. You just don't want to."

"That's the truth. I want all this to go away."

Frustrated, Max jumped up, ran his hand through his
hair, and began pacing. "What am I going to do, Anna?
I've gone through the options in my head, and I hate every
one of them. Hell, I'm supposed to play ball at State in
the fall! I'm not ready to get married. Especially to
Janine! Will I lose you? Of course, I will. Dammit! I've
ruined everything. I've ruined us, and probably Janine,
although she seems to be reveling in all this."

Max sat down beside Anna and rested his elbows on
his legs. "And then there's… the baby."

Anna thought it was as hard for him to say as it was for her to hear. The picture in her mind's eye, of Max and Janine admiring their adorable newborn, caused a softball sized knot to form in her stomach. She stood and turned away, hoping Max wouldn't notice the look of pain on her face. Anna wasn't only feeling sorry for herself; she was worried about how Max's life was being turned upside down.

He stood again and cupped Anna's shoulders from behind. "Are you all right?"

She turned with a sob, wrapped her arms around the boy she'd always loved, and buried her face in his t-shirt-clad chest. Max leaned down, settling his face in Anna's hair, loving the smell of it. His arms tightened around her, and they stood in that position for a long time, not wanting to let go. Finally, Max spoke. "I'm sorry, Anna. You'll never know how sorry."

"I'm sorry, too."

"What do you have to be sorry about?"

"I'm sorry you were such an idiot." They both laughed, grateful for a break in the tension.

Anna pulled away, wiping tears from her face. "I got your shirt wet."

"Even trade, I got your hair wet." They looked at each other and smiled, before despondency hit Max with a vengeance. Anna thought his face might be the saddest one she'd ever seen.

"What are we going to do, Anna?"

She couldn't answer, for she didn't know how either of them would survive the unfortunate turn of events.

Taking Max's hand, she pulled him toward the rock and urged him to sit beside her. "Maybe we should focus on what's best for...for the baby," she suggested.

"Yeah," Max agreed sadly. "But what do babies need? I'm sure I don't know. Parents who love each other? That's not going to happen, unless we give it up for adoption, and Janine's not going to do that. I don't think I could either. But I can't see Janine as a single mother."

Anna sat quietly, thinking. "Could some sort of joint custody arrangement be set up?"

"You mean, between single parents?"

"Yes. That's what I mean."

"Maybe, but I can't see the court favoring an unmarried teenage father of a brand-new baby. And I couldn't even pay child support unless I gave up college. And who knows where Janine would want to move? So many variables could come into play."

They both knew where this was headed. Anna wanted to run and hide, scream, jump into the river, anything to escape this discussion, but when she saw the agony on Max's face, she forced herself to stay by his side.

Max's head fell to his waiting hands before he looked up and murmured, "I guess I could marry her."

Thinking she might burst into tears, Anna turned away. When she gained control of her emotions, she turned back toward Max.

"Surely there's another way," she managed to say.

They analyzed options for what seemed like hours, trying to find an answer they could live with. Max couldn't believe this was happening. *I'm sitting here with the girl I'd like to marry someday, talking about marrying someone else. And at eighteen, no less.* But there was a child to consider and that had to be his first priority.

Maybe he could be in the child's life without getting married, but Janine could make that difficult. If he married her, no matter what happened down the road, there would be no question of his rights as a father. Max's father was an important part of his life, and he couldn't imagine not being involved in his child's life. Eventually, the father-to-be realized he had no choice but to man-up and accept his responsibility, no matter the cost to himself.

As they made their way down the hill, Max realized he was leaving behind his last opportunity to be close to Anna. He wanted to take comfort in her arms more than he'd ever wanted anything. He wanted to lose himself in her and show her how important she was to him. He wanted to forget about Janine and the baby.

But Anna was a virgin. To take her innocence and walk away would be the ultimate betrayal. He didn't even consider how unfair it would be to Janine. As far as he was concerned, she was the villain in the tale.

Before mounting the bike, Max held Anna's face in his hands and gave her a tender kiss. One kiss was all he intended. But he gave in to need and kissed her again. There was nothing innocent about the second kiss. It was filled with need and desire. When Anna responded, Max changed the angle of his head, deepened the kiss, and pulled her close.

With her arms around his neck, Anna molded her body to his, experiencing the passion she'd only dreamed of. Max put his large hands on her slender hips and pulled her close to that aching part of him, the part that had gotten him into so much trouble. The thought jerked him back to reality. Forcing himself to release Anna, Max leaned his head against hers, and they stood together, delaying their inevitable parting.

"I'm sorry, Anna, for so many things."

When they finally straddled the bike for the trip home, two things were clear to the despondent girl: she would always love Max, and Max was going to marry Janine. Instead of wearing the helmet, Anna looped her arm through the strap and held her cheek tightly against Max's strong back. She stayed that way the entire trip home, wetting his shirt, once again, with her tears.

Margie waited inside for her daughter, choosing to stay home from work after hearing the news from Carol. Her eyes filled with tears when the bike stopped at the edge of the street in front of her house. When Anna handed the helmet to Max, their eyes met, admitting all the things they wouldn't let themselves say. Max dismounted, wrapped his strong arms around Anna and kissed her fiercely.

To be given a taste of such passion, just to have it taken away was cruel, Anna thought. But she would treasure his kisses forever, reliving them again and again. Then without a word, Max and Anna silently, bravely, made their way to their respective homes, knowing their time together had come to an abrupt and absolute end.

CHAPTER SIXTEEN

When Anna moved back to Tenacity as an adult, she wasn't surprised to find Miss Sweet McGillicuddy still living in the house across the street from Max. Miss Sweet was a fifty-year-old widow the spring the Anderson and Robinson families first moved to Tenacity. She'd welcomed each family with a loaf of warm, homemade bread and a jar of fig preserves.

"I put the preserves up myself," she told them proudly. "Picked the figs from the tree in my backyard, although it's getting a little scary climbing up that ladder at my age."

Miss Sweet, it seemed, had decided to become prematurely elderly, as if widowhood automatically put her in that category.

"I'd like to have the jar back when you finish," she explained to the new families. "I'll fill it for you next summer when I put up another batch of preserves."

And she did just that— every summer, year after year, commandeering Max and Anna to endure the scratchy fig leaves to pick her treasured figs.

"Mom," young Max once asked, "Why can't Miss Sweet just buy grape jelly from the grocery store? It tastes better."

Carol stifled a laugh, understanding his position.

"She enjoys making the preserves for us," Carol explained, "and it's very nice of you and Anna to help." It seemed to Max that Miss Sweet was aptly named, because all she had to do was smile and look sweet, and people did whatever she wanted.

She claimed she couldn't drive, although Max and Anna suspected she simply preferred having someone do it for her. And she seemed to have an unlimited list of neighbors and people from church willing to run her errands and drive her wherever she wanted to go.

Max was twelve years old the first time he mowed Miss Sweet's lawn, and he was excited about earning some money. He sweated for hours, pushing the mower around Miss Sweet's yard and edging the sidewalk, doing the best job he could. Proud of what he'd accomplished, he couldn't help being disappointed when a one-dollar bill and three cookies were placed in his hands.

When Alex learned what happened, he supplemented his son's earnings with a bonus for doing a good job. The last time Max mowed Miss Sweet's lawn was the week before he graduated from high school. Like all the times before, she laid a crisp one-dollar bill in his hand when the task was done.

Max had only held a driver's license a few days when Miss Sweet assigned him the task of caring for the 1968 Camaro that was her late husband's pride and joy. She refused to sell it, although she never drove it. So it sat in her garage, virtually abandoned.

"Just crank it up every now and then," she instructed, "and drive it around the block a few times to keep the battery charged."

Max did as he was told, wishing he could take it out for a proper spin. He also changed the oil once a year and gave the old car a bath when it got so dusty you could write your name on it. Miss Sweet expressed her appreciation by giving Max a few of her secret recipe cookies.

Max was Miss Sweet's favorite source of nearly-free labor, but she didn't forget her other across-the-street neighbor. When Anna was a child, she was given the privilege of weeding Miss Sweet's front flower garden. When she was old enough to drive, she was promoted to personal shopper, a position that often came with embarrassing errands.

About six in the evening, the young author pulled her car into Miss Sweet's driveway, chuckling when she saw Max, now a dad and an architect, driving his riding mower around Miss Sweet's yard. He turned both palms up as if to say, what are you going to do? Miss Sweet had explained that the boy who normally mowed the yard was unavailable, and for a reason Max didn't understand, it had to be mowed that very day. He hoped she paid the new boy more than she'd paid him.

When Anna removed the bag of groceries from her car, it was Max's turn to laugh. He turned the mower off and yelled, "Need help?"

"No, thanks. This is all I have." Unloading her purchases in the kitchen, Anna noted nothing was being cooked and wondered why the grocery trip had been such an emergency.

"Anna dear," Miss Sweet said, "will you ask Max to stop mowing and join us in the kitchen? Here's a towel for him to dry off with. It's a scorcher out there, even this late in the day."

Anna stood on the front stoop, waving the towel to get Max's attention. When he turned off the mower, she walked over the freshly mowed grass and handed it to him.

He thanked her, took the offering, and wiped his face. "What's up?"

"I have no idea, but Miss Sweet insists she needs you inside this very minute."

Max gave Anna a crooked smile. "Whatever Miss Sweet wants." Then almost before Anna realized what he was doing, Max pulled his wet t-shirt over his head, showcasing broad shoulders, a narrow waist, and a mesmerizing happy trail leading down his flat belly. For a man who no longer played football or worked construction, he was certainly fit. Aware of Anna's appreciative gaze, Max smirked.

Rolling her eyes, she asked, "Did you perform that little strip tease for my benefit?"

"Maybe. Was it appreciated?"

"Maybe," Anna answered.

After running the towel over his body, Max produced a dry shirt and donned it before following Anna into Miss Sweet's kitchen.

"Goodness gracious!" the older woman gushed. "Look at you two! I just love y'all living across the street again. That's the way it should be. Max, sweetie, you must be starving for something to drink. What can I get you?"

"I'm used to the heat, Miss Sweet. But I wouldn't turn down a glass of cold water."

"Sure you don't want something else. Ice tea's in the fridge, and lemonade can be ready in two shakes."

"No, ma'am. Water's good."

"Well, if you're sure," she said, walking to the refrigerator. "You can stop mowing now, dear. It'll be dark before long, and the boy who normally mows for me can come in the morning."

"I'll be glad to finish, Miss Sweet. It won't take long."

"No. It's getting late, and you have other things to do. Besides, Daniel looks forward to my cookies."

Changing the subject abruptly, she said, "You'll never believe what I did." She shook her head theatrically. "Just a little while ago, I asked myself, Sweet McGillicuddy, what in the world is wrong with you?" She feigned disgust with herself. "Do you know I plumb forgot tonight is spaghetti night at church? And I made chicken spaghetti for supper. I want you kids to take it and share."

"No. You keep it, Miss Sweet," Anna said. "It'll be good tomorrow."

"I don't want spaghetti two days in a row, and I won't take no for an answer. I want you and Max to have it." After retrieving the casserole container from the refrigerator, she placed it in a waiting paper bag. "I'm sending a can of baby green peas and a loaf of French bread so you'll have a complete meal."

She gave the bag to Max before placing two large pieces of cake on a plate and handing it to Anna. "I'm out of Saran Wrap, but you're not going far, so it should be all right. It's my chocolate pound cake, the one everyone begs me to take to church potlucks."

Ushering them toward the door, Miss Sweet instructed, "Y'all go on now. My ride will be here in a minute. Just cook the casserole at three fifty for an hour and have a good night."

Nodding to his mower on Miss Sweet's front lawn, Max explained, "I'll come back for that after taking the food home."

"Good, but don't finish the lawn. I mean it. Daniel will do it tomorrow." With that she closed the door.

"What just happened?" Anna wondered aloud as they crossed the street.

Max raised his eyebrows. "Do you think Miss Sweet could be playing matchmaker?"

Anna laughed. "I'm afraid so. She'd definitely given dinner prior thought. The French bread and peas were on the grocery list she gave me this afternoon, and it didn't take two minutes for her to put the whole meal together."

"And the casserole was in a disposable pan, almost as if she'd planned to give it away," Max added with a grin.

Reaching the sidewalk, he turned to Anna and gave her the smile that made her stomach turn flips. "We can't disappoint Miss Sweet, especially after such an admirably executed covert operation. Your kitchen or mine?"

"Yours is the better option, unless you like sawdust in your food."

"No, thanks. I've had that displeasure. My house it is. Just give me a minute to shower."

Unbidden, a picture flashed into Anna's mind of water splashing onto Max's chiseled face and running down the muscled body she'd had the privilege of glimpsing moments before. Anna gave herself an excuse for the momentary lapse. *My head went there because I'm a normal red-blooded woman.*

When Anna and Max began walking toward their own homes, Miss Sweet stepped onto her front stoop and yelled across the street, "Y'all know I mean for you to sit down at the same table to eat that."

"We will, Miss Sweet," Anna said with a big smile on her face. "We just have a couple of things to do first."

"Good." With a distinct nod, Miss Sweet turned and went back into her house, while Anna and Max flashed knowing grins at one another.

CHAPTER SEVENTEEN

Max came to the door smelling of soap and aftershave, his hair still damp from the shower. Soft, worn jeans hung below his slim waist, showcasing long, muscular legs, and a faded blue t-shirt clung to his body. Anna's mind had been wandering since she'd seen Max bare-chested, and now she was imagining how it would feel to jerk that clinging shirt over his head, push him onto the sofa, and straddle him.

"Are you all right, Anna? That's the second time since we left Miss Sweet's that you've zoned out on me."

"Yeah. Fine. I'm fine. Hi." Anna silently chastised herself for the trajectory of her thoughts.

Max smiled and bent to look into her eyes. "Hi yourself. Come on in." Taking her hand, he led her to the kitchen. "How about a glass of wine? I have Pinot Grigio and a Merlot."

"Pinot Grigio sounds good. Thanks. I could use a drink after dealing with Mr. Mayfield at the grocery store this afternoon."

Max poured Anna's wine and got a beer for himself. "Let's get comfortable in the living room, and you can tell me what happened. I put the casserole in the oven before I showered, but it'll still be a while before it's ready."

Anna positioned herself at one end of the sofa while Max took the middle. He handed the wine glass to Anna and sipped his beer, his eyes never leaving hers.

"Now, tell me what happened with Mr. Mayfield."

Anna took a deep breath, still annoyed by the episode. "I'm so outdone with him. He had a stack of tabloid magazines beside the check-out register with a sign that read, 'See Local Celebrity Inside.' So, I flipped through it on the off chance it could be about me." She thrust her free hand upward in disgust. "And sure enough, there I was. I should say there we were! There was a picture of the two of us leaning against your dad's Chevy in high school and separate ones of us as adults."

"Why was my picture there?" Max asked.

"Okay. Don't let this go to your head, but the caption was 'Author returns to hometown. Could the hottie be the reason?' Where did they even get those pictures?"

"The older one was from a school yearbook," Max said. "And the recent one of me was from an architectural periodical."

"You've seen it!"

Max chuckled. "One of the secretaries at work brought it in. I may never outlive the hottie moniker."

"You love it," Anna accused. "It's definitely a good picture of you. But I don't like having my privacy invaded. And I don't appreciate Mr. Mayfield using that article to make a few dollars."

"Did you say anything to him?"

"I bought every magazine he had and gave him a dirty look."

"Well, I guess you showed him. I'm sure he learned a valuable lesson."

As irritated as Anna was, she smiled. "I know. He sold all his magazines, which was exactly what he wanted, but at least everyone in town didn't get one."

No one was more surprised than Anna when talk show hosts began inviting her to appear on their shows, and pictures of her began popping up in tabloids. When her book was published, she never imagined making any kind of promotional appearances, much less being featured on television and in magazines. Oh, she knew there might be a few book signings in small bookstores, but nothing more.

Then Ellen DeGeneres read her book and invited her to be on her show. After that, Anna was the guest everyone wanted, attracting as much attention for her beauty as for her success at such a young age.

One late night host introduced her as every man's hot librarian fantasy. Another quipped, "Gentlemen, she'll make you want to run out and get a library card." Anna thought the television appearances weren't so bad, even though they were a little frightening, but she wasn't a fan of tabloids.

When a timer buzzed, Max strode to the kitchen, took the casserole from the oven, and placed it on a trivet in the middle of the kitchen table. They served themselves and laughed about the things their neighbor had asked them to do over the years.

"I'll never forget how I itched the first time we climbed up that old fig tree," Max said.

Anna remembered. "The next year we knew to cover our arms and legs. At least she didn't send you to the store to buy granny panties and hemorrhoid cream. I used to get so embarrassed. The worst was when I had to ask the pharmacist what I should buy for menopausal symptoms. I wandered around the store for what seemed like hours, waiting for all the customers to leave."

Max laughed. "You're right. I never had to do anything like that. But I got the nasty jobs. Once she asked me to crawl under the house to get rid of a dead possum, which had been there for quite a while. Since we're eating, that's all I'll say about that."

Anna scrunched up her nose. "You think we could have told her no?"

"Nah. Pretty sure it's against the law."

"Oh yeah, I forgot about that."

They laughed and Max really, really wanted to kiss her. He didn't. Instead, he brought her up to date on old friends and told her about his latest project at work.

Offering Anna a piece of bread, before taking one for himself, he asked, "How's the bedroom project coming?" He couldn't wait for her to move in. Maybe then he could relax, knowing she was safe and was really going to stay.

Anna's face lit up. "It's finished! They painted the facings today. Knowing I wanted the bedroom finished first, I arranged for the movers to pack a split shipment. One of the containers holds my bedroom furniture and a few other items. I can have it delivered now and get the rest of my things later. I'm calling the movers in the morning."

"Good thinking. I hope the soundproofed bedroom works out for you."

"I realize living in a construction zone will be a challenge, but it will be so nice to sleep in my own bed and not have to drive to the motel every night. And I won't have to text you to let you know I'm safely locked in for the night."

"You can just open your window and yell," Max joked. "And you know you can use this house if the commotion gets to be too much. You have a key. Use it anytime." Changing the subject, Max nodded toward the bookshelf. "Think you could sign your book for me now?"

"Not yet. But I will."

"I'm going to keep asking, you know."

Max left the table to make coffee when his phone rang.

"It's Gracie," he explained. "I bought her a phone and told her to call any time." Anna gestured for him to take the call.

"How's my girl?" Max asked. He listened to his daughter and frowned. "Your mother isn't home?" Anna watched Max struggle with his agitation.

Willing his voice to sound casual, he asked, "What are Grandmother and Granddaddy doing?" He listened again, glancing at Anna, smiling to show his appreciation for her patience.

"Well, Gracie," Anna heard Max say, "I love reading to you, and you can always call me, but you know your grandparents will read to you if you ask."

Gracie whined, "I know, but I want you. Will you come get me?"

Max exhaled and dropped his head, feeling utterly powerless. "Gracie sweetheart, we've talked about this. I wish you could stay with me all the time, but it can't be that way."

He would have explained that Janine wanted time with her too, but that argument wouldn't hold water when Janine was God-knows-where. Since Gracie was with him half the time, Max thought Janine should have plenty of time to do whatever she considered so damned important. She could at least stay home long enough to put her daughter to bed.

Max walked to Gracie's bookshelf, motioned for Anna to sit on the sofa, and gallantly pushed the weightiness from his voice. "Okay, Miss Gracie, let's choose a book. I'm putting you on speaker. Anna's here with me."

"Hi, Anna. I wish I could be there with you and Daddy." The sadness in her voice revealed the reason for Max's dejected demeanor.

"Maybe we can have dinner together soon," Anna offered.

"Tomorrow? Can we do it tomorrow?"

Anna grimaced and mouthed, "Sorry."

Max answered for her. "Not tomorrow, but soon. I'm looking at the books now. Which one shall we read?"

"*Sylvester and the Magic Pebble,* Gracie said. "Or maybe *Lyle Lyle Crocodile.* No *Sylvester.*"

"Okay, *Sylvester* it is." Not giving her a chance to change her mind, he riffled through a stack of books to find the selection of the evening. Looking at Anna apologetically, he whispered, "I hope you don't mind."

"Of course, I don't mind. And I like *Sylvester.*"

Max sat on the sofa next to Anna and turned his attention to Gracie and the book. "Do you have it in front of you?"

"Ah huh."

138

"Are you looking at the page where Sylvester is sitting at the table playing with some pebbles?"

"Just a minute." Anna could hear the sound of pages turning. "Okay, I found it."

Not wanting Max to see the tears forming in her eyes, Anna went to the kitchen and began clearing the table. *He bought duplicate sets of books so he could read bedtime stories to his child. How sweet is that! And how sad!* She always knew Max would be a good dad. If only she could be Gracie's mom instead of Janine!

Listening to the man of her dreams interact so lovingly with his daughter aroused a myriad of emotions in Anna. Still healing from the injury his marriage inflicted on her, she was genuinely afraid to give in to her feelings. If Max still treated his relationships as casually as he had in high school, he posed a threat, for there was nothing casual about Anna's feelings for him.

Unconsciously, she began clearing away the stumbling blocks keeping them apart. *Maybe there is a chance for us,* she reasoned. *Max was only a boy when he treated girls so carelessly. And now he's a mature, caring man with responsibilities. Is it possible the only thing standing in our way is my fear?*

Recognizing the story was coming to an end, Anna placed coffee and cake on the sofa table and sat next to Max, determined to learn more about him that very night. She had to know if she could trust him before she opened her heart and allowed him in. When Max turned off the phone, Anna saw an apprehensive look on his face.

"You're worried about her," Anna observed.

Max resisted the urge to pull her closer. "A little." He wouldn't reveal the full extent of his concern.

"Obviously, we don't have an ideal situation, but Janine could help if she'd give Gracie a little more of her attention. I don't know why she doesn't just give me full custody."

"Is that what you want?"

"I don't know. That wouldn't solve anything. Gracie would still need time with her mother, and it's not like I could quit my job to take care of her. There's no sense talking about it. It'll never happen."

Anna put a hand on his arm. "Don't worry so much, Max. Like you said, it's not an ideal situation, but it looks to me like you're doing a great job. Gracie is a happy precocious child, who seems well-adjusted, even if the world doesn't always meet her expectations."

Max pressed his lips together and nodded. "You're right. And there's no sense obsessing over something I can't change." He sipped his coffee, visibly beginning to relax. "You remembered I use cream in my coffee."

"I pay attention," she said coyly.

Setting aside his pensive mood, Max flashed Anna a genuine smile, amazed at how the world seemed to right itself when she was near.

CHAPTER EIGHTEEN

Anna let Max enjoy coffee and dessert before beginning the interrogation she planned while he was reading to Gracie. When he put his cup down, Anna took a deep breath and began, intent on finding out if the man she loved was a man she could trust.

"Max, we've been close most of our lives, but I know almost nothing about your life while we were apart. Will you tell me about those years?" Seeing Max's reluctant expression, she added, "I can't really know the person you've become if you hide that piece of your life from me. It's part of you, and I want to know what you went through."

She doesn't know what she's asking, Max thought. He'd worked hard to put those years behind him, and the last thing he wanted was to dredge them up again. "What do you want to know?" he asked, trying to sound nonchalant.

"Everything you're willing to tell me."

"Okay. Let's see," Max said, feigning contemplation. "I knocked up a girl I didn't want to marry, married her anyway, became a dad, divorced, got a college degree, and moved back to Tenacity to be close to my daughter. Now I'm an architect and have a business with my dad." He dusted his hands together, indicating his narrative had come to an end. Anna shook her head slowly. "What?" he said with mock indignation.

Anna continued shaking her head. "You don't really think you're getting away with that, do you?"

"No, but I thought I'd give it a try."

"I want details. I'm serious about this, Max. I need to fill in the gaps."

His sigh was evidence of his reluctance, as well as his resignation. "All right. You deserve answers. What do you want to know?"

"Let's start with something easy. Did you choose the right school and was giving up your football scholarship the right choice?"

"Yes, to both questions."

Anna rolled her eyes. "Come on. You can do better than that."

He smiled wryly and stood. "I'm going to need a drink for this. What can I get you?"

"What are you having?"

"Gin and tonic."

"I'll have the same."

Returning with two cocktail glasses, he set them on the coffee table, settled himself in the middle of the sofa, and patted the cushion beside him.

"Come closer. You're too far away for a serious conversation." Max leaned toward her, put his arm companionably around her waist, and pulled her close. "Better. Now I can talk. Or at least try."

He moved his arm to the top of the sofa, in effect inviting Anna to curl against him. She wanted to snuggle, wrap her arms around his sculpted abs, but she wouldn't be derailed from her mission to uncover his past.

Max readjusted his body, angling it toward Anna, their knees barely touching. "You asked about the football scholarship. I won't lie. Giving it up was hard. I had dreams of conference wins, bowl games, parties, you as my girlfriend, the whole college experience. But my life took a turn I didn't expect, and I was determined to do the best I could with my new fate. Football was part of the life I lost, and it didn't have a place in the new one."

Max took a sip of his drink and took Anna's hand in his before continuing. "I chose Rice University in Houston because it offered a graduate degree in architecture and was far enough away that Janine wouldn't want to run home every weekend.

State has a good program, but it's where I was supposed to play football, and I knew we'd run into too many people we know. I figured if we had any chance of making a go of the marriage, we'd need to start new, away from old relationships and Janine's parents."

Anna understood his concern. Everyone in town knew how over-solicitous Mr. and Mrs. Larson were toward their only daughter.

Max continued. "Obviously, the way the marriage began was a strike against us, but for the sake of the child, I had to give it a chance. You know?" His eyes pleaded for understanding.

"I understand," Anna said. And she did. She knew Max well enough to know he'd do everything he could to make a good life for his child, including living with a woman he didn't love. It was at that moment Anna realized she might be unprepared to hear what he had to say.

"How was school? Did you have a job?"

"We packed the car before we went to the justice of the peace and left Tenacity immediately after he pronounced us married. Because we got to Houston before the influx of students in the fall, we were able to find an apartment near campus. I used my motorcycle for transportation, and Janine had the car her parents gave her for graduation.

"I took a job with the highway department for the summer. I knew it would be hard work, but I was used to physical labor. I worked with Dad's construction company from the time I was old enough to balance a piece of lumber on my shoulder, and I played football all through junior high and high school. But I'm here to tell you, repairing highways is miserable, back-breaking work. And hot! Man was it hot! At the end of the day, I was spent. All I wanted to do was drink gallons of water, eat, and sleep."

"What did Janine do while you were working?"

"Who knows. But I know what she did when I came home. She complained."

"About what?"

"Everything. But her favorite complaint was I was too tired to do anything. And she was bored, and she didn't have any friends. It was all true, but I was working my ass off, doing the best I could. To me, life wasn't about having fun anymore. We had to grow up whether we wanted to or not.

"In the fall, I found a local construction company willing to use me on Saturdays and when I didn't have class. My boss, Big Ned everyone called him, was a great guy. He said he was impressed with my knowledge of construction and my work ethic. So he introduced me to the head of an architectural firm who gave me a summer internship after my freshman year. The pay wasn't good, but it helped, and the internship was a great experience."

Without any preamble, Anna asked what she really wanted to know. "What happened to you and Janine? I mean, why did the marriage end? But maybe that's too personal."

Max rubbed his hand through his hair, obviously bothered by the question. Realizing she'd gone too far, Anna withdrew the inquiry.

"That is too personal. Forgive me," she said, silently willing him to answer.

Max was thoughtful before saying, "No. That's all right. You have the right to know." Anna watched his face while he decided how much to share. Finally, he spoke.

"I want you to keep in mind that this happened years ago. It's old news. I'm not traumatized or anything. It's just something I don't enjoy talking about. When you hear the story, you'll know why I'm asking you not to share this with anyone. I'll explain, and we won't talk about it again. Agreed?"

"Agreed, but you don't have to."

"No, it's okay." He sighed before beginning the story. "My marriage to Janine was bad. For a while I tried to make it work, but nothing I did was good enough. According to her, I spent too much time studying, too much time working, didn't bring home enough money, and worst of all, I was no fun. I was an eighteen-year-old kid trying to be an adult. I didn't have time for fun. I was preparing to earn a decent living for my child.

"Janine began going out alone, or at least without me." Max didn't give Anna the details, but he remembered, vividly, the evening Janine came out of the bedroom dressed for a party and announced she was going out.

He had looked up from his books and raised an eyebrow. "Out?"

"Yes. I've looked like a cow for months, and I finally have my figure back. I'm ready to start living again. You can spend your life with your nose in a book if you want to, but I need something more. I met some girls today at that cute little boutique I like, and they invited me to go out with them. I told them I would."

"Do you know where you'll be?" Max asked.

"No, but I'll have my cell if you need me. You can keep an eye on Gracie. You'll be here anyway. You know where the bottles and diapers are."

Max sighed. "I need to study, but I'll watch her since you've already made plans." As she started toward the door, he said, "Wait. For future reference, you need to check with me before deciding to go out. I could have a test to study for or an important project."

Janine turned a furious gaze on him. "Dammit, Max! You always have something due tomorrow! You can't expect me to stay in this house day and night playing mommy. I won't be a prisoner. Even if you're not interested in having fun, I am!"

She slammed the door as she left, making Gracie cry. Max sighed and went to pick up the infant.

"Going out became a frequent occurrence for Janine," Max said, "and I was expected to baby sit. I accepted the outings. By then, I knew the marriage wouldn't survive, so why fight it. Hell, I didn't have time to fight. I was doing well in school and was determined not to let Janine sidetrack me. I had a child to support and finishing school was the best way to accomplish that.

"I hung on to the marriage because I didn't want to lose Gracie. I was a student with a part-time job. If we divorced, I'd never be granted custody. Even joint custody would mean I'd have to pay a sitter, which I couldn't afford. I was barely making ends meet as it was. And I was afraid a judge might mandate that I pay child support. I was between a rock and a hard place. And what if Janine decided to move out of town?"

Max hesitated, dropping his head, trying to decide something. Then he looked directly into Anna's eyes.

"I'm trusting you with a secret no one knows except my parents, a couple of lawyers, and an understanding judge. It's important that you never repeat it."

"All right," she said slowly.

"It's something I never want Gracie to hear."

"Okay. I'll keep your secret."

Max downed the rest of his drink before beginning.

"It was Monday. My last class of the day was cancelled, and I returned home earlier than usual."

Anna already had an idea where this was going.

Max hesitated, then continued. "As soon as I opened the door, I heard Gracie crying. I picked her up, soothed her, and went to look for Janine. I found her in the bedroom, and you can probably guess the rest."

"She was with a man."

147

"Yep," was all Max said, but he remembered the afternoon well.

He'd opened the bedroom door to find a college boy hopping around, trying to get his pants on, his eyes large as saucers at the sight of Max.

"Who are are you?" stuttered the boy.

"I'm your girlfriend's husband!" Max said through gritted teeth, trying not to frighten the child in his arms.

"She told me she was divorced! Honest," the boy pleaded.

"Out! Now!"

The young man grabbed the rest of his clothes and ran from the house, bare chested and bare-footed, holding up his pants.

Rather than spouting excuses or apologies, as one might expect, Janine began yelling that Max's inattention was responsible for her indiscretion. That's what she called it—her indiscretion. With Gracie still in his arms, Max walked out of the bedroom, grabbed her bottle, and left the house in search of a peaceful place to think.

Anna touched his arm, bringing him back to the present. "I'm sorry, Max."

"Like I said, it's old news. I was angry. Anyone would be. I was also relieved to end the charade we'd been living. But the divorce issues still existed, and I hoped the so-called marriage would limp along until I could provide for Gracie.

"Then things got worse. After the cheating incident, Janine yelled all the time. At least it felt like she did. She must have thought if she pointed out my shortcomings often enough and loudly enough, I'd realize her cheating was my fault. I tried to let it roll off, but the constant uproar was affecting Gracie. She cried a lot, and that wasn't normal for her. You sure you want to hear all this?"

"Yes. I never imagined things were so tough for you. So, what did you do?"

"It became obvious the marriage had to end. I let her file for the divorce, but I fought for custody of Gracie, or at least partial custody. I stayed at the house and slept on the sofa, afraid Janine wouldn't take care of her.

"My co-workers at the architectural firm saved me. They turned me on to a good attorney and wrote glowing character references. It didn't hurt that several of them were prominent members of the community. Long story short, the judge gave us joint custody and did everything he could to see that I stayed in Gracie's life while I finished school. He even denied Janine the right to move to another city until I graduated. One day I'm going to find a way to let him know how grateful I am."

My parents, as well as Janine's, helped financially, and the judge counted the money Janine's parents sent her every month as income. He told her to use it on bills instead of treating it as bonus money."

"You mean her parents sent money every month, and she never helped with living expenses?"

Max tightened his lips. "Yep. She said it was her allowance, that her parents sent it, so she'd have her own spending money. Knowing that relationship, I figured it was true."

"Wow. Did Janine take good care of Gracie when she had her?"

"I saw no evidence that she didn't. Since I had her half the time, Janine was free to party on her off days. At times, she'd ask to trade days and that was all right, as long as she didn't spring it on me at the last minute."

"Max," Anna asked, "how on earth did you handle school, a job, and a child?"

"I won't lie and say it was easy, but there was a good drop-in day care facility on campus, and my boss bent over backwards to accommodate me. He's someone else I owe big."

Anna sighed. "I had no idea you had such a rough time of it."

Anxious to end the question-and-answer session, Max rushed to finish his story. "Janine moved back to Tenacity the day I graduated, and I was right behind her. I went into partnership with Dad, and it's worked out well. We incorporated an architectural component to the construction company.

"It's my job to design residential and commercial buildings and work with Dad's construction managers to make sure plans are executed properly. Since the office is this side of Clarkston, I only have a forty-minute drive. And now, my dear Anna, you're up to speed on my life—the good, the bad, and the ugly."

"Thank you for trusting me with your story." Then sheepishly, she said, "I have one last question, and I hope you won't hate me for it."

Max sighed, annoyed she wasn't ready to let him off the hook. "Okay. Ask your question."

Then she hit him with it. "Did you ever cheat on Janine?"

Max gave her an indignant look before answering succinctly and emphatically, "No." After a moment of silence, he reluctantly elaborated. "I admit to being tempted. There were some beautiful girls on campus. Some of them flirted, invited me to parties, gave me their phone numbers. But I didn't cheat.

"When I agreed to marry Janine, I insisted on three things. There would be no church wedding, no minister, and I would choose the vows. I searched the internet for vows that wouldn't be a complete lie and insisted the justice of the peace substitute them for the traditional ones. The word 'love' was completely omitted from the ceremony. I never promised to love Janine, but I did promise to be faithful." Max cocked his head and looked at Anna, still annoyed by the question. "Satisfied?"

Anna was more than satisfied; she was thrilled. *Max could be faithful! Hallelujah!* But all she said was, "Yes, thank you."

Max sat with his arms crossed. "That's all, Anna. No more questions. I've been straightforward with you, laid it all on the line, but I'm talked out. I'm off the hot seat as of now."

CHAPTER NINETEEN

"I'm sorry," Anna said. "I went too far with my questions. I apologize. I should go now. She stood to leave. This is the last night I have to drive to that motel, and I'm sooo glad."

"Me, too. You know I never liked you staying there. But you can't go yet. It's your turn."

"My turn for what?"

"To fill in the blanks."

It took Anna a minute to grasp his meaning. She hadn't expected the question, although she probably should have. Max answered her questions honestly, when he obviously didn't want to. He deserved the same from her.

Returning to the sofa, she stalled. "I don't know where to start."

"Start with high school. I know you went to the prom with Windom. Did you date anyone else?"

She wouldn't tell him she'd been so deeply in love with him and so devastated by his marriage she had no interest in dating.

"I went out a few times, but mostly I focused on finishing school early and getting a scholarship, which thankfully I received. Otherwise, I don't know how I would have gotten through college.

"Mom hadn't saved for college expenses. I'm sure she thought she'd be around to help. Her insurance policy covered the funeral and the last of her bills, but that's all. I sold her car, but the money went toward getting the house ready to rent."

"You sold the car? What did you use for transportation?"

"I took an old car to school my freshman year, but it quit and wasn't worth the cost of repairs. I sold it to a junkyard and bought a bicycle. It got me where I needed to go."

"That's the only transportation you had? What did you do when it rained?"

"I had a slicker and kept extra clothes and shoes in a plastic bag. Very chic," she joked.

Max was beginning to realize how challenging Anna's life had been. "I'm sorry I wasn't around to help. Really sorry."

"I know. You had your own problems. But you helped by coming to Mom's funeral. I don't know how I would have gotten through it without you."

Max dropped his head; regretful he hadn't done more. "I would have gone to your house, but I made a deal with Janine. If she wouldn't attend the funeral, I wouldn't see you afterward. I didn't want her there and didn't think you would either."

Anna's eyes misted when she thought about her mother. "I talked with Mom the night before she fell. She called to see if I was studying, getting enough sleep, eating right. You know, the things moms worry about when their children move away. I wish I'd told her how much I loved her, thanked her for the sacrifices she made."

Max put an arm around Anna and pulled her close. "She knew how you felt."

Enjoying his closeness, Anna continued. "Mom was all the family I had, and when she was gone, I felt lost."

"Did she ever tell you about your relatives, explain why she wasn't in touch with them?"

"All she ever said was, 'we'll talk about it when you're older.' So, I quit asking. I like to think she would've told me when I turned eighteen. But she didn't live that long. After she died, I opened her safe, sure I'd find answers. I found some jewelry, the deed to the house, and a few other papers. Nothing else. I must have relatives somewhere, but I guess I'll never know who or where they are. Maybe I'm better off not knowing."

"You must have felt so alone."

"I did. Suddenly, I had no one to depend on but myself. It was frightening. I had a recurring nightmare that I was homeless, living on the streets. Mom hadn't finished paying off the house when she died, and I didn't have renters right away. That was scary. When it did rent, it only brought in enough to make the payments. I still had to find money for insurance and taxes.

"The logical thing would have been to sell it, but it was all I had left of Mom, you, our childhood. And maybe I felt the homeless dreams couldn't come true as long as I had the house."

Max was stunned to learn how much emotional turmoil Anna had gone through. "You must have known you could depend on my parents. They told me they tried to keep in touch, but you pushed them away."

"I did, and I feel bad about that. It's hard to explain. In my mind, the past equated to pain, and your parents were a big part of my past. I know it was contradictory to avoid everyone from Tenacity while stubbornly holding on to the house. Obviously, I had issues to work through. When I finally put some starch in my back and decided to accept the past, I came home."

"So how did you live?" Max asked. "I mean, did you take out loans?"

"The scholarship paid most of my tuition, as long as I kept my grades up, and I received money from social security for a few months, until I turned eighteen. Part-time jobs paid for books, but I still had to take out a loan. Thank goodness I never got sick enough to need a doctor, because I had no health insurance."

"What kind of jobs did you have?"

"Different ones. Often a job would fit my schedule one semester but not the next, so I'd have to find something new. There were several fast-food jobs, and for a while, I washed hair and swept up at a beauty salon. I wrapped Christmas gifts at the mall, bagged groceries, and did almost anything that didn't require me to take my clothes off."

Max shivered at the thought and said almost the same thing to her that she'd said to him. "I'm sorry things were so tough for you. I had no idea."

Anna tried to sound upbeat. "Seems like neither of us had an easy time of it, but we made it through. I drove myself pretty hard, knowing my fate rested with me alone. Like in high school, I finished a year early. I chose a degree in library science because I love books. I knew it wouldn't make me rich. I just needed to know I could keep a roof over my head and not starve."

"Did you live in the dorm?"

"At first, and I enjoyed it. But after Mom died, it wasn't right anymore. Too many noisy, carefree people. I needed to study, and like you, I had no time for fun. Luckily, I found a studio apartment in a nice building not far from campus. It was small, but safe and convenient."

"Smart girl. Tell me about your friends. Was there anyone important in your life? A man?" He selfishly hoped there hadn't been.

"There was someone," Anna confessed. "A man."

"Tell me about him."

"Well," she began, drawing out the word, "we lived in the same building. My apartment was on the second floor, and his was directly above mine."

"He was a student?"

"A law student. At first, we only said hello in passing. We didn't really get to know each other until he stopped by with a pizza one night and asked if he could come in and share it with me. Amused and hungry, I invited him in, and we became friends. I think I was an oddity to him. He's the gregarious sort. People were in and out of his apartment all the time, and he didn't understand why I was such a hermit."

"Then you started dating?"

"Not exactly. He asked me out a few times. I said no, but he kept coming by with dinner."

"Why did you say no?"

"Too busy. And I might have been a little depressed."

"That's understandable. So, if you wouldn't go out with him, how did he become your important person?"

"One evening he brought a bottle of wine with the pizza."

Max interrupted. "I don't think I want to hear what happened after the wine."

"It wasn't like that. It was a night much like this. We just sat and talked." She smiled. "I was a mystery to him, and he took advantage of my lack of sobriety to unearth my secrets. I explained what happened to Mom and told him about having no relatives. Then, thanks to my loosened tongue, I told him about our childhood, your family, our teen years, and about what happened with Janine."

Max was surprised. "You told him about that?"

"I did. And felt better for it. My burden was lighter because I had someone to help carry it. That's the way it felt, anyway."

"So he became your confident, your friend."

"He did, and before he left that night, he put his arms around me and held me. Until that moment I hadn't realized how much I missed being close to someone, being touched. I felt an almost forgotten sense of wellbeing. From then on, we shared our meals more often than not. He'd bring take-out or one of us would cook."

"Did you ever become more than friends?" Max asked, hoping they hadn't.

"You're asking if we had sex. Yes," was all she volunteered.

"Why did you break up?"

"We didn't, really."

Max was taken aback. That's not the answer he expected, nor the one he wanted to hear. "So, you're still together?"

"No, not really."

Perplexed, Max asked, "Then what are you to one another?"

"We're very good friends."

"Is that all?"

"Yes. I guess. Yes."

"You don't sound sure."

When she wrinkled her nose, he tried another tactic. "When was the last time you saw him?"

"He joined me in New York when I was there for one of the morning-show interviews. We went to dinner to celebrate the success of my book."

"Okay, we're getting somewhere. When I ask the next question, I want you to remember you asked me some very personal things. Now it's your turn and I expect you to be as truthful."

"Okay."

"When the two of you were in New York, did you have sex?"

Anna reluctantly nodded.

Max promptly got to his feet and ran a hand through his hair. "I thought we were going somewhere with this," he said, motioning between himself and Anna, "and now you're telling me you're with someone else?"

"No, I'm not," she hurried to say. "Our relationship is difficult to explain."

"No shit."

"It's whatever I want it to be." Anna shrugged. "I know that sounds bad, selfish, but that's how it is. It's how he is. If I only want to be friends, that's okay with him. He knows about you. I've told him we've reconnected."

"And that's all right with him?"

"Yes, if that's what I want. He wants me to be happy."

"Huh," was all Max managed to say, unable to understand how any man would sit back and hand Anna over to someone else.

Just as Max had, when he told her about Janine, Anna left out the details of her relationship with Conner. She failed to tell him, among other things, about the night things changed between them.

Conner had asked Anna what she'd do if he kissed her. "I guess I'd kiss you back," she'd answered. So, he pulled her close, gave her a slow tender kiss, then winked before backing out of her apartment. *What an operator!* she thought. *He left me wanting more and knew exactly what he was doing.*

But even as Anna was developing feelings for Conner, she couldn't help comparing her upstairs neighbor to Max. Conner was six-foot five, refined and blond, while Max was the epitome of tall, dark, and handsome. Conner had the long lean muscles of a basketball player, while Max was the quarterback type, with broad shoulders tapering to a slim waist. Max looked manly even before he was a man. And his eyes! She could get lost in his eyes. *Stop thinking about Max,* she'd told herself. *He made his choice.* Understanding his decision didn't change a thing.

Anna knew Conner wanted to take their friendship to another level, and he'd been more than patient. She sincerely cared for him, but she didn't love him the way she loved Max. If she had sex with Conner, it would be more like friends with benefits. Could she even do that?

She'd seen girls come and go from his apartment, and it wasn't unusual for one to spend the night. Meeting Conner on the stairs one morning after listening to his bed squeak rhythmically throughout the night, Anna asked with mock innocence, "Did you have a good night?" Then before he could answer, she deadpanned, "Oh, Conner, yes, yes, yes."

Playfully, he reached for her. "Cheeky little devil."

Anna laughed as she ran down the stairs and sped away on her bicycle. The episode had been funny at the time, but if their relationship became intimate, things could get complicated. She hadn't noticed any overnight guests lately, but she was fairly sure Conner wasn't the monogamous type.

His friendship was important to Anna. She didn't want to take a chance on losing it. But that kiss had felt good, and to be honest, it had already changed their relationship.

It was almost a week after their kiss before Anna saw Conner again, and she used the time to ponder her situation. She had let go of her long-held belief that Max would be her first and forever sexual experience. That would never come to pass. He was married to Janine, and they had a child. It was a fact she had to accept.

Conner stopped by her apartment to invite her to a party he was having that weekend. "You have to come," he pressured. "You deserve some fun, and I planned it on a night when you don't have to work." Giving Anna his most charming smile, Conner cajoled, "There'll be too much noise for you to study. Say you'll come. I really want you there."

Anna decided to make an appearance. Looking in her closet for something to wear, she was glad she'd purchased clothes the summer after high school. She certainly hadn't bought anything since. She chose a fashionably short skirt and a knit top showing just the right amount of cleavage. Liking what she saw, she finished the look with a loose updo and dangling earrings.

When Anna arrived, the party was in full swing. No one answered the door, so she opened it and peered in. The apartment was crowded, the music was loud, and people were shouting to make themselves heard. The group closest to the door yelled, "Come on in!" and a slightly inebriated young man gave Anna an unapologetic once over.

Conner rushed over to discourage the attention of several men clustering around her. He eyed her approvingly. "You look beautiful." Taking her hand, he led her toward the kitchen and leaned close to be heard. "Beer? Wine?"

Anna yelled above the din. "White wine, if you have it."

Conner bellowed to a friend in the kitchen, "Rick, get my girl a white wine, will you?" Anna raised her eyebrows and cocked her head. Giving her a little smile, he answered her silent question, "Yes, that was me laying claim to you. I know I'm being presumptuous, but you're a beautiful woman, and these guys can be persistent. I'm letting them know you are off limits. Do you mind?"

Anna shook her head. "This is quite a crowd."

"My friends brought their friends," Conner said, "and I don't know half the people here."

After Rick brought Anna's wine, Conner introduced her to his friends. Since she hadn't admonished him for referring to her as his girl, he continued to do so. When a slow tune began to play, Conner set her glass on a nearby table and swept her into his arms. Pulling her close, he skillfully swayed with the music.

When he bent down and buried his face in her neck, Anna thought about her passionate dance with Max in the school gym. She would never forget that evening or her surprise at discovering Max thought of her as more than a friend.

Once again Anna found herself in the arms of a friend, a friend who was re-awakening things in her she thought were dead. And she was thinking of Max. She had to get over him. Maybe Conner could help. He was ridiculously handsome, intelligent, charming, and she trusted him. Other than Max, she could think of no one she'd rather give her virginity to.

So she welcomed his kiss in the middle of their dance and molded her body to his. Feeling her willingness, Conner grasped her shoulders and pulled away to look into her eyes. When he saw the answer he was hoping for, he asked hoarsely, "Where's your apartment key?"

"It's not locked."

"We'll talk about that later." He clasped her hand and led her into the stairwell. As soon as they were inside Anna's apartment, he pushed her against the wall, covered her body with his, and kissed her until the rest of the world melted away.

162

"Tell me you're not daydreaming about another man," Max said, jerking Anna away from her memories.

"In a way, I guess I was. I was trying to think of a way to explain what he is to me," she lied.

"Any luck?"

"There's only one thing I can say. During my time away from Tenacity, he was my only friend, and I don't know what I would have done without him."

"I guess I have to accept that" Max said. "Let's change the topic. I don't want to talk about him anymore."

Upset about the other man, but knowing he had no right to be, Max tried to lighten the mood. "So, you graduated, became a librarian, and wrote a best-selling book. Not bad. I didn't even know you liked to write."

"I've always had stories in my head. As a child, I made up stories about the father I never knew. He was a pilot, a soldier, a firefighter, a detective. The profession changed, but he always loved me and was desperate to find me." She laughed. "You know how children are. Remember the stories I used to tell you in the tree house? Those imaginary friends evolved into the characters in my book."

"No joke?"

"No joke."

"At first, I think, writing was an escape mechanism, a way to be in control of something. Then I grew to love it. It amazes me that I can write a simple sentence on a blank sheet of paper and make it grow into whatever I want it to be. The possibilities are endless."

"When did you begin writing *A World Apart*?"

"The summer after my sophomore year in high school."

"Right after I left," Max noted.

"Yep. It was my hobby. I continued working on it in college when I could squeeze it into my schedule. Most of the time my mind was... It was bridled. Yes, that's the word. My sense of purpose bridled my mind. So to write, to let my imagination soar, was a joyful experience.

"After graduating and finding a full-time job, I wrote in the evenings and became serious about completing the story. Because I worked in a college library, I knew people with connections to the literary world. A professor put me in touch with a publishing company that happened to be looking for fantasy manuscripts, and things happened quickly."

Max had expected the evening Miss Sweet set-in motion to progress differently. He'd hoped there would be kissing and maybe something more. But rather than the romantic evening he'd wished for, the night had been one of revelations, some hard to confess, others hard to hear.

"I should go," Anna said. "I don't know about you, but I'm exhausted. Tonight's conversation drained me."

"I know what you mean. But before you go, I want to ask you something. He took both her hands into his and looked directly into her eyes. "I want to take you to dinner. I want you to wear your sexiest dress, and I'll wear a coat and tie. We'll drive to Clarkston, have a nice dinner and maybe do a little slow dancing. A real date—you and me. How about it?"

Anna hesitated. Agreeing to the date, she thought, sent the signal she was ready to move forward with their relationship. Max was a wonderful giving person. Maybe too giving. Women loved him, and he loved them right back. Anna seemed stuck on that issue.

164

But he'd responded to all her questions, and she'd found no fault in his answers. Still, she hesitated. Maybe she should refuse for now. But when she imagined Max sitting at a table, gazing at her the way he was at the moment, passion nibbled at her excuses.

And when she thought of him holding her on a dance floor, her resistance fled. Everything boiled down to one simple fact. She couldn't resist the man.

Anna looked contemplative. "A real date? You and me?"

"That's the idea."

She exhaled loudly and "okay" came out hesitantly. Max was pleased. Her agreement sounded weak, but she'd said "yes."

"Friday night?"

"Okay." She looked away, thinking about how that evening might end. Max gently turned her face toward his and gave her a sweet, heartfelt kiss.

CHAPTER TWENTY

Despite Anna's protests, Max followed her to the motel. Still concerned about appearances and the tabloids, Anna insisted he refrain from walking her to her door. She'd done just fine these past years without someone watching over her.

Anna found a parking spot directly in front of her room, but the only space available to Max was at the opposite end of the motel near the service station. After parking, he dutifully waited for Anna to lock herself safely inside. He hoped it would be the last night she'd have to stay in that place.

Max noticed a gray-bearded, big-bellied guy walking in Anna's direction. When the man passed under a light illuminating the gang insignia on his black motorcycle vest, Anna's self-appointed protector went on alert. He glanced around the parking lot to make sure the man was alone, and when Max looked back, he was nowhere to be seen.

Leaving his vehicle as quietly as possible, Max watched, ready to move quickly if the need arose. His friend Leonard, who worked at the station, yelled at him. When Max put a finger to his lips and pointed toward

Anna, Leonard caught on right away and joined his friend.

Feeling exhausted, Anna couldn't wait to get a shower and crawl between the sheets. After finding her room key, she left her car, walked the few steps to her room, swiped the key card and opened the door. Before she knew what was happening, she was violently pushed, face first, onto the dirty carpet. A heavyset man strode into the room, kicked the door shut, and jerked Anna up by her hair. It was painful and shocking.

"We're going for a little ride," a gruff voice said. "At first, I was only going to take your money and that shiny new car of yours, but you're such a pretty thing, I've decided to take you, too. Me and the boys get bored out in the woods by ourselves. You can be our entertainment for a while. You won't like it much. But we will."

They were going to rape her and who knows what else. Anna's mind raced. She had mace, but it was in the purse she dropped when she was pushed. If he stole her car and took her somewhere, maybe she could throw herself out the door. If it killed her, so be it. Dying would be preferable to what he had planned, and more than likely, they'd kill her anyway. Then she remembered Max had followed. *Thank you, God. But what if this guy has a weapon?*

The pain intensified. "You're hurting me. Let go." He threw her back to the floor, causing her head to hit the edge of the bed on the way down. Blood ran down the side of her face. Before she could recover, the man emptied the contents of her purse onto the bed. After stuffing her money and credit cards into his pocket, he grabbed Anna's arm, almost jerking it from its socket, and pulled her to her feet. "Where's yer keys?"

"I...I don't know." He slapped her, without letting go of her arm, and the world started turning black. The man's thick fingers rummaged in her pockets, and his hands roamed her body, searching for the keys. Anna's repulsion prodded her to struggle toward consciousness. After throwing her to the floor again, he opened the door to peek out. *Is he leaving? Please, God, let him leave.*

The door was abruptly pushed open, and Max's large fist hit the man squarely in the face, knocking him to the floor. Accustomed to violence, the man recovered quickly, grabbing for Anna's foot with one hand, while reaching for his knife with the other. She scrambled out of reach, managing to crawl to the back of the room.

"Bathroom!" Max yelled. Understanding the command, she stumbled into the bathroom and locked the flimsy door. When the gray-bearded guy turned to face Max and found two challengers instead of one, he moved toward the bathroom door, intent on capturing a hostage.

The two men rushed him, pushing him against the wall in the back of the room. Max grabbed the attacker's head and beat it against the wall until he fell to the floor.

Kicking away the bloody knife the man dropped, Max quickly pulled off his belt and secured the culprit's hands behind his back. He rummaged in a dresser drawer, finding a scarf and a pair of leggings to reinforce the make-shift handcuffs and tie the man's feet together.

After securing Anna's attacker, Max moved to Leonard, who was lying on the floor clutching his bleeding belly. "I'm okay," the injured man said. But clearly, he wasn't. Max pulled out his cell phone and called Doc, briefly explaining what happened, and asked him to phone the sheriff on his way to the motel.

He could have called an ambulance, but Doc was closer, and Max trusted him. Doc Waller moved to Tenacity right after he finished medical school and had practiced there ever since. He was getting up in age but was still available to folks in and around Tenacity, night or day. Sometimes he saw them in his office, located at the end of his home. Other times, he went to wherever his patients needed him.

Max found a clean knit shirt in a drawer, folded it, and placed it on Leonard's bleeding belly. "Doc says to keep pressure on it. Can you do that? I need to see about Anna."

After pulling the attacker away from the bathroom door, Max called to the frightened woman. "Unlock the door, babe. It's me. It's Max. It's safe to come out." There was no answer. He tried again but got nothing. "Get away from the door," he yelled. "I'm coming in."

The door flew open with one hard kick, and Max found Anna in the dry tub, curled into a ball. "It's me, sweetheart. It's me. No one's going to hurt you. That guy is tied up, and Doc is on his way. You're going to be all right." Max didn't try to move her. He just caressed her back and spoke tender, assuring words.

Doc arrived in minutes, quickly determining the stab victim was his priority. After putting a thick sterile bandage over Leonard's wound, Doc covered him with a blanket.

"Keep applying pressure. Don't let up. You're going to be all right, but you need to stay where you are until we get some help."

Sheriff Scott Wallace rushed into the room, his hand on his weapon.

"What's happening?"

"That guy over there," Doc said, nodding toward the trussed-up man, "attacked Anna Robinson. She's in the bathroom with Max."

"Who tied him up?"

"Max, I guess," Doc said. "But I crammed a sock in the bastard's mouth. Wouldn't shut up. Kept saying he was only trying to scare the woman."

The sheriff eyed the man next to Doc. "Leonard, what the hell happened to you?"

"That son-of-a-bitch stabbed me. Hurts like the devil. The knife must be around here someplace."

"How did you get involved in this?" Scott asked, looking around for the weapon.

"I thought Max could use some help."

Finding the knife on the floor, the sheriff carefully placed it in an evidence bag he took from his pocket.

Scott took a good look at the bearded man on the floor. "I know this guy. I locked him up one night after a fight in a biker bar across the river. Looks like Santa Claus, but he's trouble. If we're lucky, this knife will get him convicted of attempted murder."

"Let me see what that weapon looks like," Doc demanded. When the sheriff held it up, Doc was relieved. "That's good. The knife blade's not that long. Leonard, my man, your fat stomach probably saved your life."

"Didn't anybody tell you it's not nice to call people fat?" Leonard joked through his pain.

"Try to stay still," Doc reminded him. "Scott, I need to check on Max and Anna. You can see them when I've finished."

The sheriff followed the instructions of the man who used to give him lollipops after his injections, and then he checked to make sure the attacker's bonds were secure. He would replace the make-shift restraints with handcuffs once the deputy arrived to back him up.

When Doc finished checking his patients in the bathroom, he told Leonard and the sheriff, "Max is fine, except for a couple of busted knuckles, but that trussed-up bastard roughed Anna up pretty good. She'll need stitches for a gash on her head, and she could have a concussion. Her arm might be broken. Can't tell without an X-ray. She won't look her prettiest for a while. I'd like to kick that son-of-a-bitch in the head a few times."

"Better not, Doc," the sheriff warned.

Sitting on the edge of the bed, Doc spoke to Leonard. "Two ambulances are on the way to take you and Anna to Clarkston General. After they look you over, you'll probably go directly to surgery. The hospital docs will take over once we arrive, but I'll be around to keep an eye on you. I'll be right behind the ambulances."

Max walked slowly from the bathroom, his arm wrapped around Anna's waist while she cradled her injured arm with her left one. Anna recoiled at the sight of the two men on the floor, her face going pale. The one in the sleeveless plaid shirt was the man she'd seen watching from the gas station.

"You okay, Anna?" Leonard asked.

Max saw the puzzled look on her face. "You remember Leonard Stewart. He works at the station. He's been keeping an eye on you."

"Yes. Leonard," she said through a split lip. "I remember. High school."

Doc was concerned about Anna. She was white as a ghost and seemed a little confused. "Max, Anna needs to lie down until the ambulance gets here. Cover her with a blanket and put a pillow under her lower legs, instead of her head. She's a little shaky. I don't want her going into shock. Keep pressure on her head wound. Heads bleed like the dickens and putting her feet up won't help. But I'm more worried about shock than the head wound."

"Scott," Max said to the sheriff. "I know you need to talk to me about what happened here. Any chance we could do it later? I'd like to go to the hospital with Anna and Leonard."

Scott nodded. "I'll probably catch up with you there. If not, I'll call you tomorrow for a thorough interview. But I need you to answer a few questions now, for the record, so I can lock this Santa doppelganger up. I'll take him on to Clarkston tonight."

Years ago, the town of Tenacity converted most of its historic two-story jail into a library, leaving the sheriff an office and two cells in the back of the building. On the rare occasions a cell was used, it was usually for a resident who imbibed too much or for trouble-making youngsters who needed a scare put into them. In the unlikely event of a serious crime, like the one that just occurred, the culprit was taken to the Clarkston jail. It was an unusual arrangement, but Tenacity was an unusual place.

CHAPTER TWENTY-ONE

The emergency room staff responded immediately when the ambulances arrived. Leonard was admitted for surgery and Anna for observation. Max stayed with Anna through the night, managing to sleep in a chair that extended into a reasonable facsimile of a bed. When he woke the next morning, he found Anna looking worse than she had the night before, her face more swollen and her bruises more pronounced.

Max needed a cup of coffee, but he wouldn't leave until Anna awoke. She could be confused or frightened, and he wanted her to know she wasn't alone. Not anymore. He used her private bathroom as quietly as possible, splashing water on his heavily stubbled face. Anna looked up when he opened the bathroom door.

"You're still here," she said drowsily through her cut and swollen lips. Carefully touching her face, she asked, "How broken am I? I don't remember what the doctor said."

Max was honest. "You have a mild concussion. You'll have to avoid physical and mental exertion for a while. You have five stitches in your head and a lot of bruising. Your face is pretty banged up, but it's nothing permanent. The X-ray showed that your arm isn't broken, and your shoulder is still in its socket, but they gave you a steroid shot. You're supposed to keep your arm in a sling for a while, unless you're resting it on something. They're only giving you Tylenol for the pain because of the concussion."

"What happened to that horrible man?"

"He's in jail. Scott wants to talk to you when you're up to it. He was here last night. Doc and I filled him in as much as we could, but Doc wouldn't let him see you or Leonard."

"Leonard Stewart?" Anna asked, remembering bits and pieces of what happened. "He was stabbed. Is he okay?"

"They sewed him up. He'll be all right. Doc says his bulging gut saved his life. Now he'll never want to lose weight."

Anna smiled and winced.

"How about a popsicle?" Max suggested.

"What?"

"A popsicle. It's something you learn when you have an active kid, an easy way to ice a swollen lip."

"Sounds good."

Max hurried to the hospital cafeteria, getting back before the doctor made his rounds. After repeating what Doc Waller had already explained, the hospitalist released Anna on the condition that she wouldn't be alone for the next few days.

"She'll be with me," Max said, surprised Anna didn't argue.

Max helped her up the steps of his home and into his recliner. "What can I get you? Water, coke, something hot?"

"Water, please." After a few swallows and a couple of Tylenol, Anna handed the glass back to Max.

"How about a bath? A good soak will help your sore muscles."

"Sounds good."

Max ran her a warm bath. "Need any help?"

"Seriously?"

"Seriously. I've seen a naked woman before."

"But you haven't seen me naked."

Not yet, he thought.

"I can manage," Anna told him. "But thanks, I guess."

"Call if you change your mind," he said, winking and closing the bathroom door.

Anna looked in the mirror for the first time since the attack. "No!"

From outside the bathroom door, Max called, "Are you all right?"

When she didn't immediately answer, he yelled, "I'm coming in," and walked into the bathroom. Still dressed, sitting on the closed toilet, Anna held her hands loosely over her face.

"Don't look at me. I'm hideous."

Max squatted beside her. "You're not hideous," he said in his most soothing voice. "You're just hurt. Nothing's broken, just bruised and swollen. It'll get better. And I've already seen you." Easing her hands away, he barely touched his lips to the less injured side of hers. "Do you need help? With anything?" he asked seriously.

She started to shake her head, but it hurt, so she said, "No. But thanks."

"I'll be in the next room if you need me. Okay?"

"Okay." Getting in and out of the tub was difficult, as was bathing, but Anna wouldn't ask for help. If Max ever saw her naked, that wasn't the way she wanted it to happen.

Anna appeared in the living room, wearing one of Max's clean t-shirts and a robe, which he had to tie for her. It felt good to be clean, but she really wished she had underwear.

Max gave her a pitying smile. She looked so helpless, all banged up with her arm in a sling. "Are you hungry? Do you want some soup?"

"I think I could handle that if you put it in a cup. I'm starving."

After Anna carefully drank the soup, Max helped her to bed, assured her everything would be all right, and lay down beside her. Both fell asleep, immediately.

The following day, Max drove to the motel to get Anna's things and check her out of that horrid place. While he was out, he stopped by Mayfield's Grocery to look for some soft, easy-to-eat food items. He hadn't been gone long when a car pulled into the driveway. The doorbell rang, followed quickly by pounding.

Anna froze. *Could it be the attacker? No, he was in jail. Have his friends come for me?* Then, the thought that something could have happened to Max motivated her to respond. "Who is it?" she said as loudly as she could without re-splitting her lip.

"Open up," a female voice said. "Tell Max to open this door now. I know you're staying here, Anna, and I won't have it. I won't let my daughter stay in this house while you're here. What kind of message would that send?"

"Max isn't here, Janine."

The pounding continued. "I demand you open this door right now. Or am I interrupting something sordid?" Afraid Janine's misconceptions could cause problems for Max, Anna opened the door and gestured for the unwanted guest to enter.

Janine's hand flew to her mouth, and she looked truly distressed. "You look awful!" She wasn't being malicious, Anna realized, just tactless.

"I need to sit down, Janine. Join me? Max really isn't here."

Watching Anna move stiffly to a chair, she followed. Positioning herself on the sofa, Janine leaned forward, studying the injured woman. "Wow. You're really hurt. And you look terrible."

Janine's comments were so guileless it was almost funny. Then she said the most unexpected thing. "I'm sorry." That was the nicest thing she'd ever said to Anna. Maybe there was a heart in that body after all. Janine looked down at her hands and, under her breath, as if talking to herself, said, "I didn't mean..."

After waiting a moment for the rest of the sentence, Anna asked, "You didn't mean what?"

"I... I didn't mean to say you look awful. I should leave. My car's blocking the driveway."

Hearing heavy footsteps run up the steps and across the porch, the women looked toward the door in time to see Max storm in, an indignant look on his face. "What are you doing here, Janine?"

Anna was the first to speak, opening her mouth just enough to form the words. "Janine wanted to make sure it was all right for Gracie to visit while I'm here." It was sort of true.

"Yes," Janine jumped in. "I thought it might not be best for her to come over now. I can keep her at Mother and Daddy's if that would help."

Max squinted, as if trying to solve a mystery, clearly distrusting the validity of the calm scene before him. Knowing how upset Gracie would be to miss her time with him, not to mention his own disappointment, Max insisted on picking her up from day care as usual. Janine was surprisingly compliant, even offering to pick her up and drop her off.

"Thanks," Max said suspiciously, "but I'll do it. The drive will give me a chance to explain about Anna before Gracie sees her."

When evening arrived, Max was tempted to put a no-visitors sign on the door and take the phone off the hook. He'd fielded questions from concerned friends all day, telling them all the same thing. Anna was attacked by someone she didn't know; she was going to be fine; and her attacker had been arrested. And no, she hadn't been raped. If Anna wanted to explain further, she could. That was up to her.

It had been a busy day. Doc came by, then Samantha, and finally the sheriff, whose visit had been difficult. Thankfully, Scott's interview was over before Max left to pick up Gracie. Things were said that a child shouldn't hear.

Max held Anna's hand during the sheriff's questioning, offering support, but when she related the attacker's plans for her, he thought he might explode. Because Anna needed him to remain calm, he pretended calmness, although she told him once he was squeezing her hand too hard.

After the sheriff left, Anna's cell phone rang in the guest room. Because she didn't bother to close the door, Max heard her side of the conversation. She kept assuring the caller she was being well taken care of and there was no reason to come to Tenacity. Max hoped the caller was satisfied. He didn't think he could handle a visit from Anna's lover.

CHAPTER TWENTY-TWO

When Max picked Gracie up from day care, he explained that someone had hurt Anna, that she looked bad, but she'd be all right. "It's our job," he told her, "to help Anna get better." The child asked a few questions, which Max answered as vaguely as possible. Then, just as Max knew she would, Gracie embraced her role as nurse and focused on what she could do to help.

Anna ate oatmeal and blueberries for supper and retired to her room. She hurt in so many places it was hard to say where she hurt most. Even putting on her pajama pants and t-shirt was a trial, but she wouldn't ask for help. She finished dressing and was crawling between the sheets of the comfortable bed in Max's guest room when he knocked lightly on her door.

"Gracie wants to read you a book before you go to sleep. Are you up to it?"

"Of course. That's nice of you, sweetheart," she said to the child. "What are you going to read?"

"You said you like *The Little House*, so I'll read that one."

The fact that Gracie didn't really know how to read wasn't a hurdle. Turning the pages, she recited what she could from memory and made up the rest. After carefully kissing Anna on the cheek, the precious child knelt by the bed and said a prayer she'd learned in Sunday School.

"And please let my friend Anna get well and be pretty again," she added.

Anna simultaneously wiped away a tear and choked back a chuckle.

"I'll be back," Max mouthed, guiding his daughter from the room. "It's Gracie's turn to get tucked in."

When Max returned, he sat on the bed beside Anna and carefully kissed her forehead.

She caressed his defined jawline. "Your Gracie must be the sweetest child in the world."

"I can't argue with you there. She's pretty special."

"That kindness came from you. Thank you for all you're doing for me."

"I like taking care of you."

He always had, Anna realized, remembering the ladder he made when he was eight. When Max got up to leave, she caught his hand. "Don't leave."

"Be right back," he said. A minute later he returned in a t-shirt and sleep pants. He crawled into bed and held Anna carefully. When it became obvious he was aroused, he said, "Just ignore it. It doesn't always do what I tell it to."

❦

A few evenings after the attack, the sheriff called. "I have information to share with you and Anna. Is this a good time to come over?"

About fifteen minutes later, Max opened the door to the sheriff. "Come in. Have a seat." Dressed in a sharply creased uniform, Scott greeted Anna before settling in an upholstered chair.

Anxious to hear what he came to say, Max started to sit but then remembered his manners. "Can I get you something, Scott?"

"No thanks. I'd like a beer, but I'm on duty."

Max and Anna sat on the sofa opposite the sheriff and waited. With his elbows on the arms of his chair, Scott clasped his hands together and began.

"As I said on the phone, I have information you should hear. Brewster, the guy who attacked Anna, says he was paid to scare her."

"You don't believe him, do you? He did a lot more than scare her."

"I know it sounds phony," the sheriff said, "but he swears it's true."

Max didn't believe it and said so. "Who would want to frighten Anna, anyway?"

Scott had an intense look on his face.

"There's more," Max guessed.

The sheriff nodded, then hesitated before speaking. "I'm going to lay this out as it unfolded so you'll know we didn't jump to a conclusion. Brewster says he doesn't know the name of the person who hired him." Scott looked at the floor, then at Max. "But he described the individual as female, blonde, pretty, small. She gave him a hundred dollars."

Max knew where this was leading and shook his head. "No." He sat back on the sofa, denying a very possible conclusion. But Anna had told him about Janine's unexpected reaction to her attack. His ex-wife didn't like Anna. Jealousy, he figured. But Anna said

Janine was truly distressed upon seeing her condition. *Could that have been remorse?*

Max stood and began to pace. "It couldn't be her. She wouldn't do that." But deep down, he knew she might. She wouldn't condone what the scumbag did, but she was perfectly capable of setting that ball into motion.

"You better sit down," Scott said. "There's something else."

Max did as he was told, knowing what Scott had to say must be important.

"Leonard saw Janine talking to Brewster at the station."

Max buried his face in his hands. "Something's wrong with that woman. I don't know what, but something's wrong."

He looked at Anna, who hadn't said a word, and took her hand in his. Then he turned his attention back to Scott.

"Have you talked to her?"

"Yeah. I just came from the Larson house. Janine says she asked Brewster if he would be around during the Christmas holidays. Said she wanted him to play Santa for day care. I guess it's possible."

"But it's six months until Christmas," Max reminded him.

"Yeah. There's that. But that's not all. Brewster picked Janine's picture from a group of fifteen others, as the one who paid him to scare Anna."

Max held his hand over his mouth as he listened. "Will you arrest her?"

"We could, and will, if Anna wants to press charges."

They both looked at Anna.

"I don't know," she said. "I need to think about it."

"Well, I can tell you this," the sheriff said. "Since Brewster says he was hired to scare you, a good lawyer would say Janine only meant to play a prank, a sick one, but a prank, nonetheless. By acting penitent on the stand and stating she had no idea he would actually harm you, she could get off with a slap on the wrist. We went to his house," Scott continued, "and it appears he lives alone. He gave us directions because he was worried about his dog. He puts her in the house when he leaves so she won't follow the Harley. That probably means all the talk about taking Anna back to the boys was simply meant to scare her."

Max felt sure his ex-wife hadn't intended for Anna to be physically hurt, but it sounded like she was ultimately responsible for the attack. He wanted to go directly to the Larsons' to confront Janine, make her aware of what she did and how much worse it could have been. He wanted to condemn her for being a bad example for Gracie and tell her how ashamed he was of her.

But Scott advised him not to, and Anna talked him out of it. She was stunned Janine could do such a thing but was more concerned about how a confrontation might affect Max and Gracie.

"It'll just make a bad situation worse," she said, "and she'll deny it anyway."

Samantha and Max did everything they could to help Anna heal and make her feel safe. Both of them took time off from work, rotating days, so she wouldn't be alone. Samantha oversaw the delivery of Anna's bedroom furniture, and Max arranged to have an alarm system installed in her house. Tenacity was a safe place, but Anna had been through a frightening experience, and he wanted her to feel secure.

After a few days of Max and Samantha's constant attention, Anna insisted they return to work. She was tired of feeling like a victim and needed to regain control of her life. She began sleeping in her own bed but spent a large portion of each day at Max's house, since Doc demanded she avoid the construction noise.

Anna's renovation crew took turns walking next door to see if she needed anything and to remind her they were only a few steps away. And every afternoon, before he left for home, Fred walked through Anna's house with her to assure her no one lurked in a closet or hid under a bed.

The ladies from church provided meals until Anna insisted they stop. After that, Max brought take-out. He ate with her, left, then returned to check on her before she went to bed. Sensing her fragility, he kept things platonic, except for one sweet good-night kiss each night. He'd waited a long time to have Anna in his life. He could wait a while longer.

CHAPTER TWENTY-THREE

It was Max's night to have Gracie, but he agreed to let Janine drop her off after a birthday dinner she was giving her boyfriend, Doug. As it turned out, Mr. Larson was the one to deliver his granddaughter. Max figured Janine was avoiding him, and that was probably for the best.

Gracie was surprisingly quiet when she got to her dad's. That concerned Max, for Gracie was never quiet. When he asked if she was all right, she said she was, but wouldn't look him in the eye. Something was wrong. There was something she wasn't telling him, and his daughter normally told him everything.

When Max dropped Gracie off at day care that morning, she'd been her usual guileless self. When she returned home that evening, she was morose and distant.

Max did the only thing he knew to do. After changing her into a nightgown, he held his daughter in his arms, sat in the chair in Gracie's room, and rocked. When her eyelids grew heavy, he tucked her into bed as usual.

He was shocked when she began struggling against the covers. "No, no!" she cried. "I can't breathe. Let me out! Daddy! Help me!"

Max pulled his panicked daughter into his arms, walked back and forth, and rubbed her small back, murmuring soothing words. Gracie clutched his neck like a drowning person clinging to a lifeline.

When her sobs diminished, he sat with her in his lap and eased her hands from his neck. "Look at me, ladybug." She looked up, her eyes red and watery, her face splotchy from crying. Max wanted to put her in his pocket and keep her there, where she'd always be protected.

"You're all right now. I've got you."

He desperately wanted to know what was wrong, but instinctively knew not to push. When Gracie rested her head against his chest, he held her a while, before trying again, "Look at me, sweetie. Why couldn't you breathe? Tell me what's wrong."

She regained some of her composure and spoke in a small voice. "I can't."

"You can't tell me?" Gracie shook her head. Max was truly frightened that something terrible had happened. "Why can't you tell me, baby?"

Looking at him with her big blue eyes, she said in a barely audible voice, "Mother said so."

Max wanted to put his fist through the wall. Not only was Janine keeping information about his child from him, she was also teaching Gracie to be dishonest. For the second time that day, he pretended to be calm when he actually wanted to punch something.

"Your mother probably said that because she didn't want me to worry," he lied. He wasn't being honest either, but he had to find out what was wrong so he could fix it.

Tears ran down Gracie's face. "You mean it's all right to tell you."

"Of course, it's all right. You can always talk to me." Gracie hugged Max as hard as she could.

"So, do you know why you were afraid to be tucked in?"

Gracie nodded. "It made me think of when Kevin and Allen wrapped me up and wouldn't let me out." Gracie breathed a sigh of relief and pent-up words spilled out. "Daddy, I was so scared. I couldn't breathe, and they left me all wrapped up." It took a while, but Max eventually extracted the whole story.

When Gracie fell asleep, he called Anna. "Can you come over? I'd be grateful. I'd go to you, but Gracie's asleep. I'll watch you from the porch." Thanks to the motel incident, Anna wasn't comfortable going out alone at night.

"What's going on?"

"I need you to keep me from killing someone."

"Who is it you want to kill?"

"I'm not sure. You can help me decide."

"Okay. Be right there." Dressed for bed in a large t-shirt, she slipped into cut-off jeans and a pair of sandals and was next door in less than five minutes. She found Max pacing the porch, hitting a cupped hand with his fist, a look on his face she'd never seen.

"I don't know what happened," she said, "but you're obviously upset. Sit down and talk to me."

"I'm not upset, dammit. I'm furious! Those boys are bad seeds," he said, trying to keep his voice down so he wouldn't wake Gracie.

"What boys?"

188

"Fric and Frac, or whatever Doug calls those demons of his."

"You're angry at Doug's kids?"

"Hell, yes."

"Max, I can't help you until you settle down and tell me what happened." To stop him from pacing, she took him by the hand, pulled him onto the metal glider, and sat in his lap. "We're sitting here until you tell me what's going on. Spill."

Max sighed and ran a hand through his hair. "I know I shouldn't have called you, but I had to tell someone. This is what happened. I tucked Gracie into bed, like I always do, and she panicked. She was scared, Anna. Really scared. It triggered something. When I asked her what was wrong, she wouldn't say."

"That doesn't sound like Gracie."

"No, it doesn't. Finally, she admitted her mother told her not to tell me. You can't know how mad that makes me. I'm Gracie's dad! How can a mother tell a child to lie to her father? I guess I shouldn't be surprised, considering what Scott said this afternoon."

"Did Gracie tell you what was wrong?"

"She did, after I assured her it was all right. I told her that her mother just didn't want me to worry. When Gracie finally started talking, she told me everything, and saying she has a good memory is a gross understatement. Janine took Gracie to Doug's house and told her to go upstairs and play with the boys while she and Doug put supper on the table. Gracie didn't want to, but Janine insisted. It's hard to believe she did that. She knows Gracie is afraid of those boys. Everyone knows what they're like, and they're eight years old, three years older than Gracie."

Seeing Max becoming more agitated, Anna rubbed his chest, hoping to soothe him. He took a long breath before continuing.

"Those little demons took Gracie into one of the upstairs bedrooms, rolled her in a rug, with her arms pinned to her sides, and left her there! From what I can gather, Janine began looking for her when it was time to eat. Gracie heard her mother calling…"

Max took a moment to control his emotions. "She tried to answer but was having trouble breathing and couldn't make herself heard. Anna, you should have seen her when she told me. She held onto me and sobbed. Kept saying she wanted me to come save her."

Max wiped unashamed tears away with the back of his hand. "She thought she was going to die. Those little bastards moved the bed, shoved her against the wall, and put the bed back into position so no one would find her."

"Oh, no," Anna said, her hand moving to cover her mouth.

"Gracie told her mother she never wants to go back to that house, but Janine assured her everything would be fine, that she and Doug would take care of her. 'After all,' she said to Gracie, 'hadn't Doug made the boys tell him where they hid her?' "

Max shook his head. "Gracie could have suffocated, and now she's afraid to be tucked into bed. And you know what Janine told her daughter? She said the boys were just playing, that boys play differently than girls. She defended the little devils!"

Anna was shocked that sweet little Gracie experienced such a traumatic incident. "Poor baby. She must have been terrified. It takes time to recover from terror like that. I know."

Max nodded. "Yeah. You do."

Still sitting in Max's lap, Anna stroked his neck and back. "So, now what?"

"I'll have to have a come-to-Jesus talk with Janine, try to make the hard-headed woman realize the seriousness of her actions. But I'm so angry, I don't know if I can be effective.

"Ordinarily, I'd say a discussion between adults should be just that, a discussion. But I don't see Janine as a normal adult. A part of her is still a spoiled child. Sometimes I think she needs professional help. Other times, I think she's just mean. I can deal with it. I've been doing it for years. But now she's hurting Gracie and you."

Max and Anna talked through the problem and decided the conversation should take place at the Larsons' so they could be included. Gracie would stay with Anna to keep her out of listening range, and Max would invite Scott to join them. Not only would he be a reliable witness to what was said, Max hoped the sheriff's presence would help Janine realize the seriousness of the situation.

The day of the dreaded talk arrived. When the assembled group took their places in the Larsons' living room, Max told himself to relax and began. First, he reprimanded Janine for telling Gracie to keep things from him.

"That can never happen again. I won't have you teaching her to lie. I'm her father, and she can tell me anything. She should never question that. And under no circumstances will you berate her for telling me about the rug incident. Not one word." Max's ex-wife blanched, unnerved that he'd found out.

Janine stood, announcing that she didn't have to sit there and listen to Max tell her what to do. She was right. She didn't. But Max had things to say, and if he had to be overbearing to get her to listen, that's what he'd do. Gentle persuasion had no effect on her. Max was intensely grateful when Scott inserted himself into the conversation.

"Janine," the sheriff said, "it would be in your best interest to sit back down and pay attention to what Max has to say." She sat, but her arms were folded over her chest, and her chin was in the air.

"Mr. and Mrs. Larson," Max said with respect, "I don't believe you're aware of what happened at Doug's house recently. I found out because Gracie panicked when I tucked her into bed. Hands clenched at his sides, he described Gracie's reaction and the reluctant revelation of her harrowing ordeal.

Max looked directly at Janine. "I need you to listen carefully to what I'm about to say." Emphasizing every word, he declared, "Do not ever leave Gracie alone with those boys. Not for one minute. And if she balks at going to Doug's, you will not force her. She can stay with me or her grandparents."

"That's crazy," Janine argued. "And unnecessary. The boys were just playing around."

At that, Max splayed his hands on the top of his head and walked away. He stood with his back to the group, fuming. She was still defending them! He wasn't making a dent in her armor. And if she didn't agree to his demands, Gracie was in danger.

"Dammit, Janine," he said when he turned around, "for once, will you think of your daughter? Do you even care about her?"

Scott came to the rescue again. "Janine, you need to be careful. You don't want a social worker up in your business. And that could happen. If a court determines that you knowingly put your child in danger, you'll have big problems."

Scott's warning was vague, but Janine stopped arguing. Instead, she left the room. A minute later, they heard a car pull out of the driveway.

Max didn't get the chance to talk to Janine about her part in Anna's traumatic experience, but he explained the situation to Mr. and Mrs. Larson. They needed to know the extent of their daughter's bad judgement so they understood the importance of protecting their grandchild.

The Larson's were appropriately appalled to learn Anna had been hurt but were sure Janine had nothing to do with it. Max and Scott looked at one another.

"And there you go," Scott said.

Janine's parents defended her, no matter what she did. Of course, she felt entitled.

CHAPTER TWENTY-FOUR

Max wanted to focus on his relationship with Anna, but life kept getting in the way. Anna was attacked by a stranger, and Gracie was attacked by Doug's eight-year-old twins. Max was dealing with the fallout from both incidences, doing his best to help both Anna and Gracie. Try as he might, he couldn't get past the fact that Janine was responsible for it all.

But finally, things seemed to be looking up. Janine was leaving Gracie with her parents or with him when she visited Doug, and Gracie was returning to her normal, happy self. Anna's injuries had healed, she was settled in her own bedroom suite, and she was regaining confidence after her traumatic experience. So one night, when Max and Anna were sitting on Anna's front porch swing, he asked if she was ready for their date.

"I am," she replied.

Pleasantly surprised she'd accepted so readily, he made a reservation at La Maison Rose, a posh restaurant in Clarkston. Unwilling to wait weeks for a Friday or Saturday reservation, he opted for the following Thursday, clearing his calendar the following day, in case the evening went as he hoped.

Anna thought a date might be just what she needed. Since that horrible night at the motel, she'd found it difficult to get excited about anything, but the prospect of a date with Max made her feel alive again. And because the remainder of her clothes had been delivered with her bedroom shipment, she had the perfect, drool-worthy dress and shoes.

Late Thursday afternoon Janine arrived at Luanne's flower shop to purchase flowers for Doug's dinner table. She was preparing the evening meal and wanted everything perfect. Doug McKinnon didn't know it yet, but he was going to be her next husband. She just had to convince him he couldn't live without her. If she had to cook a few dinners to make that happen, she could endure it.

Luanne Campbell spent mornings working on the family farm and afternoons in her beloved flower shop. The Campbell family's main crops were corn and soybeans, but they also kept a greenhouse where they grew flowers for area florists. In the small town of Tenacity, Luanne's shop never turned much of a profit, but as long as it didn't operate too far in the red, the family gladly provided the flowers.

Luanne looked up when the bell on the door jingled, pleased to have another customer. "Hi, Janine, what can I do for you?" As Janine pointed out the flowers she wanted, Luanne casually disclosed information she hoped would generate some good gossip. "Max was here a few minutes ago. Bought a nice bouquet of yellow lilies. Any idea who they're for?"

"No. And I'm sure I don't care. That man is no longer any of my business."

"But surely you know what's going on in his life."

Janine huffed, hoping to conceal her concern. "I'm too busy with Doug to worry about Max's tramp of the week." Because she kept an eye on him, she knew Max dated several women in Clarkston. That was acceptable, since he never narrowed the field down to one, never got serious. But his interest in Anna worried her.

If the flowers were for someone in Clarkston, Janine deduced, he would have bought them in Clarkston. But since he purchased them in Tenacity, they were probably for his neighbor. Max and Anna had been spending a lot of time together, and she'd stayed with him when she was hurt. Janine didn't think they were sleeping together, but they were getting entirely too cozy.

Max never openly dated Anna in high school, but Janine suspected there was more to their relationship than either of them admitted. Remembering Max and Anna's embarrassing dance at the Spring Fling, Janine pondered her failed marriage. *Max never really gave us a chance. His feelings for the "library girl" are probably the reason he didn't love me. Why didn't I see it before? Anna Robinson is responsible for my divorce.* Having worked herself into a state, Janine resolved to put a stop to whatever was happening between the two.

Driving past Max's house, she found her ex-husband leaning into his recently washed SUV, exposing his excellent jean-clad butt to passers-by. Car mats lay on the ground while he vacuumed the interior of the gleaming vehicle. The man bought flowers and was giving his car

196

a thorough cleaning. It wasn't hard to guess that he had a big date.

Janine quickly formulated a plan. Sitting at the kitchen table in her childhood home, she drank coffee with her mother, sneaking glances at the clock on the wall. The need for guesswork made her plan tricky. Arriving too early or too late could spoil the entire scheme.

When Janine felt the time was right, she pretended her phone vibrated. Executing a one-sided conversation, she pretended Max wanted their daughter for the evening.

Gracie was arranging toy animals on the windowsill when Janine rushed into her room. "Come on," she said. "Let's go. You're spending the evening with your dad."

"I thought I was supposed to be with you tonight," Gracie said, as her mother strapped her into the booster seat.

"Things change," Janine answered curtly.

Seeing Max's vehicle in the driveway, the deceitful young woman complemented herself on her timing. She pulled Gracie toward her father's front door and rang the doorbell.

Thinking it must be Anna, Max grabbed his coat and opened the door. "You were supposed to wait at your..." He stopped when he saw who stood on his porch.

Elated her plan was unfolding so perfectly, Janine suppressed a smile. Max stood at the open door, looking ever so sexy, with a surprised look on his face. Wearing a crisp white shirt and tie with a jacket thrown over one arm, he looked like a magazine ad for men's cologne. He even smelled the part. Janine remembered the scent, and for a moment, thought about how it felt to be with this man. But she'd long ago abandoned her efforts to get Max back. The stubborn man refused to forgive her one little indiscretion.

Focusing on the task at hand, Janine spoke hurriedly. "You look like you're going somewhere. I'm sorry if I'm spoiling your plans, but I'm desperate. I'm trying to get a job with a real estate firm in Clarkston, and the owner just called. She wants me there right now. She's giving me the responsibility of showing a house by myself," she dramatized. "If I do a good job, I think she'll take me into the firm. Gracie is the problem. Mother and Father aren't available tonight, and I don't know what to do with her. Please take her off my hands for the evening."

Not only was Max irritated by Janine's interference with his plans, he was angered by the phrasing of her request. Gracie looked dejected, concerned that she was a problem for her mother. Max put down his jacket and scooped Gracie into his arms, kissing the top of her head. "Gracie's never a problem. Thank you for bringing her over."

Max's date with Anna was important. He'd thought of little else since she'd accepted his invitation. But for Gracie's sake, he pushed down his disappointment. He might have tried to get a sitter had Janine not made the child feel unwanted. Now, he had no choice but to cancel the date and hope Anna would understand. Janine thanked him profusely and left with a smirk on her face.

Gracie brightened when Max suggested they take flowers to their neighbor. Anna opened the door with a smile on her face, looking beautiful in a red sheath dress and matching spiked heels. Her smile didn't waver when she noticed the small person standing next to her date.

Max's lips pressed together in a tight line, and the expression on his face told Anna what had happened.

"We brought you flowers!" Gracie exclaimed.

"They're beautiful." After giving Max an understanding glance, Anna accepted the flowers and spoke to the child. "Thank you. Come on in. I'll get a vase."

Max stifled a whimper at the sight of Anna walking away. Her dress was cut to the waist, exposing most of her back. He wanted to wrap his arms around her, nuzzle her neck, and kiss his way down her spine.

Returning quickly with the flowers, Anna surprised Max by saying, "I'm so glad Gracie is here. She can go to dinner with us." Gracie was dressed in well-worn shorts, a tank top, and flip-flops—not proper attire for La Maison Rose. "Do you have a dress at your daddy's house?" Anna asked the child.

Max shook his head, appreciating Anna's effort to make the best of the situation.

"Then we'll stop on the way and buy something. This will be fun."

"You're sure?" Max asked.

Anna retrieved her purse and her wrap from a nearby chair. "Of course, but we'd better get started. We have a lot to do."

Anna made the trip fun for Gracie. They searched billboards and license plates for letters of the alphabet. Once they found A, they began searching for B. When the game stalled at Q, Anna talked Gracie into singing her favorite songs.

Max marveled at how Anna seemed to enjoy his daughter's company. And how was it that she was more careful with Gracie's tender feelings than the child's own mother?

When Max, Gracie, and Anna walked into the restaurant, all eyes turned their direction. Max was every woman's dream in a dark suit and crisp white shirt, while Anna looked glamorous in her red sheath and matching heels.

Adorable in her new attire, Gracie admired the dimly lit restaurant. The tables were dressed in white, adorned with white tapers in silver candleholders. Red roses, silver chargers, elegant china and shining silverware completed the picture. A pianist played soft jazz on a grand piano. Gracie's eyes widened. "This is beautiful," she said quietly.

The maître d' escorted them to their table, put a child's cushion in Gracie's chair, and helped her get settled. When he told her how lovely she looked, the little girl cast a shy look toward Anna and her dad, but had a big smile on her face.

She did look lovely. Anna had dressed her in a new ensemble from head to foot. "This is my gift to Gracie," she insisted. The little girl's dress was white, with a full skirt, and the light blue bow in her curly dark hair matched the sash around her waist. White ruffled socks and white patent leather shoes completed the ensemble.

After studying the menu, Anna ordered onion soup as an appetizer, while Max chose a green salad for himself and a roasted pear salad for his daughter. As an entrée, Anna chose Red Snapper, Max went with Filet Mignon, and Gracie decided on a hamburger and fries. For dessert, it was white-chocolate cheesecake all around. Max whispered to Anna, "Can you get catsup out of a white dress?"

"We'll have to google it."

Gracie marveled at her surroundings. "This is like a princess at a ball."

Looking at his daughter and the beautiful woman at his table, Max's heart was full. "Then we must dance."

Anna looked unsure. "Are you hiding extra arms somewhere?"

"You might be surprised."

Max led the way to a small dance floor near the piano and picked Gracie up. Balancing her on one arm, he pulled Anna close with the other. Physically, it was a little awkward, but they all smiled hugely, and Max knew he was holding the two most precious people in his world. They moved around the dance floor to an old standard, Nat King Cole's 'Unforgettable,' a tune befitting the evening.

When they were seated again, the trio became aware of a young woman taking pictures with a cell phone. She shyly walked over when Anna looked at her. "You're Annaleah Robinson, aren't you, author of *A World Apart*?"

"I am."

"I'm Stephanie Rollins, and I'm a fan. I've been trying my hand at writing. I'm not very good at it, but I enjoy it."

"Well, that's the way to learn. There are sources to get you on the right track. If you'll give me your email, I'll send you some information."

Noticing she kept glancing at Max, Anna introduced him and then Gracie. The woman rejoined her group, which looked like a family gathering, smiling, and telling them what had transpired.

"That was nice of you," Max said. "I think you made her evening."

"I'll enjoy helping her. I remember what it was like to have an interest with no guidance. But I do wish people wouldn't take photos without permission. I know everyone does it these days, but when you think about it, it's rude.

"My grandmother would agree with you," Max said.

"That's because she grew up in a time when people respected one another's privacy and considered politeness a virtue. Sorry. I admit to being oversensitive about privacy."

On the way back to Tenacity, Gracie fell into a contented slumber, while the adults enjoyed the intimacy of the dark ride home. Anna watched Max's confident hands on the steering wheel, and they spoke quietly, mostly about the events of the evening.

Max thanked Anna profusely for the way she handled the little surprise who was sleeping in the back seat. It wasn't the night he envisioned, but he'd experienced the joy of seeing wonder on his daughter's face and spending time with a generous, caring, beautiful woman.

"I never imagined a fancy restaurant would delight Gracie so," Max said. "Think she'll still like Dairy Queen?"

Anna laughed. "I'm imagining a day care worker asking the children to name their favorite restaurant and Gracie declaring hers is La Maison Rose."

Despite the polite conversation, it was impossible to ignore the sexual tension in the car. You could almost taste it. Max reached over and took one of Anna's hands in his, and her body practically hummed.

When Anna traveled through the corridor that night, in the car with Max and Gracie, she remembered how it had felt to return after her long absence. She'd been excited, fearful, and more than a little confused about her compulsion to move home. She'd almost felt coerced. Now she wondered if Max was the reason. *Was something or someone pulling her home to be with him?*

Max parked in Anna's driveway and rushed to open her door, surprised the sight of her long legs and red, heel-clad feet affected him so. After helping her out, he closed the door and eased Anna against it. Then he gave her the kiss they'd both been anticipating. Passionate and a little desperate, it didn't disappoint.

Anna's arms encircled Max's neck as he wrapped one of his arms around her torso and slid the other to her hips. Holding her against him, they lingered in that place where delicious pleasure and the torture of denial reside in equal measure. Eventually, Max eased his body away from Anna. It was a struggle, for it wasn't what either of them wanted. Giving her a self-deprecating smile, Max said in a gravelly voice, "I might have gotten a little carried away."

"That makes two of us." They both had big grins on their faces.

Then Max's expression turned serious. "Anna, I want you to know I'm not playing around. I want a relationship with you."

She nodded, wondering what kind of relationship he had in mind. But who was she kidding? She wanted him so much, it didn't matter. Even if it emotionally ruined her, they were going to make love, and it was going to be soon.

"Give me a minute," Max said, "and I'll walk you to your door." After checking on Gracie, Max walked Anna onto her well-lit porch, kissed her softly, and saw her safely inside. Before he left the porch, the door reopened. "Max," Anna called.

"Yeah?"

"Do you have Gracie tomorrow night?"

"No." He hardly breathed.

"Want to come for dinner? I'll cook, but don't expect a lot since I don't have much of a kitchen."

"I don't care. I'll be here."

"Around six?"

"I'll be ready," he said, praying they had the same plan for the evening.

"Until then," he said with a cocky grin, "think about our kiss by the car, and remember how much you liked it."

"You think you're hot stuff, don't you?"

"It's not about what I think," he said with a wink, then descended the stairs with a spring in his step.

CHAPTER TWENTY-FIVE

Anna was at Mayfield's Grocery, searching for items needed for the evening meal, when she received a text from Max. **Are you thinking about our kiss**?

Anna stood in the aisle, looking at her phone, shaking her head. *I am now.* At the check-out counter, she received another text.

You didn't answer my question.

Once she settled in the car, she texted back. **Yes, I'm thinking about it. Don't you have work to do**?

She certainly did. Not finding everything she needed in Tenacity, Anna drove to nearby Clarkston. Since most of her household goods were still in storage, she bought a couple of wine glasses, a tablecloth, a single-flower vase, a candle, and a candleholder.

Back in Tenacity, she strode to Luanne's flower shop for one perfect red rose. When Luanne asked if she was planning something special, Anna wisely said the flower was a treat for herself.

At Big Mama's Café, she asked for two pieces of pie, refusing to admit who the second piece was for. But Cora must have guessed, for she insisted Anna take home a whole lemon-icebox pie, Max's favorite, and tried to pay for it herself.

That afternoon, Anna did the prep work for chicken cordon bleu, the fanciest dish she knew to make. Max didn't have to know Conner taught her how. A green salad waited in the refrigerator, as well as an asparagus dish and twice-baked potatoes, ready for the oven.

The meal hadn't been easy to prepare with the renovation crew around. Accustomed to helping themselves to the cold water and iced tea she kept in the refrigerator, they were in and out of the kitchen all day, wanting to know what she was making and who was coming for dinner. After wisely taping a Do Not Touch note to the pie box, she baked refrigerator cookies to appease the crew.

Sequestering herself in her master suite, Anna set about becoming her prettiest self, shaving her legs, washing, and fluffing her hair, painting her toenails, and applying a touch of make-up. Concluding the process, she added a light spray of perfume and donned a hot pink sundress. The workmen yelled good-bye from the other side of the locked door, and Fred assured her no one was left in the house.

Anna was confident the evening would mark a turning point in her relationship with Max. Conner, with whom she often had long phone conversations, kept reminding her she couldn't live life to its fullest as long as she made the protection of her heart a priority.

"Take a chance," he told her.

So tonight, she planned to take a chance, to trust Max and stop being so afraid of a broken heart. She would enjoy her time with him. If it didn't last, she'd add those memories to the treasured ones she already carried in her heart. *If this is a mistake*, she thought, *it's an inevitable one. Mistake, here I come!*

Waiting nervously, she mentally reviewed her "to do" list. The necessary food preparation was done, the little table on the back lawn was dressed, and Anna was polished and fluffed. Her heart jumped at the sound of the doorbell, and she hurried to start the selected music. When Anna opened the door, Corrine Bailey Rae was singing "Like a Star."

Max stood in the doorway, looking handsome in slacks and a sports coat, holding flowers and a bottle of wine. His eyes met Anna's, and for a moment, he didn't move. Then he placed the flowers and wine on the floor, took her hand, and led her to the middle of the room. Pulling her into his arms, he began dancing to the soft, romantic music. Seducing her with his moves, he twirled her, vigorously returned her to his body, and gently swayed.

Anna slipped her hand out of his and wrapped her arms around his neck, bringing their bodies immodestly close. Feeling her soften against him, Max pulled her even closer, a pattern they repeated until their bodies begged for more.

"The lights," Anna said, realizing they were in full view of the bare windows.

Max danced them to the switch. With a flick of his finger, they were immersed in darkness, the dimming of one sense seeming to heighten the others.

Then he took things a step farther by spreading a hand across Anna's hips and simultaneously moving one leg between hers. When she moaned, his mouth closed over hers with a mind-blowing, passionate kiss that made her knees go weak.

Their lips and bodies moved as though they'd been waiting for that kiss their entire lives, which, in a way, they had. Lifting her body higher, Max searched her eyes. Seeing that her desire matched his own, he backed her into the bedroom, placed her gently on the bed, and lay down beside her.

With an arm around Anna's waist and a hand in her hair, he kissed the woman in his arms. When she began fumbling with the buttons of his shirt, Max helped, pulling both his shirt and t-shirt over his head and throwing them to the floor. Anna had seen his naked torso that day at Miss Sweet's, but he was even more impressive up close and personal. And now she got to touch him.

The appreciation he saw in her eyes fueled his arousal. Max kissed under her ear and down to the hollow of her neck while his hands traveled to her shoulders. When he pushed the straps of her dress as far down as they'd go, Anna sat up, turned her back to him, pulled her hair away from her neck, and gave him access to her zipper.

Max lost his breath the moment he realized she wasn't wearing a bra beneath that sweet little dress. Then almost before either of them knew what was happening, Anna was lying on the bed in nothing but a sexy pair of panties that he would let her wear a little longer.

He was trying to control himself, go slow, make the experience good for Anna, but her impatience wasn't helping. Max couldn't remember ever being this out of control, except maybe when he was a rookie kid. The panties had to go.

When Anna began working his belt, Max left the bed long enough to rid himself of the remainder of his clothes, first taking a condom from the pocket of his slacks. He imagined she'd be shy, at least in the beginning, but there was nothing shy about the woman in his arms. She was an eager participant, and Max couldn't be happier about it.

Positioning his body above hers, he held himself up so they barely touched. "Now," Anna demanded. "Don't tease me. I want you now." He lowered into her, filling her slowly, going deep, eliciting a sharp, impassioned gasp. She moaned when he began moving inside her, slow and sure. It was heaven.

When Anna shattered, she was surprised Max didn't follow. He stayed inside her, continuing to move slowly until she climbed once more. Breathing hard, she said, "Come with me this time. Please." He was more than glad to oblige.

As they gradually recovered, neither of them could stop smiling and kissing and touching. "Umm," Anna murmured, basking in the afterglow of their lovemaking. "That was too lovely for words, Max. You're delicious." She kissed him, again.

"You're not only delicious," he said, looking into Anna's eyes, "you're addictive. I'm never going to get my fill of you."

When he began kissing his way down her body again, Anna asked, "Should we make time for dinner? I cooked."

"We'll make time, but I'm not ready to let you go. Do you know how long I've wanted you?"

"No, but I think I've wanted you since I reached puberty."

Max laughed. "What a coincidence. That's when I started wanting you."

Anna joined in the laughter as her hand swept over a scar on Max's leg. "How did you get this?"

"You remember Jeremy Smith. When we were eleven or twelve, old enough to know better, we decided we'd slide down that big hill near his house on a makeshift sled. It had been raining, the hill was muddy, and I had the honor of being the first to go down—on a big piece of tin."

Anna's hand flew to her mouth. "Oh, no."

"It worked like a charm, except I was headed for a tree at the bottom of the hill and had to bail. I rolled away in time, but the tin bounced off the tree and came back at me. Luckily, I only got nicked, but that was the end of tin sledding. His dad threw our sled in the back of his truck and hauled it off somewhere. Jeremy was mad because he didn't get a turn. I got four stitches and a tetanus shot, but at the time, I thought it was worth it."

He looked at Anna lecherously. "I showed you mine; now you show me yours. You must have a scar or two somewhere." He searched her body with his large warm hands.

Anna pointed to a scar on her thigh. "You were present for that one." Max placed a gentle, wet kiss on the small imperfection, making it hard for Anna to concentrate. "Remember when I had a bicycle accident and landed on a rock in front of Mrs. Weatherly's house?"

"Afraid not," Max said succinctly, his kisses moving higher up her leg.

"Well, I do," Anna continued a little breathlessly. "You moved our bikes off the road and let me lean on you while I hopped home with blood running down my leg. Then you went back for the bikes. You were such a chivalrous little guy."

"You mean I didn't pick you up and carry you home."

"You were just a boy. You hadn't reached your full physical potential." In a mock sultry voice and a come-hither look, she said, "But you're all man now." Wiggling closer, she crooned, "As a matter of fact, I think you're at your full physical potential right this minute."

"You think?" was all he said, before covering her mouth with a searing kiss and going for round two. Or was it three?

Once they recovered, Anna said, "We need to eat."

"We do," Max agreed.

"And we have to get dressed," Anna reminded him. "There are no curtains on the windows, and I'll have to turn the lights on to finish our meal. When I began sleeping here, I put make-shift rods over the front windows. At night, I throw sheets over them, but I haven't done that tonight."

"Where are they? I'll do it."

"In the lower cabinet, to the right of the stove."

"Got it," he said, getting dressed.

At the little table she'd put in the backyard, the new lovers talked and flirted through the salad course, while potatoes and asparagus baked in the oven. Max was impressed with the table setting and told her so.

"I still have to cook our main course. You can wait out here under the stars or watch me in the kitchen."

"I'll watch you, of course. You're very watchable, you know."

Inside, Max picked up the wine and flowers he'd unceremoniously left on the floor and presented Anna with the bouquet of yellow lilies. "They were fresh when I arrived, but someone distracted me. I even brought a vase."

"Good thinking. The only one I have is the bud vase on the table." After quickly arranging the flowers, Anna cooked the chicken cordon bleu in a skillet on her mother's old stovetop.

"That didn't take long," Max commented.

"I did the time-consuming part earlier." Anna thought the hardest part of meal preparation was having everything ready at the same time, so she patted herself on the back when the meat, potatoes, and asparagus were ready almost simultaneously. The asparagus may have been a little overcooked, but it wasn't bad.

"I have something to ask you," Anna said when they finished eating.

"Okay. Shoot."

After a brief hesitation, she gathered her resolve. "You've been divorced for what…four years?"

"About that."

"I didn't hear a word from you all that time. I wouldn't have been hard to find. Why didn't you contact me?"

Max sighed. "I wanted to. I really did. I thought about it a lot, but you were so hurt when I left. And when you distanced yourself from my parents, I knew you were furious. I didn't think you'd want to see me, and to be honest, I didn't want to face your rejection."

"I wasn't angry, Max. I was trying to cope. I needed to forget about us and knew I couldn't if I kept in touch with your parents. I imagined them showing me photos of you and Janine, smiling at your beautiful child, their grandchild. There was no way I could congratulate them."

"They wouldn't have done that."

"I know they would never hurt me on purpose. It was just too hard. It broke my heart to let go of them. I missed them. I needed them, especially after Mom died. To say I was conflicted is an understatement. But in the long run, I chose to try to move on with my life."

Max hung his head. "I'm sorry. I know the words are inadequate, but that's all I know to say."

"Look at me," Anna said. "That's in the past. We both made mistakes. Big ones. But it's time to let them go and move on." Hesitantly, she added, "Maybe this time, we can do it together."

Max's relief was palpable. He pulled Anna up from her chair, wove his fingers with hers, and kissed her. The kiss was sweet, grateful, passionate, and full of promise. Before long, they were back in the bedroom. The pie would have to wait.

Propped on an elbow, Max looked at the beautiful woman in the bed beside him. He couldn't believe his luck. He and Anna were together after being apart for years. He vowed never to let anything separate them again. "Are you going to let me spend the night?"

"Sure. You know, this won't be the first time we've spent the night together."

It took him a minute to remember. "But this time, no sleeping bags."

Anna turned on her side to face Max, "I don't think our mothers knew what to do when we wanted to spend the night together."

"Now that I have Gracie, I understand their dilemma. I have to hand it to them. Sleeping bags on the back porch was a creative solution." Max snuggled close to Anna and nuzzled her neck. "But this arrangement is much more to my liking."

"Mine too," Anna said, before falling asleep and dreaming of the man beside her.

CHAPTER TWENTY-SIX

Saturday morning, Anna awoke to find her favorite person watching her. He was really in her bed. It was the fulfillment of a dream she thought would never come to pass.

Eyes sparkling with appreciation, Max's hands roamed her body, and it wasn't long before they began their day in the same intimate way they ended the night before. Once they entrusted their bodies to one another, it took effort to get out of bed and do anything else.

When Anna forced herself to leave their cozy cocoon, Max leaned on an elbow and watched her slip a long t-shirt over her naked body. "I'll bring a pair of drawstring pants over, if that's not being too presumptuous," he said, donning his trousers. That's assuming you enjoyed last night enough to warrant a repeat performance."

"Is that what that was to you? A performance."

"No. I didn't mean it that way. Please don't overanalyze what I say. I'm not the most eloquent guy in the world. Just know that I'm crazy about you, Anna, and no one else. I've wanted this a long time."

"I am pretty bad about overanalyzing," Anna admitted. "Sorry. Bring anything over you want. I'll enjoy seeing your things in my house. But now, I'm hungry. If you'll make toast, I'll do the eggs." Then coyly, she said, "I wouldn't mind if you left your shirt off."

Max stood so close to Anna they were almost touching, but he didn't reach for her. *Handsome devil knows how tempting he is,* Anna thought, restraining herself from running her hands over his body.

"And why don't you want me to finish dressing?"

"Because I like to look at you," she said without hesitation. Max smirked, appreciating her boldness.

"The sentiment is mutual, I assure you."

Anna turned toward the kitchen, finding it hard to believe Max was standing in her house, half dressed, and had made love to her most of the night. But her satisfied body, still feeling the delicious vestiges of their lovemaking, was verification that it truly happened.

Over breakfast, they decided the time had come to visit the Andersons. Max phoned his mom while Anna listened to his side of the conversation. "Mom, are you fixing lunch tomorrow?"

Anna whispered, "After lunch. Don't make her fix lunch for us."

Tapping her affectionately on the nose, he ignored her suggestion. "If you don't mind, I'm bringing a friend, a woman who is very special to me." He listened and replied like a good southern boy, "No, Ma'am. That's all I'm going to say. We'll be there shortly before lunch. Love you, too. See you tomorrow."

He had a self-satisfied look on his face. "It's all set. Mom and Dad are going to be thrilled to see you. They've worried about you through the years."

Anna grimaced. "I'm sorry. Do you think they'll be mad at me for staying away so long?"

"Nah. They'll just be glad to see you. Can we do something together today?" He grinned. "Maybe something that doesn't involve a bed. Not that I'd mind that. Not at all. But I wouldn't want you to get the idea that sex is all I want from you."

"You want something more from me? What might that be?"

"Everything. I'm greedy that way. I want every bit of you. So, is there anything special you'd like to do? Maybe something you've wanted to do but haven't gotten around to?"

"I've never gone tubing."

"Really? Everybody's floated the Tanakbi at one time or another."

"Not me."

"You never went tubing with a group of kids?"

"Nope."

"Why not?"

Anna thought about what she should tell him. "Okay. Think about what you did on those trips when girls were along? How would you have felt if I was with one of your guys?"

"That wouldn't have happened. They knew to leave you alone."

"There you go. You wouldn't have wanted to see me with one of your guys, and I didn't want to see you with another girl."

Max rubbed the back of his neck. "I did ruin your high school years."

"I wouldn't use the word ruin. But you definitely influenced them."

Max took her hand and pulled her up from her chair. He glanced up and down Anna's body, covered only by her oversized t-shirt. "You'd better put on some pants before I change my mind and take you to bed."

Anna raised her eyebrows before heading to her closet. "Getting kind of bossy, aren't you?"

The grin on Max's face was as wicked as it was sexy. "Yeah, but you like it." It was true, heaven help her. She did.

Max called around until he found a truck inner tube. "We mostly used tractor tubes when we were kids, but a truck tube will be big enough for the two of us."

Max changed into swim trunks at his house, gathered a few items for the trip down the river, and returned to find Anna in the kitchen, wearing a faded, red t-shirt over a navy two-piece. She wished she could dazzle Max in her baby blue bikini and matching cover-up, but that wouldn't fare well in the river.

"What's that?" he asked, nodding toward the plastic bags she held.

"Pimento cheese sandwiches. I put them in sandwich bags, thinking we could put them in a larger bag and tie it to the float."

Max held up a dry sack made for that purpose. "Like this?" His phone dinged with a text. After glancing at it, an expression came over his face that Anna couldn't read.

"Go ahead and answer. I don't mind."

"No need. It's nothing urgent." Driving out farm road, they passed the Windom farm, then veered onto the grassy shoulder. They drove down a steep dirt path, used by generations of Tenacity residents, and followed it into the woods.

After unpacking Max's vehicle, they walked down a well-worn path, reminding Anna of trips to the swim hole on the west side of town. "You'll need sunscreen," he reminded her.

"Already done."

"Well, that's disappointing. That was my excuse for getting my hands on you."

Anna smiled seductively. "Who said you need an excuse." After setting down the items she was carrying, she slowly pulled her shirt over her head and proficiently executed a model's walk toward Max. Or maybe it was a stripper's walk.

"You're asking for it," he said, dropping the inner tube. "We're in the woods. Alone. By ourselves. With no one around."

"Sooo?" Anna crooned.

Max moved close to Anna and began kissing her face, avoiding her lips. His mouth traveled down her neck, across the tops of her breasts, and back to her face. Anna threw her arms around his neck and kissed him passionately, their bodies pressed together.

Max wanted nothing more than to take their kissing session to its natural conclusion, but Anna would be mortified if someone walked up the path and caught them in the act. Besides, Max reminded himself, the outing was meant to prove he was interested in more than sex. Reluctantly pulling away, he nodded toward the river.

"Come on. You'll never float the Tanakbi at this rate." So they picked up their gear and finished the walk to the river.

After tying the necessary items to their float, Anna situated herself on the tube. Max pushed off the bank and jumped on, sitting across from Anna for balance. Their feet dangled in the water while the current seized the tube and launched the couple on their excursion.

"We put in," Max explained, "just below what we generously call a waterfall, so it's fairly swift here. It'll be calmer soon."

Anna looked at the beauty surrounding them, listening to the sounds of nature. Occasionally, she could hear the engine of a vehicle, but the woods between the river and the road muffled the sound.

"This is so peaceful, so quiet. I should find a spot out here to write." Then she remembered. "Where's that place you took me on your motorcycle? You know, that last day? The bluff overlooking the river."

"It's farther from town, on the other side of the Tanakbi. I'll take you again if you like. I haven't been there since that day. It's such a beautiful spot; it would be good to make new memories there. But I'd worry about you coming out here alone. There are areas, especially on the other side of the river, that could be dangerous. In a little while, we'll float past the Easy Breezy, alias the Sleazy Breezy. The law finally shut the place down, but the building is still there."

"I've heard of it. Did you ever go inside before it closed?"

"Hell, no. That was a good place to get murdered. There used to be a sign on the side of the building warning people not to enter unless they were armed. Among other things, the place was a brothel, welcoming lowlifes of every persuasion. It's been closed for years, but its stories persist.

"When Doug, Janine's Doug, was a kid, his father would make him row across the river at night and sneak in the back door to buy cheap liquor. Nobody cared about his age. His dad got stabbed there. Killed.

"Keep an eye on the left bank for the path that led to Doug's house. You'll see how far he had to travel on this river at night, and he was only a boy. His dad was a piece of work, an abusive alcoholic. The house isn't there anymore. A few years back, Doug got the volunteer fire department to burn it for practice. Said he never wanted to see the place again."

"Is Doug like I am, with no family other than his boys? I guess his brother's still alive. After his father died, his brother was arrested for driving the get-a-way car for a bank robbery a couple of counties over. He said he didn't know what they were up to; they just told him to leave the car running and wait. So he did. Who knows?"

Anna kicked her legs in the warm water. "I didn't realize Doug had such a terrible childhood."

"He did. And I have to hand it to him for doing what he's done with his life. He started working at the Baptist church in town when he was about twelve, after school and on weekends. I know because my family was there almost every time the doors opened. Anyway, Doug knocked on the preacher's door and asked for a job. Said he wasn't asking for a hand-out, but he was asking for help. He promised to work hard. And he did.

"He walked or hitch-hiked the three or four miles between his house and the church. When Brother Evans found out, he made sure somebody happened along that road every day when Doug was walking to work. The preacher drove him home.

"When Doug's dad was killed and his brother was arrested, the minister gave Doug the room in the church basement and made sure he had what he needed. He probably would've given him a room in his house, but with all the preacher's kids, there wasn't one. Somehow, they kept the arrangement under the social workers' radar." Max lifted his chin toward a low-roofed, unpainted building in the distance. "That's the Sleazy Breezy ahead."

Anna feigned a shiver. "It looks creepy, like a hangout for zombies. I wonder what it's like inside."

"Rumors say there are secret rooms and tunnels they used for hiding bootleg liquor and girls when the law came around. I admit to being curious, but there are no trespassing and danger signs all over the building. I've heard it's often occupied by vagrants, despite the warnings." The building was intriguing, but Anna was glad when they passed the place.

"Getting hot?" Max asked. "You can lower your body into the water if you hold on to the tube. But don't turn loose. I don't want to lose you. Sliding into the center of the tube, he coaxed Anna down with him. Holding onto the tube with one arm, he pulled her close with the other. Treading water, bare legs grazing bare legs, the proximity of their bodies was tantalizing.

When Anna let go of the tube to put her arms around Max, her side began to rise, and she had to grab it to avoid flipping. Their bodies were close, their intimacy new, and their desire intense, yet Max never moved beyond kisses and some tempting body brushes.

Refusing to allow his passion to spin out of control, Max hopped back onto the float. While Anna was occupied with getting out of the water, Max glared at his phone, which kept beeping from inside the waterproof case. If not for Gracie, he'd turn it off, but he wanted to be available if she needed him.

Anna righted herself in time to see Max end a text. "Ready for a sandwich?" he wanted to know. Handing her one, he asked what she wanted to drink, never mentioning the text. Anna couldn't help wondering why.

Later, he jerked his chin downriver. "We'll be taking that curve in a few minutes. The river will want to take us to the outside of the bend, toward the right bank, but we need to stay in the middle. As soon as we round the bend, start paddling toward the left bank. Hard. Your paddle is hanging there beside you. We'll aim for the sandbank at Mill Village, then walk home, get my old truck, and retrieve the SUV."

Max leaned forward and crooked his finger at Anna. They kissed, no hands style, then leaned back. "When we get home, we'll have to think of something else to do," Max said suggestively.

That "something else" had been on their minds all day. The tubing trip was fun. It was also an exercise in patience. They'd been half dressed, wet, and excruciatingly close for a good part of the day. They were aching to be in one another's arms, yearning for the privacy a locked door could provide.

CHAPTER TWENTY-SEVEN

Mary Beth Stringer managed to ring Max's doorbell while holding a basket containing a warm casserole. His car was in the driveway, so when no one came to the door, she put down the basket and called.

Max sat up in Anna's bed and grimaced when he looked at his phone. "Oh. Hi, Mary Beth. You are? Sorry, I didn't hear you. I must have fallen asleep. Give me a minute." Max jumped up and pulled on his pants. "Mary Beth Carlson is at my door." Anna found his shirt and threw it at him. "Thanks," he said, jamming his arms into the sleeves and giving Anna a quick kiss. "Be right back. Don't move."

Max ran through Anna's backyard, then through his back door. After running a hand through his tousled hair, he took a couple of deep breaths and opened the front door. Mary Beth drew in a breath of appreciation at the sight of Max, his feet bare, his shirt unbuttoned. "I thought you might be ready for another casserole," she said sweetly, handing him a basket containing a steaming aromatic dish.

Max smiled, not realizing the effect he was having on the woman. "Thanks, Mary Beth. I appreciate your thoughtfulness. The food you bring is always delicious, but you really shouldn't go to all that trouble."

She flushed. "Oh, that's all right. I enjoy cooking." A little shyly, she said, "I heard you and Anna are together. Is that true?"

"Yeah. We're getting there. We have a lot of history."

Mary Beth looked disappointed but said with as much sincerity as she could muster, "Then I hope it works out for you."

"Thank you. I appreciate that."

Still holding Mary Beth's offering, he arrived in Anna's bedroom. "I brought food, but I'm pretty sure this is the last of the casseroles."

"Why is that?"

"Mary Beth heard I'm off the market, and I verified it." Putting the casserole on the bedside table, he crawled into bed with Anna. "I'm sure gonna miss those casseroles," he teased.

"Then I'll just have to think of a way to console you."

Still at Anna's on Sunday morning, Max called Gracie to let her know he was thinking of her. It was a quick call since she was getting dressed for Sunday School. On the Sunday mornings Gracie spent with Janine, they attended the Baptist church. It was the church Max grew up in, but when he returned to Tenacity after college, he joined the Methodist congregation to avoid Janine. He took Gracie

225

to his new church on special occasions and for day care, but their Sundays were often spent visiting his parents.

Satisfied Gracie was all right, Max sprinted from Anna's back door to his own. After showering and dressing at home, he ran up Anna's front steps and rang her doorbell like a proper suitor. His beautiful neighbor opened the door wearing a pretty print dress, her hair hanging loosely down her back. She looked so pretty that Max couldn't resist kissing her. Soon, one hand was reaching under her skirt while the other found her zipper.

"Max Anderson," Anna giggled, "you're insatiable."

"I am with you. Does that bother you?"

"Not in the least. Do we have time?"

"If we make it a quickie."

"A quickie it is." Kissing, they staggered toward the bedroom.

Max and Anna were all smiles as they left Tenacity. They'd never been so happy, but Anna couldn't help wondering where the relationship was headed. They were an exclusive couple now. She felt sure of that. She should be satisfied. But try as she may, Anna couldn't keep her mind from jumping all the way to happily ever after.

Max was excited about taking Anna to see his parents. They had loved her since she was a child, and they'd be thrilled to learn he and Anna were together. The last time they saw her was after Margie died. They drove to Anna's dorm room to deliver the news, and Carol stayed with her in Tenacity to help make funeral arrangements.

He thought about how fortunate he was to have his parents. They'd stood behind him when he discovered he'd be an eighteen-year-old father and when he gave up his football scholarship. When he and Janine divorced and he was trying to get joint custody of his daughter, they were there for him. They even helped financially after the divorce so Max could finish school and remain part of Gracie's life.

He'd always had their support and was beginning to understand Anna's extreme reaction to her mother's death. Margie was a great mom, but her refusal to share information about her relatives had left Anna feeling abandoned and isolated. Yet, she emerged from that dark time in her life as a lovely, confident person, and Max admired her for it.

Alex and Carol lived in an older neighborhood. The homes, built mostly in the Forties, showcased established, well-kept yards shaded by old oak and hickory trees, their limbs trimmed to avoid electric lines. The Andersons' Clarkston home, larger than the one Max lived in, looked warm and welcoming with rocking chairs and ferns on a wide front porch.

Opening the door of his parents' home, Max announced their arrival. "Mom, Dad, we're here." His mom came out of the kitchen with a dish towel in her hands. She didn't yell Anna's name, as Max expected. Instead, she dropped the towel and softly, tenderly murmured, "Anna," as her eyes filled with tears. "Oh, sweetie, how I've missed you."

Tears ran down both women's faces as they hugged. "Miss Carol," was all Anna could say. She loved Max's mom, and the warm embrace from her mother's best friend was a little like a hug from her mom.

To lighten the mood, Max said, "How about me? Don't I get a hug?"

"Of course, my baby boy," Carol teased, standing on her toes to reach him. Dad is out back in his garden, looking for the best tomatoes to slice for lunch. You know how he is about his tomatoes."

Max mimicked his father, "Today's farmers grow tomatoes to look pretty and hold up during shipping. They don't give a damn about how they taste."

Carol chuckled. "Go on out there and surprise him. I'll be in the kitchen."

Anna always thought having a dad would be the most wonderful thing in the world, but having Alex in her life seemed almost as good. When she and Max were kids, he never seemed to tire of his two young shadows. He flew kites with them, set up a badminton net in the backyard, helped them plant a garden, and even taught Anna how to ride a bike. But helping Alex wash the car was undeniably their favorite activity. Everyone got a turn with the hose, and no one escaped getting drenched.

"Dad," Max said.

When Alex looked up and saw Anna, a huge smile came over his face. "Well, if it isn't our Anna banana." He brushed the dirt off his hands, stood, and opened his arms. Anna flew into them, loving the affection she felt in his embrace.

"When Max said he was bringing someone home with him, I hoped it was you. We've missed having you in our lives." Alex gave his son a man-hug and picked up the juicy, red tomatoes he'd left on the ground. "Let's go inside where it's cool. Carol cooked a nice meal for us."

Anna peeked into the modern, country-style kitchen. "Need any help, Miss Carol?"

"Thanks, but everything is about done." Carol hugged Anna again. "I'm so glad you're back. And I see you've made our boy happy. Thank you for that. That girl who gave birth to Gracie did everything she could to make his life miserable. Still does when she can. Help me put these glasses of tea on the table, and I think we'll be ready." Carol walked through the dining room to the living area where Alex and Max were half-watching a football game. "Y'all ready to eat?"

"We're starving," Alex said, moving quickly from his recliner.

Max held Anna's chair for her, like the gentleman he was. When they were all seated, the small group held hands while Alex asked the blessing, adding a special thanks for Anna's return. For the most part, the conversation was light, dotted with fond memories and good-natured teasing. Then Carol asked Anna how she was doing after the incident at the motel. "We wanted to come check on you, but Max said you didn't need company."

"It was a bad experience, but I'm all right, thanks to Max."

Carol shook her head. "Who was that terrible man, anyway?"

At first, no one spoke. Then Anna looked up and said, "He was a member of a gang. I won't tell you what he said he was going to do to me. Now he's saying he was only trying to scare me, but it sure felt like he meant business."

Max noticed Anna's hands shaking. "Excuse me," she said, leaving the table. Max followed her into the hallway, held her in his arms and rubbed her back until she felt in control. "I'm okay," she said, "I just needed a minute."

When they returned to the table, Max was holding Anna's hand. He let go of it, to hold her chair for her, then repossessed it. Anna apologized for leaving the table so abruptly. "I thought I was all right, but for some reason, the fear came rushing back."

Apology was written all over Carol's face. "I'm sorry I brought it up. Of course, you're upset. Anyone would be."

Max changed the subject. "This stewed squash is delicious, Mom. You outdid yourself. You should try it Anna."

"I can't," she said, grinning.

"Oh," Max said, letting go of her hand. They all laughed, glad for the chance to relieve the tension brought on by Carol's question. After everyone helped clean up in the kitchen, they retired to the living room. Before they sat, Max's phone vibrated. He looked at it but didn't answer.

"Work again?" Anna asked. Max gave her a slight nod.

"Who's calling you at home?" Alex asked. "There's no reason for that."

"It's all right, Dad. We can talk about it at the office." Alex dropped the subject but seemed perplexed.

Anna walked over to a built-in shelf and picked up a framed photograph. "Gracie told me you had this." It was a picture of Max and Anna in front of the ladder Max made for her when he was eight.

"I remember taking that," Alex said. "That was the day I met a spunky little girl sitting on a tree limb with my son. I knew right away the two of you would be great friends."

Standing beside Anna to look at the picture, Max put his arm around her waist and pulled her to his side. "I was smitten from the start." They gazed at each other, enthralled by one another's smiles.

For the remainder of the visit, the conversation bounced between Max and Anna as children, Gracie, Anna's book, Max's work, and Alex's backyard garden. Heavy topics like Janine, Margie's death, and Doug's boys were carefully avoided.

When Max and Anna were backing out of the Anderson's driveway, Alex looked at his wife and said facetiously, "I think they might be sleeping together."

"Ya think?" was Carol's response. "They couldn't keep their hands off each other."

When Alex joked that he'd thought of offering them a bedroom, Carol batted his chest playfully. Then a serious look came over her face. "I hope everything works out for them. Heaven knows, those two deserve some happiness. But I can't help being afraid Janine will interfere in some way."

Monday morning Max traveled to work as usual. He drove the same route, parked in his normal spot, poured break room coffee into his designated cup, and headed to his office. Everything looked the same; his routine hadn't changed; but his world was different. He was different. The past weekend changed everything.

Over the next couple of months, Max and Anna were seen together at Lucky's Catfish House, Big Mama's Café, the Bar None, and a couple of restaurants in Clarkston.

It wasn't hard to figure out what was going on between them. The way they looked at one another and the familiarity in the way they touched gave them away. But no matter what conclusions people drew, Anna and Max continued their back-door policy concerning sleepovers. Living next door to one another definitely had its advantages.

CHAPTER TWENTY-EIGHT

Max and Anna were making scrambled eggs, sausage, and biscuits for supper when his phone rang. "Gracie girl!" Max answered with a smile. But when he heard her sobbing plea for help, his face went eerily pale. "I'm on my way, baby. You'll be all right." He was walking out the door as he spoke. After quickly turning the stove off, Anna followed.

Clearly distressed, Max explained the situation as he drove. "Gracie's in trouble. Something about the boys locking her in furniture and setting it on fire."

"What?"

Max tried to calm himself. "Surely that can't be. But something's happening. She's very upset, scared. Thank God she has her phone with her."

"Just hurry," Anna urged.

In front of Doug's house, Max's car lurched to a stop. He ran down the sidewalk with Anna right behind him. Banging on the front door, he bellowed, "Janine! Let me in! Now!" Anna rang the doorbell.

When Janine and Doug calmly opened the door, Max experienced his first doubt that the situation was as dire as he initially believed. But his daughter had been hysterical.

"Where's Gracie?"

Looking confused, Janine said, "She's in the house somewhere, playing with the boys."

Without asking permission, Max peered into one room after the other yelling, "Gracie! Where are you?" Arriving at one of the upstairs bedrooms, he heard banging from inside a wardrobe and a muffled voice. "What the…"

He reached the wardrobe in a couple of long strides and tried to open the locked door. Anger poured from him. "Where's the damned key?" he roared.

Doug, who'd followed him upstairs, said, "I, I don't know. Normally, it's in the door." Then he yelled, "Boys!" They didn't answer.

Anna, who was standing just inside the bedroom door, exclaimed, "Oh no! Max look!" She pointed to an electric heater sitting under the wardrobe, turned to high. The furious dad ripped the cord from the socket, visibly trying to control himself. "It's okay, baby," he said to his child. "You're okay. The fire is gone. We just have to find the key. It'll only be a few minutes."

A little voice came from inside the wardrobe. "It's really hot in here."

Max turned to Doug and said, in a quiet, menacing voice, "If you don't find that key in the next two minutes, I'm tearing this piece of furniture apart."

When Doug left to find the key, Janine stood outside the wardrobe and spoke to her daughter, "Gracie, you're going to be all right, honey. The boys were just playing. They wouldn't really hurt you." Max turned such an enraged glare at Janine that she backed away and went silent.

When the key was found and Gracie was released from the wardrobe, Max scooped her into a protective hug. The child wrapped her arms so tightly around her daddy's neck, the jaws of life would have had trouble prying her loose. Burying her face in his shirt, she sobbed. In spite of his tightly clenched jaw, Max managed to say, "I'm taking her with me."

Anna drove them home, busying herself in the kitchen while Max rocked his daughter. When Gracie fell asleep, Max joined Anna in the kitchen. She hugged him tightly, then took his hand and led him to the sofa.

Smoothing his hair, she asked, "Is she all right?"

"She's asleep. I don't know if she's all right."

Anna shook her head. "I can't believe Janine took Gracie into that situation again. What was she thinking?"

"Who knows. Something about Janine is off. She doesn't seem able to view things from anyone else's perspective. She's the most self-centered person I've ever met."

"I have it on video," Anna said.

"What?"

"I recorded what happened tonight. I got the whole thing: the heater turned on under the wardrobe, Janine defending the boys, and Gracie's reaction when the door was unlocked. I thought you might need it someday."

When Janine appeared at her ex-husband's house the following day, Anna entertained Gracie while her parents talked outside.

Max had to find a way to make his stubborn ex-wife see the seriousness of their situation. "Janine, we had this talk. You have to keep Gracie away from Doug's boys. They're terrorizing her."

His ex-wife rolled her eyes. "You're exaggerating."

"Exaggerating!" Hell, those little monsters rolled her in a rug, almost smothering her, and tonight they locked her in a wardrobe with a lit heater under it. Can't you see what could have happened?"

Janine continued defending the twins. "Don't call them monsters. They are mischievous, and they don't always use good judgment, but they aren't bad boys."

Max barely contained his fury. "Mischievous? Gracie could barely breathe in that rug. And the wardrobe could have caught on fire, or she could have suffocated. Can you imagine how hot it was in there? What does it take to convince you those boys are dangerous?"

"You're overreacting, but I'll talk to Doug about the boys."

"Oh, yeah, that'll do it," he snorted. "Doug doesn't have the slightest idea how to control his children. You have to keep Gracie away from them. Why didn't you leave her with me or your parents last night?"

Janine looked away, refusing to listen. Max turned her chin toward him so she was forced to look at his troubled face. "Janine, you hear me, and hear me good. Don't take Gracie to Doug's. She can never be left alone with those boys. And right this minute, she needs to stay

236

with me. She's traumatized about last night, and to be perfectly honest, she's afraid to go home with you."

"She can stay for two days. Then I'm coming for her." She sighed, dreading Max's reaction to what she had to say next. "I guess this is as good a time to tell you as any. Doug asked me to marry him, and I accepted." She held out her hand, displaying an engagement ring. "We're going to be a family, so the kids have to learn to get along."

Max clasped his hands behind his head and looked toward the sky, silently asking for help. He felt powerless. Afraid of what he might say if he opened his mouth, Max turned and walked into his house. He knew what he had to do. He had to obtain sole custody of his daughter.

Max phoned his mother, brought her up to date on what was happening with Gracie, and asked her to elicit help from Lana, her social worker friend.

Lana was glad to help, not only providing contact information for Mark Collins, the best family law attorney in the region, but also calling to ask if he'd take Max's case as soon as possible. Since the attorney had worked with Lana on several occasions, he knew she wouldn't ask if it wasn't important. He agreed to consider the case that same week.

Max texted Janine that he and Gracie were out of town, ignoring her responding texts and calls. After leaving his daughter with his parents, Max drove to Jackson to meet with attorney Mark Collins. Mark was affiliated with a firm in Clarkston, as well as in Jackson, but Max chose to drive the extra miles to lessen the chance that someone would see him and report to Janine.

In the attorney's office, he explained his concern for his daughter's safety, laying out as many details as he could think of, including what he knew of Janine's role in Anna's attack. Then Max showed him the video from the wardrobe incident.

After listening carefully, Mark asked, "What can you tell me about your ex-wife as a person? What would other people say about her?"

Max tried to paint an honest picture. "In my opinion, she's an unfit mother, but I doubt we'd find anyone to testify to that. Everyone knows her parents spoiled her, but the family is well thought of. The fact remains," Max reminded the attorney, "she's delusional when it comes to her fiancé's boys."

Mark sympathized. "You certainly have reason to be concerned, and you've done a good job of gathering evidence, but facts can be manipulated in a court of law. The evidence you have is incriminating, but a good attorney could convince a judge that the kids were playing, and the boys didn't realize the danger.

"He could say your daughter over-reacted. He might deny your petition in favor of counseling for your ex-wife and her future family. If the mother's parents are influential, as you insinuated, that could be a factor. It shouldn't be, but sometimes is."

"What about Janine's role in the motel attack?"

"That hasn't been proven in court," Mark reminded him. From what you say about the guy who perpetrated the attack, his testimony wouldn't carry much weight. And he only accused your ex of asking him to scare someone. I don't believe introducing that would help your case, and it could appear that you're grasping at straws."

Collins leaned back in his chair and steepled his fingers. "Based on what you've told me, I agree your daughter would be better off with you, but your case could still be difficult to win. It's hard to take a daughter from her mother. Then there's the fact that you'd have to leave her in day care while the mother is able to keep her at home—whether she does or not. I know it's unfair, but that doesn't change the perception.

"If we go to trial and lose, there would be a long wait to get it on the docket again. I can take the case, if you want to move forward after our conversation, but I can't tell you we'll win. We could," Collins said, "but when the injurious behavior emanates from minors, it's hard to say. I'm sorry I can't be more positive. You have a difficult decision to make." He stood and shook Max's hand. "Here's my card. I'm writing my personal cell number on the back. Don't hesitate to call if you need me."

On the drive home, Max thought about his options. There weren't many. So the next day he met Doug at his office next to one of the Wag-a-Bag stores. After pouring out his fears for his daughter, he asked Doug to consider consulting a counselor and gave him the list of therapists his mother's social worker-friend had provided.

Doug readily admitted his shortcomings as a disciplinarian and agreed to seek help. But when Janine heard what Max had done, she showed up on his porch, spewing indignant threats. She was furious. After a long conversation, in which Max presented every rationale he could think of, Janine agreed not to take Gracie to Doug's house until a professional deemed it safe. Max breathed a sigh of relief for the reprieve and hoped for a miracle.

CHAPTER TWENTY-NINE

Every year Janine's parents had a big Fourth of July bash in their backyard and invited half the town. Because the Larsons' house backed up to the river, it provided the perfect spot for shooting fireworks. Max dreaded the event, knowing Janine would be there. But Gracie was excited about her grandparents' party, and Doug would be there with his boys; so Max had to go, and he wanted Anna with him.

Anna was also reluctant to attend, but Max needed to be there, and he'd made it impossible to say no by extending the invitation in Gracie's presence.

"Please come," the child begged. "It will be so much fun. Grandmother and Granddaddy are going to put lights in the backyard and everything. Please."

How could she refuse? Anna had fond memories of attending the Larsons' Fourth of July parties as a child, but the invitations ceased when she was in middle school, a circumstance for which Janine was undoubtedly responsible.

Attending the Larsons' party with Max was tantamount to officially announcing their couple status, so Anna wanted to look her best. The day of the party, she sat at her vanity, assessing her appearance. The trip down the Tanakbi and time spent planting flowers had given her skin a healthy glow. And her hair looked good, thanks to a recent trip to the hairdresser for highlights. She just needed a little eye make-up, some pink blush, and cherry-blossom pink lipstick to compliment the polish on her toes.

Satisfied she looked her best, she stepped into a baby blue sundress that fit her slender waist and showed off her long legs. Strappy sandals completed the outfit. After a quick spray of lightly scented perfume, she declared herself ready.

When the doorbell rang, Anna cast a quick look in the mirror, took a deep breath, and opened the door. Max stood there in all his male glory, tanned and gorgeous in khakis and a navy golf shirt that showed off his muscular arms. Anna thought with amusement that a woman's knees shouldn't go weak just from looking at a man. Females always made fools of themselves over Max, and Anna hoped he couldn't tell how he was affecting her.

Unaware Max was having the same reaction to her, Anna wondered why he stood in the doorway—staring. When she looked down her body to see what was wrong, he finally managed to speak. "Wow. You look beautiful. You're perfect."

"Thank you, kind sir," she replied breezily. "You're not so bad yourself." She picked up her contribution to the occasion, a caramel cake she'd purchased from a bakery, and announced she was ready.

"So am I, beautiful girl. So am I."

As they walked into the Larsons' backyard, Max kept a warm, possessive hand on the small of Anna's back, and she marveled at how his touch made her feel feminine and cherished. She placed the cake on a table, located near the gate, then looked up to see Max's ex-wife heading their way. Janine greeted them warmly, but Anna recognized it for the face-saving move it was.

"She's up to something," Max said so only Anna could hear.

Janine touched Anna's arm and gave her a huge smile. "Don't you look pretty today. It's so nice to see you here."

Max felt like rolling his eyes. *And so it begins.*

"Hi, Max," Janine said in an intimate voice. And before he knew what was happening, she pulled his head down and planted a proprietary kiss on his lips. Max pulled away, looking uncomfortable. Then he took Anna's hand in his and folded it to his body.

Gracie bounded up. "Daddy!" Max bent down to catch his leaping daughter, and then stood, holding her easily on one arm. She wrapped one of her little arms securely around his neck and gave him a wet kiss, reaching for the beautiful woman at his side. "Anna, you came!"

"Of course, I did. I couldn't miss your big party." Gracie blessed Anna with one of her little girl kisses before running off to play with the other children. She was having a ball, not standing any place for long.

Gracie's obvious affection for Anna infuriated Janine. Max and Gracie were her family, not Anna's. *She*

242

may want my family now, Janine thought, *but she'll know the score by the end of the day.* Janine smirked at no one in particular. *When my plan goes into effect, I'll have Max and Gracie, as well as Doug. Max may have left my house and my bed, but Gracie will always bind us together.*

When Doug appeared at Janine's side, she possessively latched onto his arm. The twins ran past her without a glance. "Those boys," she said, attempting to hide her embarrassment at their indifference, "always so full of energy. Why don't you get them something to eat, Doug? I'll join you in a minute." She didn't want him to see what was about to happen.

Once Doug's boys arrived, Max knew he'd have to keep a closer eye on Gracie. Scanning the crowd for his daughter, he saw two women he'd been dating walking toward him. Anna saw him blanch before he cast an angry look at his ex-wife. "Janine, what the hell have you done?"

Satisfied, she smirked. "I thought you'd want all your girlfriends here, and I knew Anna would want to meet the other members of your harem."

Max couldn't hide his anger. *How the hell did she even know about them?* "Janine, do you ever think of anyone but yourself? Obviously, your intention was to hurt Anna and me, but did you consider, for even a moment, how this might make them feel?" He nodded in the general direction of the approaching women. Janine walked away from the angry man, content to watch events unfold from a distance.

With one arm around Anna, Max pulled her close and whispered in her ear. "It's all right, babe. I'll explain. Just wait here." He forced his arm to leave her waist and took her hand, averse to losing the feel of her. "Please don't leave. I'll explain," he repeated. I need to speak with some people—some women. When we go home, I'll tell you anything you want to know."

Max looked intently at Anna. She had to have heard what Janine said, but her expression didn't hint at what she was feeling. "Please say you'll wait." Anna was a little stricken at what she assumed was happening but said she'd wait. He tried to smile his appreciation, without much success. Her remote expression worried him. Max kissed her cheek, walked toward the two women, and prayed that Anna would understand.

The approaching women watched as Max let go of the beautiful woman's hand and turned toward them with a look of misery on his face. Both women slowed their pace, their smiles turning to looks of concern. They were intelligent women, and it wasn't a huge leap to guess they'd unwittingly become part of a plan to hurt Max. Neither was it difficult to ascertain that the small blonde, sporting the Cheshire cat grin, was the one to blame for his discomfort.

Anna wasn't sure what was happening. *Who are those women?* she wondered. *Was I foolish to let myself dream that Max and I might have a future together? He never said that's what he wanted. Was it all in my head?* Part of her wanted to run away from whatever was happening, despite her promise, but part of her needed to see the drama play out.

Grateful Angie had managed to melt into the crowd, Max approached Jennifer. She was one of the most beautiful women Anna had ever seen, tall and slender with olive skin and a sleek dark ponytail sitting high on her head. A model, Anna decided. The woman listened intently to Max with a sympathetic look on her face, her hand clasped warmly on his arm. Seeing the closeness between them made Anna's heart ache, but she couldn't stop watching.

Finally, the woman affectionately kissed Max on the cheek and walked over to Anna, who was glued to the spot where she stood. Smiling, the poised young woman said in an unconsciously sultry voice, "I'm Jennifer, a friend of Max's. You're lovely. I'm happy he's found someone he really cares about." She smiled before returning to the crowd of people.

Max glanced up to see her join Jeff Windom. She'd told him she was staying at the party to visit with a friend. *Does she have something going on with Windom too*, he wondered?

Max's musings were interrupted when Gracie abruptly grabbed his leg. "Base," she yelled to the children chasing her. "My daddy is base." Max slowed Gracie down enough to ask if Doug's boys were staying away from her. She nodded, "Yes, sir. And if they bother me, I'm going to scream as loud as I can. And you can come save me."

"That sounds like a plan," he said, as Gracie ran away giggling.

Anna looked up in time to see a blond woman approach Max. When she began caressing his arm, Max briefly took her hand in his. The initial shock of what was happening was beginning to fade, and unadulterated jealousy was replacing it. The second woman was soft, petite, and curvy, with short curly hair. Even from where

Anna was standing, she could tell that the woman's large eyes, which she kept batting at Max, were bright blue.

It was hard to watch his interaction with her. She kept touching him, sending signals no man could miss. No matter what words came from her mouth, her body said she was ready and willing. When their conversation came to an end, the blond gave him a big warm hug, pressing her ample breasts against him.

No, Anna thought. *Surely that woman's not coming to speak to me. Doesn't she know I don't even want to be here?* Sauntering up to Anna, the buxom blond took her hand and smiled sweetly. "Hi, I'm Angie. Max and I are very close." Anna resisted rolling her eyes as the woman continued. "I don't have to tell you what a special man he is. Be good to him. He deserves it." The blond gave the taller woman an unwelcome hug and then left with a little wave. "Bye, hon." Now Anna knew the woman couldn't be trusted. *Did she really say, "Bye, hon"?*

Max dreaded the conversation with Anna. None of this should have happened. As usual, it was Janine's fault. Her actions put the women he'd dated in an embarrassing situation and him in a completely miserable one. Then there was the possibility Anna wouldn't understand, which was obviously the reason Janine pulled the stunt in the first place. He didn't think he could ever forgive his ex-wife.

While Angie was talking to Anna, Max was looking for Gracie. He breathed a sigh of relief when he saw her near the balloon twister at the eastern end of the Larsons' spacious yard. Doug's boys were on the western side.

He'd almost reached Anna when he heard, "You hoo, Max." It was Janine, pointing her finger toward the backyard gate with a satisfied smirk on her face.

Max groaned aloud when he saw Josie. He would have to talk with her, but first, he'd touch base with Anna. When he took her hand, she accepted it, but he felt her reluctance.

Anna kissed him on the cheek, giving Max quickly rescinded hope. "That was for the benefit of those who've been waiting for my reaction. I didn't miss the look of triumph on Janine's face when you noticed those women. I thought she might actually crow. So I won't give her, or anyone else, the pleasure of watching me make a scene."

"I'm so sorry," Max said, "but I need to…"

"I know. I saw. Go do what you have to."

Max walked toward the late arrival; his shoulders slumped. Josie gave him a heartfelt hug. "You look like the weight of the world is sitting on your shoulders," she said, in her lilting Caribbean accent. "Tell me what has made your heart so heavy." He told her what Janine had done.

Because Josie was understanding and easy to talk to, Max had shared some of his history with her. She knew about his marriage and how it had interfered with his plans to be with the girl next door. She understood the seriousness of their reconciliation and sympathized with his distress over the events of the day.

"I'm sorry, Max. Your ex-wife isn't a nice person, is she?"

He shook his head. "No, she's not. Because she's Gracie's mother, I normally take whatever humiliation she has to dish out, but this time she's gone too far."

About that time, Gracie ran to him and hugged his leg. "Daddy, are you all right? You look sad."

"I'm not sad," he lied. "Those twins haven't bothered you, have they?"

"No, Daddy. I'm going to scream if they do. Remember?"

"I remember. Gracie, this is my friend Josie. Josie, this is my daughter."

"I'm happy to meet you, Gracie. I've heard a lot of nice things about you. Your daddy loves you very much."

"I know," she said matter-of-factly. She looked at Josie thoughtfully. "I like the way you talk. And you're pretty."

Max knelt down to Gracie's level. "I need to speak with Josie for a few more minutes." He gave his daughter a kiss on each cheek and pointed to Anna. "See Anna over there? Will you give her one of those kisses and tell her it's from me?" She kissed her daddy, then taking her task seriously, ran to do his bidding.

"Gracie's adorable," Josie said, watching the child deliver her daddy's kiss. "And Anna's beautiful." Noticing Max and the woman looking her direction, Anna glanced away, as if something caught her attention. "I'm going to miss you, Max Anderson," Josie said.

"I'll miss you too, Josie. You're an exceptional woman."

"May I meet your lady?" They walked together, but before they reached Anna, Josie put a hand on Max's chest to stop him. "You stay here. It's time for girl talk. Don't worry. I have your back."

Anna watched curiously. The tall woman with a regal bearing was an unusual beauty, with dark eyes and skin the color of café latte. She was older than Anna first thought. *No one can accuse Max of having a type,* she thought.

"Hello pretty lady," Josie said, in an accent Anna couldn't identify. "So you finally came back for your man. I have always known he was yours. He told me about you. He also told me what happened here today. I hope that does not change your feelings for him."

She looked directly into Anna's eyes. "That man over there is a good man. And for one as handsome as he, that is an accomplishment. If you decide you don't want him, you tell him to give me a call. I will take that man in a heartbeat." She started to walk away but then turned. "And try to protect him from that ex-wife of his." Not quite able to muster a smile, Anna nodded. She thought she'd like Josie under other circumstances.

Anna was having trouble grasping all that just happened. *Was Max dating three other women while he was dating her? If they hadn't shown up today, would he have even told her about them?* She couldn't help wondering if present-day Max was just an older version of the oversexed schoolboy who'd caused her so much pain.

Max walked Josie to the gate and hugged her before returning to Anna. He was bone weary. *I try to be a good person, a good father,* he thought, *so why does life keep kicking me in the gut?*

CHAPTER THIRTY

"Will you stay for the fireworks?" Max asked Anna, sounding defeated. "I can't leave while Doug's boys are here."

"I'll stay," she said, taking his hand. Max thought she may have softened a little. Or maybe she felt as tired as he did. At least there was no need to talk during the fireworks. They lay on a blanket with Gracie between them, looking up at the sky, the excited child talking enough for all of them.

Max and Anna sleepwalked through the rest of the evening and rode home in silence. After parking in Anna's driveway, the disheartened man walked quickly to the other side of the car to open the door. He wasn't fast enough. She was already out of the car, walking toward the house. Max followed quietly.

When they reached the porch, Anna turned to confront him. "Do I even want to hear what you have to say?"

"I hope so. I'll tell you anything you want to know. Just hear me out."

Anna gestured to the swing, where so many other events in their lives had unfolded, and got right to the issue. "Who were those women?"

Max knew he had to get this right. "They are women I was dating before you returned."

Anna's face was expressionless. "At the same time?"

"Well, not together."

Anna wasn't amused. "You know what I mean."

"Yes, I know what you mean and yes, I dated all of them within the same period of time."

"Did you sleep with all of them?"

Max hesitated, knowing Anna wouldn't like his answer. Then he looked her in the eye and answered unapologetically. "Yes."

Anna knew it was illogical to feel hurt, but she did. Part of her wanted to hurt him right back. She shook her head, looking as though she might get up to leave.

"Wait, please. Let me explain."

"What's to explain? You slept with them. All of them. I thought you'd changed."

"Please listen. Let me try to make you understand."

Anna sighed impatiently, secretly hoping he could say something to make things better. "All right. Give it your best shot. I'm listening."

"Okay," Max stalled. "Good. As you know, my marriage to Janine was horrible, and I wasn't ready to jump into a new relationship. I met Jennifer first. She's an architect I worked with on a project."

"Which one was she?" It shouldn't make any difference, but Anna wanted to know.

"The one with the long ponytail."

The model, Anna thought.

251

"We met for drinks a couple of times, started dating, and eventually began a relationship.

"You mean you started having sex."

"You could put it that way," Max said warily. "But I was straight with her from the start. She knew I wasn't looking for anything serious. We agreed the relationship wouldn't be exclusive. We got together occasionally, on weekends when I didn't have Gracie. Not every time, just sometimes.

Later, one of the guys at work wanted to fix me up with his wife's sister. That was Josie, the one from the Caribbean. She's a linguist. She translates written material and sometimes serves as an interpreter. We had the same talk. I told her I dated another woman, and she understood. We had the same arrangement about dating other people."

Max wanted to leave the swing and pace but forced himself to sit still and face Anna. "A while later, I went to a bar with some guys after work and met Angie, who is a high school math teacher. We had the talk, and before I knew it, I was dating three women who all happened to live in Clarkston. It's a big enough place that we didn't usually run into each other. I did see Jennifer at a restaurant once, when I was with Angie, but she had a date, too.

"I really didn't go out with any of them that often. I have Gracie every other weekend, and there were three of them." Max didn't know why his last statement made Anna angrier, but it obviously had.

He kept talking, hoping he'd happen upon the right words. "Anna, I care for each of them. They're nice women, but the relationships were casual. They understood that from the start. In fact, Angie has dated this one guy several times, and I think they may be getting serious."

Anna didn't believe that for a minute. Curvy cutie was probably trying to make him jealous.

"But you're not still dating them?"

Getting frustrated, Max shook his head. "Of course not. They know I'm with you now."

Anna narrowed her eyes. "But they didn't know that until today, did they? Were you dating all four of us at the same time?"

"No. I've been a little busy lately." Max forced the sarcasm from his voice. I just hadn't gotten around to telling them about you. Don't be angry about this, Anna. I haven't seen any of them since you returned. Yes, I dated them. And yes, we sometimes had sex, but they were fine with the situation. Think about it. I've been divorced four years, and I'm not celibate. I didn't do anything wrong."

If things had happened differently, if they hadn't shown up today, I would have told you I occasionally dated some women, and I think you would have understood. It's just the way it happened. I know it looks bad."

Anna sighed. "How do I know you won't be with them again...or with other women?"

"No, Anna. It's only you now."

She seemed not to hear. "It's so easy for some people. Casual sex, I mean. But I'm not made that way. Max, I can't be like them. I won't share you. I couldn't do that."

He put his arms around Anna and pulled her close. "I know that, and I only want you. Please understand and give me a chance." Max lifted her chin and gave her a tender kiss. He ached to take her to bed, kiss her senseless and make her forget the events of the day. But he needed to tread carefully.

Tired and emotionally drained, Anna gently brushed the side of his face as she stood. "All right, you have your chance, but now I need to sleep." Looking at him with sad eyes, Anna said goodnight and went into the house. Max was worried. She said she'd give him a chance, but the look in her eyes said she thought he'd bungle it.

A week later, the phone rang. Samantha was calling. She was working in a fashionable Clarkston boutique on River Street until her teaching job began in the fall. The pay wasn't great, but the deductions on clothing made up for it. "I'm between customers right now," Samantha said, "I'll have to hang up if someone comes in. Have you heard from Max?"

"No. It seems Janine accomplished her goal."

"To cause trouble?"

"Yes."

Max had called the day after the Larsons' party, but Anna didn't answer. Instead, she texted that she wasn't ready to talk. A few days later, he texted that he missed her. Anna didn't respond. Other than that, they hadn't communicated for a full week.

"Are you worried?" Samantha asked.

"Of course. I thought he'd changed. Now, I'm not so sure. And I don't know what to do."

Samantha noticed some women standing near the door of the shop. "Anna, I think someone's coming in. Never mind, they passed on by. I don't know what to tell you. What I do know is that you need to forget about Max for a while. Meet me for lunch. I only have an hour off, but you could get some shopping done while you're here."

"I can do that. Should I pick you up at the boutique or meet you somewhere?"

"There's a new café down the street from the store. Let's meet there. I usually bring my lunch and eat in the backroom, but Chez Nous is supposed to be really cute. I've been wanting to check it out."

"Sounds good. I'm looking forward to it. Thanks for being my friend, Sam."

Anna arrived at Chez Nous a little before noon and chose a corner booth, which was partially obscured by a trellis-style room divider. When Samantha entered the restaurant, Anna stepped away from the booth and waved to get her friend's attention.

"I see my favorite celebrity chose a spot out of the view of the paparazzi."

"I don't think we need to worry about that. This booth just seemed cozy."

They placed their orders and were chatting happily when Anna's face paled and her heart began to pound. Samantha followed her gaze to see Max walk in with a blonde in a bright blue, low-cut dress, his hand gentlemanly at her back.

When Anna spoke, her voice was shaky. "It's the curvy blonde from the party. The one who couldn't keep her hands to herself."

"What's Max doing with her? I thought he explained to those women that he was with you?"

"That's what he said." Anna's breathing became rapid and shallow as she watched Max slide into a booth across from the sexy blonde. The rest of the room faded away.

"What do you want to do? Should we leave? Anna, are you all right? Anna," she said, shaking her friend. When Anna finally looked at her, Samantha asked again, "What do you want to do?"

"We'll sit here, eat our lunch, and watch."

"Don't you think that's a little masochistic?"

"Maybe, but I can't do anything else."

Anna couldn't eat the salad she ordered or look away from Max and curvy cutie, who sat in an easily observed booth across the room. The bouncy blonde still had wandering hands, and Max didn't seem to mind. In fact, he did a little hand and arm touching himself. It hurt Anna to see how comfortable they were with each other, smiling, laughing, touching.

At one-point Max took Angie's hand in his, looked directly into her eyes, and spoke seriously about something. *If only I could hear what he was saying,* Anna thought. But her heart was pounding so loudly she couldn't have heard him if she'd been sitting in his lap.

Even though it made her late for work, Samantha stayed with Anna until Max and the woman got up to leave. Anna threw some money on the table, slid out of the booth, and followed Max out of the restaurant. She watched as the woman pressed her body against Max, put her arms around his neck, and kissed him more intimately than was appropriate for public display.

Anna had been upset since she met the women at the party, but now she was angry. She walked toward the couple, in time to hear the woman say, "A little something to remember me by."

Max's response was, "Can't forget that."

"You won't have to," Anna said, walking past. "You can have her." She heard Max's footsteps behind her, seconds before he grasped her arm, "Anna! Anna! Stop and talk to me."

"I heard all I need to hear."

"I was telling her good-bye."

"Maybe so, but you sure seemed to regret it. I should never have trusted you. I feel sick. Go away." Instead, Max followed Anna to her car. He thought she'd finished rebuking him, but she turned and added, "It's obvious you don't really want to break up with blondie. So don't. In fact, you should keep them all. It would be selfish of me to keep such a stud to myself."

Max was astounded at her accusation. Rummaging in her purse, she dammed the key fob for not being in the right place. Max grabbed it the minute she pulled it from her purse and put it in his pocket. Anna slid behind the steering wheel of her car and sat, hurt and angry.

When Max settled in the passenger seat, she held out the palm of her hand and demanded, "Key."

"I'm not letting you drive when you're upset." He'd never seen Anna like this. She was usually calm and rational. She listened as Max took out his phone and told someone at the office that he didn't know when he'd be back. "You'll have to call and reschedule," she heard him say.

"I'm all right, Max. Go back to work."

"There's no way I'm going to work. We have to talk. You're trying to end our relationship, which has hardly begun, and I don't even know why."

Anna's hand flew to the top of her head, and she looked heavenward. "The fact that you don't understand is proof this isn't going to work."

"I'm not accepting that, Anna. I may be dense, but you have to explain to me what I did that was so wrong. I just told Angie I can't see her anymore. Why does that make you angry?"

"I thought you told her goodbye at the party."

"I couldn't brush them off like that. They deserve better," Max explained.

"Give me the keys and get out of the car."

"I don't want you driving. You're too upset."

"I'll be all right if you'll just let me go!" she screamed. Max gave in and put the key in her hand, then hurried to his car to follow. But the traffic lights worked against him, and he lost sight of her.

CHAPTER THIRTY-ONE

Max drove home to Tenacity and waited for Anna all afternoon. He phoned a ridiculous number of times but got no answer. *Where could she be? Maybe she had an accident.* It was getting late, and he was about to phone the sheriff when he thought to call Samantha. Without saying hello, he asked, "Have you heard from Anna?"

Sam pointed to the phone and mouthed, 'Max'. Anna shook her head. She didn't want to talk. Then Samantha said, "Yes, she's here with me at the farm. I'll get her." Anna threw her a disgusted look. Covering the mouth of the phone, Sam said, "I couldn't do anything else. He's worried. I was afraid he'd try to report you as a missing person."

Anna took the phone and Sam listened to one side of the conversation. "I'm sorry you were worried. Yes, I know we should talk, but not now. I need to spend time with Sam. Good night, Max. I'm hanging up."

He was relieved Anna was safe but was worried about her state of mind. There'd been no intimacy in her voice. None at all. She could have been talking to a stranger. Compelled to act, he drove to Samantha's.

Leaving the highway, he traveled down the narrow road leading to the isolated farmhouse at the end of the road. Max had always liked the place. When he looked at it, he could almost hear the voices telling John-Boy 'good night' on that old television show.

Chickens clucked their disapproval and dogs barked their warning as Max pulled into the gravel area near the house. Only a single porch light lit the doorway, until he reached the steps. Then motion activated lights flooded the area and Samantha stepped out carrying a shotgun. She looked like she was deciding whether to shoot him or let the dogs have him.

"Queenie! Hot Shot!" she yelled. "Leave the man alone. Go on," she said, motioning for them to back off. They obeyed but continued barking.

"You're not going to shoot me with that cannon, are you?"

"No, but I probably should. After dark, I always meet unexpected guests this way. I'm usually alone out here, and a shotgun is more impressive than a pistol. Plus, your aim doesn't have to be as good."

"I'm glad you're taking that precaution, but I really have to talk to Anna."

"She doesn't want to see you."

"I know. But she misunderstood, and I need to explain."

"You can try." She went inside, while Max waited on the porch. When Anna appeared in the doorway, Max saw she'd been crying. He wanted to hold her and tell her everything was all right, but obviously it wasn't.

She motioned for him to enter. He sat on the sofa, while she took one of the chairs opposite him. When Anna asked Samantha to stay, her friend dutifully took the other chair. The two women listened as Max repeated the explanation he gave earlier that day. He was at Chez Nous with Angie to break up with her, and he didn't understand why Anna was so upset. Seeing her discouraged look, he rephrased his explanation, which got him nowhere. They were no closer to fixing the misunderstanding than before he arrived.

Samantha interrupted Max's floundering efforts to explain his actions. "I know this argument is none of my business, but I've known both of you most of our lives, and I believe y'all are meant to be together. Maybe I could mediate, like I learned in school. I'm no expert, and the little training I received was geared to children, but we could try."

Max and Anna agreed to the experiment, so Samantha began, hoping she could help her friends. "Our first goal is to determine the cause of this disagreement. We're trying to get to the core of the problem, and it might not be as obvious as you think. When I ask a question, I'd like you to think about your answer carefully. Then articulate it as well as you can. And there are stipulations. You must avoid drama at all costs; no exaggerations, no raised voices, and you can't get angry and walk away. Agreed?"

"Agreed," they said quietly.

"Anna," Samantha said, "tell Max what made you angry today, and don't say it's obvious." Anna took a deep breath before speaking. "Sam and I were having a nice lunch when you walked in with the blonde you said you'd broken up with."

"I keep telling her," Max said to Samantha, "I couldn't brush them off with the few words I spoke at the

Fourth of July party. I needed to explain more thoroughly, end things more politely."

Anna rolled her eyes. "Humph. You were polite, all right."

"Tell Max what you mean by that."

Anna didn't need any encouragement. "It didn't look like you were breaking up. It looked like you were on a date."

"Go on," Samantha urged.

"It looked like..." Anna began.

Samantha stopped her. "Remember to talk to Max, not me."

Anna looked directly at the confused man. "You were both laughing, having a great time."

Max stood. He couldn't believe what he was hearing. "You mean you're mad because she wasn't upset? Would you feel better if she'd cried or been angry?"

"No, but I would feel better if she looked like she believed you, like she knew you were serious about being committed to me. But that's not what I saw happening. You left the door wide open, so you can waltz back in anytime you wish. That's not breaking up."

Max was exasperated. "I broke up with her, with all of them. Have you broken up with that guy you see?"

"That's different. There is nothing to break up. He's a friend."

"With benefits," Max said under his breath.

Anna turned to Samantha. "This is a waste of time. He's either determined not to understand or unable to."

"My friend," Samantha reminded her, "you agreed not to walk away. And I think we're making progress.

Max says he broke up with the woman. Do you object to that?"

"Of course not."

"Then, could we say the problem is how he broke up with her, how they interacted?"

"Bingo."

"Then tell us," Samantha urged, "exactly what you objected to? Can you break it down to specific actions?"

"Let's see," Anna said sarcastically, theatrically touching a finger to her chin. "It could have been the laughing, the flirting, the touching. Oh, and let's not forget the kissing."

"Angie kissed me, not the other way around. Would you have preferred I pushed her away?"

"You told her the kiss was unforgettable."

"I was trying to let her down easy, to be nice. What's wrong with that? I didn't want her to feel bad."

"So, you made me feel bad." They were both raising their voices, in spite of Samantha's rules.

"I didn't know you were there."

"Well, think of it this way," Anna tried, "do you believe the people in the restaurant thought you were breaking up with that woman or did they think you were having lunch with your girlfriend?"

"When did you start worrying about what other people think?"

"Oh, I don't know. Maybe it was when pieces of my life started showing up in magazines. How do you think the tabloids would interpret your lunch date?"

"Is that what this is all about?"

"No! Anna shouted. "That's not what this is about, although it's true I'd rather not be known as the gullible girl who was stupid enough to think Max Anderson would choose her over other women. We convey our feelings and intentions through the way we act, as well as what we say, and you treated her like she was the most important woman in your life. You treated her the same way you treat me."

Max sat, head down, legs apart, elbows resting on his thighs, silently considering all Anna said. Upon drawing a conclusion, a pained look came over his face. "You don't trust me," he said, lifting his head to look at Anna. "That's it, isn't it? You don't trust me."

No shit, Sherlock, Anna thought, before considering the question seriously. "I'd trust you with my life," she said. "But you're right. I don't trust you with other women, especially someone you've been sleeping with. You have to admit, your track record doesn't give a girl confidence."

Max thought about what she said. "I'll give you that. But you have to believe that since you've come back into my life, it has only been you. I only want you."

Samantha sat quietly, until she realized neither Max nor Anna intended to speak. "All right, it seems we've gotten to the core of the problem," she said sadly. She looked at Max. "Anna doesn't trust you. The next step of this process is to think of ways the problem might be solved. I need you to brainstorm, throw out any solutions that come to mind. I admit to being out of my element here. My experience is limited to classroom and playground disagreements when I was practice teaching."

"I don't know what solution there could be," Max said, "unless she wants me to change who I am, or avoid talking to other women?" Anna rolled her eyes.

"No exaggerations," Samantha reminded them. "Since the two of you seem to be at an impasse, I'm going to interject an observation. Max, you can be a flirt. I'll go so far as to say you're an accomplished flirt."

"I thought you were supposed to be impartial."

"I don't believe I'm taking sides," Samantha said. "I'm simply stating a fact. "You've always known how to interject a little amorous attention into your dealings with women. I imagine it's a skill that's served you well."

Max defended his behavior. "Women like the way I treat them. It makes them feel good about themselves. What's wrong with that?"

Anna sat quietly, content to be left out of the conversation.

"Let me ask you this," Samantha said, looking pointedly at Max, "Would you have acted the same way with your luncheon companion if you'd known Anna was watching? Don't answer too quickly. Think about it and answer honestly. Remember, the point of this conversation is to solve a problem, not place blame." She repeated the question slowly. "Would you have acted the same way if you'd known Anna was watching?"

After a brief pause, Max admitted, "Maybe not."

"Your answer tells me you knew your conduct would be offensive to Anna, yet your behavior didn't change because of that knowledge. You say you only want to be with her. I believe the time has come for you to make an important decision. Do you want to please all women or one of them?"

Max narrowed his eyes. "And then again, maybe Anna could just trust me. I feel like the two of you have ganged up on me, and you're trying to change who I am."

"Not at all," Samantha said, refusing to admit she was taking Anna's side. "We've identified a problem and are trying to find a solution. Would it be possible for you to tone down the flirting a little? If you need a ruler by which to measure your behavior, pretend Anna is there with you." Max had no answer. Emotionally spent, he was through talking.

The process had accomplished at least one thing. Anna was no longer angry. Unfortunately, her anger was replaced with despondency. She looked lovingly at Max. "You are a kind person, and I see how that characteristic could possibly impact the way you behave with women. Maybe the flirting is an innate part of you that will never change." A tear slid down her face. "Unfortunately, I don't think I can live with that."

Disappointed her effort to help her friends hadn't been more effective, Samantha announced she was going to her room. "The downstairs bedroom is available to anyone who needs it."

Max stood, halting Samantha's departure by affectionately clasping her arm. "Thanks for trying," he said, before kissing her cheek.

She turned to Anna and shrugged. "He did just make me feel better." The smiles of the three friends contradicted their sad demeanor.

As soon as they were alone, Max enfolded Anna in a loving embrace, her head tucked under his chin. Her arms automatically wrapped around his firm torso, and they stood that way a long while, each of them praying it wouldn't be the last time.

Max pulled back to tenderly close his lips over hers, rejecting the urge to deepen the kiss. "Don't give up on us. We'll figure this out." Reluctantly, he released his hold on Anna and walked out the door.

CHAPTER THIRTY-TWO

Everyone working in the offices of Anderson Architecture and Construction heard the impact of shattering glass. Investigating the source, Alex looked through the plate glass window of his son's office and saw him pacing, an anguished expression on his face. Upon entering, he noticed broken ceramic pieces scattered on the floor. "What the hell happened here?"

"I threw the damned vase on the floor." Max pointed to his computer and resumed pacing. There was an email on the screen from Anna. Alex took Max's gesture as permission to read. "When you do something," Anna wrote, "you do it thoroughly. This is no exception. Not only have you hurt me; you've also humiliated me."

"Click on the attachment," Max said with resignation. Alex watched a video of Max having a meal with a beautiful architect they'd previously worked with. When that faded away, another scene replaced it, showing Max at the same restaurant with a dark exotic beauty. Next, Max was holding a sexy blonde's hand. The finale was a kiss with the blonde and a confrontation with Anna. The headline read "Three-Timing Player Breaks Author's Heart."

"When was this video taken, son?"

"The one with Anna was taken yesterday."

"I thought she was important to you," his father said.

"She is."

Confused, Alex asked, "Then why are you dating other women?"

Max looked exasperated. "I wasn't dating them. I was breaking up with them."

Alex frowned. "That doesn't look like breaking up to me."

"Not you, too? Why doesn't anyone believe me?"

Turning his palms skyward, Alex said sarcastically, "Did you watch the video?"

Max's conversation with his dad didn't go any better than the one the night before. No one understood. Even his father was critical of his behavior. And the comments on the website were scathing.

He had to admit it looked incriminating. *Who the hell made that video?* he wondered. *And why?* Anna was fairly well known, but she wasn't a high-profile celebrity. And she wasn't even there when the first two videos were recorded. Someone had followed him, and he couldn't imagine why. Then he thought of Janine.

Later that day, when Max saw Fred's crew leave for the day, he summoned Gracie, who was playing in her room. "Let's go ask Anna to join us for dinner." Acutely aware he was in danger of losing the woman he treasured, Max and Gracie walked next door to issue the invitation. He was shamelessly using his daughter to coax Anna into joining them. That wasn't playing fair, but he'd do almost anything to keep her from slipping away.

Their pretty neighbor rose from a porch rocking chair as father and daughter approached. She greeted Gracie warmly before lifting sad eyes to Max's hopeful ones. Gesturing for him to sit in the chair she'd vacated, Anna situated herself on the porch swing—physical evidence, Max thought, of the emotional gap between them.

Anna patted the space beside her. "Gracie, come sit with me."

Gracie hopped onto the swing, smiling up at the woman who was becoming increasingly important to her. "Will you eat supper with us? Daddy's going to cook hamburgers."

Anna put her arm around the little girl's shoulders. "Thank you for inviting me, but I'm waiting for someone." Normally, Max would've let his inquisitive daughter ask, but he couldn't stop himself. "Who's coming?"

"A friend from college," was Anna's less-than-complete answer.

"What's this friend's name?"

"Conner. His name is Conner."

Disconcerted that she was waiting for a man, Max, nevertheless, attempted a teasing tone. "Just how good a friend is this Conner?"

Anna answered without apology, her tone serious. "A very good friend."

As if on cue, a black Porsche came to a halt in front of Anna's house. When the door opened, confident loafer-clad feet hit the ground, and Conner's lean form unfolded from the sporty vehicle, looking no less sexy for the slightly rumpled look acquired on his trip. Max almost groaned aloud at the sight of the tall, tanned, classically handsome man, knowing instantly he was the type of man women went crazy for.

Conner looked up, pushed back a thick blond lock that fell forward when he got out of the car, and cast a dazzling smile at Anna. His long arms opened wide for the woman who hurried down the steps to greet him. Sweeping her into an embrace, he kissed her mouth firmly, while Max watched helplessly, jaw clinched, fists at his side.

Anna put her hands on Conner's chest, gently pushing him away. "Hi," she said sweetly, then nodded toward the porch. "We have guests."

"Max?" Conner guessed.

"That's him," she said succinctly.

With an arm around his friend's waist, Conner strode toward the porch and said without rancor, "Let's go meet this Max fellow I've heard so much about."

Stricken by the sight of Anna in the arms of another man, Max forced himself to unclench his fists and tried, not quite successfully, to wipe the scowl off his face. The intimate way they looked at one another and the way they touched told Max this was the undefined relationship Anna told him about.

When they reached the top of the stairs, Conner released his hold on Anna, as she introduced the men without making eye contact with either of them. Conner confidently put out a hand. "It's good to finally meet you, Max."

Max shook his hand, more than a little discomposed. To make matters worse, he noticed Conner started to wrap his arm around Anna's waist, as if from habit, then caught himself and returned it to his side. *Look at me, Anna,* Max silently demanded, but she intentionally avoided his gaze.

Conner knelt down to Gracie's level. "Who is this beautiful young lady?"

Gracie didn't hesitate. "I'm Gracie. Why did you kiss Anna?"

Amused, Conner said, "Because I like her." Gracie continued in an accusatory tone. "My daddy likes her, too," she said in her direct manner, "and so do I." Max put his hand on Gracie's shoulder, a gesture intended to put an end to the interrogation, but Gracie charged on. "She's not your girlfriend."

This time, Max stopped her. "I'm afraid Gracie hasn't developed a filter," Max said to Conner.

The child looked up. "What's a filter, Daddy?"

Max caressed her head and shook his own. "I'll tell you later, but before we go, I need to talk with Anna. Stay on the porch with Conner a minute. I'll be right back." Taking the hint, Conner stayed put, as Max took Anna's hand and led her into the house. Once inside, he held her chin in his hand so she had no choice but to look into his pleading eyes. "He's not going to stay here tonight, is he?"

"We haven't talked about it."

"Please, Anna, give us a chance. You and I belong together, and you know it. At least I hope you do." He looked at the floor before returning to her eyes. "Don't sleep with him. Okay?"

Waiting for her answer was excruciating. "Okay," she finally said. He held her face in his hands and kissed her. She kissed him back, but the kiss was more restrained than it would have been before the Jennifer, Angie, and Josie debacle.

Max returned to the porch, feeling better for having Anna's promise, and forced himself to be polite. He and Gracie needed to leave. He couldn't bring himself to tell the other man it was nice to meet him. So he just said, "Conner," and nodded farewell. But he did shake his hand, noting it could easily palm a basketball. Max cast a last pleading glance at Anna before picking Gracie up and walking home.

For the first time in his life, Max was experiencing devastating, gut-wrenching jealousy. Who knew it was physically painful? After putting Gracie to bed, he poured himself a drink and stared at the liquid, astonished at the despondency he was feeling.

Max was astute enough to see the irony in the situation. Anna must have felt the same way about the women who showed up at the Larsons' party. And he'd trivialized her feelings, accused her of being unreasonable. He'd screwed up big time. Max racked his brain for a plan to regain her trust, hoping it wasn't too late. He would start with a sincere apology for being dismissive of her feelings. Beyond that, he had no idea.

When Conner offered to take Anna out for dinner, she almost suggested they eat at home. Then she remembered the whole town had probably seen the video, and she wanted everyone to know she wasn't hiding in her room, crying herself to sleep.

Conner was suitably impressed when Anna introduced him to Lucky's Catfish House but hoped the animals would stay away from his car. He was a southern boy, but the Savannah restaurants he frequented were quite different from Lucky's. When the musicians took a break, Conner brought Anna up to date on his upcoming move to Clarkston.

When Conner Wilmington's father realized his son wouldn't be bullied into joining the family firm, good ol' dad asked his college roommate to offer Conner a job, which happened to be in Clarkston, Mississippi. Because both families owned vacation homes on St. Simons Island, the young attorney had met his new boss on a number of occasions.

Matthew Jacobson was a good enough guy, when he wasn't talking with Conner's dad about the good old days at Duke. Conner knew Jacobson would send full reports on his progress, but if the arrangement satisfied Will Wilmington and got Conner out from under his dad's thumb, he was fine with it. Coincidentally, the job was near Tenacity, where his friend Anna lived.

Conner hadn't planned to travel to the area for another month, but when he spoke to Anna on the phone and heard how upset she was, he drove over early. Knowing her history, he'd hoped her return to Tenacity would bring her a sense of peace. Instead, it had turned her life upside down.

Conner was willing to offer support and help in any way he could. And while in the area, he'd take the opportunity to become familiar with the town he was going to work in. He needed to find a place to live. He liked Tenacity but he didn't want to drive forty-five minutes to work every day, and he'd rather live in a place with at least a little nightlife.

After putting Gracie to bed, Max sat on his front porch, watching the house next door. Earlier, Anna and the GQ model went somewhere in the black sports car Max secretly coveted. They were back now, and he seriously wanted to know what was happening. Anna's promise was the only thing keeping him from barging in on them. Since sleep was out of the question, he sat in the glider, anxious and miserable, as he waited for the man to leave.

Anna sat in one of the two kitchen chairs in the house, while Conner sat in the upholstered chair she normally kept in her bedroom. At six foot five, Conner had been one of the shorter players on the Tar Heels basketball team, but he was too tall to comfortably sit in one of her kitchen chairs for any length of time. "I should tell you," Anna said, "I told Max about us. I mean, that we've been together, in that way."

Conner gave her a crooked smile. "You mean, you told him we had sex?"

"Sort of. I told him about us, but I didn't give your name. He doesn't know I was talking about you."

"Honey," Conner said, "believe me, he knows."

"Why do you say that?"

Conner made a show of clearing his throat. "Didn't you see the way he looked at me? What did he say when the two of you went in the house?"

"He asked me not to sleep with you."

275

Conner chuckled. "He knows all right, and you can bet he's one miserable son-of-a-bitch right now. He's suffering, sitting over there wondering what's going on between us. Don't worry," Conner consoled when he noticed Anna's unease. "He'll live through it, and he might be a better man for it. He'll appreciate you more. Now let's talk about what's going on with you. From your emails and phone calls, I gather you and Max have hit a snag."

"It's worse than that."

"Okay. Tell ol' Conner what's wrong?"

Anna rolled her eyes but was glad to have someone to talk to. "I let myself think our relationship might go somewhere. And that seems to have been a mistake." She related the story of the party and the three women Max's ex-wife invited.

"Whew!" Conner exclaimed. "I'm starting to feel sorry for the guy. His ex must be some piece of work."

"Yeah, she is. Always has been."

"And Max couldn't see that?"

"Couldn't or didn't care. Not until it was too late."

"Let me get my facts straight," Conner said. "He says he hasn't dated other women since you returned, and he only wants to be with you? Do you think he's lying?"

Anna gave it some thought. "No, I don't think so."

"Do you think he treated the other women unfairly?"

"I guess not, even though I think sleeping with three women is wrong. He says they knew about each other. They all wished us well, although one of them obviously didn't mean it, and another told me she'd be glad to take him if things didn't work out between us."

"Sounds like a good recommendation to me."

"You would think that. You're both pretty boys with too much power over women."

"Maybe that's your type," Conner joked. "Getting back to the business at hand, let me get this straight. You're upset because he had sex with those women while the two of you were apart, just as you did with me. Is that right?"

Anna narrowed her eyes, but said, "Right," dragging out the word.

Conner took her hands in his familiar ones, looked warmly into her eyes, and said, "So it hurt you to see him with women he cares about, who also care about him. You were jealous."

"Yes," she reluctantly admitted. "But the video."

"I watched the video. The man knows how to pour on the charm. I'll give him that. He told you the video showed him breaking up with them, even wrote that on the website where it was posted. Do you believe it?"

"I do. But the way he acted with them…"

"Maybe he treated them that way because he cares about them. Not the way he cares about you, obviously. He gave them up for you. Maybe you should give him a chance, see if you can work things out." Conner pulled her up from her chair and hugged her.

Anna sniffed. "I love you, Conner Wilmington."

"And I love you, Anna. If that fellow next door is the one you want, then he's the one you should have. But if I keep you against my body much longer, I can't be held accountable for my actions. You're still the sexiest woman I know."

Anna moved away from Conner and looked up at him, smiling through her tears. With his hands on her shoulders, Conner bent down and looked directly into her eyes. "I have a reservation at a motel not far from here. Not the one you stayed in," he rushed to say. "Will you be okay if I leave now?"

"I will. Thanks for coming."

Conner winked. "How about I take you out for breakfast before I leave in the morning?"

"I'd like that."

He gave her an almost chaste kiss. When he reached his car, highlighted by a near-by streetlight, he glanced at the house next door. He'd bet good money Max was sitting on the porch, waiting for him to leave. So he turned toward the dark porch and saluted, before folding his body into the Porsche and pulling away.

CHAPTER THIRTY-THREE

The next morning, Conner picked Anna up before the construction crew arrived. "Where to?"

"To Big Mama's, of course. Once you've been there, you'll have been to every restaurant in Tenacity."

"You mean there are only two places to eat in town?"

"That's all."

After parking on Main Street, Conner remarked on the location of city hall. "I've never seen a road just stop like that, in front of a building."

"Town history says the spot was once a dumping area for loggers. They unloaded logs into a shoot that propelled them down the bluff into the river. Later, to keep people from accidentally driving into the river, they chose to build City Hall in that spot."

"And no one's ever driven into city hall?"

"Not yet. At least there's room for a U-turn."

Lying outside Big Mama's was a big, lanky hound dog, who raised his floppy-eared head and wagged his tail when they approached. "Who do you belong to?" Conner asked the dog.

"That's Buddy," Anna said, relating the story she'd been told. "He used to belong to Miss Honeywell. After she died, several people tried to adopt him, but Buddy likes his independence. Half the town feeds him, and the store owners leave water out for him."

"Smart guy."

"Oh, and Buddy goes to church every Sunday. He stands out front and greets people as they arrive and doesn't leave until the service is over."

"What denomination is he?" Conner joked.

"He's non-denominational. Divides his time between the Baptists and the Methodists."

"Not Catholic?"

"No. He's Protestant, but that may be because those are the only churches located within his roaming area."

When they entered the diner, Conner looked around appreciatively. "Has it always looked like this?"

"Since the Fifties, I'm told."

"I didn't know places like this still existed."

Anna spoke to a group of regulars, calling them each by name, and then chose a booth. Cora sashayed to their table. "Who's your handsome friend?"

"Cora, meet Conner Wilmington, a friend from college. Conner, this cheeky woman, who rarely bothers with the order pad in her apron, is Cora Thompson. I can't remember a time when she didn't work at Big Mama's."

Conner smiled and offered his hand. "Nice to meet you, Cora."

"Has nice manners, too. This one could give Max a run for his money." Winking at Conner, she said, "Honey, you make me want to be young again. But who am I kidding? I can't even remember being young. Had a kid on my hip before I was eighteen. But I guess you didn't come here to gab. What can I get you this morning?"

After she took their order, Cora headed toward the kitchen, not moving as quickly as she once did.

"I understand why you moved back," Conner said. "It's a nice town. Friendly. And you have roots here. Plus, it's charmingly quirky."

Hearing the jingle of a bell, they looked up to see Samantha walk through the door. Anna stood, hugged her friend, and invited her to join them. "Samantha Susanna Lindsey, meet Conner McArthur Wilmington."

Small talk followed the introduction until they noticed a man standing near their table, busily snapping photos. "How do you feel about the videos of Max with other women?" he asked Anna. "Who are you having breakfast with? Who cheated first, you or Max?"

"Tabloid journalist," Anna explained unnecessarily. "Why are you bothering me?" she asked the man.

Conner stood, towering over the smaller man. "You need to leave. We're here to have a quiet breakfast."

"I have as much right to be here as you do."

"If you refuse to go," Conner warned, "I'll be forced to expropriate that expensive camera."

"What?"

"Seize. Commandeer. I'll take your camera."

"You do that," the man snarked, "and I'll sue your ass off." Conner stepped closer, conjuring his most ominous expression. "Mister, you should never threaten an attorney with a lawsuit, and that's what you just did."

"Okay, okay, I'll leave. I should have enough to make her happy anyway," the man said, as he hurried to his banged-up car.

After he left, Anna asked Conner, "Would you really have taken his camera?"

"Hell, no. He could have sued my ass off." They all laughed.

Anna smirked. "And you were going to do what with his camera? Expropriate it?" They burst into laughter, again.

When Conner got up to pay the cashier, Samantha nodded his direction and gushed. "When I saw that man, I thought I'd pee in my pants. Oh, my. "He's all three B's," she sighed, "blond, built, and beautiful! Wherever did you find him?" She didn't stop for an answer. "If you don't want him, give him to me."

Anna laughed at her overly dramatic friend. I'm not sure anyone can really have him, but you're welcome to give it a try.

"No, really," Samantha said, "how do you know him?"

"He lived in the apartment above mine when I was in college."

"You're kidding. Did the two of you, you know?" Anna said nothing.

"You did! You dog!"

"I never said anything of the sort."

Sam's eyes were wide. "But you did."

Once Conner and Anna were settled in Conner's little black sports car, he said, "Your friend Samantha is cute. I didn't see a ring on her finger. Is she dating anyone?"

"Want me to set you up?"

"Maybe," was Conner's surprising answer. Anna thought the two would be an odd pair, but they were obviously attracted to one another.

Samantha would be a second-grade teacher at Tenacity Elementary School in the fall. She lived on the farm where she grew up and still got up every morning to feed the animals.

Conner was from an affluent, old Savannah family, with ancestors who probably came over on the Mayflower. Sometimes there was no explanation for attraction.

"Turn left here," Anna said on the spur-of-the-moment. "The guy with the camera said he should have enough photos to make her happy. I'm just wondering..." Anna directed Conner to drive by the Larson home, and sure enough, that banged-up car was parked in the driveway. "If Janine had that man watching us today, she's probably responsible for the videos. That would explain a lot."

After seeing Conner drop Anna off at her house and drive away, Max texted her. **Are we okay?**

Probably.

I'll take that, he texted back. Then he left to drive Gracie to day care.

CHAPTER THIRTY-FOUR

Gracie cried and begged. "Please Mother, please! Don't make me go. They'll be mean to me! Please. Please! Let me stay with Daddy. He said I don't have to go to Doug's. He said I could stay with him." Janine promised Max she wouldn't take Gracie to Doug's until a counselor deemed it safe, but she hadn't gotten around to finding one, and her parents weren't home to babysit.

Besides, she was sure the boys wouldn't act up after the talking-to Doug gave them. Gracie would be fine. Now that she and Doug were engaged, the kids had to learn to get along. And she and Doug would be right there in case the boys got rambunctious.

Gracie cried as Janine dragged her to the car. "I have to get my cell phone. Daddy told me to always take my cell phone."

"Remember what happened the last time you took your phone? You got everyone upset."

When they arrived, Janine had to bodily remove Gracie from the car. "I'm disappointed in you, young lady. Stop acting so ugly. Wipe your eyes and be polite. I won't leave you alone with the boys if that'll make you feel better."

Gracie nodded. "Don't let them get me, Mother. Stay close to me."

Doug was on the back patio, getting the barbecue grill ready, and the boys were playing tether ball. "We're here," Janine singsonged. Doug came from the backyard and gave her a peck on the lips. Tousling Gracie's hair, he asked, "How are you today, pretty girl?" Gracie, who clung tightly to her mother's leg, answered in a small voice, "I'm okay."

Doug smiled at the child. "Come on back. I already have the grill going. I've warned the boys they better be on their best behavior."

They had a nice, normal backyard barbecue until Janine and Doug began taking the dirty dishes to the kitchen. Gracie followed her mother back and forth between the backyard and the kitchen, until Janine finally said, "Gracie, stop following me like a little duckling. Just stay here on the patio. I'll be back in a minute."

Gracie cast a look at Allen and Kevin to find them grinning at her. Inside, Doug took the opportunity to pin Janine to the kitchen counter and kiss her as he'd wanted to all evening. When the adults didn't immediately return to the patio, the boys flew into action.

They were prepared. One boy stuffed a sock into Gracie's mouth while the other tied it in place with a dishtowel. The two eight-year-olds dragged little Gracie to the side of the house, tied her hands behind her back, and threw her into a bed of poison ivy. They told her in great detail what it would do to her.

Proving they weren't the sharpest tacks in the box, they picked leaves from the vines and rubbed them on Gracie's arms, legs, face, and body. When they realized they were poisoning themselves, they decided it would be all right as long as they washed their hands.

Thankfully, when they rubbed it on Gracie's face, she instinctively closed her eyes. The little devils even put some under the cloth they'd tied over her mouth. Then one of them began to laugh. "Let's put some in her pants so she'll go around scratching there." They laughed hysterically.

When Allen and Kevin heard Doug's call, they warned Gracie not to tell anyone what they did. "We don't want a little sister," they told her. "Just stay with your dad." They quickly tore the cloth off her mouth, untied her, and left the terrified child lying in the poison leaves. After hiding the restraints in the ivy, the boys ran across the front yard to the opposite side of the house and pretended they'd been there all along.

Doug looked at the boys suspiciously. "Where's Gracie?"

"Not sure," one boy said.

"Don't know," said the other.

When Gracie failed to answer Doug's call, he and Janine began searching. Not finding the child in the yard or in the house, Doug questioned the boys, who convinced him they knew nothing.

"She didn't want to come tonight," Janine said. "She could have tried to go to her dad's." After advising Allen and Keven to call his cell if they saw Gracie, Doug drove Janine around the neighborhood and down the roads leading to the two houses Gracie called home.

Finally, Janine made the call she'd been dreading and tried to sound casual. "Max, has Gracie gotten in touch with you?"

"What happened?" he snapped.

"We were at Doug's. I was watching her but…"

Max didn't let her finish. "Dammit. I told you not to take her there. What have they done to her?"

"We were all in the backyard. One minute she was there, and the next she was gone. Don't worry. We'll find her. I just wanted to see if she was with you."

Max bellowed, "How long has she been missing?"

"I wouldn't go so far as to say she's missing."

"Hell, Janine, how long has it been since you last saw her? Never mind, let me talk to Doug."

"Why do you want to talk to Doug?"

"Just get him!"

"All right," she whined.

Doug took the phone. "Yeah, Max, any idea where she might be?" Max's anger subsided, somewhat, upon hearing the concern in Doug's voice.

"Do something for me, Doug. Interrogate the hell out of your boys. I have a bad feeling they know what happened to her."

"Okay, Max. Yeah, I will."

Max wasn't convinced he'd follow through. "Doug, I know you try hard to be a better father than yours was, and I admire you for that, but right now you need to put the fear of God into those boys. You know how it's done."

Doug swallowed hard. *Does everyone know about my old man? No time to think about that.* He got the message and knew Max was right. He turned the car around and headed home.

On his way out the door, Max pulled out his phone, punched in the code for Anna, and told her Gracie was missing. "Call me if you see her."

"I'm walking out the door," she said. "Pick me up." They drove around the neighborhood looking for any sign of the child, returning often to Max's house in case she showed up. It would have made sense for Anna to stay home and keep watch, but Max thought she might be the only thing keeping him from losing his mind.

Anna phoned Janine's parents after getting their number from Max. They hadn't seen any sign of their granddaughter. "Please call if she shows up," Anna said. "We're scared half to death."

The next person they notified was Sheriff Wallace. "I understand," Scott said, after Max explained the circumstances. "I'll lock up the office and call in the deputy. We'll knock on some doors in McKinnon's neighborhood. Find out if anyone has seen anything. Call me with updates, and I'll do the same."

"Thanks, Scott. She wouldn't run off without a reason. Something happened, and I know McKinnon's boys had something to do with it. They've hurt her before, and Gracie's afraid of them."

"I'll drive over and talk to them," Scott said. "See what they know."

"Thanks. Don't let those little shits fool you. They may look innocent, but those boys are little demons."

"If they know anything," Scott said, "I'll get it out of them. The gun and handcuffs can be pretty intimidating."

"I appreciate your help." The entire time he talked to Scott, he was scanning one side of the road while Anna scanned the other.

"Stop here," she said. "I think I saw something." They jumped out as soon as the car jerked to a stop, calling for Gracie, praying they'd found her. A brown dog emerged from the bushes, wagging his tail, and their spirits fell. Max looked around just in case, trying not to think of worst-case scenarios. He'd never been so afraid or felt so helpless in his life.

About an hour and a half after Janine's call, they made another slow pass-through Mill Village. Seeing something on his front porch, Max pulled into his driveway and ran up the steps. Gracie was curled in a ball against the door, scared, and shaking.

"Gracie, it's Daddy. Are you all right?" Max braced for Gracie's leap into his arms, but she just lay there, seemingly unaware of his presence. He picked up his daughter and cradled her in his arms, his heart aching, his mind searching for an explanation.

The little girl was quiet, except for an occasional whimper. Something was very wrong. Max took her inside for a better look while Anna let the other searchers know they'd found the missing child.

Turning his head toward Anna and away from his daughter, he said quietly, but menacingly, "Tell Janine if she comes here, I won't let her in. I can't put into words how angry I am."

Like everyone else, the sheriff breathed a sigh of relief when Anna relayed the news. "I spoke with the McKinnon boys," Scott said. "They admitted to rubbing poison ivy on Gracie. There's a bunch of it at one end of their house, and I could tell some of it had been pulled up. They said they were just playing around. When I asked if they wore gloves, they looked at one another and ran to wash their hands."

"Thanks for the help, Scott. I'm hanging up now. I need to tell Max."

The worried father gently nudged Gracie to sit up. He turned her unresponsive face toward his and said softly, "Gracie, I need you to speak to me. Can you tell Daddy what happened?" No response. Her eyes were unfocused, like a doll's. It was frightening. With feigned patience, Max tenderly coaxed his daughter back from wherever her bright little mind had retreated.

Max closed his eyes and let out a breath, thanking God Gracie was coming out of her stupor. When she became aware of her dad, she tried to speak, but sobs made her words unintelligible.

Holding his daughter firmly, Max rocked back and forth. Anna caressed her head, softly singing an Irish lullaby her mother used to sing to her.

Gracie pulled back and smiled through her tears at the woman she'd grown to love. Anna smiled back and took the child's small hand in hers. Then she noticed Gracie's wrists.

"Look, Max. Her wrists look like something was tied around them."

His jaw clenched when he saw the red marks. Desperate to know the details of his daughter's ordeal, he instinctively understood the need for patience. The wait was excruciating. "I'm here, sweet girl," Max told his child.

He continued rocking slowly, until Gracie began to speak, her words punctuated with small sobs. "Daddy, they put poison leaves on me and put a cloth in my mouth so I couldn't talk."

"Did they tie your hands?" When his daughter nodded, Max became so furious his body shook. Determined not to further traumatize his child, he managed to control his emotions—but barely.

Forcing himself to calm down, at least outwardly, he gently coaxed information from his shattered daughter. Eventually, the grim details emerged. At one point, he placed Gracie in Anna's arms and walked onto the porch. Something like a growl came from his direction, and Anna thought she heard a flowerpot hit the sidewalk.

When Max returned, he valiantly replaced his grim expression with a small smile for Gracie. He had no idea how much poison ivy she'd been exposed to, but it was time to give her a thorough bath.

Together, Anna and Max painstakingly soaped and rinsed every inch of the listless child. They toweled her dry, put her in a soft cotton nightgown, and Anna dried her hair. Max rocked Gracie to sleep and then dozed on the sofa beside Anna, repeatedly checking on his daughter for signs of a reaction.

Exhausted, they fell asleep about three in the morning. Max jerked awake at first light and hurried to check on Gracie, chastising himself for falling asleep. He paled at the sight of her.

Her face, eyelids, and lips were swollen, and her face was dotted with angry red patches. He picked up her little body, blanket and all, and nudged Anna awake. "Get the car," he said frantically, trying not to wake his daughter. "We're taking Gracie to Doc. The keys are on the counter. You drive."

Anna gasped when she saw Gracie's face and hurried to follow Max's directions. Doc Waller answered his front door in his robe and slippers, still half asleep, but came instantly awake at the sight of the little girl in her daddy's arms. "What'd she get into?"

"Poison Ivy," was all Max said. They hurried through the house to the clinic at the far end where Doc gave the child a cursory exam. He opened a drawer to retrieve a tube-like device and several pre-filled syringes.

Adding them to his medical bag, Doc announced, "We're going to the hospital. Here," he said, handing Anna a couple of reflective medical emergency signs. "Put one of these on each side of the car. I'll put this one on the back," he said, referencing the sign still in his hands. Anna, you drive. Max, you and I will sit in the back with the little one." The whole process only took a few minutes, but it would take thirty-five to get to the hospital. Maybe thirty, that early in the morning.

As soon as Doc eased into the car, he said, "Drive! Don't take any chances, but don't be afraid to break the speed limit. If law enforcement stops us, we'll ask for an escort." Turning to Max, Doc said, "Talk to me. Tell me what happened here?"

Max relayed the details, while Gracie moaned in her sleep. She'd been moaning for a while, but the moans were getting more intense, and she was clawing at her body. "I don't understand why she's still asleep," Doc said. "Did you give her anything?"

"I gave her Benadryl last night. Well, really, it was around two this morning. Was that the right thing to do?"

"Fine. That was fine."

Doc Waller entered the emergency room lobby in his robe and slippers, confidently delivering instructions as he went. "Take this child to a room immediately," he told the orderly with the gurney he'd called ahead for. Dr. Shoemaker's expecting us. "Max, put her on the gurney. We'll follow. You too, Anna."

"Who's that in pajamas?" an emergency room receptionist asked the older woman sitting next to her?

"That's Doc Waller."

"He can't just come in here shouting orders, can he?" Without waiting for an answer, she stepped from behind the Plexiglas barrier and hurried toward the doctor. "Doctor Waller, you need to check in at the desk. We have procedures." He produced the admission papers Max had completed on the way to the hospital and thrust them toward her, never slowing his pace. "Here you go."

Nonplussed, the young woman walked back to her booth. "He can't do that, can he?" she asked a second time.

"Honey, Doc Waller does whatever he wants."

The younger woman frowned. "How does he get away with it?"

"He's old for one thing. Old people can get away with a lot. And he knows most of the medical personnel here. He brought some of them into the world, treated some when they were kids, and he's been the only doctor in Tenacity for years."

"So he gets to do whatever he wants?"

"Sort of. He knows who to call."

An ER nurse produced the smallest hospital gown she could locate, knowing it would still swallow the child's small frame. When Anna and the nurse removed

Gracie's nightgown, they saw the full extent of the damage.

The child's father was the picture of devastation. His chin fell to his chest, his hands covered his eyes, and his entire body slumped. Those horrid boys had smeared the child's entire body with poison ivy. They hardly missed a spot. Tears ran down Anna's face, as she imagined the terrifying attack the sweet child endured.

The nurse hurried away, returning quickly with a hospital doctor who, thanks to Doc Waller, was already familiar with the facts of the case. After examining Gracie's small body, he appeared grim. "Her skin's reaction to the poison will likely continue to worsen for a while," he explained. Anna's hand flew to her mouth and Max's face grew ashen.

"The child is lucky you bathed her thoroughly and gave her antihistamine," he continued. "That was exactly the right thing to do. And Doctor Waller gave her a critical shot of epinephrine. We're treating her for severe allergic reaction," the hospitalist said, "focusing on preventing further damage from the initial contact with the poison. Among other things, that means no scratching.

"We'll keep her in the hospital a few days, treat the rash and the blisters that will inevitably appear, and make her as comfortable as possible. We're giving her medication to numb the itching, which will cause her to sleep. I prefer not to give strong painkillers to children, but in this case, I see no recourse. It's hard to know what to expect in a case like this, because the exposure is so extensive. We can see rashes and blisters, but we have to watch for more indiscernible symptoms. If she begins to sweat, becomes nauseated, or has difficulty breathing, you must alert medical personnel immediately. Are you all right?" the doctor asked Max. "You look a little pale."

"Yeah," he said. "I'm just afraid for Gracie." Feeling Anna's hand slip into his, Max held on to it like the lifeline it was.

Glancing at Doc Waller, the hospitalist said, "We normally limit visitation in this area, but we'll skirt the rules this time. Additional eyes on this patient can't hurt. The medical staff will constantly monitor her vital signs, and a doctor is always stationed in this unit. Inform medical personnel of any changes, no matter how small. The nurses' station is just across the hall."

Anna noticed how much older Doc had been looking lately. "Don't you want to sit?" she asked him, once the hospital doctor left. "We got you up early."

"I'm fine. Margaret's coming to pick me up shortly. I'll rest then."

"Doc," Max said, "I'd like to step out for a couple of minutes before you leave. I have a few calls to make."

"You do what you need to," Doc said. "I'll be here a while longer."

As soon as Max stepped out of the emergency room, he pulled out his phone and decisively punched in Mark Collins's number. "This is Max Anderson," he told the attorney, "I want to file for full custody of my daughter as soon as possible. She's not safe with her mother."

CHAPTER THIRTY-FIVE

Upon hearing the latest development, Mark said succinctly, "That should do it. I'll get you temporary custody until we can go before a judge. Let me know when Gracie gets out of the emergency room. I'll need to see her."

Before returning to his daughter's room, Max called his mother.

"Where are you?" Carol asked, sounding upset. "Janine's been calling, saying she can't get hold of you and something about Gracie being missing. We've been so scared. I've been calling, but you didn't answer."

"Sorry I worried you, Mom. My phone's been turned off. ER rules. Things have been happening pretty fast." Max summarized recent events and discouraged his parents from coming to the hospital. "Anna and I are already pushing the rules by staying in the ER, and I don't want to give them an excuse to kick us out. Doc is with us. I'll keep you updated."

Carol offered to drive to Tenacity to get fresh clothing and essentials for Max and Anna, but before she hung up she said, "Max, I understand your reluctance to call Janine, but you have to let her know what's going on.

As much as you wish otherwise, she's Gracie's mother, and you're legally bound to tell her, if for no other reason."

Max knew she was right. He picked up the phone and made the call. When she answered, he held the phone away from his ear and endured the rant, only half listening until a question required a response. "Are you listening to me, Max?"

"Yes, Janine. Now are you ready to stop talking and find out about Gracie?"

"I am. Talk."

"She's in the hospital, thanks to your negligence."

Janine's only comment was, "I'll be right there." She hung up before Max could tell her not to come, and she wouldn't answer his calls.

Anna sat beside Gracie's bed, wearing yesterday's clothes and watching Max pace. He was exhausted, worried, angry, and about to interact with the woman he blamed for his daughter's condition.

Anna said what was on her mind, even though she knew Max wouldn't want to hear it. "I understand why you're upset with Janine, but you need to take a deep breath and calm down before speaking to her. No good can come from facing her in the state you're in now."

"I know you're right," Max said, trying to keep his voice down, "but I'm so damned angry right now I could wring her screwed-up, self-centered neck."

Knowing hospital personnel wouldn't deny entry to a child's mother, Max stood in the hallway, hoping to head Janine off before she marched into Gracie's room. As soon as she walked into the ER, Max hurried down the hall and grasped his ex-wife's elbow, firmly escorting her out the door she'd just walked through.

Janine saw the fury in his eyes and steeled herself for a verbal onslaught. His quiet voice didn't disguise his anger. "I'm not going to tell you to go away. I want you to see that helpless little girl lying in a hospital bed and understand the damage your disregard for her welfare caused. Then you can leave. Dammit, Janine. I told you."

He took a deep breath and forced himself to calm down before continuing the castigation. "I told you not to leave her alone with those boys. I warned you they're dangerous. And you ignored me. I'm her father, and you just ignored me."

"Let go of me. I have the right to see my daughter."

"You do that," he said through gritted teeth, "and then get the hell away from here. I've got this."

Janine pushed the ER doors open and found Gracie. Max was right behind her. Anna witnessed the look of horror on Janine's face when she saw her daughter. She inhaled quickly, her hand flew to her mouth, and she went pale. Then, like a chameleon, Janine swallowed hard and forced her features into an undefinable expression, her new persona completely belying her initial reaction.

Surprising Anna further, Janine sounded almost cheerful when she spoke. "Oh, baby," she cooed, "Mother's here now. You're going to be fine. The doctors will help you get better; then we'll go home, and I'll take care of you. Everything will be all right."

The child was resting quietly before her mother arrived, thanks to the drugs she'd been given, but at the sound of Janine's voice, she began turning her head rapidly from side to side and moving her feet, as if trying to push away from danger.

Despite the distortion caused by the swelling, her agonized sounds became recognizable words. "No, no, no! Daddy, Daddy!"

When she began gasping for breath, Max yelled, "We need help in here! She can't breathe!" He rushed to his daughter's side, stroked her head, and spoke softly. "It's okay, sweet girl. Daddy's here. I won't let her take you. I won't let anyone hurt you."

When medical personnel came in with a hypodermic needle and a breathing tube, Max held up a hand. "Wait," he said. "She's breathing more easily now. She just got upset."

Max shot an accusing look at Janine, which softened at the sight of her. She was standing in the corner, looking like a child herself, tears in her eyes. Then she straightened and walked from the room without a word.

After Gracie was moved out of the emergency room, attorney Mark Collins came to the hospital with Conner Wilmington, a new attorney in the Clarkston law firm with which he was affiliated. Mark shook Max's hand and then Anna's. "I'm Max's attorney," Mark said to Anna, "and you are?"

Conner stepped in. "This is Anna Robinson. She's the friend I told you about." When the attorneys turned to look at Gracie, they were horrified. The child was sleeping, but her eyes were obviously swollen shut, and her lips were abnormally distended.

Mark photographed Gracie's face before handing the camera to Max and directing him to take pictures of his daughter's body. "We need quality pictures we can enlarge." He saw Max's reluctance. "It's necessary if we're going to convince a judge your ex-wife is unfit. You can cover her genitals."

Anna spoke, anger flashing in her eyes. "Oh, they didn't forget that area. It's awful."

"I know this sounds callous," Mark said, "but we can use that. It makes this a sexual attack, which judges take very seriously." Anna saw Max cringe. "We'll also need video of the child trying to eat and talk. The judge needs to see the damage done to this child. Otherwise, he won't believe it. And get a copy of the doctor's report."

Seeing the anguish in the father's eyes, the attorney said, "I'm sorry to be so blunt, but that's what you're paying me for. And try to get someone in here who can document what she's going through emotionally."

Seeing that Max was barely holding himself together, Conner joined the conversation, trying to help. "Anyone would be traumatized by what Gracie's going through, and she's just a little bit of a thing. A psychiatrist or a counselor can help her cope with what's happened and explain how you can help. Call me when you have the pictures. I'll come by and get them. I'll want to check on Gracie, anyway."

"Get the things I asked for as soon as possible," Mark said. "It takes time to get hearings on the docket, but as soon as you send me those pictures, I'll get an emergency order granting you custody until the trial.

"Try to get good close-ups of the damage, without worrying about your daughter's modesty. I don't have to tell you there's a lot riding on this. I asked Conner to do it, but he assures me you and Anna can handle the job." Max nodded his thanks to Conner.

Before leaving, Mark shook hands with his client and Anna. But Conner hugged Anna and patted Max on the back, handing him his card. "I wrote my private number on the back. Call if I can help in any way. Gracie and I bonded on Anna's front porch. She's a special child, and I'm sorry this is happening to her."

After a difficult week at the hospital, Gracie recovered enough to be released, although she still didn't look well. Dry, pink splotches remained on her face and body, her spunky demeanor had disappeared, and thanks to several days of nothing but liquid nourishment, she'd lost weight.

Max took his daughter home, relieved she was better and that he'd been given temporary custody. Janine called but didn't try to see her. Since Gracie wasn't physically or emotionally ready to return to day care, Anna stayed with her during the day, or Max dropped her off at his Mother's, which wasn't far from his office. Because he missed work when Anna was attacked and when Gracie was in the hospital, he couldn't afford to take more time off.

Anna cooked dinner for Max, Gracie, and herself every evening before going home to spend time on her book. Nothing romantic transpired between Max and Anna, except an occasional, nearly platonic kiss. They'd never really made up after the Fourth of July debacle and hadn't resolved any of their issues. But Gracie needed to be cared for, and that took priority.

Once she began feeling better, Anna tried to think of something to put the sparkle back in the little girl's eyes. It would soon be September, and Anna wanted Gracie to be well in spirit, as well as body, before kindergarten began. Remembering an article she'd read about horses being used in therapy, Anna called her high school friend, Jeff, to ask if he had a horse gentle enough for a child to ride. He did and was anxious to help.

After her first riding lesson, Gracie couldn't wait to tell Max about the experience. She begged to ride every day, and it didn't take long for her enthusiasm for life to reappear.

Max phoned Jeff to thank him for putting excitement back in his daughter's life. "I owe you," he said sincerely. "I won't forget what you've done. Thanks to you, Gracie's my spunky little girl again." Max only hoped the riding lessons weren't providing the opportunity for Jeff to move in on Anna.

CHAPTER THIRTY-SIX

The hearing date came much earlier than Max expected, and he was grateful the excruciating wait was over. He was nervous. If this didn't go his way, he had no idea how he'd protect Gracie.

Janine sat on one side of the courtroom with her attorney, while Max sat with Mark Collins and Conner on the other. The bailiff instructed everyone to rise and introduced a pleasant-looking, gray-haired man as the presiding judge. Judge Carter wasted no time getting started. "Is the attorney for the petitioner ready?"

"I am, Your Honor. I'm Mark Collins, for the petitioner. My client, Max Anderson, presently shares custody with his ex-wife, Janine Anderson. He's asking for sole custody of their five-year-old daughter, Gracie, and restricted visitation. Gracie has suffered both mental anguish and physical harm at the hands of Doug McKinnon's eight-year-old twins, Kevin, and Allen. Although Mr. Anderson has repeatedly asked his ex-wife not to take Gracie to the McKinnon home, she persists in doing so, exposing the child to danger."

The judge peered over his reading glasses. "And by danger you mean…" He glanced at his notes. "Allen and Kevin McKinnon."

"Yes, Your Honor. The child's mother has yet to admit the boys are a danger to Gracie. My witnesses will testify to incidences of Allen and Kevin McKinnon's cruel treatment of the five-year-old, one of which resulted in an emergency trip to the hospital, where she spent an entire week. My client fears for his daughter's safety if his petition isn't granted."

"Who is speaking for Mrs. Anderson?" the judge asked.

Justin Mills, a tall, thin attorney wearing dark-rimmed glasses, introduced himself and then proceeded with his opening statement. "Mrs. Anderson loves her daughter, Your Honor, and would never knowingly do anything to cause her harm. She is engaged to marry Doug McKinnon. Because Mr. McKinnon's twins and Gracie are to be siblings, my client believes the children should spend time together, get to know one another. But Mrs. Anderson wants what is best for her daughter and will do whatever is required to satisfy the court."

"Mr. Collins," the judge said to Max's attorney. "Call your first witness."

"I'd like to call Max Anderson, the child's father, to the stand."

Max took the stand and told the judge about Gracie's panicked reaction when he tucked her into bed. Then he recounted the rug incident, as she'd related it to him. Max barely managed to control his emotions when he explained how Gracie thought she was dying and wanted her daddy to save her. "I felt helpless. I feel helpless. The legal system has imposed restrictions on me that prevent me from keeping my daughter safe."

"You mean the shared custody arrangement," the judge clarified.

"Yes, sir. When my ex-wife has Gracie, I'm powerless to keep my daughter away from dangerous situations."

"Was that the only time Kevin and Allen harmed Gracie?" Max's attorney asked him.

"No, it wasn't."

"Tell the court what else happened."

Max explained what happened the night Gracie phoned him from inside the wardrobe, and Mark introduced Anna's video as evidence. The judge took the time to view it, but reserved comment. Lastly, Max spoke of the events that occurred the night he found Gracie curled on his front porch, including the trip to Doc's and the harrowing ride to the emergency room.

Janine's attorney cross-examined, emphasizing that Max was not present at the time of the so-called rug incident, and his second-hand information was from a five-year-old. He also made sure the judge understood there was no actual fire during the wardrobe incident, and continually referred to it as a prank.

When cross-examining Max about the poison ivy incident, Janine's attorney wanted to know where Max acquired the medical knowledge qualifying him to make judgements about Gracie's condition.

Then he asked Max if Gracie's trauma could have resulted from getting lost after she ran away from the McKinnon home. Max was tempted to tell the attorney he didn't have the medical knowledge to make that determination but knew a smart mouth wouldn't win him any points with the judge.

Janine's attorney insinuated that Gracie over-reacted to the events because she didn't have siblings and didn't understand how to play with other children. Thanks to Mark's prior instructions, Max managed to avoid an outburst, but his angry expression and clenched fists left no doubt about his feelings.

Continuing with his cross-examination, Mr. Mills asked Max to explain his childcare plan. "Wouldn't you feel bad about taking the child from her grandparents' home and leaving her in the care of strangers all day?" He wanted to know what time Max got off work and how long it took him to get from his office to Gracie's day care.

Max explained that the day care workers weren't strangers, and Gracie went there because she loved it. But the attorney had made his point.

After Max's testimony and cross-examination, Mark Collins, Max's attorney, called Anna as a corroborating witness to two of the incidents. On cross-examination, Mr. Mills pointed out, as he had with Max, that Anna hadn't been present when the events occurred and was only witness to the aftermath.

"How do you know Gracie didn't voluntarily get into the wardrobe?" Mr. Mills asked. "It could have been a game of hide-and-seek that went bad."

"You should be ashamed of yourself," Anna said to the attorney, "for arguing to put a sweet child in danger." Judge Carter reprimanded Anna, while Max mentally high fived her.

Doc Waller was called to the stand. He explained why he rushed Gracie to the hospital and described the physical and mental trauma she'd endured the following days. Doc had visited every day she was in the hospital and consulted with the hospitalists on a regular basis. Mark submitted into evidence copies of Gracie's medical records, pictures taken during her hospital stay, a written report from Doc Waller, and a hospital psychiatrist's report.

The hospital psychiatrist testified that Gracie had been severely traumatized and explained that the incident could cause anxiety and interfere with her ability to trust. In his cross-examination, Mr. Mills pointed out that the psychiatrist hadn't seen Gracie since she left the hospital and had no way of knowing if she'd experienced the described symptoms.

"I have no other witnesses," Mark told the court, regretting he'd called the psychiatrist.

Justin Mills, Janine's attorney, quickly called his first witness. "I'd like to call Janine Anderson, Gracie's mother, to the stand. Janine gave an academy award-winning performance. She was humble, repentant, and claimed she would do whatever the judge deemed necessary.

"Doug and I are engaged," she said. "We love each other and want to marry and blend our families—when the time is right. But we agree Gracie's welfare comes first."

Max reprimanded himself for underestimating Janine's acting ability. When the judge asked her about the events Max previously described, she gave tearful, perfectly plausible explanations for how things got out of hand.

"Allen and Kevin aren't bad boys," she explained. "They're just energetic and love to play tricks. Yes, their tricks are sometimes inappropriate, but they'll learn. Doug is a good father, but he is only one person. He's had to be both mother and father. But soon they'll have me, too. I'll be there to help guide them. We'll provide a good home for all our children."

Max wanted to jump out of his chair and shout that she was lying, but he'd do nothing to cause the judge to look on him with disfavor. Mark was tough on Janine in his cross-examination, making her admit she'd forcibly taken Gracie to Doug's when the child begged to go to her dad's. Janine also admitted she hadn't watched the children as closely as she should have and that she promised Max she wouldn't take Gracie to Doug's until a counselor deemed it safe. "So you lied to him. How do we know you're not lying to the court as well?"

"If you promised to see a counselor," the judge interjected, "why didn't you?"

"I intended to, but I was looking for the right one."

Max spoke softly to Mark, who stood and said, "My client tells me he provided you with a list of counselors recommended by a social worker. Did you contact any of them, Mrs. Anderson?" Janine admitted she hadn't gotten around to it.

Once the cross-examination was over, her attorney called Janine's fiancé. As Doug walked to the stand, Mr. Mills handed the judge a glowing character reference from a minister he worked for when he was young. He needed the judge to view Doug as a good person who wanted what was best for Gracie. After highlighting his accomplishments, Mr. Mills gave Doug the opportunity to explain the events that occurred in his home from his viewpoint.

Mark was ready for the cross-examination. He listed the twin's offenses before asking, "Mr. McKinnon, do you approve of their behavior?"

"Of course not."

"Then how do you explain what they've done?"

Doug rubbed the back of his neck, looking uncomfortable, and said, "I guess I don't know how to handle them." The judge looked surprised at the honest assessment. Doug continued, "My wife left me when the boys were two years old. I know that's no excuse. I've tried to be a good dad, but sometimes I can't make them behave."

Mark had hoped Doug would unsuccessfully try to justify his sons' actions, but he hadn't. So he focused on Doug's shortcomings as a disciplinarian, painting him as an unsuitable stepfather. "When they do something they shouldn't," Max's attorney asked, "what do you do?"

"I tell them why it was wrong and that they shouldn't do it again."

"Is that all?" the judge asked.

"Yes, sir. Should I do something else?"

"What did your parents do when you did something wrong as a child?" the judge asked.

Doug glanced around the room, as if looking for an exit, then sat up straight and answered without emotion. "My father beat me, sir, and I won't do that to my children. I know about the cycle of abuse and that behavior stops with me."

The judge nodded, beginning to understand. "What do you mean, exactly, when you say your father beat you?"

Doug sighed, obviously uncomfortable, and answered in a monotone. "Bruises, black eyes, bloody noses, a couple of broken bones."

"I see," the judge said. "And your mother? Tell me about her."

"She was a good woman," Doug said. "Made sure we had hot meals and clean clothes. She taught us right from wrong and took us to church. My mother deserved better than she got. I asked her once why she married Daddy, and she said they were happy when they first married, that he was good to her and held down a job. Then he was injured on the oil rig, couldn't work, and alcohol eased the pain. You can guess the rest."

"I understand your dad wasn't a role model for parenting, but what about your mother? What did she do when you misbehaved?"

"She spent most of her time trying to keep us safe. When Daddy went after my brother or me, she would step in, usually getting the beating he would have given us. We would never have disobeyed her. Never."

"You referred to your mother in the past tense. Am I correct in assuming she's deceased?"

"Yes, sir. My father killed her." Everyone looked shocked, including the judge.

Seeming to forget why he was in court, Doug went on to say, "Oh, they never proved it. Nobody really tried. But I know. He went after us that night, and like always, she stepped in. She made us promise not to leave our room, no matter what we heard. We should have helped her, but we did what she said.

"Daddy was hitting her. We heard the front door slam, and then everything was quiet. We never saw her again. He said she left us, that somebody came to get her, and she just left. But she wouldn't have done that."

The judge didn't speak right away. Then he said, "I'm sorry to have made you relive your tragic childhood, but it helps me understand the situation. This letter I'm holding is from a minister who couldn't say enough good things about you. It appears you've overcome an abundance of adversity. I commend you for that."

"I promised my mama," Doug said, remembering a long-ago conversation.

Mark regretted the questions he'd asked, for Doug's revelations made him a sympathetic character in the judge's eyes.

CHAPTER THIRTY-SEVEN

At attorney Mark Collins' request, the judge granted a fifteen-minute recess. In the hall, Max's attorney explained to Alex and Carol, and even Conner, that he needed to speak with Max and Anna alone. Then he ushered them to a private room and presented his assessment of the situation, as honestly as he could.

"Today, I'm sorry to say, hasn't gone as well as I hoped. Mrs. Anderson came across as a concerned, loving mother, and Judge Carter expressed admiration for her fiancé. The judge also seemed bothered that you would need to put your daughter in day care for the entire day, while her mother doesn't work outside the home. I know, I know," he said, showing Max his palms. "She would probably be in day care anyway. And there's nothing wrong with that. I'm just saying that could be a factor in the judge's decision."

Knowing he had a short time to make his point, Mark took a breath and soldiered on. "Now if you were married, Max, I believe you'd have a good chance of winning. But if you remain single, your chances of getting custody seem slim. I'm guessing the judge will recommend counseling for your ex-wife's new family. If he believes that will solve the problem, he may determine that spending time in a family environment would be in your daughter's best interest.

"I can't suggest you and Anna get married for the sake of the child. But I can say, if you were already planning to marry, doing it now could make all the difference. Today would be good. If you were to marry and it didn't work out, I'd advise you not to end it too soon. It couldn't look as if you married for the wrong reason."

Max took Anna's arm, gently leading her away. "What do you think?"

"About what?"

"About getting married—today. You heard what Mark said."

"But…"

Max spoke excitedly. "We could do it. It'd be great. Yeah, we'd be rushing things a bit, but we could definitely do it."

Puzzled, Anna asked, "Didn't we break up?"

Max smiled for the first time all day. "Nah. That was just a little tiff."

Anna rolled her eyes. "To you maybe."

Max kissed her lips lightly and said in a cajoling voice, "We've always loved each other. Haven't we?"

Anna had to admit they had, but she was troubled. "This is too fast. We don't have time to plan or talk about expectations."

"We'll wing it, figure it out as we go. We can do this, Anna. It'll be good."

This is crazy, she thought, but she and Max had an unspoken pact. When one of them was in trouble, the other stepped up to help. And what would happen to Gracie if Max didn't get custody? Anna understood that marrying under these circumstances would be complicated. And it wouldn't be a real marriage. She'd have to keep reminding herself of that.

To be joined with the man she loved and have that come to an end would be painful, but it would be preferable to subjecting little Gracie to a lifetime of Janine's neglect and poor decisions. Anna had survived devastation before. Maybe she could do it again.

She was only sixteen when Max destroyed her dreams by marrying Janine, and she wasn't much older when her mother died and left her alone. Anna had felt deserted, devastated. Now, she was a grown woman, stronger. Max might get custody without marrying, but there was a chance he wouldn't. It was a chance neither Max nor Anna was willing to take.

Anna sat with Max's parents in the courthouse hallway, while Max, Conner, and Mark strode toward the courtroom. "You can't let her do that," she heard Conner say to Mark. She glanced toward them to see an indignant expression on Conner's face. Max winked at her before walking through the courtroom doors.

Once court reconvened, the attorney revealed the upcoming nuptials to the judge. "I object," Janine yelled. "This is the first anyone has heard of this engagement. They're just saying that so Max will get custody. Those two will do anything for each other."

"Which is a component of a healthy marriage," the judge said. Then he asked Max's attorney, "Why is this the first I've heard about a marriage?"

Mark explained the couple had been keeping the engagement secret because of the paparazzi.

"Forgive me for not knowing, but why would the paparazzi be interested."

Janine grabbed her attorney's phone since she hadn't been allowed to bring hers into the courtroom and pulled up the offending blog. After scanning the tabloid article, her attorney quickly presented it to the judge. Max went pale.

"Your Honor," Max said. But the judge gave the signal for him to wait until he finished watching the video.

"Mr. Anderson, do you know what I just viewed?"

"Yes sir, I could hear some of it."

"Why were you out with these women if you're engaged to someone else?"

"That was a complete misunderstanding, Your Honor."

After Max explained he was telling the women he couldn't see them any longer, the judge said matter-of-factly, "That's not what it looks like." Max actually blushed. "What do you have to say about that, Mr. Anderson?"

"Many people, Your Honor, have expressed that opinion. My fiancé, members of my family, friends, acquaintances, and complete strangers on the web have informed me my communication style is inappropriate. I'm working on it."

"Good idea," the judge said, a hint of a smile appearing on his face. "Mr. Anderson, am I to understand your fiancé wrote a book that made her a target for the paparazzi? That seems very unusual for an author?"

315

"Anna wrote *A World Apart*," Max said, "a highly successful book that a production company is considering making into a movie. It is unusual for an author to have such notoriety, but Ellen DeGeneres liked the book and asked Anna to appear on her show. People liked her and other talk shows wanted her. I guess you could say she was a hit, so the tabloids became interested."

"Bailiff," the judge said, "I need to see Miss Robinson again." Judge Carter was deviating from normal hearing procedures, but as the presiding judge, that was his prerogative.

"I thought you looked familiar," he said to Anna when she returned to the courtroom. "My daughter is a fan. I think there are a couple of magazines lying around the house, permanently turned to your picture. And I saw you on television once. Thank you for representing our state so well." After asking Anna how she felt about being a stepmother, the judge called for a recess.

"This is a difficult case," he told the bailiff privately. "I don't have a strong feeling either direction. I need to talk with the child in my chambers. If I'm still not sure what to do, I'll observe her with each of her parents." The plan was a little unorthodox, but he was determined to make the best possible decision. Giving custody to the father could unjustly separate a mother from her child. But if he didn't, he could be putting a little girl in danger.

During the hearing, Gracie read books and enjoyed cookies and milk with Mrs. Dudley, the state-appointed child advocate. When notified, the woman took Gracie to the judge's chambers and settled her in one of the two leather chairs facing his desk. Mrs. Dudley sat unobtrusively in the back of the room.

316

After meeting the man who introduced himself as Judge Carter, Gracie immediately asked a question. "Hi. Where's your robe? The judges on television always wear robes and have a hammer so they can bang it on their desk." Judge Carter smiled, realizing he was about to have an interesting conversation with a bright child.

"I took my robe off, but I can put it back on if you like."

"No, sir, that's all right. You're probably more comfortable without it."

The judge grinned and began, "Gracie, do you know why you're here?"

"I know you want me to answer questions."

"That's right. Are you ready?"

"I am," she answered. "Daddy told me I might get to see you. He said I'll do fine."

"Did your daddy tell you anything else before you came today?"

She tapped her finger against her temple, thinking. "He said to answer the questions the bestest I could, but he knew I would do fine because I like to talk."

The judge didn't try to hide his smile. Summoning his most affable manner, he said, "I know sometimes you stay with your mom and sometimes with your dad. Tell me what you do when you stay with your mom?"

Gracie thought for a second. "I watch television and color or play with my dollhouse. And sometimes I read. I can read some words by myself now. But not everything."

"Is there something special you like to do with your mother?"

She thought about it. "Sometimes she reads me a story before I go to bed, but she's usually at Doug's house."

The judge wrote on his notepad. "And what do you do when you stay with your dad?" Gracie's face brightened. "We have fun. I help him cook, and we put big puzzles together, and Daddy reads to me and I read to him. My daddy's funny," Gracie volunteered, "and he loves me a lot. He tells me all the time."

"I'm sure your mama loves you too," coached the judge.

"I think she does," Gracie answered matter-of-factly. "But sometimes she forgets to say it."

Judge Carter wrote on his notepad again. "I see that you go to Miss Katie's school."

"I do," she exclaimed. "Who told you that?"

"A little bird." Gracie giggled. The judge continued with his questions. "Who takes you to school?"

"Daddy takes me when I stay with him, and Grandmother takes me when I'm at her house."

"Does your mother ever take you to school?"

"Sometimes, but she usually needs to sleep. She stays late at Doug's house and that makes her tired."

"Is Anna ever at your dad's house when you're there?"

"Sometimes she eats supper with us. Do you know Anna?"

"I've met her. Do you like for Anna to visit?"

"Oh, yes! She's the bestest, and she's my friend. We read books together. She's a li... I don't know the rest of that word, but it means she works in a liberry. But not right now."

The judge shifted to a more threatening topic. "Do you ever go to Doug's house with your mom?" Gracie's entire demeanor changed. She pulled her feet into the chair, making herself as small as possible. Shaking her head, she spoke almost in a whisper. "I don't want to go to that house again, not ever."

The judge gently persuaded Gracie to relate her version of the events involving Allen and Kevin McKinnon. With coaxing, she talked about how hard it was to breathe when the boys rolled her up in the rug and about how they tried to burn her up in the furniture and how hot she got. It was clear the events were harrowing experiences for the child. But when Judge Carter asked about the poison ivy incident, she curled her small body into a ball.

"Can you tell me what happened?" he asked again.

"Kevin and Allen want to kill me. I don't want to talk anymore. Where's my daddy?"

"You'll see him in a little while. I'm sorry I upset you, Gracie. You've been very brave to talk to me about Kevin and Allen."

From his conversation with Gracie, the judge gathered quite a bit of information about her relationship with her parents, but he wanted to see for himself how she interacted with them. Janine entered the room and sat in the chair the judge gestured to. She smiled at her daughter, who sat on the edge of the other chair, her little legs dangling, seeming to have recovered from the recent discussion about the twins.

"Hello, Judge," Janine said, "I hope Gracie has been behaving herself."

Judge Carter smiled at Gracie. "She's a lovely young lady." Getting down to business, he said, "We're here in my chambers, Mrs. Anderson, so I can get to know the parties involved on an informal basis. This may seem a little irregular, but I want you to ask Gracie a question. You choose the topic. Ask whatever you want, but it should require more than a yes or no answer."

Janine thought for a minute and then said, "I know you don't like going to Doug's house, Gracie, but the boys didn't realize you would react to the poison ivy the way you did. They got some on them, too. And did they ever complain!"

"A question," the judge reminded.

"Okay," she said slowly, trying to think of something. "You like Doug, don't you?"

"He's all right," Gracie said. "But I don't want to go to his house again. Kevin and Allen will hurt me. They hate me."

"They don't hate you sweetie."

"I want to stay with Daddy." Janine looked at the judge, trying to gauge his reaction.

"You need to learn to get along with the boys."

Gracie shook her head violently. "I want to stay with Daddy."

After Janine left the room, Max was called in. Gracie jumped out of her chair and ran to him. Max scooped her into his arms and stood, holding his daughter, until the judge indicated he should sit. He sat, situating Gracie in his lap. She cupped her hand around her father's ear and whispered.

"Okay," Max said. "Judge, we have a bit of an emergency. Is there a bathroom nearby that Gracie could use?"

"Of course. She can use mine. Its right through that door," Judge Carter said, gesturing.

After Gracie assured Max she could handle the task alone, he waited in his assigned chair.

The child returned to her father's lap. "I remembered to wash my hands."

"Good job. Now let's listen to Judge Carter." It was the first time, the judge noted, the child had looked completely relaxed since entering his chamber.

After hearing the same instructions his wife received, Max guessed the judge wanted to see how he and Gracie interacted. So he asked, "What have you been doing with Mrs. Dudley?"

Gracie was a chatterbox, describing the puzzle they worked on, what Mrs. Dudley was wearing, and what they ate. "Is Anna with you?"

"Not right now." He didn't think it was the time to talk about the upcoming ceremony.

"Aww."

After asking a few more questions, the judge thanked Max for his cooperation and nodded to Mrs. Dudley. "Gracie," the judge said, "I'd like you to spend a little more time with Mrs. Dudley while the adults talk. I enjoyed meeting you."

"I joyed meeting you, too. You're nicer than Judge Judy. She's kinda mean sometimes."

CHAPTER THIRTY-EIGHT

After the verdict was read and the hearing was adjourned, Conner pulled Max aside, explaining he needed to talk to him alone. "I apologize for my timing," he said. "I understand this is an important day for you, in many ways, but I have something to say, and I need to say it now."

"Shoot," Max said impatiently. "Anna and I need to get a marriage license and wedding rings. Judge Carter is marrying us at three."

"In that case, I'll be straightforward, no beating around the bush. You know Anna and I had an intimate relationship—in the past," Conner emphasized. "But first and foremost, I'm her friend. I always will be." The last part of that statement sounded like a warning, with a silent "and you better get used to it" tacked on the end.

Max stood quietly, his arms crossed over his chest, trying not to behave like the jealous lover he was. "Get to the point."

"Anna was a lost soul when I met her," Conner said. "Her only family was gone, and for a reason I've never understood, she pulled away from everyone in her past, people who could have helped her deal with her grief. I lived in the apartment above hers, and it took a Herculean effort to get to know her. She kept to herself, rarely said more than hello to anyone in the building, never dated, and had no close friends. She attended class, studied, and worked. Nothing else. She closed herself off from everyone. A misguided effort to protect herself, I presume."

Pleased he had Max's attention; Conner continued. "Even after we became friends, she didn't fully let her guard down. I was afraid she never would. Then she returned to Tenacity and reconnected with you. Talking with her on the phone, I could tell she was letting you in, allowing herself to be vulnerable, which is ironic since you..."

The normally articulate attorney searched for a way to say what needed to be said that wouldn't get him punched in the face. Coming up blank, he blurted it out. "I hate to lay this on you, especially today, but man, you crushed her."

Irritated that Conner presumed to know Anna better than he did, Max clenched his jaw. He would have walked away, if not for Conner's obvious concern and sincerity.

"Meeting your girlfriends," the young attorney said...

Max interrupted, "I wish everyone would stop calling them that."

"Call them what you want, but that really knocked Anna off balance. Her reaction scared me. That's why I rushed to Tenacity. If she erects that shield of hers again, I'm afraid it'll never come down. And that can't happen."

"I suppose you're going to tell me how to prevent that," Max said, with more than a little sarcasm.

"Give me a few more minutes. Listen to what I have to say. Then decide for yourself what you should or shouldn't do. Anna used to share stories about you and life in Tenacity, and her feelings were written all over her honest face. I knew from the start her heart belonged to you. But you weren't there. And I was."

Max really wanted to deck the blond pretty boy. He'd been itching to do it since first laying eyes on him, but knowing Conner was sincerely worried about Anna, he listened.

"The way I see it, you can resent my relationship with Anna, or you can thank me for being there when she needed someone. At first, we were only friends. Eventually, it became more. But we were never really committed to one another, at least not in the romantic sense."

Max really wanted this conversation to end. "Is there a point you're trying to make?"

"Let me finish. It's important." Max looked away, sighed, then looked back, his eyes narrowed. Conner correctly interpreted his reaction as, *I really hate this but go ahead.*

"I'm pretty sure she knew I saw other girls," Conner said, "and I don't think it really bothered her. She never said anything if it did. But from you, my friend, she needs commitment. If you can't give her that..." Conner stopped before completing the sentence. "She's waiting over there—yours for the taking. She always has been if you ask me. I can't tell you what to do, but I'm asking you not to hurt her. I'm truly afraid she might not recover. If you mess up, man, you're a damned idiot. And not that you care, but I'd never forgive you."

Conner shrugged. "I don't know what else to say. I'm out of my element here. Obviously, what you do is up to you and Anna, but I thought you should know what she went through when you weren't around and how important it is that you treat her with care."

Max took a breath and held it, before letting it go. "Okay. I hear you. Thank you for being her friend when she needed one. But you'll never be that kind of friend again. Understood?"

"Understood," Conner said, relieved to have finished the most difficult argument he'd ever presented.

After Max and Anna obtained a marriage license, Judge Carter married them in his chambers that very day. In attendance were Carol, Alex, Gracie, Mark Collins, and Conner, who promised not to interfere. Samantha arrived at the last minute, with a frazzled look on her face. It hadn't been easy, but she'd managed to get away from work for the occasion.

Max, his parents, Anna, and Gracie picked up fast food from a Dairy Queen near the courthouse and walked to a park. They ate at a picnic table under a large oak tree, while Max tried to think of the best way to tell Gracie what happened that day. He eased into the conversation by asking, "How did your visit with Judge Carter go?"

"It was all right. He was nicer than Judge Judy. And he didn't wear a robe. Why did he ask so many questions?"

Max glanced at Anna. Seeing the request for support in his eyes, she rested her hand on his leg. "Well, Max said, "he wanted to get to know you." After a pause, he added, "And he wanted to make sure he understood what Kevin and Allen did to you."

Gracie squished up her face. "Why did he want to know that?"

Max placed his hand over Anna's and squeezed, praying he'd find the right words. "It's like this. I don't want your mother to take you to Kevin and Allen's house anymore."

"Me neither," Gracie chimed in.

"Your mother sees things differently. After she marries Doug, she'll live with him. Because Allen and Kevin live there too, your mother believes all of you should learn to get along."

"No, Daddy. No. They're mean, and they'll hurt me. Don't make me go back to that house."

"Calm down, Gracie. You aren't going back there. I'm trying to explain. Because your mother and I couldn't agree, it was up to the judge to make the decision, and he believes it would be best for you to live with me."

"All the time?"

"Yes, but you'll still spend time with your mother."

Gracie sat thinking, then said, "Mother might be sad."

"I'm sure she will be." Max made a feeble effort to defend her. "You know your mother would never want you to get hurt. It's just that she believes Allen and Kevin won't bother you anymore."

"I understand," Gracie said, sounding quite adult. "Sometimes, when Mother doesn't like something, she pretends it away."

Max was amazed at his daughter's insight. "I know what you mean, smart girl. I know what you mean."

"Who's going to pick me up from school every day?"

"Anna's going to do that so you can leave day care earlier." That's one thing Max and Anna did talk about. Gracie would continue going to day care, to create undisturbed writing time. "Now that Anna and I are married, she'll live with us."

Anna made a mental note to discuss living arrangements. The renovation was almost complete, and she was anxious to occupy the entire house."

"Yay!" Gracie exclaimed, looking adoringly at her father.

"Do I have two mothers now?"

"Anna is your stepmother."

"Like in the Cinderella story." She grinned mischievously.

"Yes," Anna said, tickling the child and cackling like a witch, "and if you're not a good little girl, I'll turn you into a pumpkin."

"That's not what happens in the story," Gracie laughed. Everyone smiled at their easy interaction.

Carol spoke to the newlyweds. "Your dad and I have a wedding gift for you and Anna—a little bit of a honeymoon. We reserved a room for you at The Marguerite for the next three nights. Clarkston may not be your first choice for a honeymoon, but we thought it might do—under the circumstances. And you have a reservation at the hotel dining room for seven o'clock tomorrow night. Order what you like. It's our treat. Gracie can stay with us. She has play clothes at the house, and if she needs anything else, we'll go shopping."

"What a hardship!" Max teased. "I know how the two of you hate to shop."

"No, Daddy. We like to shop. It's fun."

"If you say so." With a genuine smile on his face, Max thanked his parents. Anna was still a little stunned about everything that was happening. After a quick trip to Tenacity for things they needed, they checked into the hotel. *Max is acting like we've been planning this marriage for years,* Anna thought, *instead of hours.*

She glanced at the gold wedding band they'd hurriedly purchased that afternoon and wondered what Max expected from their honeymoon. His kiss, only steps away from the hotel desk, answered her question.

Anna was conflicted. She loved Max. There was no question about that. And he was the most handsome man she knew, except maybe for Conner. But Conner never bewitched her the way Max did. Her attraction to the man she just married was so strong, she wondered if some magical force propelled her toward him.

On the other hand, she wasn't completely over what Max referred to as a little tiff. At least he'd somewhat admitted his behavior with the women on the video was inappropriate.

That night, after a long day in the courtroom, they enjoyed a superb meal with good wine and avoided talking about the things they needed to discuss. After dinner, they strolled hand in hand along the river walk, stopping here and there to share a kiss. It had been a couple of months since they'd had sex, and by the time they reached the hotel, their anticipation had approached a pinnacle. The moment the door of their room closed behind them, they began stripping off their clothes.

After falling into the large, multi-pillowed bed, Anna basked in the feel of the man looming over her; his scent, his hard body against her softer one, his hands and lips on her skin. Anna had missed their intimacy, their passion. She'd missed Max. They'd seen each other often, but they'd been distracted by the custody hearing, Janine's scheming, and Anna's mistrust after the Fourth of July party.

Lingering in the afterglow of mind-blowing sex, Anna chuckled softly. "I wonder how many couples have honeymoon-sex that doubles as make-up sex."

Max propped on one elbow, his impressive chest on display. "Have we made up? Have you forgiven me for, for…?" Finally, he settled on the word "everything."

"Yeah," she said sweetly. "That's behind us. We have other things to think about now."

The newly married couple may have thought about other things, but they didn't discuss them. They swam, took walks, and made love, avoiding any topic that might disturb the sweet cocoon they'd wrapped around themselves.

Their second morning at the hotel, Anna finally picked up her phone. Seeing Samantha had phoned several times, she reluctantly called her back. As expected, her friend didn't mince words. "What in the world do you think you're doing?"

"Max and I got married."

"I know that, and I said nothing at the courthouse, just as you instructed. Now I'm asking, "How can you be broken up one minute and married the next?"

"We made up."

"I'll say. Do you know what you're doing?"

"Probably not, but the honeymoon sure is fun." Max came out of the bathroom with a crooked grin on his face. Obviously, he'd been listening.

"I can see," Samantha said, "you're in no mood to share. But I expect a full explanation when you return."

CHAPTER THIRTY-NINE

The first few weeks of Max and Anna's marriage were spent in Max's home, but knowing how Anna anticipated the completion of her own, Max insisted they shift houses as soon as it was finished. The renovated home was beautiful. Fred and his crew did an outstanding job. Max didn't know who was more excited about the move, Anna or Gracie.

Anna found it thrilling to see her ideas transformed into reality. She'd planned every detail, often when she should have been sleeping, and worked with Fred every step of the way. She'd selected appliances, banister styles, baseboards, crown moldings, tiles, bathroom fixtures, light fixtures, cabinets, cabinet hardware, and much more.

When Anna planned the renovation, she thought she'd be living alone. Rooms were repurposed and walls taken out, leaving her with only two bedrooms, one of which was in the attic.

Max insisted he and Anna take the sound-proofed master bedroom on the ground floor, which left the attic room for Gracie. The room was great, with a sitting area and a private bath, but Anna was afraid Gracie would feel insecure so far from the adults. So she pondered the situation and came up with a solution. She would get Gracie a roommate.

She drove to a large metal building about an hour away and told the attendant at the no-kill shelter she was looking for a small to medium-sized dog.

"Before we look at the smaller dogs," the woman said, "I want you to see one that was brought in yesterday afternoon, a real sweetheart. The groomer just arrived to clean her up. She's skin and bones, filthy, a real mess. But with love and care, she'll be beautiful.

"She's been living in the woods near a gas station, which makes me think a traveler lost her. Judging from how thin she is and the condition of her coat, I'd say she's been on her own for quite a while. She's so matted that we'll have to shave her. There's no chip, and I've checked all the lost dog sites. If someone was looking for her, they've given up."

After taking Anna to the grooming room, the woman left to take care of another prospective adopter.

"What breed do you think she is?" Anna asked the groomer.

"Hard to say for sure with her coat so matted, but she's probably part poodle. That breed mats badly if not groomed. She may be one of those designer dogs. It's popular these days to mate different breeds to poodles.

"I'd take this one home myself if I didn't already have so many. She's well-mannered and appreciates everything we do for her. I'd bet money she once lived in a loving home."

Before the groomer turned on the clippers, Anna stooped beside the dog. "Hello, darling. What happened to you?" The dog slowly wagged her tail and tentatively licked Anna's hand. When the matted animal looked up at her with intelligent, soulful eyes, Anna knew she wouldn't be leaving without the skinny, dirty dog.

"I like her. May I stay until you've finished?" She wouldn't take a chance on someone else getting this dog. She watched the groomer shave the entire animal, leaving as much hair as he could on her head and ears. The dog stood unflinching, enduring the ordeal like a pro. Clearly, this wasn't her first grooming experience.

The volunteer was impressed when she returned and observed the dog's dignified demeanor. "That's one classy lady," she commented. "We have an on-call vet who can check her out and give the required shots if you want to take her home." Smiling at Anna, she said, "I know love when I see it." Noticing the way the dog watched Anna, she added, "And it appears the feeling is mutual."

Regulations say we have to keep her for five days, in case an owner comes to claim her, but you can foster her for that time period, assuming you meet the requirements. On the sixth day, she'll be yours. You'll be required to have her spayed, but I'll be surprised if this one hasn't already had that done."

The groomer spoke up. "No problem there. I saw the scar when I shaved her belly."

"Let's do it," Anna said. "I think the abandoned lady and I are meant for one another."

When Anna returned from completing the paperwork, her clean, wet dog was sprinting around the grassy area behind the shelter, drying her short white hair. Seeing Anna, the dog ran straight to her. Instead of jumping, she sat, waiting for instructions.

When Anna pulled up to Gracie's day care with a large dog in the back seat, the child's eyes got big as saucers. "Go ahead and get in," Anna said. "She's gentle."

But Gracie stood in place, stunned. "Is that a dog?"

"Gracie, meet Classy Lady—Classy for short."

"She's big," Gracie said. "Who does she belong to?"

"Well, she's agreed to be my friend, and she'll be yours too if you like. She's going to live with us. Try to move a little faster, sweetie. There's a line of cars behind us. Classy might lick you, but she won't hurt you." Anna held the dog's collar while a day care worker helped Gracie get situated in her booster seat.

The child couldn't stop staring at the big white dog. "She doesn't have much hair."

"She will. It'll grow. Her hair was so matted that the groomer had to shave her. Go ahead. Pet her. She likes it." A minute later, Gracie giggled, and Anna knew the child and dog were bonding. *That didn't take long.*

When Max came home to the recently renovated house, Gracie rushed to him. "You won't believe it, Daddy. We have a dog!"

Max did a double take when he saw the large animal. "Anna, what happened? I thought you were going to get a small dog."

She dried her hands on a dishtowel and moved from the kitchen portion of the room to the living area. "I did, too, but this one wanted to come home with me."

"Told you that, did she?"

"Yep. It was love at first sight. Max, meet Classy. Shake his hand, Classy." The dog walked to him, sat regally, and offered a paw in greeting."

"What the? You taught her that today?"

"She already knew. Must have had a good home once. Her manners are impeccable."

Max shook Classy's paw. "What is she?"

"Probably a standard poodle mix. She's sweet, young, well-trained, and won't shed. What more can you ask? We'll have to have her groomed though."

"Where did you get her name?"

"A woman at the shelter called her a Classy Lady, and I thought it fit."

When Max moved to pick Gracie up, Classy calmly stepped between them. When he moved to get around the dog, she stood between them again.

"Anna, look at this. The dog doesn't want me to go near Gracie."

"Aww. She's being protective." When Anna told Classy it was okay, the dog moved away.

"Well, I'll be," Max said. "I think she's assumed the role of Gracie's protector. I can't fault her for that."

When Gracie became preoccupied with Classy, Max pulled Anna close and kissed her. Real or not, their life together was good. She was Max's wife, living in her childhood home with the man she adored, and they had a lovely little girl and a big white dog.

Being Max's wife was everything she could imagine. Their nights were filled with passion, and their time spent as a family was joyous. All she had to do was forget that Max only married her to get custody of his daughter and that her perfect life had an unknown expiration date.

A few weeks later, Anna was leaving Mayfield's Grocery when she encountered Janine and the twins on the sidewalk. "Is that your dog," one of the boys asked. "Can we pet it?"

"You'll have to ask her," Anna said. The twins looked puzzled but stooped to talk to the dog. Classy stood, letting them know who was boss, and allowed the petting.

"What kind is she?" Janine asked.

"Maybe I'll have a good answer to that question when Classy's hair grows. The vet thinks one parent was probably a Standard Poodle, but the other is a mystery."

"Whatever it was, it must have been big, Janine said. She was trying to make polite conversation but was obviously frazzled.

"Is something wrong?" Anna found herself asking.

"Kevin has a counseling session this afternoon, and I don't have a place for Allen to stay. Day care won't be open long enough since we have to drive almost an hour each way. I guess I'll have to cancel."

"Your parents can't keep him?"

Janine shook her head.

"How about Deborah, who works mornings at the day care center?"

"Tried. I've tried everyone I can think of."

Not wanting Kevin to miss his appointment, Anna said, "I have a rather bizarre idea, and it's a long shot at that. But if Gracie agrees, and only if Gracie agrees, maybe I could watch him. She feels safe with Classy at her side, and since it'll only be one of the boys, it's possible she'll give her consent."

When Anna picked Gracie up from day care, she explained the situation. "It's important that the boys see the counselor. He's trying to teach them to behave properly. But if it makes you uncomfortable to have one of them in our home, I'll tell your mother we can't do it."

"Will you and Classy be there?" Gracie asked.

"Of course."

"Okay," she said. "I want the boys to behave better."

Max isn't going to like this, Anna thought. *Not at all.*

CHAPTER FORTY

Janine escorted Allen to Anna's door, thanked her for the favor, then hurried to the car where Kevin waited. Looking around, Allen said, "Wow, this looks like something in a magazine. I like it." Charmed, Anna reminded herself this was one of the little boys who treated Gracie so cruelly.

She immediately explained the rules to Allen. "Stay in this room unless I say otherwise. Be nice to Gracie, and keep your hands to yourself. And don't pet Classy without asking. She doesn't know if she can trust you yet. You'll have to prove to her that she can."

"Will she bite?" Allen asked.

"If someone tries to hurt Gracie, I think she will."

The afternoon went better than expected. They baked cookies and homemade dog biscuits, and Anna read a book with a child on each side of her. Allen clearly loved the attention and behaved well. It was hard to imagine this innocent-looking child hurting anyone, and Anna wondered if his twin was the troublemaker.

The kids were in the kitchen watching Anna chop supper vegetables when Max walked in. Anna knew he wouldn't be thrilled to see Allen, but she hadn't expected the fury she saw in his eyes. After sending Anna an accusing look, he rushed toward Gracie, intending to scoop her into his arms.

Maybe Classy saw the look in Max's eyes, or maybe she sensed his anger, but for some reason, she took a protective stance in front of Gracie and growled. Anna watched Max clench his jaw and curl his hands into fists. Then he plopped onto the sofa, leaned his head back, and closed his eyes. "I guess I am a little out of control," he said, accepting the beer Anna thrust toward him.

Allen stood nearby, watching. "Allen," Anna said after Max settled down, "you need to tell Gracie's dad what you told her. And remember, no excuses. Accept responsibility for what you did." Allen looked at the floor. "No, look at Gracie's dad. You can do this, Allen."

The boy swallowed hard, looked at Max's angry face, and soldiered on. "I'm sorry me and Kevin hurt Gracie."

When Max said nothing, Anna suggested Allen read some of Gracie's books, while the adults talked.

"What are you doing Anna?" Max asked. "Playing psychiatrist? You know how I feel about those boys."

"Would you like to know what happened?" Lowering her voice, Anna related the events of the afternoon. "I thought it was important for Kevin to keep the appointment."

Max shook his head in disbelief. "You're being played, purposely avoiding speaking Janine's name in front of the children.

"Why would she do that?" When Max sent her a disbelieving look, she whispered, "You think she's trying to cause trouble between us? I really don't think that was it." Max looked at the ceiling, asking for divine intervention.

"Well, I do," he said, "and it worked."

"Don't be angry. It turned out well. Allen," she said in a louder voice, "tell Mr. Anderson what we did today."

Allen was hesitant but did as Anna asked. "We ate cookies that didn't come from a bag, and they were really good. Me and Gracie helped make them. At our house, cookies come in a bag. We made different cookies for Classy. I didn't pet her today, 'cause she was guarding Gracie. I wish we had a dog. Buddy came to our house one time, but he didn't stay."

"Wonder why," Max muttered under his breath.

"Thank you, Allen," Anna said. "That was nice."

The boy looked at her with sad eyes and asked, "Can I pet Classy before I leave?"

"Yes, but not yet."

Max sighed. "I'm taking Gracie and going to the other house."

"Janine will be here soon. Don't you want to stay and let Gracie spend a minute with her mother?"

"No."

Before Max could get off the sofa, Janine came to the door. When she saw her daughter, she knelt on the floor and held out her arms. "Baby. Gracie baby. I miss you." She kissed her daughter over and over.

Classy stood close while mother and daughter embraced. "I miss you too, Mother." Max almost felt guilty for not allowing them more time together, but then reminded himself that Janine couldn't be trusted.

The judge allowed Janine two, three-hour visits and one, four-hour visit per week, to be supervised by her parents. Anything more than that was up to Max.

Allen stood alone, watching his future stepmother hug her daughter. When Anna put her hand on his shoulder, he moved closer, and Max might have let his heart melt toward the boy just a fraction. After mother and daughter visited briefly, Max told Gracie it was time to go.

"Where are we going?"

"Out."

Gracie hugged her mother again, patted Classy, and told Allen good-bye, which surprised Max. "Anna, aren't you coming?" Gracie asked.

"She has something else to do." Max grasped his daughter's hand and tugged her toward the porch.

On her way out the door, she looked back. "Remember, Anna, you told Allen he could pet Classy."

"I'll pick up supper," Max dispassionately called over his shoulder, leaving his wife and ex-wife with the demon child.

When Max and Gracie returned, Gracie ran into the house before her dad. "We got fish from Lucky's," she yelled, "and I got to pet the bunnies." Anna walked quietly from the bedroom, not looking at Max, knowing she'd unsettled their precarious imitation of the perfect life.

After they both told Gracie good night, Anna said, "Max, we need to talk."

"If you say so." He sat in a chair instead of on the sofa with his wife and waited for her to speak.

"I know you think I was wrong to keep Allen today, but Gracie agreed to it, and it was good. He was well-behaved. Gracie was a little guarded at first, but she didn't seem afraid. She took a big step today toward overcoming her fears."

"Ever hear that fear is a biological reaction to a dangerous situation?"

"Yes, but today's situation wasn't dangerous. I never let Gracie or Allen out of my sight."

"How can you even use those two names in the same sentence? You saw what they did to her."

"I know. But maybe we can help the boys learn to behave in more acceptable ways."

Max stood and started to pace. "Do you hear yourself? You want to help the little monsters who terrorized Gracie. They could have killed her. Have you forgotten that?"

Anna followed Max as he paced. "Of course not. But Gracie lives in the same town as the twins and won't be able to avoid them forever. Maybe, by providing a safe environment for the children to interact, they can learn to treat each other with respect—with proper direction, of course. Heaven knows, they need all the help they can get."

Max decided to sit again, so Anna returned to the couch. "I had a thought today," she said, then held her hands up in a stop gesture. "I know this will sound like I'm playing psychiatrist, but I'm going to say it anyway. Maybe the twins were motivated by jealousy. That's obviously no excuse for what they did. But they've never had a mother, at least not one they remember, and when they're about to get one, they discover a pretty little girl already has a claim on her. Allen seemed starved for my attention this afternoon." On a roll, Anna spewed out her plans. "I want to keep Kevin when Janine takes Allen to his session."

Max glared at her. "Then I'll find someone else to watch Gracie."

"That will defeat the purpose. They need to be in the same room. Talk to your daughter. If she says she was afraid today, I'll tell Janine to try to find someone else. But I think today was good for Gracie."

"All right. I'll talk to her if it'll make you happy. But Anna, you're overstepping. You had no business doing what you did today without checking with me. I'm Gracie's father. I have custody, and I'm the one who makes the decisions regarding her welfare." His statement was a punch to the gut, and Anna's expression reflected it.

With tears flowing down her face, Anna whisper-shouted so she wouldn't wake Gracie, "You better make sure you explain that to the next woman you consider making your wife."

Anna knew she was being overly dramatic, but she felt hurt. And angry. And abandoned. Her voice grew louder, more insistent. "I'm all too aware I have no claim on your daughter. And to make sure I wouldn't forget, you just made that perfectly clear. But you need to be aware of a few things, too. You can try to shield your daughter from life's challenges, from the influence of others, but you won't be doing her any favors. And if you discourage her from having a relationship with her mother, there'll come a day when you'll be sorry. That's all I have to say. I'll be in my office," she said, leaving the room.

Max buried his face in his hands, wondering what just happened. What did Anna mean about his next wife? He took a shower and thought about what they'd both said. After drying off, he slipped into a pair of drawstring pants and a t-shirt and knocked on Anna's office door.

When she opened it, her eyes were red from crying, and Max immediately pulled her into his arms. "Let's talk," he said, leading her toward the bedroom.

"No, the living room," she insisted. He looked and smelled too good for a conversation in the bedroom.

Sitting on the sofa next to the woman he married, Max took both her hands in his. "I'm sorry, Anna. It's just that seeing one of those boys in this house with Gracie was a surprise and a hard pill to swallow. I shouldn't have gotten so angry."

He looked at their joined hands before meeting her eyes. "I'm sorry I said what I did about making decisions for Gracie. You certainly have the right to an opinion about her welfare. I'm used to making decisions on my own. So are you. We both have some adjusting to do." She'd give him that. She hadn't consulted him before agreeing to help Janine. But that had been a conscious decision. She knew he'd disapprove.

Max cocked his head and smiled. "Can you forgive me?" Anna said nothing. "Just know I'm sorry, and I'll try to do better. And that's the last I want to hear about another wife."

Max kissed her and led her to the bedroom. This time, she didn't resist. After he apologized with words, he apologized with his body. He made love so tenderly, so sweetly, Anna believed she was the only woman he'd ever want, and the two of them would live happily ever after. In Max's arms, the world was a perfect place. If only that feeling could last.

At the custody hearing, Judge Carter saw that the McKinnon family desperately needed professional help. He mandated counseling, hoping it could save the family and prevent a permanent rift between mother and daughter. Two afternoons a week, Anna kept one of the boys, while the other attended his session. Doug and Janine also saw the counselor and seemed grateful for the opportunity.

Surprisingly, Max never again mentioned leaving Gracie with someone else, nor did he complain about finding one of the twins in the house when he came home. Anna knew he didn't like it, but he accepted it. Gracie must have given the arrangement her approval.

One afternoon, when picking up one of the boys, Janine asked, "Anna, do you have a minute to talk?" As usual, she'd left the other twin with her mother. Max might allow Gracie to interact with one of the boys, but never both.

"Sure," Anna said, wondering what was on Janine's mind. "Let's go to the backyard so the kids can play on the swing. That'll give us some distance while we're keeping an eye on them. Classy." The dog came quickly, looked up, and waited for instructions. "Watch Gracie," Anna instructed. Classy ran toward the children and sat, watching.

"That dog is amazing," Janine said. "She acts like she knows exactly what you're saying."

"I think she does. It's like she's possessed by some intelligent, benevolent spirit, sent to watch over us. Now what is it you want to talk about?"

Max walked in about that time and stood in the hallway, watching the children and Classy. Then he heard Janine ask, "Why are you doing this, Anna? I've given you every reason to hate me, yet you're helping when others won't. Why?"

"Because I love Gracie and Max," Anna said without hesitation. She paused to gather her thoughts. "First, I have to tell you, I believe the custody arrangement is exactly as it should be. I'm not suggesting anything else.

"Your actions and the boys' treatment of Gracie have had some undesirable consequences beyond the obvious. Max can't seem to get over his anger about what happened, and at times, Gracie is more fearful than a little girl should be. I want Max to be happy again and Gracie to be the confident child I first met. She's getting there.

"And I want you to have a healthy relationship with your daughter because Gracie needs that. I also hope your relationship with Doug works out. All those things have a common denominator. They all hinge on the twins learning to behave properly. Think about it. Max's anger, Gracie's confidence, your relationship with your daughter and with Doug. All those issues are affected by the twins' behavior.

"I want those boys to become kind, considerate men of good character. I know there's goodness in them. I see it. But right now, they're heading down the wrong path. They need to experience the gratification of treating others with kindness." Anna looked down at her hands. "I'm sorry. I didn't intend to preach a sermon."

"No, that's all right. I asked." Janine appeared pensive, then decided to entrust Anna with some of her most private thoughts. "You know, this custody thing was inevitable. From the start, it was the two of them—Max and Gracie. When she was born, I was still a child myself. I'd never been around children and had no idea what to do with such a tiny, fragile human. What if I did the wrong thing and hurt her?"

Anna was surprised at the turn of the conversation and that Janine was confiding in her. But that's what was happening, so she listened. Maybe the counseling sessions were responsible for the change.

"Max wasn't any older than I was," Janine continued, "and I don't think he had any more experience with children than I did. But somehow, he always knew what to do. Gracie would be this red-faced little goblin, screaming her head off, and nothing I did would help. But the minute Max took her in his arms, she transformed into a cooing, contented little cherub."

Janine shrugged. "I felt extraneous, an outsider, and finally I gave up. Really, I turned Gracie over to Max a long time ago, but I keep trying to be part of her life. I know Max doesn't believe it, but I love Gracie. I mean, she grew inside me. You know? I'm her mother."

Janine blinked back tears. "I don't know where we go from here. I want a relationship with my daughter, but I also want a life with Doug. He wants that, too. We know the odds are stacked against us, but we're not giving up. What you're doing for us really helps. Thank you."

Wow! Anna thought. *Am I in some alternate universe? This is an entirely different Janine.* Anna knew the woman was a master manipulator, but for some reason, she took the disclosure at face value. Janine was hard to unscramble, but Anna believed there was a side to her Max had no idea existed.

Anna waited until Gracie was playing in her room to present her plan to Max. Not sure if it was valiant or foolhardy, she forged ahead. "I want to have a cookout in the backyard...with you, Gracie, Janine, Doug, and the boys." She rushed to say, "I'm not suggesting you forgive Janine or let Gracie go to Doug's or anything of the sort. I just think it would be good for Gracie to see her parents attempting to get along. And you'll be there to set Allen and Kevin straight if they start to misbehave."

Anna steeled herself for his reply. He'd probably refuse any such interaction, but she had to try. Her time with Max and Gracie was growing short. He was spending more and more time away from home and was preoccupied and secretive. Anna could read between the lines. She had to help before it was too late.

Max surprised Anna by agreeing to the picnic. He wasn't happy about it, but he agreed. She invited Samantha and Conner to round out the group, and at the last-minute thought to invite Miss Sweet, who was thrilled to be included.

Max never revealed he'd heard Anna's conversation with his ex-wife. Not only was he surprised at what Janine had said, he was touched by Anna's words and impressed by her grasp of the situation.

She'd gotten to the core of some complicated issues and translated them into one goal, even if it was an

348

ambitious one. He wasn't happy about the role she expected Gracie to play in achieving that goal, but now he understood his wife's motivation. So as long as his daughter was safe, he'd try to go along with Anna's plans.

The day of the cookout was the first time Anna observed Kevin and Allen together. What a difference! Each of them was cooperative and mannerly without the other. But together, they were rowdy, tussling, rolling-on-the-ground boys. When they wrestled and pounded each other, Doug ignored them. Classy, however, barked her displeasure.

"Kevin, Allen," Anna yelled, "you're upsetting Classy. You need to settle down." When they didn't, she yelled, "Now!" Everyone turned to look at her, and Max couldn't stifle his smile. Anna began spouting orders. "Kevin, get the paper plates from the kitchen and put them on the serving table. Allen, you get the napkins. Gracie, make sure they know where to put them." Anna kept finding things for them to do, which she could have done much more easily, but the children enjoyed the responsibility and it kept them out of trouble.

After Janine, Doug, and the twins went home, Max came up behind Anna and wrapped his arms around her. Nuzzling her neck, he said, "You did good today. The party wasn't half bad, thanks to your hard work. I appreciate all you did to keep the boys under control."

She turned and looked at him with wide eyes. "Who are you, and what did you do with Max?" He just gave her his sexiest smile.

Both Conner and Samantha stayed to help clean up, which Anna appreciated. Miss Sweet offered, but seeing how tired she looked, Max talked her into letting him walk her home. Anna was tired, too. Entertaining one of the twins was nothing compared to watching them both. Their energy was exhausting. Now she knew why Doug was prone to ignoring the boys. It was purely self-preservation.

CHAPTER FORTY-ONE

Before Conner and Samantha left, there was a knock on the door. "Come in, Angela," Anna said.

Angela looked around. "I'm sorry. I didn't realize you had company. There are extra cars parked next door, but not here."

"It's confusing," Anna said. "We use this house, but the other driveway comes in handy. Stay. You know everyone except Conner. Angela Bryant, meet Conner Wilmington. Conner's an attorney in Clarkston and has been my friend for many years. Angela is our local librarian. When I cancelled my old answering service account, she agreed to handle my fan mail and the website."

"That's why I'm here," Angela said. "I found something I think you should see, but maybe I should tell you about it another time."

"These are my best friends. They can hear whatever you have to say."

"All right. I told you your old answering service sent a box of letters from people claiming to be related to you. I planned to throw them away, like you asked me to, but I couldn't resist looking through them first. I found this."

She handed Anna a photo that looked astonishingly like the young author. "The man who sent this said it's a picture of his mother when she was in her twenties. He thinks she might be your father's sister. He goes on to say that the wife of the man he thinks is your father disappeared with their two-year-old daughter during a custody battle. The woman looks so much like you, I had to show you."

When the picture was passed around, everyone was amazed at the resemblance. "You should follow up on this, Anna," Conner said.

Anna shook her head and held up her hands, palms toward her friends, as if that would stop the discussion. "I should never have told that reporter about my background. After that article was published, letters poured in. I hired someone to look into the most promising ones.

"Some letter writers were people who liked my book and only wanted to meet me. Others had sinister intentions if my investigator was correct. Thank goodness, I had the good sense not to try to meet any of them. Many of the letters were sad, from people legitimately looking for lost loved ones. But there were too many. I gave up the search and asked my answering service to throw away letters from people claiming to be related. I'm surprised they didn't follow my instructions."

"I agree with Conner," Max said. "We should look into this. I can't believe how much this woman looks like you. The man who wrote the letter—where's he from?"

"The return address is Savannah, Georgia," Angela told him.

"That's where I'm from," Conner said. "What's this guy's name?"

"Steven Stewart."

Conner looked astonished. "I think I know the family. If it's the Steven I'm thinking of, his mother was a Fairchild. His grandfather was, maybe still is, a judge, and the judge's wife is a society fundraiser type. She and my mother have probably served on some committee or board together. If you like, I'll call and see if she knows anything."

"Do it now," Samantha urged. "I can't wait."

"I'll try. If she's busy, she won't answer. If she answers, the call may take a while. I'll go out back so I don't bore you with the requisite mother-son talk. When my mother gets me on the phone, she won't let me go until I tell her what I've done every day since we last talked. It takes a while to fabricate that many G-rated stories."

Angela offered to leave, thinking she might be intruding on a private moment, but Anna insisted she stay. "You started this; you can stay to see it unfold."

They heard Conner say, "Hi, Mom," as he walked into the backyard and closed the door. Anna busied herself with pouring coffee and offering cookies, while the group waited impatiently. When Conner walked back inside, he joked, "For some reason, I feel like people are staring at me."

"People always stare at you," Anna quipped, "and you know it. Quit stalling and spill."

He smirked because she was right. "Well," Conner began, "Mom has heard a story, but, of course, it's only gossip."

Samantha was almost bouncing in her chair. "Don't keep us waiting. Talk," she demanded.

Conner smiled at her exuberance and glanced at the paper in his hand. "I can't believe Mom remembered all these names. I had to write them down. According to the high matron of the Savannah grapevine, otherwise known as my mother, the letter-writer's mother is the daughter of Sinclair and Elenora Fairchild.

"I remember meeting them at an event in our home. They're a formidable looking pair. He's a big guy with a past-his-prime belly. She's tall and slender and looks like it might hurt her to smile. Elenora and Sinclair had two children, the letter-writer's mother, whose name is Anna Sue, and Anna Sue's older brother, Charles.

"According to Mom, Charles married a girl his parents considered beneath him because her family lacked money and prestige. Charles and his wife had a child. Mom thinks there was a divorce, but she doesn't know what happened to the wife and child."

"Did she remember the woman's name?" Anna asked.

"Sorry. She didn't. But I think you should look into this."

"I've always wanted to see Savannah," Max lied, "and it's time we took a vacation."

"I don't know," Anna said. "I'm not sure."

"What?" everyone said in unison.

Samantha couldn't believe it. "You've always wondered about your background. This is a chance to learn your mother's big secret. You have to pursue it."

Max agreed. "Conner, would you feel comfortable calling this Steven guy, make sure he's the person you think he is? You could explain the situation at our end and see what he has to say."

"Sure. I'll try him tonight. It shouldn't be hard to get his number."

Things were moving fast, but Anna drifted with the current. When Conner called the following evening, Anna put him on speaker so Max could hear.

"He's the person I thought he was," Conner said. "I think the three of us should go to Savannah. I know the town, and I've met Steven. I need to visit home anyway. You and Max can stay with my family. It's a big house, and they'd love to have you. Just let me know when you're ready."

Max would have declined Conner's offer, but Anna accepted before he got the words out of his mouth. And he had to admit, Conner might come in handy.

The following weekend, with Gracie and her four-legged shadow safely settled at her Mimi and Paw Paw's, Conner, Max, and an extremely nervous Anna sat on a plane headed to Savannah. Max held his wife's hand and talked more than usual, trying to keep her mind off what was to come.

After getting settled in the beautiful old Wilmington home in Savannah's historic district, Conner's dad treated them all to dinner at a charming restaurant near the river.

"How lucky you were," Anna said to Conner, "to have grown up in this gorgeous town."

"If your mother hadn't disappeared with you," Max said to Anna. "You might have grown up here as well."

Anna smiled at her husband. "It's beautiful here among the historic mansions and moss-hung oaks, but I wouldn't trade my childhood in Tenacity for anything."

Max took her hand in his. "As far as I'm concerned, you landed in exactly the right place."

This feels like we're a real couple, Anna thought, reminding herself not to fall more deeply in love with her husband.

The following day, Conner, Anna, and Max waited for Steven and his mother at a restaurant on River Street. Watching the front door, Anna said, "I'm so nervous I could jump out of my skin." Holding her hand, Max pulled his wife close, hoping to comfort her.

She was looking at Max when Steven Stewart and his mother, Anna Sue, approached the table. They greeted Anna so warmly and seemed so genuinely glad to meet her that she felt better instantly. As the new arrivals situated themselves at the table, everyone noticed the strong resemblance between Anna and Anna Sue Stewart. The woman was older now than in the picture, but the resemblance was still uncanny.

After placing their lunch orders, Steven and his mother listed the players in the family drama and explained that Anna's father was out of the country. "We wanted to meet you first, anyway," Mrs. Stewart said.

"Because we're nicer," Steven joked. When Anna Sue gave him the mother-look, Steven said, "Well, it's true."

Anna Sue explained. "My parents are stern, proper sorts, and they think your father can do no wrong. But the truth is, he treated your mother poorly. He was openly unfaithful and expected Olivia to grin and bear it. He's grown up a lot since then."

"Olivia?"

"Yes. If our assumptions are correct, your mother was born Olivia Felder. She was my good friend. That's how Charles met her. I'd hoped to see her again someday. It breaks my heart that she's no longer with us."

Anna thanked her and then asked, "Were you still close when she left?"

"We were. I loved you and your mother. I hated to lose you both. But I don't blame Olivia for leaving."

"Do you think she named me after you?

"I'd like to think so. She gave you that name after she left. When you were born, my mother insisted they name you Rebecca, after her mother, and Charles went along with it."

"Whoa," Anna said. "When we learned about you, I realized my last name had been changed, but knowing my first name was changed, too, is kind of a shock." Anna hesitated before saying, "I need to ask you something."

"All right." Anna Sue could see her niece had something weighty on her mind.

"I understand why Mom took me and left. But why do you think she refused to tell me about my family when I was older? I don't understand why she kept me from you."

"I don't know." Then Anna Sue gave the question more thought and shrugged. "Maybe she was concerned about how you'd react. Or more likely, she dreaded facing Charles and my parents."

"She could have been afraid of facing charges and going to jail," Conner added. "Taking you the way she did was illegal, and she must have broken several laws to change your identities."

The group talked through lunch, continuing the conversation over coffee. Anna and the Stewarts filled in one another's information gaps, speculated on the likelihood of their suppositions, and began the process of getting to know one another.

Finally, Anna Sue brought up a subject she hoped wouldn't spoil the rapport they were establishing. "Have you thought about having a DNA test done? It would tell us if our conjecture is true. I took the liberty of making arrangements at a near-by medical facility if that's something you'd like to do. But only if you want to. No pressure."

Conner's mother met them at the door, anxious to know what happened. "They were nice," Anna shared. "And we had a DNA test done. Of course, we won't know the results for weeks."

"What's your impression?" Mrs. Wilmington asked. "Do you think they're your family?"

"It certainly seems so. My resemblance to Mrs. Stewart is strong, and she gave me copies of photographs." Anna took the pictures from her purse and handed them to Conner's mother. "If she's right, they're pictures of my mother and me with my father. The woman could be my mother, but I've never seen a picture of her at that age, and the photos were taken from a distance. The Fairchilds have other pictures, but Mrs. Stewart, Anna Sue, only has these. The baby could be any baby. My coloring is more like the man's than my mother's, and I could have gotten my height from him, but I'm trying not to jump to conclusions."

"Would you like them to be your family?"

"It would be a relief to know where I came from. I've imagined all sorts of things through the years. And it would be nice to have relatives, even if we're not close."

Knowing his mother was desperate to know everything, Conner filled her in. "Charles, the man we think is Anna's father, is out of the country. According to the Stewarts, who were brutally honest about their family, Charles ran around on his wife. And when she tried to divorce him, he threatened to take their daughter.

"Since his father was a judge from an old Savannah family, Charles' wife believed he could make that happen. So she disappeared with the child. She was clever, and they never found her. If the story is true, our Anna was born Rebecca Fairchild, and her mother's real name was Olivia."

"That's an amazing story," Mrs. Wilmington said, "and knowing the Fairchilds, it rings true. They're a powerful family with impressive connections."

A few weeks later, Anna called Conner to tell him she would get the results of the test at the end of the day and would phone with the result. "Not on your life," Conner said. "I'll leave work early and be at your house between four thirty and five." At five o'clock, Anna, Max, Conner, Samantha, and Angela all sat in Max and Anna's living room, waiting for the phone to ring. Not understanding what was going on, Gracie simply enjoyed the party atmosphere.

Anna answered the phone when it rang, and everyone got very quiet. "Are you sure?" they heard her ask. After ending the call, she turned to the people in her living room, who were sitting on the edge of their seats, and said, "It's true. I'm the offspring of one Charles Sinclair Fairchild."

Everyone cheered and congratulated Anna with hugs. Max opened a bottle of champagne and toasted Annaleah Fairchild Robinson Anderson. No one mentioned the name she was given at birth, but Max and Conner were both thinking about the bureaucratic paperwork the discovery could generate.

In bed that night, Anna snuggled next to Max and talked about her mother. "I don't know how to feel. On one hand, I'm angry with Mom for keeping my family from me. Having only one relative, I've always felt something was missing. Not knowing who or where they were left a hole, an empty place I had no way of filling. And I've told you how hard things were after she was gone.

"On the other hand, she gave up everything for me. My parents may have still been legally married when Mom died, unless my father filed for divorce due to desertion. I guess that explains her no dating policy. If she'd filed for divorce, he might have found us."

Anna wiped tears away before they could leave her eyes. "It makes me sad to know my mother was denied the opportunity to have a man in her life," Anna said, grateful for the time she had with her temporary husband. Max could think of nothing to say that would help, so he kissed her and consoled her the way he knew best.

When the phone rang, Anna hoped Max wasn't calling to say he'd be late again. That had happened a lot lately. Sometimes he stayed at work so long Gracie had to stay up past her bedtime to see her dad. Max said he was catching up on work he'd put aside during the custody hearing. Even so, Anna didn't believe he had to stay quite so late. Her instinct told her something else was going on.

She couldn't fault him for not calling. Max always let her know when he was going to be late. But he was secretive. Sometimes, when he got a phone call, he'd glance at the screen and walk into the yard before answering. He said he didn't want to bother her with talk of work, but Anna could see the signs. Her time with Max and Gracie was coming to an end, and she might as well get ready for it. Max was interested in another woman.

Anna wasn't surprised. After all, he hadn't really wanted to get married in the first place. He'd done it for Gracie. She understood but was upset at the prospect of losing what she'd come to think of as her family. She was exactly where she wanted to be, living in her beautiful home with the man she adored and a cherished stepdaughter. But soon, if her hunch was right, she'd have to leave it all.

When Anna agreed to the marriage, she knew it would be temporary, but she wasn't ready for it to end. She could probably drag things out if she ignored Max's absences and gave him his freedom, but sharing him would be more than she could bear.

Anna was surprised to find the caller wasn't Max, but Janine, with surprising news. The statement Doug made during the custody hearing, about his mother's death, stimulated renewed interest in the case.

An investigative team scoured the woods behind Doug's childhood home for evidence that his mother died there. And they found it. For years, her bones had been lying beneath a spot people used as a fire pit, concealed by burned logs and ashes. DNA from Mrs. McKinnon's hairbrush, which Doug took from the old house before he had it burned, matched the DNA in the bones. Janine was calling to invite Max and Anna to Mrs. McKinnon's funeral.

When Max returned home, Anna told him about the call. "Janine wants us to attend the funeral next Sunday afternoon. She's afraid there won't be many attendees, since Doug's mother died so long ago, and she doesn't want him to be disappointed."

"What?" Max said. "Janine is actually thinking of someone other than herself?" He agreed to go, making it clear he was attending for Doug's sake, not Janine's.

The following Sunday, Miss Sweet stayed with Gracie and Classy while Max and Anna traveled a few miles out of town to the white wooden church Doug and his brother attended when they were children.

Janine shouldn't have worried about the number of attendees. Doug's brother, Mike, was there with his wife and daughter, looking as if he'd turned his life around after the mistake that put him in prison. And a good number of the church's congregation came to give Doug and Mike's mother a proper send off, sincerely sorry Mary Alice McKinnon had met such a violent end. Many of them remembered the sweet woman who had done her best to raise good, God-fearing sons despite the worst of circumstances.

Taking Max's hand, Anna led him to the far end of the front pew. He sighed but followed his wife. Before the minister spoke, the family stood at the front of the church, shaking hands and accepting condolences from those in attendance. Janine hadn't even known Mrs. McKinnon, but Doug wanted the entire family in the line, and he considered her family.

It didn't take long for the twins to get bored. Instead of shaking hands, they got creative with hand slaps, thumb hooks, fist bumps, and anything else they could think of. Anna caught Janine's eye, offering with gestures to take the boys out of the line. Janine whispered to Doug, and they both nodded. Anna took a twin's hand in each of hers. She sat beside her husband, putting one boy on his far side, and the other next to her.

The boy beside Max looked up at him sheepishly. A few minutes later, he began slowly sliding off the seat. Max placed one big hand on the boy's chest, setting him squarely back on the pew. Both boys contented themselves with swinging their feet, which seemed to be allowed.

After the boy beside Anna whispered in her ear, she walked with him through a nearby door to the men's room. When they returned, the other boy pointed to himself and then to the door.

"You need to take him," Anna told Max. "It's a one-toilet bathroom. While I waited outside, this one decided to pee on the toilet paper instead of in the toilet. I found another roll, but it's the last one."

Max scowled when Anna said, "You'll need to go into the bathroom with him to make sure he behaves. Pretty sure that's Kevin. You can't just ask them. They think it's funny to give the wrong name."

Max dutifully went with Kevin into the bathroom. Sounding like he meant business, he instructed, "Pee directly into the toilet. Nowhere else."

While Kevin was going about his business, the boy asked, "How big is your tally wacker?" Max was glad he didn't have liquid in his mouth. If he had, he would've spewed it all over the wall.

"Why on earth would you want to know that?"

"My daddy has a big tally wacker." Max hid a smile and wondered who taught him that particular term. The boy seemed to like using it. *It might be fun,* Max thought for the first time, *to have a little guy around. Maybe Anna and I will have a boy someday. If we do, I'll be sure to teach him a better term than tally wacker.*

Kevin hadn't exhausted his supply of questions. "Do you think my tally wacker will be big when I grow up?"

Max had to hide his smile again. "Sure it will."

"Don't you have to use the bathroom?" Kevin asked Max.

"Nope," he said, eyeing the curious child.

After the service, Max spoke to Doug." I took one of your boys to the bathroom earlier. Inquisitive little guy."

Doug winced. "That would be Kevin. Sorry. He's going through a phase. Thanks for coming today and for helping with the boys. The way you and Anna are helping us is extraordinary, especially after all that's happened. You'll never know how much we appreciate it."

Max recalled Anna's answer when Janine asked why she was helping with the boys. She'd been right about everything. Lately, he hadn't felt so angry. Now that he had Anna by his side and knew Gracie was safe, a weight was gone from his shoulders. He didn't even mind attending the funeral. It felt right to support Doug, and he had to admit the little demons could be entertaining. Surprisingly, he found he could even tolerate being in the same room as Janine.

CHAPTER FORTY-TWO

Monday afternoon, Samantha sat on her porch watching for Max's SUV. When she saw him coming down the road, she jumped in her car and followed him to the construction site. Samantha had kept Max's secret for months. It had been difficult, but it was about to get impossible. He had to know things were spinning out of control.

"Hi Sam. How's it going?" Max said, closing the door of his vehicle.

Without answering, Samantha lit into the man standing in front of her. "Max Anderson, you might be the most obtuse man I know."

"Hello to you too. What's got your tail feathers in a flutter?"

"I broke Anna's rule today and interrupted her writing time. She was crying." Samantha didn't tell him his wife was sitting at her computer, trying to decide where her next home should be.

Max frowned, having no idea what was wrong, but Sam didn't give him a chance to ask questions. She jabbed her finger at his chest. "If you don't do something, you're going to lose her."

He looked confused. "What?"

"I know how hard you've been working on this surprise for her. But she doesn't understand your absences. You've been neglecting her, and she has totally misinterpreted your actions. You have to do something."

"I'm an idiot," Max said.

"Yes you are. You need to talk to her. Now."

Max got back in his vehicle and drove to Mill Village. When he walked in the front door, Gracie threw her arms around his legs and looked up with sorrowful eyes. "I made Anna cry. I didn't mean to."

"Where is she?"

"In the bedroom. She closed the door." Max was anxious to talk with Anna, but he couldn't leave his daughter just yet. Sitting on the sofa with Gracie in his lap, he listened as she related the story.

"I made Anna cry. But I don't know why. I asked her if I could call her Mama, and she started crying and ran to the bedroom. Did I do something wrong?"

Max pulled his daughter close. "Anna was simply happy. That's all. Sometimes women cry when they're happy."

"She didn't look happy."

"I'll go check on her. You stay here with Classy. Why don't you work on that puzzle we started last night?"

Anna was lying on the bed she shared with Max, crying and thinking about what just transpired. She'd been working in the kitchen when Gracie said, almost shyly, "Can I ask you something?" There was a serious tone in her voice that caused Anna to stop what she was doing and give the child her full attention.

"Of course, you may. What do you want to know?"

"Well, I know Mother is my mother, and you are my stepmother. I know that."

Realizing Gracie had something weighty on her mind, Anna stooped to her level, held the little girl's delicate hands in hers, and looked into her pretty blue eyes. "What is it, darling?"

"I was just thinking, since I call Mother, Mother, maybe, if it's all right with you, I could call you Mama or something."

All Anna could do was nod and hug Gracie tightly. She managed to sob out "thank you," before running into the bedroom and shutting the door behind her. *What have Max and I done? We tried to do what was best for Gracie, but she'll feel hurt and abandoned when I leave. She won't understand.*

Max opened the bedroom door and found Anna curled on the bed, sobbing like her heart was breaking. He sat beside his overwrought wife and moved her to his lap. With his strong arms wrapped around her, he pulled her against his chest.

"What's wrong, honey? Why are you so upset?" When she didn't answer, he tilted her chin up and looked into her distraught, tear-stained face. "Please tell me what's wrong."

Seeing that Anna hadn't regained control of her emotions, he just held her, rocking their bodies side to side. When her sobs finally subsided, and Max felt her body relax, he shifted her to face him. Trying once again, he tilted her chin up so she was looking into his eyes.

Very quietly, emphasizing each word, he asked, "Anna, what's wrong?" She saw the concern and confusion on his beautiful face and tried to formulate an answer.

"I'm sorry, Max," she sobbed. "I tried, but I can't help it. And we're going to hurt Gracie. She thinks this is real. And I want it to be. I'm sorry, but I do."

Max realized something was dreadfully wrong but had no clue what it might be. Confused, he asked earnestly, "Anna, what are you talking about? I don't understand. How are we going to hurt Gracie? What isn't real?"

Anna looked at him with sorrowful eyes. "You know what I'm talking about, Max."

"No, Anna. I don't."

"This marriage," she said through a sob.

Confused, becoming upset himself, Max asked, "What about this marriage? Anna, aren't you happy?"

"Yes. I've never been happier." *I have to agree with Gracie,* Max thought. *That's not what happy looks like.*

"I'm sorry," Anna continued, "but I don't want it to end. I don't. I'm sorry."

Astounded, Max said in a confused voice, "Well, neither do I. What's all this about? You know I love you, don't you?"

"Do you?"

Max looked astonished. He couldn't believe what he was hearing. "Of course, I do. Don't I make you feel loved? Don't I show you every night?" Raking his hand through his hair, he said, "I must be terrible at this."

"No, You're wonderful! I've never experienced anything so beautiful. You must know you're great at sex."

"I'm great at sex?" Astounded at her words, Max was beginning to understand that Anna had no idea how much he loved her. Looking into her sad eyes, he said, "Sweetheart, we don't just have sex, we make love. And I've never made love to anyone else in my life."

"But you were married, and there were other women."

Max shook his head. "Baby, Janine and I weren't in love. We were just a couple of stupid kids having a good time. Because we accidentally made that wonderful little girl in the next room, I stepped up to the plate and did what I thought was right. I admit I tried to love Janine, but I just couldn't. And she didn't love me either, although she may have thought so. Anna, I've never been in love with anyone but you."

Horrified at what was becoming increasingly clear, Max was determined to correct the misunderstanding causing Anna's pain. Holding her head between his big hands, looking directly into her eyes, he asked quietly, "Anna, why do you think I asked you to marry me?"

She tried to look down, but he held her head in place. "Look at me," he said in a voice that was soft but demanding. He asked again, "Anna, why do you think I asked you to marry me?"

She answered in a quiet voice. "So you could get custody of Gracie."

Max grabbed her and pulled her close, holding so tightly he almost hurt her.

"No, Anna. No. I love you. Don't you know that? I wanted to marry you because I love you. I want to spend the rest of my life with you. The custody hearing just put a rush on things."

Running his hands through his hair, he was almost sick with the knowledge that he'd caused Anna so much pain. "How could I have bungled things so badly? I'm sorry." He spoke with a catch in his voice. "Anna, I knew I wanted to marry you the moment you came back to town. Even before that. Hell, I probably knew it the night we danced in the gym, when we were teenagers.

"But I wanted to give you time to know me—not the child or the teenager you used to know, but this me. I wanted to take you on romantic dates, make you fall in love with me, and ask you to marry me, without the cloud of the custody issue hanging over our heads. It didn't seem fair to ask you during all the conflict," he said with a self-deprecating laugh.

"I've been working on a surprise for you, ever since you returned. I was going to show it to you and then propose, ask you to spend the rest of your life with me. Maybe it wasn't the best plan, but that was my plan."

Max knew he had to lay everything on the line, allow himself to be vulnerable. He tried to explain. "When it looked like I might not get Gracie, I got scared…"

Anna interrupted him. "I know. I understand. It was the right thing to do."

"That's the second time doing the right thing for Gracie has hurt you, starting with my marrying Janine." He searched her face. "Do you believe me, Anna? Do you believe I love you?" Anna threw her arms around his neck and kissed him.

Pulling back, he looked at her and asked, "Did you just say you believe me, and you love me back?" Anna smiled and nodded. Relief flooded him, and the tightness around his chest began to loosen. But just to make sure, he asked, "Are we okay?"

With a smile that reached her eyes, an emotional "yes" tumbled from her lips. Max sighed with relief and gently wiped away Anna's tears. He held her a long time. When she finally pulled back from the embrace and looked up, Max pushed her tear-dampened hair from her face.

"Let me run a bath for you," he said, "and get you a glass of wine." Totally spent from the turbulence of her emotions, she nodded. "I'd like that." Anna let Max undress her and help her into the warm inviting water. After placing a glass of wine on a small table beside the tub, he set out a fluffy towel, Anna's favorite pajamas, her robe, and slippers.

"There's one more thing I need to know," Max said. "You didn't believe me when I told you I loved you?"

"I wasn't sure. You mostly said it in the throes of passion or before you hung up the phone."

"Really? I guess I was so accustomed to avoiding the words. I grew up hearing my dad tell Mom he loved her, and I knew he did. I told myself I'd never use those words unless I meant them, and I haven't. I've said them to my parents, to Gracie, and to you. No one else."

"No one?"

"No one."

Max couldn't believe what a mess he'd made of things. How had he let it happen? He could never make up for the unthinkable misunderstanding, but he was sure as hell going to try—starting now. He hoped the bath would give him time to implement a plan that was forming in his mind. Max kissed Anna, told her he loved her, and encouraged her to take a long soak. Then he hurried from the room to share his plan with Gracie. Together, they began making preparations.

Anna was grateful for the bath. She laid her head against the curve of the claw foot tub and wondered how she'd managed to completely misjudge the situation. Even though she believed what Max just told her, she found it difficult to reverse her way of thinking so quickly.

When she was much younger, she believed she'd have a life with Max. But the day he married Janine, that changed. Trying to accept what happened, Anna told herself, daily, that a life with Max was only a dream, something that would never happen. Lying in the warm bath, she wondered if she'd repeated the refrain so often that the words became ingrained in her psyche.

It seemed she and Max had both let old ways of thinking affect their relationship. He hadn't been generous with the words she needed to hear, while she hadn't let herself believe she could have the man she loved. Now, Anna thought happily, it was time to change those damaging habits.

When she entered the living room, her eyes had to adjust to the dim light. Night had fallen, and the room was dark, except for the candles Max had lit. Anna didn't know where he'd found so many. The excited little girl gestured to a chair in the middle of the room. "Sit here. Sit here." Wondering what was happening, she did as she was told and looked into Max and Gracie's smiling faces.

Her hand flew to her mouth as Max got down on one knee and held up a diamond ring. She looked into his beautiful moist eyes and heard him say, in the most earnest voice she'd ever heard, "My beautiful, beautiful Anna, I love you very much. I know I don't deserve you, but I'm asking anyway. Will you marry me again and be my wife forever?"

"Yes," she sputtered, "oh, yes." Max slipped the ring onto Anna's finger and gently pulled her into a heartfelt embrace. They kissed until they heard Gracie giggle. Once Anna's brain began to function again, she asked, "You already had the ring?"

"I did. I got it from Mom a while ago. It was my grandmother's. I wanted to propose when I presented my surprise to you. I've been working hard on it, trying to get it finished instead of coming home when I should have. I'm just now realizing what a bad idea that was. Knowing I made such a mess of things, I simply couldn't wait any longer to put this ring on your finger."

Anna felt guilty for doubting him, for not trusting him. She'd been so wrong. Her next statement had the sound of a question. "But you didn't give it to..." Remembering Gracie, she didn't complete the sentence.

There was love in his eyes when he explained. "I never even considered it. This ring was meant for the woman I love, the woman I would spend the rest of my life with. It was meant for you." Anna kissed Max again, wetting his face with her tears.

He rushed to add, "But if you'd rather have a new one...choose it yourself, we can do that."

"No. I love it. It's perfect."

"We're not quite finished," he said, seeing how anxious Gracie was. He gestured for Anna to sit in the chair again. "Okay, Gracie. You're up."

Gracie walked toward her, hands behind her back, a serious expression on her adorable face. She mimicked Max, bending on one knee, and held out a single rose from a bush that grew in the yard. Gracie looked up at Anna and said, "Will you be my Mama forever?"

Anna managed to sob out, "Yes. Oh, yes, sweet girl. I'll be your mama forever." With tears running down her face, she hugged the adorable child.

"Are you happy?" Gracie asked.

"Yes. I'm very happy."

"I thought so. Daddy says sometimes ladies cry when they're happy."

CHAPTER FORTY-THREE

As soon as spring peaked around the corner, Carol invited her daughter-in-law to join her for tea and scones at a quaint little coffee shop near her home. As Anna expected, it didn't take long for Max's mother to ask about wedding plans. She'd witnessed the courthouse marriage, but everyone knew what that was about. The church ceremony would be about love and commitment, and Carol was anxious to participate.

"Have you chosen invitations yet?" Carol asked. "I'll help address them if you like.

"Thanks. I appreciate the offer, but... I should fill you in on our plans. Max and I have given the wedding a lot of thought. In fact, I've been surprised at how involved your son has been. We've made some rather unorthodox decisions. I just hope we haven't veered so far from tradition that you'll be disappointed."

"I'm intrigued. Fill me in."

Carol noticed her daughter-in-law's apprehensive expression. "Don't look so worried. I'm sure whatever you and Max have planned will be fine. It's your wedding, not mine. Just tell me about it. I can't wait to hear."

"All right," Anna said, drawing out the word. "We booked the church for an afternoon wedding, and we're only inviting family and close friends to the ceremony. But we're inviting the entire town to a reception at Mill Village Park. That's the reason we planned the wedding in the spring."

Carol didn't hide her surprise. "The entire town?"

Anna smacked her lips together. "Yup. I'll handwrite invitations to the ceremony, but..." She paused. "You'll think the next part is strange."

"Maybe not. Go on."

"I know none of the etiquette experts would approve, but we're going to put a blanket invitation in the church bulletins, and I'll make posters for Big Mama's and Mayfield's grocery." Anna paused to judge Carol's reaction.

"That should work."

"It gets more nonconformist," Anna warned.

"Go ahead. So far, I haven't heard anything too outrageous."

"On the flyers and posters, we're going to explain that Max and I will provide roast beef, fried chicken, iced tea, cake, and ice cream, and we're asking the reception guests to bring a side dish. I hope you don't think that's too tacky."

"In other places, it would raise eyebrows," Carol said, "but somehow, a potluck reception seems appropriate for Tenacity."

Anna breathed a sigh of relief. "Oh," she continued, holding up a finger to indicate she wasn't finished. "Guests will need to bring lawn chairs and drinks if they want something other than tea. And their dancing shoes, of course. We've already booked a band from Yazoo City, and we'll rent some wooden dance floors."

Carol nodded. "I'm sure there'll be no shortage of ice chests in truck beds and car trunks. Sounds like a party to remember. Y'all have really thought this through. What will you do if it rains?"

"We'll move to the gym. But only if there's a tornado, hurricane, or torrential rain. Otherwise, it's the park."

Carol smiled. "Have you thought about your dress?"

"We're calling this a wedding celebration. So instead of a traditional white dress and veil, I'm wearing a celebration dress. I'm not sure what that's going to look like. I just know it'll be celebratory."

They both smiled and Carol reached across the table to fold her hand over Anna's. "I love you, you know."

"I know," Anna said with glistening eyes.

"And I love you and Alex." Her voice quivered. "You've always been family to me." They were quiet for a moment, unable to speak, thinking of Anna's mom, Carol's best friend.

When Max insisted on planning the honeymoon and refused to disclose the destination, he had no idea he would be causing such a serious clothing dilemma. Months before the wedding, Anna began asking what she should pack. Max thought she might actually stomp her foot when he explained, with exaggerated patience, "Honey, everyone knows you don't need clothes on a honeymoon."

Anna folded her arms across her chest. "If you don't want to see me walking down some beach in a down-filled coat or wearing shorts on a ski slope, you'd better give me a hint—a good one."

Max held up both hands. "All right, all right. Pack what you would wear around the house."

"Really? That's your hint?"

"It is. And it's a good one."

"I'm not packing what I wear around the house. You'll have to do better than that."

"How about this? Call Samantha and ask her."

Anna looked incredulous. "You told Sam and she said nothing?"

"I asked her not to. Well, that's not exactly accurate. I threatened to fill her house with baby mice if she even thought about giving you a hint."

Anna called Samantha. When her friend told her to pack the same type clothing she would wear around the house, Anna hung up on her. Max leaned against the door frame, arms folded, legs crossed at the ankles, and smirked. Anna narrowed her eyes.

"All right. It looks like I'll have to guess, but if I'm embarrassed, I'm buying all new things—very expensive things." Max chuckled.

As Anna walked toward their bedroom, Max spoke to her back, a sincere tone in his voice. "You're going to love the surprise. I promise. And I'll be the only one to see you."

Anna stopped and turned around. "Now that was a decent hint. You promise I'll like it?"

Max walked to her and caressed her arms. "I promise you'll love it," he said, punctuating each word with a kiss to a different part of her face. The finale was a passionate kiss to her lips, taking all of Anna's irritation with it.

At Samantha's insistence, Anna agreed to spend the night before her wedding at the farmhouse. "You look nervous," Max said when he dropped her off.

"I just hope I've remembered everything." She ticked items off a mental list. "Lights are on the gazebo, and Jeff and Conner will set up the tables in the morning. The ladies from the church are handling the food and tea, and Jeff volunteered to help the band get set up."

"Relax, Anna. Everything is taken care of. You've thought of everything."

"And my honeymoon suitcase is in the SUV," Anna said, still ticking things off her list.

"Yes. You saw me put it there."

Anna had only been away from Max a few hours when she began missing him. She wouldn't see him again until they said their vows at 4:00 the following afternoon, and she had something important to tell him.

Sam looked into her friend's eyes. "You'll survive. And so will Max."

"Are you a mind reader now?"

"Always have been," she joked. "Wine?"

"No. It'll wake me in the middle of the night. I'll have enough trouble sleeping as it is."

Samantha nodded, uncharacteristically keeping her suspicion to herself. Retrieving a stack of videos from a shelf, Sam reminded her friend of their agenda. "We'll watch a couple of chick flicks, turn in early, and spend tomorrow making ourselves beautiful."

Anna's face lit up when she heard Max's ring on her phone. Looking at Sam apologetically, she held up a finger and walked toward the guest bedroom. Sam smiled and shook her head as her friend crooned, "Hi baby."

"You'd think you two hadn't seen each other in a year," she yelled.

After promising Max she'd call before she went to sleep, Anna settled on the sofa, pulled a blanket over her lap, and asked a question she'd meant to ask earlier. "I was wondering, where does that new road go?"

An odd look passed over Samantha's face, and she hesitated. "What new road?"

"You know. The one we passed right before we got to your house."

Sam tried to change the subject. "That shows how long it's been since you've visited. It's been there for months. After the wedding, you'll have to bring Gracie out here. There'll be kittens soon. One of my barn cats is pregnant. I really have to get her spayed."

"You didn't answer my question. Where does the road go?"

"It's just a timber trail," Sam lied. "Mr. Wallace is having some trees cut."

"I've never seen a timber road that nice," Anna said.

"I know. I thought the same thing." Samantha changed the subject again. "Okay. It's time to choose:

Friends with Benefits, *Twilight*, *No Strings Attached*, *When Harry Met Sally*, or *Dirty Dancing*?"

Max's ring woke Anna at eight the following day. "Good morning, wife." Are you ready to get married?"

"Not quite," she said sleepily. "I have to open my eyes first."

"If I was there with you, I'd wake you up properly."

"Hmm. Sounds like an offer I couldn't refuse. Unfortunately, we'll have to wait until tomorrow—for you to wake me, I mean."

"Looks like. But it'll be hard," he said, using the sexy teasing voice that always turned her on. Anna could almost see the delectable smirk on his face and wondered if men ever outgrew raunchy innuendo.

"So what are your plans for the day," Max asked, "other than marrying the man of your dreams?"

"Your mother is bringing Gracie over so we can all get beautiful together. I promised to paint her fingernails. Pale pink," she rushed to explain. "And Sam's going to fix her hair since they both have all those curls. I expect the excitement level to rise a few notches when she gets here."

Max chuckled. "Yeah, she's pretty pumped. I hope she doesn't wear Mom and Dad out before we return from the honeymoon."

"And I ask once again, where are we going on said honeymoon?"

"I shouldn't have said the word. You know I can't tell you."

"Uhh! You mean you won't tell me. I can't believe you're so determined to keep me in the dark."

She heard Max's deep chuckle before he said, "I'm going to hang up now. I just wanted to say good morning and tell you I miss you."

"I miss you, too. I miss waking up with your arms around me. And your morning kisses. And other things," she said playfully.

"Mmm," Max hummed. "Wanna have phone sex?"

"No. I'm getting married today. Bye." Anna heard Max's rich laughter before turning off her phone.

Gracie walked slowly down the aisle, one foot directly in front of the other, like a miniature, slightly wobbly runway model. Proudly wearing a pink sundress with white leather shoes and lace-trimmed little girl socks, Gracie carried a basket of rose petals, which she conscientiously distributed onto the worn hardwood aisle.

When she reached the front pew, Gracie handed the basket to Max's mom and then solemnly took her position beside her father. She looked up at him, smiling adorably. Placing a hand on her shoulder, he bent down and whispered, "Good job."

Conner turned around from his place on the second row to watch the maid of honor walk slowly down the aisle on the arm of Max's father, the best man. Sam's full-skirted, above-the-knee dress duplicated the style of the bride's, while its mint-green color complimented her fair complexion and strawberry blonde curls. Conner wondered, belatedly, if Samantha had a date for the reception. But date or no date, he vowed to spend some quality time with the lovely Samantha and maybe get a slow dance or two.

From where Anna was standing in the vestibule, she could see Max smiling proudly at his daughter. She couldn't decide which was Max's best look. Sometimes she thought he was hottest in soft jeans and a t-shirt. Other times, her choice was khakis and a dress shirt with the sleeves rolled up to show off his strong forearms. Really, the man was hot in anything, but today, her choice was a dark suit, dress shirt, and tie.

When "Mendel's Wedding Chorus" began, the entire congregation stood and turned to watch Anna walk down the aisle. She was simultaneously smiling and fighting tears. Max wore the same expression, somehow adding proud and utterly smitten to the look.

Anna had thought seriously about who should walk her down the aisle. Max's dad was her first thought, but since he was the best man, that wouldn't work. Her second thought was Conner, an idea she immediately discarded, knowing how Max would feel about that. So Anna walked proudly down the aisle alone to join the man she would spend the rest of her life with.

Anna hadn't told Max what she'd be wearing, just that it was her own design. A celebration dress, she'd called it. When he finally took his eyes off his wife's face and noticed her dress, a huge smile spread over his face. Anna was perfect, and the dress was perfectly Anna.

It was a 1950's style, fitted at the waist, with a full skirt that fell just above-the-knee. The neckline was high in the front, plunging to the waist in the back so Anna could feel her husband's hand on her skin when they danced. The dress, printed with tulips in shades of pink, orange, purple and yellow, was definitely celebratory. The flowers bordering the bottom of the dress were bold, with the pattern becoming smaller and sparser as it traveled toward the top. Her stilettos were mint green, as were the flats she chose for the reception.

When the minister asked who would give the bride away, you could almost hear the guests holding their breath. Then Carol, Alex, and Cleo, who had worked in Anna's home since Anna was six, simultaneously answered, "We do." It was an emotional moment, which would have been more intense had everyone known that the tall stranger with glistening eyes sitting in the third pew was the bride's father.

After being pronounced husband and wife, Max and Anna shared a restrained kiss, for the sake of those present, and turned toward the minister. Then Gracie came forward, stood between her father and Anna, and placed her small hands in theirs.

"We're not quite finished," the minister said. Looking down at the bright little girl in front of him, he asked, "Gracie, do you take Anna as your second mother, to love, honor, and obey?"

"I already do," she said proudly.

The congregation chuckled and the minister smiled. "Anna, do you agree to love Gracie and share the responsibility of her upbringing with her birth parents?"

Anna looked lovingly at the child staring up at her. "I do."

"May God bring love and acceptance to each member of this blended family,"

The congregation said, "Amen." Janine walked to the front of the church, as planned, smiled at Anna and Max, then took Gracie's hand and led her to the pew. The gesture was meant to symbolize Janine's approval of the arrangement. Anna thought the smile seemed a bit forced, but she appreciated the effort.

When the recessional began, the happy couple walked quickly through the double doors leading into the foyer, hurried downstairs, then doubled back to the sanctuary for photographs. Knowing Max would stop along the way to kiss his bride, Samantha brought the necessary items for quick make-up repairs before pictures were taken.

While friends and relatives waited outside to shower the happy couple with water-soluble confetti, Max's parents thanked Judge Carter for attending the ceremony and for all he'd done for their family.

"It's rewarding to see," he told them, "that sometimes I get it right."

Soon the happy couple appeared and ran to Doug's beautifully restored 1960 convertible for the trip to the park. Max kissed Anna, more thoroughly this time. Then he took off his coat, loosened his tie, and kissed her again, all to the tune of whistles and cat calls.

As the convertible approached Mill Village Park, the crowd cheered, and Anna unsuccessfully tried to blink back tears. It looked as if the entire town had shown up, and the partying had already begun. Max led Anna through the boisterous crowd amidst shouts of congratulations and a few lusty, good-natured remarks.

They ascended the steps of the gazebo, and the band began playing "All of Me Loves All of You." Max pulled

Anna into his arms for the first dance of the evening and softly sang the chorus to his wife. The noise of the crowd disappeared as Max and Anna Anderson only had eyes for one another.

"Hey, lovebirds," someone shouted when the dance was over. It was Conner, standing with a group of strangers, motioning for Anna and Max to join them. Not strangers. Anna knew two of them, and her heart began beating wildly as she regarded the people standing with Steven and Anna Sue. Anna was about to receive the surprise of her life.

After hugging the bride and groom, Anna Sue introduced them to a tall, slender stranger who'd been hanging back, a little overwhelmed. "Anna," Anna Sue said dramatically, "this is my brother, Charles—your father. He returned early from Europe to be here today."

At first, only shock registered on Anna's face. Then came the tears. Her father took her into his arms. "I'm sorry I've missed so much of your life. You can't know how grateful I am to have found you and how happy I am to be here."

Anna wiped the tears from her face. "You'd think there would be a limit to the number of tears I could shed on this ridiculously wonderful day."

There was still another surprise. Her father introduced her to her grandparents, who seemed much nicer than she'd been led to believe.

While they were talking, they heard the band's lead singer say, "We have a request from Gracie Anderson. For young Gracie, who just taught me the words to this song, here's the Hokey Pokey." *Yep*, Max thought, *my daughter has regained her confidence.*

When the next slow dance began, Charles Fairchild tapped Max on the shoulder. The bridegroom bowed out, with a smile for the woman he loved. *This day is surreal,* he thought. *Anna is dancing with her father, the twins are teaching Gracie to do the floss, and Doug is actually keeping an eye on his boys.*

CHAPTER FORTY-FOUR

The party was still going strong when Max and Anna slipped away. "Now will you tell me where we're going?" Anna asked.

"Not yet, but soon." He drove east on Main Street, which turned into Farm Road. Then he turned right onto the gravel road that ended at Samantha's house.

"Why are we going to Sam's? I didn't forget anything.

"We're not going to Sam's."

There were no other houses on that road, so Anna was puzzled. When Max turned onto the narrow drive Samantha had identified as a timber road, Anna was further confused. "You're not taking me camping, are you? You promised I'd like your surprise." Max said nothing but kept driving along the narrow, uphill road until he reached a pretty log cabin with small white lights strung across the front. "How lovely. I had no idea this was here. Who does it belong to?"

"It's yours. I built it for you. For us."

"Oh, Max! You did this?"

"Not by myself. I've had Dad's men working on it ever since you returned. I was planning to propose here, whcn it was finished, but since I jumped the gun on the proposal, I thought we could use it as a honeymoon cottage. I hope you're not disappointed. If you like, we can go on a trip later."

"Disappointed? Heavens no. The cabin is wonderful. I can't believe you did this."

"Want to go in?"

"Of course."

They went up a few steps to a deck and then walked to the door. "It's not finished," Max warned.

"Let's go in. I want to see."

Max opened the door to a large open room with lots of windows, a brick fireplace at one end, and a beautiful, fully equipped kitchen at the other. He scooped Anna into his arms and carried her over the threshold.

"I'm not the best at putting my feelings into words," Max told his bride, "but building this cabin is my way of saying I love you."

"I love you, too. I can't believe you did this. It even has furniture."

"I bought a few pieces so we could stay here for our honeymoon but I thought you'd want to choose the rest." Max put her down and kissed her, clearly ready to get on with the honeymoon. But Anna couldn't stop looking around.

"How is there a fire in the fireplace?"

"Samantha," was Max's succinct answer."

Then he opened the door to a large master bedroom and bath. There were dim fairy lights strung across the room and rose petals on the bed. Anna's expression asked Max if he was responsible.

"All the special touches are compliments of Samantha. And possibly Conner, since I noticed his car in her driveway. This is presently the only bedroom, but I plan to add more. We have two sleeping options tonight, the bedroom or the porch."

"The porch?"

Max led her onto a large screened-in porch, sparkling with fairy lights. A double bed sat at the end, sprinkled with rose petals.

"I can't believe you did this. It's wonderful. It feels like an enchanted cottage."

Max wanted to high-five himself. That was exactly the reaction he was hoping for. "Wait until morning." Pointing into the darkness, he explained. "If you stand right here on the porch and look west, you'll see where we are."

"Where are we?"

"On a beautiful hill overlooking the corridor."

"Really?" Anna squealed. "Then the cabin really could be enchanted. Thank you, Max. You know how special the corridor is to me."

"I do. I looked at several plots of land, but when I saw the view from this place, I knew it was the one. We can enjoy this cabin for the rest of our lives." He felt Anna nod against his chest.

"I have a surprise for you, too. Stay here." She rushed to the bedroom to retrieve Max's copy of *A World Apart* from her suitcase.

He chuckled. "You finally autographed your book for me." He opened it, moved to a spot with more light, and began to read.

My dearest Max, I greet each morning with a smile, knowing I'll see your handsome face, hear your voice, and feel your strong arms around me. What an amazing way to begin each day! I'm blessed to be your wife and grateful for the privilege of navigating this journey through life with you. Thank you for the joy you bring to my life, for your love, for sharing sweet Gracie with me, and for our growing family. We enter this stage of our lives with the knowledge that our love is complete and irreversible. What a wonderful feeling that is! I fell in love with you when I was six years old. It's a condition that will remain for the rest of our lives.   Your Anna, forever

Anna watched Max's features change with his emotions. She saw love, understanding, gratefulness, and finally confusion. "Our growing family?" he asked, the question mirrored on his face.

Anna nodded.

"Are you getting serious about having a baby?"

Anna nodded, a smile on her face.

"You're not…already?"

Anna nodded again, a bigger smile on her face. Then she couldn't get the words out fast enough. "I've been dying to tell you. I was at the doctor's office for a routine exam, and he wanted to do a blood test. He called after you dropped me off at Samantha's yesterday. I suspected, but I wasn't sure until then. I didn't want to tell you over the phone, and we haven't been alone all day. I've been about to burst with the news. It was hard not to tell Sam and your mother, but I had to tell you first." Anna clasped Max's hands and studied his stunned face. "You're happy, aren't you? I know we didn't plan this. Is it too soon? Tell me it's not too soon."

Max wrapped his arms around his wife, burying his face against her neck. "No, no. I mean yes, I'm very happy. Just surprised. I love you, Anna. More than you know." He pulled back to gaze at her beautiful face, a serious expression on his own.

"Thank you," he said earnestly, "for everything; for loving me and forgiving my mistakes, for treating Gracie like she's your own. And for carrying our child that I'm gonna love like crazy." Max's eyes glistened and his voice took on a reverent tone. "I'm having a baby with the woman I love. That's how it's supposed to be."

They were both remembering his devastation the first time he learned he'd be a father. He had only been a boy—a boy who wasn't in love with the baby's mother. Despite all the anguish Janine's pregnancy caused, Anna was proud of the way Max handled the situation, proud of how he stepped up to the plate and accepted his responsibilities.

"Anna," Max said, a sense of wonder in his voice, "after all that's happened to keep us apart, we're finally together. Really together."

"We are," she agreed, looking radiant. Max pulled his wife onto the porch bed. "We'll christen this one first." He held her warm body close, covered her lips with his, and their legs entwined with familiar pleasure. Overcome with love for the woman in his arms, Max searched for words that would adequately reveal the depth of his feelings. Finding none, he abandoned the pursuit in favor of his preferred form of expression. He might have trouble explaining how he felt about his wife, but he sure as hell could show her.

Passion overtook conscious thought, as Max eagerly began the pleasurable task of igniting every cell in Anna's body. He needn't have worried about translating his feelings into words. For silently, they shared memories, forgave regrets, acknowledged desires, and pledged their love to one another and the family they were creating. Max belonged to Anna unconditionally, and he meant for her to know it.

There is sex, Max thought, *then there is this.* When he joined his body with Anna's on that special night, in that enchanted place, the feeling was so many levels above anything he'd ever experienced that no words existed to describe it. So he told his wife he loved her with every thrust, every sensual stroke, and when they returned to earth, Max felt a sense of peace he hadn't known existed.

With Anna's head on her husband's chest, the lovers held one another, basking in the afterglow of their lovemaking, reluctant to surrender the satisfaction of the moment. Eventually, Anna began to feel the cold of the early spring evening. Max gave her his shirt, slipped on his pants, and they went inside.

"Hungry?" he asked. "Neither of us ate a proper meal at the reception."

"I'm starving. What do we have?"

"I stocked the refrigerator," he said, opening its door, but there's a stack of plastic containers in here I don't recognize." Putting them on the island counter, he discovered a smorgasbord of leftovers from the reception. "Samantha's been a busy girl."

Max disappeared into the bedroom, returning with a warm robe and slippers. "I bought these for you, thinking you might want to leave them here." His gaze roved over Anna's body as she returned his shirt and slipped on the soft robe.

"This feels wonderful. Thank you."

"You could bring some other things up here, too, so you don't have to pack when we come for a visit. There's a small laundry room, but no washer or dryer yet. I thought you might want some input into that decision."

After they ate, they walked around the cabin while Max pointed out some of the features he was especially proud of. "I made the cabinets from wood recovered from the Tanakbi. The logs were probably underwater a hundred years before someone hauled them to the surface. All that time at the bottom of the river made the grain especially beautiful. The wood for the flooring and the brick for the fireplace came from an old house in Vicksburg. It's unfortunate it was torn down, but I was glad to get the materials. The fireplace mantel was made from a tree that fell during Hurricane Katrina."

"Max, it's all beautiful. You did a wonderful job. We should put a plaque somewhere, telling where all the materials came from."

"I have a lot more to do. We have regular power and water, but I'd like to have the capacity to gather power through solar panels on the roof. I also plan to dig a well."

"Are we preppers now?"

"Not exactly. But I wouldn't mind having the capability to convert to an off-the-grid lifestyle in case we ever need it."

"You've been reading those dystopian novels again," Anna teased.

"Well, yeah, but it can't hurt to be prepared. When storms take out our electricity, we can come up here. Enough talk about the house. We're here for three whole days, without a nosy little pixie named Gracie. We can run around naked if we like."

"I don't like, but if you do, I'll be glad to watch."

"You would, huh?" He pulled his wife close, and they reveled in the knowledge they were pledged to one another forever and were having a child together.

Max took Anna's hand, pulled her to the master bedroom and onto the bed. "I thought you'd want to see how comfortable our new mattress is."

"Oh, is that why we're here?"

"Of course. Why else?"

Max leaned against the headboard and clasped his hands behind his head, while Anna stretched out on her back. Propping on her elbows, Anna turned her face upward, delighting in the gentle breeze flowing over their bed. "Magic is in the air," she whispered, nodding toward an open window.

Looking the direction Anna indicated, Max saw a soft beam of moonlight spilling into the room and gauzy curtains stirring in the night air. He smiled. His Anna was romantic to the core. "Is that a good thing?" Max asked. "Having magic in the air?" Knowing he was about to get a discourse on the metaphysical, Max enjoyed the moment. He liked seeing his wife in this contemplative mood.

"Oh, yes," Anna said, her eyes wide. "You believe, don't you?"

Max slid down beside Anna, rested on one elbow, and kissed her lips lightly. "I believe in you."

Mimicking his position, Anna looked at Max and tried to explain. "I believe there's magic in our world. You never know where you'll find it. I usually feel it in places of beauty, but it also exists in shabby places where love triumphs over its surroundings."

Anna tried to gauge Max's reaction to her musings. He was either interested, pretending to be interested, or just sated from their lovemaking. So she continued.

"Some people aren't open to magic. It can be all around them and they don't recognize it. Some who see it know it by a different name. And unfortunately, there are those who ignore it." Anna cast her eyes downward and spoke quietly. "They don't believe it's meant for them."

The look on her face nearly broke Max's heart. Her voice was little more than a whisper when she said, "I was like that for a while."

Max sat up and pulled his wife into his arms. "That's called hopelessness. I know a little about that myself." He kissed the top of her head before pulling back to look at her. "You know how sorry I am, don't you?"

"For what?"

"For the pain I caused you. Caused us both. For not being there when you needed me." Max pulled the woman he loved more tightly to him. "But I have you now. You're my magic, and I'm going to do my damnedest to be yours."

Anna thought Max's kiss must have been the sweetest one anyone ever received. His hands slid beneath her robe, roaming up and down her back, as if to soothe. Continuing south, his large capable hands slipped

397

under her hips, lifting her onto his lap, raising the temperature of the room several notches. Max just held his wife and kissed her.

Consumed with the need for more, Anna threw off her robe, relieved Max of his shirt, straddled him, and began moving rhythmically. It didn't take long for him to flip her onto her back and nimbly remove his pants. Soon the couple was lost in another exquisite cloud of passion.

The phenomenon that occurred that night was proof, as far as Max and Anna were concerned, that magic exists, for when their bodies merged, so did their souls. They had made love many times before, but on that night, as never before, they understood they were irreplaceable halves of a whole, essential to one another's happiness.

Blissful and sated, Max lay with his wife in a boneless tangle of limbs, pondering what they'd just experienced. Never had he been bombarded with such a clear message. Only one experience had come close.

He was a hormonal young teen when it happened. It was the day he stopped walking Anna home from school, choosing instead to accompany a pretty girl from his class. As they walked, something or someone spoke to him. Or maybe it was his overzealous conscience conjuring the thought. But the message was so clear and intense, it felt like a warning. "Anna belongs in your life," the voice said. That was all Max heard, but he never forgot it.

At fourteen, he couldn't understand what was happening, but now he knew it was a premonition. The path leading to this time and place wasn't straight or smooth, and much of the trek had been painful. But Max and Anna found their way back to one another. And they knew, beyond a shadow of doubt, that this all-encompassing blending of heart and soul had been destiny's plan from the start.

If you enjoyed Max and Anna's story, please leave a review on Amazon. Your opinion will help new readers discover *A Lovely Condition*.

Anita Blount's Tenacity Series will continue with *The Proper Choice*, the story of Anna's best friends, Samantha and Conner, who are working out a few issues of their own. Read about what's coming at **anitablountbooks.com**.

Acknowledgements:

First and foremost, I thank my husband, **Buff Blount**. Without your guidance, help, understanding, and patience, *A Lovely Condition* would never have been published. You'll never know how much I appreciate you.

When I needed someone to help get my project off the ground, my youngest brother, **Brad Barr**, stepped up to read my manuscript and make the first corrections. Thank you, Brad, for being a supportive brother, as well as a knowledgeable and experienced journalist.

An unexpected source of help came from a childhood friend, whom I've only had the pleasure of seeing a few times since college. On one of my rare phone conversations with **Susan Guilbert Thayer**, I mentioned the book I'd written. When she asked to read it, I mailed her the manuscript, having no idea she would be such a valuable source of encouragement and advise. Thank you, Susan, for helping with the book, caring about punctuation, and being a true friend.

A big thanks to my daughter, **Wendy Blount**, and to **Don Fillingame** for taking the time to read my manuscript, check for mistakes, and offer advice.

A special thanks to **Tracey Hudson Countz**, who offered advice and took care of the technical aspects of the publishing process.

And I must thank award-winning author **Johnnie Bernhard**, who lives on the Mississippi Gulf Coast. Thank you, Johnny, for your valuable advice.

The lovely watercolor on the cover of the book was painted by Hattiesburg, Mississippi artist, **Bobby Walters**. Thanks, Bobby, for carefully actualizing Anna's house as I envisioned it. You're a talented artist, and I appreciate your contribution to *A Lovely Condition*.

Anita Blount is a Mississippi native who spent thirty-three years as an Army spouse before returning home with her husband, Buff.

After seeing much of the world, she appreciates the charm of the Deep South and the idiosyncrasies of its people. Her writing epitomizes that appreciation.

Anita is a mother, a grandmother, and a former elementary school teacher. *A Lovely Condition* is her first novel.

You can visit Anita's website at
www.anitablountbooks.com.

Made in the USA
Middletown, DE
25 January 2022

59612175R00243